Sunfall

Book Six of The Chronicles of Parthalan

Jennifer Allis Provost

Bellatrix Press

CAST OF CHARACTERS

Aeolmar – First Hunter of Parthalan and commander of the Palace Contingent. Mate of Latera. Father of Mara, Ember, and Tor.

Alia – commander of the Northern Contingent.

Alluria – mate of Caol'nir. Mother of Aeolmar.

Alyon – priestess of Asherah in the mortal realm.

Argent – prior First Hunter. Killed at the Battle of Esguth.

Asgeloth – *mordeth-gall*, Ehkron's whelp. Killed by Latera.

Asherah – Queen of Parthalan and Lady of Tingu. Mate of Finlay. Mother of Finlay Torim.

Atreynha – High Priestess of Teg'urnan.

Attia – royal *saffira-nell* and Asherah's confidant.

Avinor – King Markham's youngest son. Brother to Iruna.

Bron – hunter in the Palace Contingent. Brother of Luth.

Caol'nir – Mate of Alluria. Former *con'dehr*. Son of Tor. Father of Aeolmar.

Caol'non – Son of Tor. Twin brother of Caol'nir. Former *con'dehr*.

Clea – Sky Goddess. Mother of Nyshanti.

Cydia – Moon Goddess. Former mate of Olluhm. Mother of the fae.

Ehkron – former *mordeth-gall*, Asgeloth's sire. Killed by Elvasla.

Elia – Latera's sister.

Elkin – Second Hunter. Mate of Innetha.

Elvasla – former Lady of Thurnda and ancestor of Latera. Killed Ehkron in the mortal realm.

Ember – Lady of Tingu. Mate of Leran. Younger daughter of Latera and Aeolmar.

Esguth – *mordeth* who attacked Teg'urnan. Killed by Aeolmar.

Finlay – King of Parthalan. Mate of Asherah. Father of Finlay Torim.

Finlay Torim – Prince of Parthalan. Asherah and Finlay's son.

Gilson Cadoret – Captain of the Ganneran Guard.

Grelk – King of the Trolls. Master blacksmith.

Harek – former Prelate. Executed for treason.

Innetha – huntress in the Palace Contingent. Mate of Elkin.

Iruna – youngest child of Markham. Sister of Avinor.

Ish h'ra – The Deliverer. A member of the old gods, she was persecuted by Olluhm.

Jannei – Latera's sister.

Kemen – hunter in the Palace Contingent. Son of Krylle.

Krylle – priest of the old gods. Father of Kemen.

Leran – Lord of Tingu, son of Lormac.

Latera – First Huntress of Parthalan and the *deva'shi*. Mate of Aeolmar. Mother of Mara, Ember, and Tor. Killed the last *mordeth-gall*, Asgeloth.

Lormac – former Lord of Tingu. Father of Leran. Former mate of Asherah. Killed on the Day of Sadness.

Luth – hunter in the Palace Contingent. Brother of Bron.

Mallia – former matriarch of the palace's healers.

Mara – eldest daughter of Latera and Aeolmar.

Markham – last king of Parthalan directly descended from Olluhm and Cydia. Father of Iruna and Avinor. Killed by a usurper who was then killed by Sahlgren.

Mersgoth – *mordeth* who marked Alluria, and went on to kill her, Caol'nir, and six of their children. Eventually killed by Aeolmar.

Natreus – former king of the dark fae. Defeated in battle by Asherah.

Nu – Sun God prior to Olluhm. Father of Nyshanti.

Nyshanti – Goddess of Dawn, lover of Ish h'ra. Also called Torim.

Olluhm – Sun God, former mate of Cydia. Father of the fae. He cast the old gods from the sky and installed himself as the All Father.

Priya – daughter of Elvasla and Tarac. Mate to Tor.

Rahlle – former royal sorcerer, one of Cydia and Olluhm's original twelve children. Hasn't been seen since shortly after Asherah took the throne.

Sahlgren – former king of Parthalan who betrayed his people. Executed by Asherah.

Sarelle – former High Priestess of Teg'urnan who acted in collusion with Sahlgren.

Sarfek – sorcerer, brother of Harek. Killed by Latera.

Sasha – Latera's youngest sister.

Solon – the child sun, first born of Olluhm and Cydia.

Surya – huntress in the Palace Contingent.

Tor (younger) – Latera and Aeolmar's youngest child. Named for his grandsire, who was the Prelate of Parthalan.

Tor (elder) – former Prelate of Parthalan. Father of Fiornacht, Caol'non, and Caol'nir. Mate to Priya.

Torim – Asherah's companion, killed on the Day of Sadness. Also called Nyshanti.

Wren – an herbalist. Latera's oldest sister.

Prologue

Nyshanti Speaks

Nyshanti is not the first name I was given. I suspect it won't be the last.

When I was a babe my mother, the sky goddess Clea, called me her little sunbeam. Fitting, since my father, Nu, was the sun, and all my life I've been told about how much I resemble him. Therefore, it was no surprise when I came of age, and my burgeoning abilities to manipulate and color light mirrored his. By the time I was grown, I preceded him each morning as the dawn, and eventually all referred to me as Nyshanti, Bringer of Light, and Herald of the Sun.

One day I met Ish h'ra, and she did not refer to me as Nyshanti, or Sunbeam, or any of the other names given to me by my parents and siblings. She called me beauty, and sweetheart, and other names that made my cheeks warm and my belly flutter. Those early days with my Ish h'ra were warm, and happy, and we were content.

Then Olluhm came.

Not I or anyone else had ever heard Olluhm's name, then he was suddenly everywhere we turned. Some said he was a disgraced god from another realm, while others claimed he was a power hungry mortal magician driven insane by his own conjurings. Wherever he came from, he'd set his sights on becoming a god, and that was how we knew he was truly mad. No one in their right mind would desire godhood, not with the demands that came with it, and the people one was beholden to protect and nurture as if they were one's own children. You were either born to godhood, or you lived a normal life. But Olluhm wanted power, and in his eyes the ultimate power was the sun.

My father.

Olluhm warred against my father for an age, sending plagues and disasters against him and the land. When my father defeated that first volley, Olluhm cast a black pall over the sky that created a darkness so absolute that crops withered and died, and our people went mad with fear. After Father restored light to the land, Olluhm made it rain for endless gray days, and the resulting deluge washed away both humble dwellings and majestic mountains.

No matter what torment Olluhm devised, Ish h'ra always stood beside my father, and she always foiled him. She would light fires to combat Olluhm's darkness, dam rivers to keep the floods at bay, and do whatever was needed to ensure her people's survival. When Olluhm saw how the people adored Ish h'ra, his rage and jealousy got the better of him, and he formed his most diabolical plan yet.

He cursed Ish h'ra's people, and made many of them into what we now know as demons.

Most of the population evaded the curse, since Olluhm lacked the power and the skill to decimate an entire race. But the damage had been done, and since a god's power is derived from their worshippers, Olluhm had at last seriously wounded not only Ish h'ra, but all of the old gods. The first to fall was my father, the sun.

It was noon, and my father was at the apex of his journey when Olluhm pulled him from his chariot and flung him to earth. Olluhm then stole my father's chariot and continued on the sun's path. In his weakened state, my father wasn't able to reclaim his chariot. Humiliated, he and a contingent of his followers retreated to the island of Ysr, with the help of the troll king, Grelk.

My mother and my siblings withdrew soon after, as did the rest of the gods, until only Ish h'ra and I remained. They all begged us to follow them, since Olluhm's madness knew no bounds, but Ish h'ra refused. Her people needed her, and she swore to defend them for as long as there was breath in her body. As for me, there was no way I would leave Ish h'ra. And I didn't, not when we were cursed to be mortals, or when we were captured by demons and Ish h'ra lost her memory, but I kept my own. I remembered everything, and I knew The Deliverer was still inside the woman now called Hillel, and knew she would come back to me. I only needed to be patient.

Then another tragedy occurred, one that I hadn't foreseen. During the time I was called Torim, my mortal body died, and my soul reverted to that of a goddess. Being that I had no form to anchor me, and my shrine in Dremmsvard and long since been occupied by another who had been imprisoned there by Olluhm, my soul eventually found residence in Ish h'ra's temple in the mortal realm. It was a quiet, safe existence which mirrored my early days when I was only the dawn, and not The Deliverer's lover.

How I missed being in her arms.

But things are changing once again, and Olluhm's time is at long last coming to an end. Soon, I will return to Parthalan, and I will see my Ish h'ra again. We won't be as we once were; too much time has passed, and too much has happened. Nevertheless, I still love her with all my heart, and I will make good on my word to help her defeat Olluhm one final time.

Soon, Ish h'ra, all of our patience and planning will come to fruition. Soon.Nyshanti is not the first name I was given. I suspect it won't be the last.

When I was a babe my mother, the sky goddess Clea, called me her little sunbeam. Fitting, since my father, Nu, was the sun, and all my life I've been told about how much I resemble him. Therefore, it was no surprise when I came of age, and my burgeoning abilities to manipulate and color light mirrored his. By the time I was grown, I preceded him each morning as the dawn, and eventually all referred to me as Nyshanti, Bringer of Light, and Herald of the Sun.

One day I met Ish h'ra, and she did not refer to me as Nyshanti, or Sunbeam, or any of the other names given to me by my parents and siblings. She called me beauty, and sweetheart, and other names that made my cheeks warm and my belly flutter. Those early days with my Ish h'ra were warm and happy, and we were content.

Then Olluhm came.

Not I or anyone else had ever heard Olluhm's name, then he was suddenly everywhere we turned. Some said he was a disgraced god from another realm, while others claimed he was a power hungry mortal magician driven insane by his own conjurings. Wherever he came from, he'd set his sights on becoming a god, and that was how we knew he was truly mad. No one in their right mind would desire godhood, not with the demands that came with it, and the people one was beholden to protect and nurture as if they were one's own children. You were either born to godhood, or you lived a normal life. But Olluhm wanted power, and in his eyes the ultimate power was the sun.

My father.

Olluhm warred against my father for an age, sending plagues and disasters against him and the land. When my father defeated that first volley, Olluhm cast a black pall over the sky that created a darkness so absolute that crops withered and died, and our people went mad with fear. After Father restored light to the land, Olluhm made it rain for endless gray days, and the resulting deluge washed away both humble dwellings and majestic mountains.

No matter what torment Olluhm devised, Ish h'ra always stood beside my father, and she always foiled him. She would light fires to combat Olluhm's darkness, dam rivers to keep the floods at bay, and do whatever was needed to ensure her people's survival. When Olluhm saw how the people adored Ish h'ra, his rage and jealousy got the better of him, and he formed his most diabolical plan yet.

He cursed Ish h'ra's people, and made many of them into what we now know as demons.

Most of the population evaded the curse, since Olluhm lacked the power and the skill to decimate an entire race. But the damage had been done, and since a god's power is derived from their worshippers, Olluhm had at last seriously wounded not only Ish h'ra, but all of the old gods. The first to fall was my father, the sun.

It was noon, and my father was at the apex of his journey when Olluhm pulled him from his chariot and flung him to earth. Olluhm then stole my father's chariot and continued on the sun's path. In his weakened state, my father wasn't able to reclaim his chariot. Humiliated, he and a contingent of his followers retreated to the island of Ysr, with the help of the troll king, Grelk.

My mother and my siblings withdrew soon after, as did the rest of the gods, until only Ish h'ra and I remained. They all begged us to follow them, since Olluhm's madness knew no bounds, but Ish h'ra refused. Her people needed her, and she swore to defend them for as long as there was breath in her body. As for me, there was no way I would leave Ish h'ra. And I didn't, not when we were cursed to be mortals, or when we were captured by demons and Ish h'ra lost her memory, but I kept my own. I remembered everything, and I knew The Deliverer was still inside the woman now called Hillel, and knew she would come back to me. I only needed to be patient.

Then another tragedy occurred, one that I hadn't foreseen. During the time I was called Torim, my mortal body died, and my soul reverted to that of a goddess. Being that I had no form to anchor me, and my shrine in Dremmsvard and long since been occupied by another who had been imprisoned there by Olluhm, my soul eventually found residence in Ish h'ra's temple in the mortal realm. It was a quiet, safe existence which mirrored my early days when I was only the dawn, and not The Deliverer's lover.

How I missed being in her arms.

But things are changing once again, and Olluhm's time is at long last coming to an end. Soon, I will return to Parthalan, and I will see my Ish h'ra again. We won't be as we once were; too much time has passed, and too much has happened. Nevertheless, I still love her with all my heart, and I will make good on my word to help her defeat Olluhm one final time.

Soon, Ish h'ra, all of our patience and planning will come to fruition. Soon.

Chapter One
Mara Speaks

It wasn't supposed to be like this.

I was supposed to hold myself chaste until I met my soul's true mate, then I would give him the one gift only I could give, just as Cydia had given her gift to Olluhm. After the claiming we would be bound, have many, many children, and spend our lives in happiness.

None of that happened.

I pressed my hand against my belly, feeling the small but firm curve that hadn't been present a few sennights past. While we were at The Seat, and the elves had celebrated the life-affirming ritual of Madoc'na, I spent the night with Kemen. Mind you, I hadn't chosen him, but apparently such formalities were unnecessary. He claimed me, then he went off and died battling orcs and trolls in the Northern Waste while his seed sprouted in my womb. If I ever encounter Kemen's shade, I will throttle him for leaving me.

And now we Parthians were on the last leg of our long, exhausting return journey home to Teg'urnan. We'd left Tingu almost two moons ago, and the size of our party, coupled with the many carriages needed for transporting the sick and wounded, had necessitated our slow pace. One of those carriages had been especially reserved for Finn, who'd been gravely injured while defending The Seat from a second party of orcs that had attacked while Leran and the rest of Tingu's legion were away. If it hadn't been for Finn's quick actions, and my sister Ember's strong leadership, I don't think we would have prevailed.

Since I'd been caring for Finn ever since he was pulled from battle, his pale curls darkened with blood and dust, it was only natural for me to travel in the carriage with him. What I hadn't realized was that the carriage's constant rolling, bumping gait would agitate both my gut and my bones, making me a sick, sore, retching mess. I couldn't wait to get back to the palace, where I could have a bit of privacy and sleep in my own bed.

When our procession stopped for the first night, and the tents were raised, I followed Finn into his. The other healers followed him, too; I daresay he yearned for privacy more than I did. But while Finn was technically my charge, I hadn't gone with him into the tent to tend his wounds. All I'd wanted was a quiet, non-moving bedroll where I could sleep away the tensions of the day. For the first few nights, that tactic worked.

Then the dreams began.

They weren't nightmares, not really, but they were vivid, and disjointed, and every day I woke more exhausted than the last. Those vivid dreams, coupled with the uncomfortable carriage, had pushed me to the very edge of my sanity, and I was even closer to breaking. The only thing that calmed me, and the tiny life inside me, was Finn's presence.

Sometimes, when my dreams were especially bad and disturbed us both, we woke up lying in the same bedroll. Finn would hold me, and gentle me, and eventually I could sleep again. While I occasionally stirred when Finn came into my bed, I never remembered going to his, the awful dreams having rendered me senseless. And Finn didn't only look after me at night. During the day when we traveled in that merciless carriage Finn held my hand, and told me stories, and kept me from screaming and wailing and wanting to throw myself off a cliff. Soon enough, it was plain that I was no longer taking care of Finn, and he was the one caring for me.

I often thought about the time he'd kissed me. It had been mere moments before he went out, alone and armed only with a crossbow and a sack of bolts to defend The Seat from the invaders; and about what happened after the battle, when he'd been wounded and near death, and he told me he loved me. We hadn't kissed again, and we hadn't talked about what he'd said, and honestly, that was for the best. Finn needed to work on his recovery and not burden himself with me and my problems. Finn will be just fine once we return to Teg'urnan. As for me and my baby, we'll also be fine. Somehow.

Gods, Kemen, I really do want to throttle you. It wasn't supposed to be like this.

I was supposed to hold myself chaste until I met my soul's true mate, then I would give him the one gift only I could give, just as Cydia had given her gift to Olluhm. After the claiming we would be bound, have many, many children, and spend our lives in happiness.

None of that happened.

I pressed my hand against my belly, feeling the small but firm curve that hadn't been present a few sennights past. While we were at The Seat, and the elves had celebrated the life-affirming ritual of Madoc'na, I spent the night with Kemen. Mind you, I hadn't chosen him, but apparently such formalities were unnecessary. He claimed me, then he went off and died battling orcs and trolls in the Northern Waste while his seed sprouted in my womb. If I ever encounter Kemen's shade, I will throttle him for leaving me.

And now we Parthians were on the last leg of our long, exhausting return journey home to Teg'urnan. We'd left Tingu almost two moons ago, and the size of our party, coupled with the many carriages needed for transporting the sick and wounded, had necessitated our slow pace. One of those carriages had been especially reserved for Finn, who'd been gravely injured while defending The Seat from a second party of orcs that had attacked while Leran and the rest of Tingu's legion were away. If it hadn't been for Finn's quick actions, and my sister Ember's strong leadership, I don't think we would have prevailed.

Since I'd been caring for Finn ever since he was pulled from battle, his pale curls darkened with blood and dust, it was only natural for me to travel in the carriage with him. What I hadn't realized was that the carriage's constant rolling, bumping gait would agitate both my gut and my bones, making me a sick, sore, retching mess. I couldn't wait to get back to the palace, where I could have a bit of privacy and sleep in my own bed.

When our procession stopped for the first night, and the tents were raised, I followed Finn into his. The other healers followed him, too; I daresay he yearned for privacy more than I did. But while Finn was technically my charge, I hadn't gone with him into the tent to tend his wounds. All I'd wanted was a quiet, non-moving bedroll where I could sleep away the tensions of the day. For the first few nights, that tactic worked.

Then the dreams began.

They weren't nightmares, not really, but they were vivid and disjointed, and every day I woke more exhausted than the last. Those vivid dreams, coupled with the uncomfortable carriage, had pushed me to the very edge of my sanity, and I was even closer to breaking.

The only thing that calmed me, and the tiny life inside me, was Finn's presence.

Sometimes, when my dreams were especially bad and disturbed us both, we woke up lying in the same bedroll. Finn would hold me, and gentle me, and eventually I could sleep again. While I occasionally stirred when Finn came into my bed, I never remembered going to his, the awful dreams having rendered me senseless. And Finn didn't only look after me at night. During the day when we traveled in that merciless carriage Finn held my hand, and told me stories, and kept me from screaming and wailing and wanting to throw myself off a cliff. Soon enough, it was plain that I was no longer taking care of Finn, and he was the one caring for me.

I often thought about the time he'd kissed me. It had been mere moments before he went out, alone and armed only with a crossbow and a sack of bolts to defend The Seat from the invaders; and about what happened after the battle, when he'd been wounded and near death, and he told me he loved me. We hadn't kissed again, and we hadn't talked about what he'd said, and honestly, that was for the best. Finn needed to work on his recovery and not burden himself with me and my problems. Finn will be just fine once we return to Teg'urnan. As for me and my baby, we'll also be fine. Somehow.

Gods, Kemen, I really do want to throttle you.

Chapter Two

Finn adjusted Mara where she lay in the crook of his arm, and smoothed her soft auburn hair back from her face. She'd fallen asleep shortly after the carriage started rolling, and it was the first peaceful sleep she'd had in days. What's more, they would be back home in Teg'urnan by sun rest, which meant she could sleep in her own bed that night, and not in a drafty tent.

He would give anything for one more day of travel, and one more night with her.

Finn had loved Mara for as long as he could remember. He had wanted to tell her for so long, but the time was never seemed right. Either she was with Kemen, or there was that disastrous incident between him and Ember, but then he and Mara were in Tingu together and he felt he could finally bare his heart, and he had the perfect place to do it: Madoc'na.

He had everything planned out, down to how he would find her in the midst of the celebration, and how he would take her aside and finally tell her how he felt. But Mara hadn't attended the celebration, and all of Finn's declarations went unsaid.

A few days after the celebration, The Seat was attacked, and since he figured he was going to die anyway, Finn drew up his courage and kissed Mara goodbye. Not only had she kissed him back, he'd survived the battle and Mara had become his constant companion while he fought his way back from his injuries. Once Finn had recovered enough to get around on his own, he resolved to find the time to talk to Mara, but she began getting sick.

Her symptoms were minor at first; she was more tired than usual, and certain foods bothered her. Finn assumed her fatigue was due to her constant vigilance over him, and truth be told he wasn't fond of elfin foods either. Then the trip home began, and Mara became plagued with nightmares. A few sennights ago, they were so bad she crawled into his bed for comfort. Finn had turned to her, his chest against her back, and thought the moment had finally come for him to tell her how he felt. He slid his arm around her waist, but when his hand moved over her belly he paused.

There was a curve, a swell that had not been present before.

Finn spent the rest of the journey staring at Mara's midsection whenever she was sleeping, which was often. When she slept flat on her back, or when she was outside and the wind flattened her clothes against her body, the swell was noticeable. What's more, it was growing.

Mara was with child, and Finn was certain no one knew but him.

The carriage jostled Finn out of his thoughts as the procession turned onto the royal road, and he saw the gray spires of Teg'urnan for the first time in more than half a year. He'd missed his home, but he had no idea what lay ahead for him or any of his family. His mother, Queen Asherah, had finally regained her memory, and her true identity as Ish h'ra, The Deliverer. She was once the leader of the old gods and the sworn enemy of Olluhm, who was the patriarch of the current Parthian gods. Finn laughed to himself; of all things he thought he might one day become, being the son of a god was not on that list.

Mara stirred at his laughter, and he soothed her. She'd no sooner settled against him when Elkin, the Second Hunter, rode out from Teg'urnan's gate. He stopped before Aeolmar and they exchanged a few tense words, then Elkin sought out the king and queen. While Finn wondered what was going on, Latera, Aeolmar's mate and Mara's mother, approached the carriage window.

"Is Mara awake?" Latera asked.

"She's just fallen asleep," Finn replied, moving away from Mara as he pulled back the curtain so Latera had an unobstructed view of the interior, and her daughter. "What's happening?"

"It seems we have some visitors waiting for us in Teg'urnan," Latera replied. "Or at least, I do."

"Who is it?"

"My sisters. They came here from the mortal realm, looking for me."

That news surprised Finn, since very few traveled between realms. "That's rather unusual. Is them being here a good thing?"

Latera gazed toward the palace square. "I certainly hope so."

Chapter Three

Latera watched as Finn woke Mara, and told her they were about to pass through the palace gates, and almost wished he'd let her sleep. Mara had seemed perfectly healthy when they set out from Tingu, but she'd grown weak and pale during the journey home. Latera hoped her daughter was merely showing the strain of caring for Finn, and that after she spent a few nights sleeping in her own bed, and resumed eating good food rather than travel rations, her health would improve.

Mara waved at her mother through the carriage window, and Latera put her latest worry aside as she urged her horse through Teg'urnan's dark iron gates. As she passed beneath the statues of the stag and doe, her gaze landed on a sight she never thought she would see in Parthalan. Two of her sisters, Elia and Jannei, were standing in the center of the square, waiting for her.

Latera paused for a moment as Asherah and Finlay entered the square followed by Ember and Leran, with Finn and Mara's carriage rumbling behind them. As the royal members of the party entered

Teg'urnan with all the associated pomp, Latera walked her horse toward her sisters.

"Girls," Latera called as she dismounted, then she paused. The women waiting for her were just that—grown women, not the children she'd last seen in Gannera. "What's happened?"

"You haven't seen us in half a lifetime, and the first thing you say when you see us is what's happened?" Elia snapped. Jannei began apologizing, but Latera waved it away.

"It has been a long time," Latera conceded. "How are you?"

"Us? We're fine, I suppose." Elia eyed Latera. "We've been told your *second* daughter is the queen of the elves."

"Yes, Ember is the Lady of Tingu," Latera said. "I've a son, too, if you'd also like to berate me about his existence."

"Elia just wonders why we've never met them," Jannei said. She'd always been their peacemaker.

"I can't just hop from one realm to another," Latera began, but Elia shook her head.

"You haven't returned home in all this time because of Father, is that right?" she asked.

"In a word, yes." Latera looked between the two of them, and asked, "Where is Sasha?"

"That's why we're here," Jannei replied. "No one knows. We thought she might have sought sanctuary here, with you."

"What do you mean, no one knows where she is?" Latera demanded, then there was a commotion near the palace steps.

"What's happening over there?" Elia asked.

"I don't know," Latera replied, then she reached out to Aeolmar with her mind.

Mar, what's going on?

Finn. He fell on the steps.

Is he all right?

He seems to be. Your sisters are here?

Two of them. Sasha is missing.

I will be right there.

Bring Wren?

I will. It will be a Ganneran reunion.

"Aeolmar is on his way, along with Wren," Latera said. "How long has Sasha been missing?"

Jannei sighed. "We have much to tell you."

***

It took a maddeningly long time to get everyone sorted out and introduced, and for Elia to express her full displeasure over Latera having borne two additional children they hadn't ever met. Eventually, Latera and her sisters, Wren included, sat in the royal receiving chamber along with Asherah and Finlay. Mara and Finn had both retreated to their respective rooms, while Aeolmar was helping Leran and Ember settle into their temporary chambers. As for Latera's son, Tor, he was at the *sola* showing off his new troll sword.

"You're certain Finn will be all right?" Asherah asked Wren, once they'd settled around the map table.

"It was just a tumble," Wren reassured her. Wren, in her role as a healer and herbalist, had taken over Finn's care from the elfin healers once she arrived at The Seat. The elves appreciated her efforts, and all agreed that Finn benefitted greatly from Wren's knowledge. "Let him have a good night's sleep, and in the morning he'll be perfect again."

Asherah squeezed Wren's hand, then she turned her attention to Elia and Jannei. "I understand you two have come here seeking your youngest sister. We've been away from Teg'urnan for some time, but my *saffira-nell* assures me she hasn't been here."

After Latera quietly explained what a *saffira-nell* was, Elia said, "Thank you for checking with your staff, my lady. We're beginning to lose hope of ever finding our Sasha."

"How did she come to be missing?" Finlay asked.

"Our father married her to an awful man out of spite," Jannei replied. "Apparently a treaty was signed with his kingdom long before any of us were born, and this man was supposed to marry Latera."

"Father married Sasha off to Gannok?" Latera demanded, and Elia and Jannei nodded. "She can't possibly be old enough for marriage! And to that soft headed boor!"

"We didn't thing she was at a marriageable age either, but while she's the youngest of us she's also the craftiest," Elia said. "She knew she couldn't stop the union, so she presented him with a bit of lore claiming they couldn't consummate the marriage until they were both in Gannok's home country."

"What does the location have to do with their marriage?" Finlay asked.

"Nothing at all," Elia replied. "Sasha made it all up as a way to fend him off, and it worked. The fool was determined to bed her as soon as possible, so he cut the celebration short and they left for his home in The Highlands a few days after the ceremony in Gannera. At some point, Sasha fled, and we haven't seen or heard of her since."

"And you thought to look for her in Parthalan?" Latera asked.

"Father sent out the guard, and she isn't any place to be found in Gannera," Elia said.

"We thought she might have paid a sorcerer to send her across the veil," Jannei said. "According to Gannok, when Sasha disappeared she took a great deal of his coin with her."

Latera chuckled; leave it to Sasha to not only humiliate Gannok, but rob him blind in the process. "Is that how you got here? Hiring a sorcerer?"

"No, we went to your temple," Jannei replied, nodding to Asherah. "The priestesses helped us, and here we are."

"Here you are, indeed," Latera mumbled.

"While you were in the temple, did you speak to the oracle?" Asherah asked. "Or hear tell of something called a lodestone?"

"We did not ask to see the oracle, and do you mean Priya's lodestone?" Jannei countered.

"Yes, the one Elvasla's daughter used to travel between realms," Latera replied.

"Everyone knows where it is, and it's not in the temple," Jannei said. "It's at Gannera castle."

Asherah blinked. "It's where?"Latera watched as Finn woke Mara, and told her they were about to pass through the palace gates, and almost wished he'd let her sleep. Mara had seemed perfectly healthy when they set out from Tingu, but she'd grown weak and pale during the journey home. Latera hoped her daughter was merely showing the strain of caring for Finn, and that after she spent a few nights sleeping in her own bed, and resumed eating good food rather than travel rations, her health would improve.

Mara waved at her mother through the carriage window, and Latera put her latest worry aside as she urged her horse through Teg'urnan's dark iron gates. As she passed beneath the statues of the stag and doe, her gaze landed on a sight she never thought she would see in

Parthalan. Two of her sisters, Elia and Jannei, were standing in the center of the square, waiting for her.

Latera paused for a moment as Asherah and Finlay entered the square, followed by Ember and Leran, with Finn and Mara's carriage rumbling behind them. As the royal members of the party entered Teg'urnan with all the associated pomp, Latera walked her horse toward her sisters.

"Girls," Latera called as she dismounted, then she paused. The women waiting for her were just that—grown women, not the children she'd last seen in Gannera. "What's happened?"

"You haven't seen us in half a lifetime, and the first thing you say when you see us is what's happened?" Elia snapped. Jannei began apologizing, but Latera waved it away.

"It has been a long time," Latera conceded. "How are you?"

"Us? We're fine, I suppose." Elia eyed Latera. "We've been told your second daughter is the queen of the elves."

"Yes, Ember is the Lady of Tingu," Latera said. "I've a son, too, if you'd also like to berate me about his existence."

"Elia just wonders why we've never met them," Jannei said. She'd always been their peacemaker.

"I can't just hop from one realm to another," Latera began, but Elia shook her head.

"You haven't returned home in all this time because of Father, is that right?" she asked.

"In a word, yes." Latera looked between the two of them, and asked, "Where is Sasha?"

"That's why we're here," Jannei replied. "No one knows. We thought she might have sought sanctuary here, with you."

"What do you mean, no one knows where she is?" Latera demanded, then there was a commotion near the palace steps.

"What's happening over there?" Elia asked.

"I don't know," Latera replied, then she reached out to Aeolmar with her mind.

Mar, what's going on?

Finn. He fell on the steps.

Is he all right?

He seems to be. Your sisters are here?

Two of them. Sasha is missing.

I will be right there.

Bring Wren?

I will. It will be a Ganneran reunion.

"Aeolmar is on his way, along with Wren," Latera said. "How long has Sasha been missing?"

Jannei sighed. "We have much to tell you."

***

It took a maddeningly long time to get everyone sorted out and introduced, and for Elia to express her full displeasure over Latera having borne two additional children they hadn't ever met. Eventually, Latera and her sisters, Wren included, sat in the royal receiving chamber along with Asherah and Finlay. Mara and Finn had both retreated to their respective rooms, while Aeolmar was helping Leran and Ember settle into their temporary chambers. As for Latera's son, Tor, he was at the sola, showing off his new troll sword.

"You're certain Finn will be all right?" Asherah asked Wren, once they'd settled around the map table.

"It was just a tumble," Wren reassured her. Wren, in her role as a healer and herbalist, had taken over Finn's care from the elfin healers once she arrived at The Seat. The elves appreciated her efforts, and all agreed that Finn benefitted greatly from Wren's knowledge. "Let him have a good night's sleep, and in the morning he'll be perfect again."

Asherah squeezed Wren's hand, then she turned her attention to Elia and Jannei. "I understand you two have come here seeking your youngest sister. We've been away from Teg'urnan for some time, but my saffira-nell assures me she hasn't been here."

After Latera quietly explained what a saffira-nell was, Elia said, "Thank you for checking with your staff, my lady. We're beginning to lose hope of ever finding our Sasha."

"How did she come to be missing?" Finlay asked.

"Our father married her to an awful man out of spite," Jannei replied. "Apparently, a treaty was signed with his kingdom long before any of us were born, and this man was supposed to marry Latera."

"Father married Sasha off to Gannok?" Latera demanded, and Elia and Jannei nodded. "She can't possibly be old enough for marriage! And to that soft headed boor!"

"We didn't think she was at a marriageable age either, but while she's the youngest of us, she's also the craftiest," Elia said. "She knew she couldn't stop the union, so she presented him with a bit of lore claiming they couldn't consummate the marriage until they were both in Gannok's home country."

"What does the location have to do with their marriage?" Finlay asked.

"Nothing at all," Elia replied. "Sasha made it all up as a way to fend him off, and it worked. The fool was determined to bed her as soon as possible, so he cut the celebration short and they left for his home in The Highlands a few days after the ceremony in Gannera. At some point, Sasha fled, and we haven't seen or heard of her since."

"And you thought to look for her in Parthalan?" Latera asked.

"Father sent out the guard, and she isn't any place to be found in Gannera," Elia said.

"We thought she might have paid a sorcerer to send her across the veil," Jannei said. "According to Gannok, when Sasha disappeared, she took a great deal of his coin with her."

Latera chuckled; leave it to Sasha to not only humiliate Gannok, but rob him blind in the process. "Is that how you got here? Hiring a sorcerer?"

"No, we went to your temple," Jannei replied, nodding to Asherah. "The priestesses helped us, and here we are."

"Here you are, indeed," Latera mumbled.

"While you were in the temple, did you speak to the oracle?" Asherah asked. "Or hear tell of something called a lodestone?"

"We did not ask to see the oracle, and do you mean Priya's lodestone?" Jannei countered.

"Yes, the one Elvasla's daughter used to travel between realms," Latera replied.

"Everyone knows where it is, and it's not in the temple," Jannei said. "It's at Gannera castle."

Asherah blinked. "It's where?"

Chapter Four

Asherah Speaks

"What do you mean, it's at the castle?" Latera demanded, as I glanced at Finlay. No one in Parthalan, Thurnda, or Tingu knew the whereabouts of the semi-legendary lodestone, the exact item I needed to gain entry to the shrine in Dremmsvard, yet its location was common knowledge in the mortal realm?

"Of all places," Finlay murmured, proving his thoughts mirrored mine.

"I don't recall anyone discussing priceless elfin relics while I lived there," Latera continued.

"And you were stolen when you were what, ten?" Elia countered. I didn't know if Elia's short demeanor was due to the stress of crossing the veil, worry over her missing sister, or if she was generally this disagreeable, and I was starting to not care. I preferred my guests to be polite, at least for a day or two.

"The lodestone is a part of Latera's statue," Jannei, the much nicer sibling, offered.

"There's a statue of you in Gannera?" I asked.

"It's not of me," Latera replied. "It's a statue of Gannera's first king, whom I'm named after." She eyed her sisters. "Is it the spear he's holding?"

"Yes, the lodestone is the spearhead," Elia said. "Why in the world do you need it? And it's not like *you* could get it, anyway. Father has been furious with you ever since the epic debacle you made of your last visit."

"Father's opinion doesn't matter," Latera said. "We need to get the lodestone so we can kill a few gods, and no one in Gannera will stand in our way."

Elia rolled her eyes. "Of course you want to do something dramatic with it. Can't you ever be normal, like the rest of us?"

"You mean boring?" Latera countered.

Wren glanced at my hands where they clutched the edge of the table, my knuckles long since gone white, and asked her sisters, "Would you like to see if your rooms are ready?"

"That would be lovely," Jannei said.

Wren smiled apologetically at Finlay and myself, then she herded her other three siblings out of my receiving chamber. "I don't know if we could handle all five of those sisters at once," I said. We could hear them arguing in the corridor, and while Latera was the warrior Elia held her ground. "They're like a herd of angry goats, butting heads as often as they draw breath. And that's not even all of them! If the fifth makes her way here, it will be a catastrophe."

"Does this mean you will be crossing to Gannera?" Finlay asked.

I turned to Finlay, saw the concern in his summer blue eyes. "I don't think that would be wise," I replied. "We need to look after Finn, and we've been away from Teg'urnan for so long, and..." I swallowed my half-hearted excuses, and spoke the truth. "I really don't want to see

Nyshanti. Not yet, not until I understand a bit more of who I was. Who I am."

Finlay approached me, and slid his arms around my waist. "You'll have to deal with her eventually."

"Yes, I know, but eventually doesn't have to be tomorrow." I laid my head on his shoulder. "Am I being cowardly?"

"Never," he said, his lips against my ear. "Sher, you are the bravest person I've ever known."

"Then why do I feel like I'm hiding?"

"Are you hiding, or waiting to confront her until you have all the information?" he countered.

I drew back and regarded him. We were nearly the same height—I was slightly taller, but Finlay claimed that was my imagination—so it was easy for me to meet his eyes. "Do you really think it will be a confrontation?"

"I suppose that depends on Nyshanti. She must have a reason for waiting in the mortal realm all this time. We just need to learn what that reason is." He tucked my cheek against his neck, and I tried to forget all that we'd learned and all that we still needed to accomplish, and just be content in his arms.

"We have a lot to do, don't we?" I asked.

"We certainly do, my goddess." Finlay gave me a final squeeze, then he stepped back and grasped my hands. "How would you like to begin?"

"I think we should speak to Atreynha," I replied, naming Olluhm's High Priestess that oversaw the Great Temple. "I can't in good conscience plot to overthrow her master without first discussing it with her."

"How do you think she will react?" Finlay asked.

"I have no idea."

Finlay moved to summon our *saffira-nell*, Attia, so she could in turn summon Atreynha. "Best get on with it, then."

Chapter Five

"I believe these are the same rooms I stayed in last time I was here," Leran said as he strode into his and Ember's guest chamber. Like all of the rooms in Teg'urnan, it was spacious and filled with light. This room had the additional benefit of being in the royal wing, and thus far removed from the noisier areas of the palace.

"You remember that trip?" Ember asked, as she followed her mate inside.

"I do. And I remember that it was a very good trip, and I was glad I'd come." Leran had made that journey to attend Asherah's jubilee. It was where he'd first met her new mate, Finlay, and learned that Asherah was with child. Leran never would have guessed that the babe would grow up to be Finn, his brother in all but blood.

Leran turned to his mate's father, who had walked them to their rooms. "Thank you for showing us the way, Aeolmar."

Aeolmar nodded. "Of course. If you need me, I'll be in the *sola* keeping Tor out of trouble."

"Too late for that," Ember said, and Aeolmar smiled.

"Most likely," he said, then he left and shut the chamber door behind him.

As soon as they were alone in their chamber, Leran pulled Ember into his arms. "Alone, at last."

"As if being alone has ever been one of your requirements," she teased. They'd been surrounded by people during their journey to Teg'urnan, sometimes even in their tent. It had led to a few rushed, if exciting, encounters.

"It wouldn't have mattered as much if you could learn to be quiet."

Ember laughed, and pressed her face against his chest. "I could blame that on you."

"You could." He tilted up her chin and kissed her. "Want to work with the Sala?"

Ember slid out of his arms, and pulled off her boots. "If you'd like."

They'd worked with the Sala almost daily during the journey from Tingu, and they'd both leaned much about how the five stones in the armband functioned. Their ultimate goal was to use the Sala to rebuild The Gate of Tingu, which had been destroyed when orcs attacked The Seat.

Leran had learned more about the Sala in these last four moons than he'd learned in his entire life, and he credited every one of his successes to his mate. She was as eager to learn the workings of the Sala as he was, and she frequently thought of new ways to enhance their connection to the artifact. One of Ember's first discoveries had been that their feet being in contact with the ground greatly enhanced the experience.

"Although, we're so far up from the ground we'll probably only learn about Teg'urnan's stones." Ember glanced toward the open balcony doors. Their apartment was on the second floor near the Great Temple. "We could go outside, but then we would risk getting interrupted by anyone and everyone."

"Then for now we'll learn something new about Teg'urnan, and later we can take a walk outdoors, find a secluded spot, and learn something else," Leran said.

"As you say, my love," Ember said, and Leran's heart warmed. He would never get used to having such a perfect mate.

They rolled back the carpets and sat in the center of the room on the bare floor, which was the same smooth gray stone that comprised the rest of the palace. "Nowhere else have I encountered stone with such a finish," Leran said, gliding his hand across the floor. "It's as smooth as Grelk's finest blades."

"The stories say that Olluhm shaped every stone by hand, and built Teg'urnan as a love token for his mate," Ember said, as she removed the Sala from her arm and set it on the floor between them. "Cydia lounged on the altar as he set the stones one at a time, watching him as he worked."

Leran leaned forward and kissed her. "Would you like me to build you a palace?"

"And give up living at The Seat? Never." She cupped his face for a moment, then she lowered her hands and sat a bit straighter. "Now pay attention. Let's see what the stones decide to tell us."

"Yes, beloved."

With that, the Lord and Lady of Tingu closed their eyes, and focused their awareness first on the Sala, then on the stones it sat upon. The first thing Leran learned was that while the palace was old, it wasn't nearly as ancient as The Seat. That knowledge didn't surprise him, since the fae were a much younger race than the elves. He probed deeper, and found a hint of black among the gray stone palace.

Blackness, or darkness?

He didn't know if that thought was his, or his mate's, or if it had come from one of his ancestors that regularly spoke to him through the Sala. Leran reached for Ember's hand, grateful when he felt her fingers slide against his palm. Together, they plunged further into the history of the stones.

"It's definitely darkness," Ember murmured; then the thought had been hers. "I've never thought of Teg'urnan as anything but a home filled with light and love."

"There's darkness everywhere," Leran began, then he fell silent as he watched the images the stones showed him. He saw a tall man, long of hair and limb, pull stone after stone from a cauldron of magic. The man, proud and boastful, kept showing off the stones, each more perfect than the last, to someone just out of Leran's view. Then the images changed, and Leran saw the woman.

She was beautiful, with tawny hair and large, pale eyes, and she was frightened. Leran pushed his awareness toward her, and realized she wasn't just frightened, she was exhausted and in pain, both from the child she'd recently borne and the shackles around her ankles.

The woman was a prisoner.

"This isn't right," Ember said, her fingers trembling against his. "Cydia wasn't chained to the altar. It was where Olluhm fed her honey. It was where she bore their children."

"The stones don't lie," Leran said. "They're showing us what happened."

Ember released Leran's hands, then she got up and walked away from him and the Sala. He followed her out to the balcony, and wrapped his arms around her.

"Those people we saw," he began. "They are your gods?"

She nodded, then she turned around and pressed her cheek against his chest. "The stories say they were in love, but that wasn't love. Olluhm treated her like a trophy. She was his prisoner."

"Why would the stones choose to show us that memory?" Leran wondered. Based on Teg'urnan's great age, and the many events that had taken place within its walls, the stones could have shown them any number of scenarios.

"These rooms are very close to the Great Temple," Ember said. "The stones have probably been waiting for eons to show someone the truth of what happened. The truth behind the lies." She leaned back so she could meet his eyes. "Do you think Asherah will be able to stop Olluhm?"

"I think she can," Leran replied. "Asherah has proven, time and again, that she can do anything."

Chapter Six

Aeolmar Speaks

I closed the door to Ember and Leran's lodgings, and smiled as I walked down the corridor. Never would I have thought to pair Leran with my sweet, fiery daughter, or anyone else for that matter, but Ember was like her mother in that every thought and emotion played across her face. When Ember looked at Leran, her face told me she loved him, and was loved in return.

They were happy together, and that made me happy. Despite the many mistakes I've made in life, as long as my children and my mate were happy, I knew I'd done something right.

I stopped by the *sola*, and saw Tor showing off his new troll-forged sword. He'd won it in Tingu, and had put it to good use when we fought the trolls. Much like my daughters, my son was growing up, too. I wasn't sure how I felt about that.

Since Tor didn't need me hovering over him, and I already knew that Mara was resting in her chamber, I turned toward the wing of guest rooms to seek out my mate and her sisters. I'd been as shocked as Latera was when Elkin told me we had visitors from Gannera; as far as

I was aware, the only Gannerans that had ever been to Teg'urnan were Latera and Wren. Now, that number was doubled.

I turned the last corner before the guest wing, and saw Latera walking toward me. She smiled when she saw me, and I quickened my pace. When we reached one another she slid into my arms like she belonged there. Which, of course, she did.

I opened my mouth to speak, and paused. "What is it?" she asked.

"I was about to thank the gods for you, but I realized I don't know who I should be thanking," I replied. We'd recently learned so much about Olluhm, who was once thought to be our great and noble elder sun, but now we knew better. I didn't want to thank him for anything except leaving us alone.

"You could always thank Asherah," Latera said, smiling up at me. "Or be like an elf, and stop following gods altogether."

"Leran always says elfin women are brilliant," I said, then I kissed her. My beautiful, much loved elf. "Is Wren still with the other two?"

"Yes, poor thing," Latera replied, then she grew serious. "Mar, I know where the lodestone is. It's part of a statue in Gannera Castle."

I frowned, since Gannera Castle was exactly where Latera did not want to go. "Did Elia and Jannei give you any insight as to where Sasha might be?"

"No, but there aren't that many places she could hide successfully. Wren and I believe we can find her, but even if we can't, we can at least secure the lodestone for Asherah."

"Only you and Wren?" I tightened my arms around her. *I know you'll be safe if you go there without me, but I want to protect you.*

"It will be easier to move around Gannera with just the two of us. You stand out too much." *I need you here, for the children.*

"I don't stand out that much." *Our children our grown.*

"Yes you do. You're bigger than everyone else." *They're still our babies.*

I kissed the top of her head. "You're right. They are." Since she would soon be leaving me for the mortal realm, I did what I loved and Latera hated. I lifted her in my arms and carried her down the corridor. She thumped my shoulder with her fists, but I only laughed.

"Put me down, you oaf," she demanded, as she pummeled my chest.

"Never." *When are you leaving for Gannera?*

Probably in the morning.

Then I have an entire night to try and convince you to stay.

Latera laughed and left off beating me long enough to slide her arms around my neck. We were almost all the way to our chamber when Asherah's *saffira-nell*, Attia, found us.

"Attia," Latera greeted from her perch in my arms. "Something tells me you're not here to wish us a good evening."

"Sadly no," she replied. "Our goddess would like to see you, and a few others, as soon as you can get yourselves to her chamber."

"She told you she's a goddess?" Latera asked as I set her on her feet.

Attia shrugged. "As if we hadn't already known."

With that, Attia continued on to retrieve whomever else Asherah wished to speak with. I looked longingly at our closed chamber door, and sighed.

"I had such plans for tonight," I lamented.

"And we can get to all of them," Latera said, as she tugged me toward the royal wing. "We just need to put this latest gathering behind us."

***

Latera and I were still laughing when we entered the royal receiving chamber. Along with Asherah and Finlay, Ember and Leran were already present. Our daughter approached us as soon as we'd crossed the threshold.

"We were working with the Sala and Teg'urnan showed us something," she said, without preamble.

"Something good?" Latera asked.

"Something about Olluhm and Cydia," Ember replied, then she glanced at the doorway and fell silent. I turned, and saw Olluhm's High Priestess, Atreynha, enter the room.

"Hello, everyone," Atreynha said. "Ember, what did the stones show you?"

Ember bit her lip, and glanced at me. I nodded, since Atreynha was one of the kindest people I'd ever met. I couldn't imagine her reacting in anger, no matter what Ember said. It was Leran who replied.

"The stones showed us their memory of Olluhm as he created the palace," Leran said. "Cydia was reclined on the altar stone, as the stories said, but she wasn't lying in comfort. She was chained."

"Chained?" I repeated, not that I doubted Leran's words. Ember had explained to me how the Sala worked, and that it could relay to its wearer the memories etched into whatever bit of earth or stone it was in contact with. Whatever the Sala had shown them had happened, no doubt about it.

Atreynha stepped forward, and touched Ember's arm. "I'm afraid you saw the event as it truly unfolded," she said. "Perhaps we should sit."

Sit we did, all of us clustered around Asherah's map table. The queen took her place at the head of the table, while Finlay stood behind her, a king standing guard over a goddess. Once we were settled, Atreynha spoke again.

"The stories say Cydia willingly went to Olluhm, but that was not the case," Atreynha began. "When he saw her sleeping in the green meadow, he was entranced by her beauty… But she wanted nothing to do with him. Undeterred, he took her, and got twelve children on her."

"How could you serve such a monster?" Asherah asked. Her fists were clenched, her knuckles white and straining.

"When I first took my vows, I did not know the truth of the matter," Atreynha replied. "In fact, I knew nothing of his true nature until after Caol'nir destroyed the original altar stone."

Leran glanced at me. "Your father destroyed the stone Cydia was chained to?"

I nodded. "He did it to save my mother."

"Caol'nir saved many of us during the Battle for Teg'urnan," Atreynha said. "I shudder to think would have become of Teg'urnan if he hadn't breached the temple doors that day. However, once the pieces of the old altar had been hauled away, those of us who remained noticed a marked change in the temple. It was warmer, and brighter, as if a great well of sadness had been removed."

"Cydia's sadness," I murmured, and Atreynha nodded.

"Though she was sired by Olluhm, your mother had no love for him," Atreynha continued, now speaking directly to me. "Alluria was always drawn to Cydia, our glorious moon, and sought to learn more about her. After Alluria left the temple for the last time, I recalled her interest in Cydia and descended into the vaults to increase my own knowledge of our mother goddess. It took me many days and nights, but I at last persuaded the stones to show me the truth of Cydia, and you are correct, child." She patted Ember's hand. "How I wish you weren't."

"She was a prisoner," Ember said. "Olluhm saw her sleeping in a green meadow, and he... and he..." Ember's throat worked. Latera reached across the table and grasped her other hand. "It was terrible, what happened to her."

"After Cydia bore their twelfth child, Olluhm desired a new mate," Asherah began, speaking in the rote way that told me she was reciting one of her memories from her time as The Deliverer. "If you can call what was between Olluhm and Cydia a mating. He ranged northward, driving his stolen chariot across the sky as he sought the daughter of the god he'd taken it from. He desired her, desired Nyshanti."

"Is that why you fought against Olluhm?" I asked. "To keep him from Nyshanti?"

Asherah shrugged. "It was one of many reasons. After I made it plain that Olluhm would never touch a hair on Nyshanti's head, and Cydia was made unavailable to him, he began that ridiculous custom of visiting a priestess at every dark moon." Asherah blinked, and the goddess left as the queen returned. "I'm sorry, Atreynha, I meant to speak to you before I began rambling on about my past lives. It seems that I'm Olluhm's greatest foe."

Atreynha nodded. "The Deliverer. How long have you known?"

"How long have you known?" Finlay countered.

"Since you were bound, actually," the High Priestess replied. "It took some effort to bind the two of you together, and near the end of the ceremony I realized that Asherah was holding part of herself back. I questioned why, and meditated on the answer."

"And your answer was that Asherah is one of the old gods?" Finlay asked.

"Actually, I first determined determined that Torim was Nyshanti," Atreynha said. "Once I understood that, I realized who you were.

Are." Atreynha beamed at the queen. "I hoped you would return soon. Cydia's been waiting for your help for a very long time."

"What sort of help does she need?" I asked.

"They fought, Cydia and Olluhm did, and he imprisoned her in a shrine in the north," Atreynha replied. "It was once the home of Nu, the sun god."

"Is that why the moon's red?" Latera asked. "Because Cydia was imprisoned?"

Atreynha's face darkened. "No. It's been that way ever since Olluhm claimed her against her will. Perhaps, when she's freed, it will revert to the clear white light that once shone over Parthalan."

"And Parthalan will be a land of truth and honor once more," came a voice from the doorway. I turned, and saw Caol'non, my father's brother, stride into the room. "Forgive me my lateness. I'd forgotten just how large Teg'urnan is."

"Caol'non," Atreynha said, rising to greet him. "I never hoped to see you again, yet here you are."

"My lady," he said, bowing before her. "I understand the *con'dehr* are no more, but I remain your servant."

"As ever, I'm grateful for your time, and your sword," Atreynha said, then she faced Asherah. "What would you have me do, my lady?"

"For now, nothing," the queen replied. "We must not alert Olluhm to my true identity in any way. Have things in the temple carry on as usual." She laughed shortly. "I've been here in his palace all this time, and in his arrogance he never noticed."

"The best place to hide is in plain sight," I said. "If he were a true hunter, he would understand that."

"Speaking of hunting, I can leave for Gannera tomorrow and begin the search for the lodestone and my sister," Latera said. "If that's all right with you, Asherah. I know me searching for Sasha wasn't part of our plan."

"And what sort of *deva'shi* would you be if you didn't rescue your sister?" Asherah countered. "What do you need to bring to Gannera?"

"Just a few supplies, and Wren," Latera replied. "We'll go to the mortal realm, find what and who we're looking for, and return as soon as we can." Latera paused, then asked, "Would you like us to bring a message to Nyshanti?"

Asherah frowned. "No. Anything I have to say to her, I will deliver myself."

I set my hand on Latera's back, and did my best to remain calm. Mark my words, this trip to the mortal realm was a bad idea.

Chapter Seven

Asherah Speaks

With our immediate plans sorted out, everyone stood to leave. Aeolmar was understandably disappointed that Latera would soon be leaving for Gannera without him, and they quietly slipped out of the room. I imagined they wanted to say their farewells in private. Next, Atreynha and Caol'non left for the Great Temple, which would be something of a homecoming for the former *con'dehr*. Atreynha was certainly happy to see him; indeed, I'd never seen her smile so much.

Lastly, Leran and Ember stood to leave, and I said, "Wait."

They paused, and turned back to me. "Is there something more we need to discuss?" Leran asked. "Tell me what I can do for you."

"Actually, there's something I can do for you." I took Finlay's hand, and we walked toward a glass-paned door set against the far wall of my receiving chamber. "Please. I'd like to show you my garden."

"Yes, let's go to the garden," Ember said, as she tugged Leran toward the door. "It's the most magical place in Parthalan! Finn and I played here every day as children."

"I remember," I said, and Ember was right. My garden was indeed magical, in that the surroundings changed to suit your mood. Within my garden, which by all accounts shouldn't have been much larger than my bedchamber, one could scale mountains, or lounge at the edge of the sea, or nap in a meadow teeming with wildflowers.

I didn't want to show Leran any of these places, fabulous though they were. Instead, I led everyone to a small, clear stream, and the gray boulder that sat beside it. I faced Leran, and said, "This is where I buried Lormac."

Leran stilled, then he turned from me to the boulder. "Under here?" he asked.

"Next to it." I gestured to the area between the boulder and the stream. "Here."

Leran sat on the ground and pressed his hand against the dirt. Ember knelt beside him, and slipped the Sala off of her forearm and placed it onto his. After a few silent, agonizing moments, Leran met my gaze.

"Have you ever told anyone he's here?" he asked.

"Only Finlay," I replied. "We both thought it best to keep it between us, and let him have his rest."

Leran nodded. "Da appreciates that. He also likes this location."

My breath caught in my throat. I understood that Leran and Ember could speak to their elfin ancestors through the Sala, but messages from those who had passed on never ceased to unnerve me. "Does he?"

"It's the stream," Ember said. "Lormac says that the sound comforts him." She turned to Finlay, and said, "He likes you, too, my lord."

Finlay blinked. "You're certain?"

"Da says Asherah chose well, and that you've been a fine mate to her," Leran said. "He says you take very good care of her."

Finlay bowed his head. "Thank you, Lormac. That means a great deal to me, but I have to say that Asherah takes care of me, too."

Leran laughed softly. "That's always been her way."

I smiled, because Leran was right. It was my way to care for people, and right now I could best care for Leran, and Ember, and Lormac, by giving them time together.

"Stay as long as you'd like," I said, as Finlay and I moved toward the exit. "Ember, do you remember the way out of the garden?"

She nodded. "I do."

With that, Finlay and I left them alone to enjoy their reunion.

Chapter Eight

Mara Speaks

The morning after we returned to Teg'urnan, I was woken by the news that my mother was leaving.

"What do you mean, you're going to Gannera?" I demanded, my voice going shrill. "We haven't even been home for a full day!"

"I know, but Sasha is missing." Mama cupped my cheek with her hand. "She needs my help."

I nodded, not trusting my voice. Or my eyes, for that matter, since I worried I would burst into tears at any moment. Even so, my emotions must have been plain on my face.

"Mara, what's wrong?" Mama asked. "What do you want to tell me?" When I didn't answer, she added, "Is it about Kemen?"

Sobs erupted from me, and Mama pulled me into her arms. "I'm so sorry," she soothed, rocking me like a baby. "You miss him a great deal, don't you?"

I shook my head. "I don't, but…"

I drew back and wiped my eyes. I should have told Mama about the baby right then and there, but she was about to embark on a journey to an entirely different realm. She needed to concentrate on finding Sasha and the lodestone, not on me.

"Can we talk when you're back?" I asked, instead of telling her what was really happening. "I don't want to keep you."

"We can talk now," she said. "I always have time for you."

She did always have time for me, and that fact sent another hot tear sliding free of my lashes. "I want to talk, too, but I don't quite know what I want to say. Well, I do, but I don't have the words yet. Does that make sense?"

Mama smiled. "It does. And yes, we can absolutely talk once I return."

I hugged her, careful to not let her feel my belly. I was so grateful for my kind, understanding mother. "Thank you, Mama."

"Of course." She stepped back, and wiped my cheeks with a handkerchief she kept tucked in her sleeve. "Do you feel up to walking Wren and me to the Hill of Torim?"

I nodded. "Yes, Mama. I'll see you off." The Hill of Torim was where Mama always began and ended her journeys to Gannera. At the crest of the Hill was a tear in the veil that led directly to a spot on Gannera's palace grounds. "Wren's going, too?"

"Yes. The lodestone is on the castle grounds, and she has a closeness with one of the sentinels. We're probably going to need his help."

Closeness... "Do you mean Gilson, the guard Wren was hopelessly in love with as a girl? Does Bron know Wren's going to be seeing him?"

Mama gave me an exasperated look. "Wren claims there's nothing between her and Bron but friendship."

"Interesting idea of friendship." I located my shoes, and sat to put them on. "Where on the grounds is the lodestone?"

"It's on the statue of King Latera."

I giggled like a child. "I still can't believe you're named after a man."

"As are you, Mara," she said, then she held out a hand and pulled me to my feet. "Let's get going. I'm sure your father's already up there, worrying."

The walk from Teg'urnan to the Hill of Torim was pleasant enough. The way had been paved with round stones that matched Teg'urnan long ago, and benches sat on either side of the causeway so those climbing could rest as needed. During the spring and autumn festivals hawkers set up temporary shops and stalls along the path, and sold everything from refreshments to love spells.

There weren't any stalls present today, probably because with the royal family so long away from Teg'urnan, visitors had dwindled as well. Therefore, Mama and I had an unobstructed view of the crest of the Hill, and the knot of people waiting for us: Papa and Tor, Ember and Leran, Auntie Elia and Auntie Jannei, along with Wren and her good friend, Bron.

"Would a friend walk you all the way up a hill for a last goodbye?" I murmured.

"Hush," Mama said. "If Elia and Jannei hear you, they'll interrogate Bron mercilessly while Wren and I are away." My lower lip quivered when she said away, and Mama squeezed my hand.

"I will be back soon, and then you can tell me anything and everything that's on your mind," she said. "If you're ready to, that is."

"And if I'm not?"

"Then I'll wait." Mama stopped walking, and pulled me into her arms. "I will come back to you as soon as I can. I promise."

"I know you will," I said. "I'm just going to miss you so much."

"I'll miss you too, my brave one."

We parted, and resumed walking. When we reached the rest, and I noticed that Wren had a satchel slung over her shoulder, and what looked like a small sack of hay on the ground next to her feet. "What's all that?" I asked.

"Meadow hay," Wren replied. "According to Elia, the king burned the meadow we usually get the hay from, and it's vital to the spell we use to cross the veil. Apparently he filled in the pond, too."

"You really angered Father this time," Elia said, and Mama rolled her eyes.

"He angered me, too," she said, then she turned to Ember. "I'm sorry I'm cutting our time together short."

"It's all right," Ember said. "Go rescue Auntie Sasha, then all of you can come visit us in Tingu." They embraced, then Mama moved on to Tor.

"Be good, my warrior," Mama said, and Tor enveloped her in a great bear hug. Bron similarly embraced his friend Wren—rather chastely, I noted—then Mama went into Papa's arms for a longer goodbye.

Mama and Papa, Ember and Leran, and now Wren and probably Gilson, I thought bitterly. *Everyone is pairing off, while I remain alone.* I stood there with my hands balled into fists to resist touching my belly, and biting the inside of my cheek to keep from crying. Screaming. Throwing myself at one of these pairs and demanding to know how they so easily found love when it evaded me at every turn. I looked away, lest my face or a stray gesture betray my thoughts, and wished Finn were there to hold my hand.

Chapter Nine
Latera Speaks

After an all too short goodbye, Wren and I crossed the veil from Parthalan to Gannera. Once we were in the land of our birth, the first thing we did was cough.

"Elia was right," Wren said, with her eyes squinting and tears running down her cheeks thanks to the smoke lingering in the air. "The king has been burning the fields."

"And he destroyed the pond." The lovely pond I'd played near as a child was gone. Now it was a flat, barren field, thus ruining the once-lush landscaping that surrounded it, and as a final insult, he'd burned the meadow hay down to the ground. That last bit proved tricky, since meadow hay had a habit of reseeding itself, and growing back just as quickly as it had been destroyed. According to Jannei, Father retaliated against the hay's fertile nature by setting controlled burns on the field on a regular schedule. Based on the amount of soot and smoke present, these burns happened often.

"Are you sure you have enough of the hay to get all three of us home?" I asked.

"I have enough to bring ten people back to Parthalan with us," Wren said, as she lifted the sack onto her back. Being that it was filled with hay, it was very light, but it made for an awkward shape. "Let's get moving before the guards notice us standing around in this ash bin."

We slipped around a break in the castle wall, and made our way through the woods to the village at the base of the hill. At the inn, where we stopped for breakfast and to hear the local news, Wren hired a messenger to deliver something to the castle guard.

"What did you tell him?" I asked, since the message was earmarked for Wren's former lover, Gilson.

"Oh, nothing much," she began, as she stirred honey into her bowl of porridge. "Only that we're here, and in a short while we'll be invading the castle in order to steal a priceless relic that's conveniently set smack in the middle of the courtyard. I also asked him to please not murder us on sight."

"That last part will be most helpful." I sipped my tea, which was hot and sweet and just as tea should be. "Should we hire horses, or walk to Asherah's temple?"

"If we walk, we'll stand out less," Wren replied, and she had a point. The villages directly outside the castle walls were some of the poorest areas of Gannera. Horses in this part of the realm were a rare luxury, indeed. "Didn't you tell Aeolmar to stay behind because he stood out too much?"

"Yes," I said, my voice filled with regret. Aeolmar remaining in Parthalan while Wren and I completed this mission was the right decision, but I already missed him terribly. "I did."

***

Wren and I walked for the rest of the day before we reached Asherah's temple. The single mortal sun had just set when we saw the temple's gray spires in the distance, and we decided to camp for the night. The Great Temple in Teg'urnan remained closed from dusk until dawn, and while I didn't know if this temple followed the same practice, I had no wish to disturb the priestesses. Besides, Wren and I were exhausted.

After a long and much needed rest, we were up and waiting in the temple's courtyard as the sun rose the next morning. I tried to wait respectfully, but when the priestesses opened the doors, they caught me tapping my foot.

"Forgive me," I blurted out, standing at attention. Alyon, the High Priestess, smiled.

"All is forgiven, Latera," she said, as she ushered us inside. "Hello to you too, Wren. We wondered how long it would take for you to arrive after the first two sisters left us. I assume they made it to Parthalan with no problems?"

"They did. Thank you for helping them." Once inside the temple, I looked around the small chamber for Sasha, and frowned when I didn't see her. "I don't suppose you have my youngest sister here, too?"

"Unfortunately, not any longer," Alyon replied.

"So she was here," Wren said, and Alyon nodded.

"Sasha arrived the day after Elia and Jannei left for Parthalan. We were willing to offer her sanctuary, but she worried the temple is too close to the castle."

I had to agree with Sasha's assessment. When our father wanted to find someone or something, he was relentless. "Do you know where she went?"

"Yes. We sent her on to Tarac."

Tarac was the kingdom named for and founded by my ancestor El-vasla's mate after she'd been killed by Ehkron. It was also the kingdom that had exiled my mother. "Why did she choose Tarac?"

"It was happenstance, really," Alyon replied. "A tinker and his wife had stopped to worship our Asherah, and they were already planning to travel on to Tarac. Sasha paid them to take her along in their covered wagon."

The thought of my baby sister hopping into a wagon with a travel-ing tinker made my gut clench. Then again, she had managed to escape from Gannok's retinue, and evade both his and our father's soldiers. I supposed if anyone could make it to Tarac just fine, it was Sasha.

"About worshipping Asherah," I began. "May we see the oracle?"

"Of course," Alyon replied, as she swept her arm toward the small arched doorway that led to the oracle's chamber. As Wren and I passed under the arch, I noted the name Nyshanti carved into the stone.

"Torim has been here all along, hiding in plain sight," Wren mur-mured. "Just like Asherah has been in Parthalan."

"So it appears."

The chamber was dark, and the pool in the center of the floor was still as glass. Wren and I sat beside the water's edge, and waited.

And waited.

"Perhaps she isn't here," Wren suggested, after what felt like an interminably long time.

"Where else could she be?" I countered. "She's a noncorporeal goddess bound to a temple. It's not like she's off visiting Asherah."

"I wish I was able to visit her."

I squeezed my eyes shut, because of course Torim—or rather, Nyshanti—chose to appear just as I said something impolite. "Why can't you visit her?" I asked.

Nyshanti melted out of the shadows and sat on the edge of the pool, and I was once again awed by her beauty. She had thick golden hair not unlike the sun's rays, warm brown skin, and large eyes that you could easily lose yourself in. It was no wonder she'd been Asherah's first love.

"There is no place for me in Parthalan," Nyshanti replied. "After Olluhm captured Hillel and me, and then cursed us to inhabit mortal forms, he walled up a goddess in my shrine. Now my mortal body has turned to ash, yet there is no room in my shrine for my spirit to reside. As such, I must remain here."

"Is Cydia in your shrine in Dremmsvard?" I asked, and Nyshanti nodded.

"My one and only shrine, set inside a temple once dedicated to the true sun," Nyshanti said. "Olluhm trapped her inside of it long ago."

"What would happen if we free her?"

Nyshanti's face darkened. "If you free Cydia, I fear Olluhm will once again pursue her, and I shudder to think what he would do. But yes, were she to be freed, I would be able to return to my rightful home."

"About that," Wren began. "If we were to somehow make Olluhm accountable for his actions, what would happen to the sun?"

"You're worried Parthalan would be plunged into darkness?" Nyshanti asked, with barely contained mirth.

"Better to ask now, rather than risk darkness later," Wren said.

Nyshanti smiled. "I do appreciate your forethought. As for the daylight, I highly doubt the child sun, Solon, would abandon his duties. He is a good man, easily as kind and honorable as his mother is, and he loves the Parthian people."

"Your father was the sun before Olluhm, is that right?" I asked.

"Yes. My father was and is the true sun," she replied. "He went with the first wave of refugees from Parthalan to Ysr. He may be there still."

"Then we have much to do," I said. "We will find Sasha and get the lodestone, then we will return to Parthalan and sort out your shrine and the suns so you can return." I paused, wondering if I assumed too much. "That is, if you want to return?"

"I do," Nyshanti said. "More than anything, I wish to look upon Parthalan again." She dragged her slender fingers through the water. "How is Hillel?"

"She's remembered a great deal about her former life," I replied. "She has a mate now, and a son. They're both called Finlay."

"I am glad. Her happiness makes me happy." Nyshanti straightened. "I have no doubt you will find your sister, and that you will retrieve the lodestone. When you arrive at my shrine in Dremmsvard, the lodestone will grant you entry. Remember, it is the key."

"It is the key," Wren and I replied in unison. "Once we're inside, how will we free Cydia?"

"Once you open the doors she will probably free herself," Nyshanti replied. "As for me, I will join you when I am able to manifest either in or near my sanctum."

"Thank you," I said. "Before we go, is there anything we might do for you?"

"Just carry out your mission," Nyshanti replied. "Once the shrine's doors are reopened, everything else will be set to rights."

Chapter Ten

The day after Latera and Wren left for the mortal realm, Mara aimlessly wandered Teg'urnan's bright halls. It saddened her that her mother was gone on her mission to Gannera, and Mara still desperately wanted someone to talk to, but when she went to Ember's chamber it had been empty, as had her father's, and even Innetha's. It seemed that everyone had more important things to do than spend time with her.

Now that's just pathetic.

Since she didn't want to be holed up in her chamber all day, Mara decided to walk the palace corridors until she either found something better to do, or her feet hurt too much to continue. When Mara passed by the healers' ward she overhead Wren's assistant, Chandra, talking about Finn's latest injuries.

"What's happened to Finn?" Mara asked, and she stepped inside the ward.

"What hasn't happened to the poor boy?" Chandra countered. "He was doing much better after his fall, so I sent a *saffira* to his chamber with his lunch instead of bringing it myself. Somehow, a bowl of soup ended up in his lap, the *saffira* ended up in tears, and now Finn won't let anyone tend to the burns on his leg." Chandra sighed, and rubbed her eyes. "Now Attia's with the girl—who is hysterical, by the way—and Finn is all alone."

Mara's heart clenched; Finn had had so many setbacks of late, and the last thing he needed was a burned leg on top of everything else. "I'll go to him," Mara said. "Where's the burn salve?"

"It's in his room," Chandra replied. "I left it there after he threw me out. Good luck, Mara."

Mara nodded her thanks, then she rushed across the palace to the royal wing, and Finn's rooms. She found his door locked, which was unusual, so she knocked.

"Finn?" Mara listened for a moment, then she knocked again. "Finn, please open the door." When the only response was silence, Mara placed her palms flat against the door and whispered a charm her father had taught her long ago, then the lock slid open. She stepped inside the darkened chamber, and called out, "Finn? Finn, it's me, Mara. Chandra told me what happened." She saw his lunch tray on a table near the hearth, with what was left of the food long since gone cold and forgotten. "Finn, please. Where are you?"

"Here."

Mara followed the sound of his voice, and found Finn in his bed with his upper body propped up against the headboard. His pale blond curls were tousled, and his eyes, black like his mother's, stared toward the window. He was wearing a loose white tunic, and the rumpled bedclothes were drawn across his lower half. "Come to check on your favorite invalid?"

"I came to check on my friend." Mara sat on the edge of the bed. "Chandra told me you were hurt, and that she tried to help, but you sent her away."

"I don't need her help."

"Finn—"

"Do you know, by the time we got here, my leg was nearly healed," he began. "I was so excited to get out of that carriage, to walk around under my own power... and in my excitement I took a bad step, and fell flat on my face in front of the whole of Teg'urnan. Suddenly I was an invalid again."

"Wren said you didn't break anything—"all the

"I didn't, but she recommended I rest. More rest. At least for a few days, just to make sure I was well. So I traded that carriage for this room, but it was fine. Just a few more days. Then, the *saffira* who brought me lunch dropped a bowl of soup in my lap and I screamed so loudly half the palace came running with their healers and their bandages, and here I am, yet again an invalid." He faced her, and she could see red spots on his neck and chest where the hot soup may have splashed him. "I hope no one punishes the *saffira*. It really wasn't her fault."

"Attia's with her," Mara said; it was well known that Attia looked after all of the *saffira* as if they were her own children. "She'll be all right."

Finn nodded. "Good."

"Does it hurt?"

"Yes. Quite a bit."

"Will you let me help you?" When Finn remained silent, she took his hand. "Please, Finn. I know what it's like to be in pain, and if I can help lessen yours, I'd like to."

"I've missed you these past few days," he admitted.

"I missed you, too. The rest of the palace has been utter chaos. I miss our quiet times in the carriage."

The corner of his mouth twitched. "You do not. You hated that carriage."

"The company was good, even if the accommodations were awful. May I see the burn?"

He finally met her gaze. "It's in a rather awkward place."

Mara glanced down at his lap, and understood. "Oh! Do you not want me to look... there?"

Finn shrugged. "I suppose it doesn't matter. It's not like you don't know what a man looks like."

Mara was taken aback by his blunt comment, but he was in pain. "All right. Um, let me get the supplies."

Mara found where Chandra had left the burn salve and bandages, and brought everything back to Finn's bed. She laid out her supplies, and drew the bedclothes aside. The top of Finn's thigh was angry and red, and she could tell the burn continued upward.

"I'm going to lift up your shirt," she warned, then she bared him to his waist. The top of the burn wasn't as bad as she'd feared, but it was uncomfortably close to his groin. She wondered if the location of the burn was why he'd sent the healers away.

Mara opened the jar of ointment and began dabbing it onto the burn. "I don't think we'll have to bandage it," she said as she gently swabbed his skin. "From what I understand, burns are better off left uncovered. It should be healed in a day or two."

"I'm to leave it uncovered for a few days? Me going about the palace with a bare arse will cause even more of your dreaded chaos."

Mara glanced up, saw his grin. "Your smile tells me you're already feeling better."

"Dearest Mara, only you can make me smile when I'm in this much pain." Mara returned his smile, then she wiped her hands on a rag and moved to return the salve to a side table. Finn caught her wrist, and asked, "When are you going to talk to me?"

"About what?"

"About anything," he replied. She tried to tug her wrist away, but he had her in an iron grip. "About when we kissed, about everything that happened in Tingu." He pulled her closer, and continued, "About the baby."

Mara gasped and yanked her wrist free. "Why did you say that?"

"One night, in the tent, you were having nightmares," he began. "You usually came into my bed when you had them. On one particular night you did, and when I woke I put my arm around you, and I… I felt your belly." When Mara stared at him, red-faced and trembling, he continued, "I wasn't trying to find out something you wanted to keep hidden. It just happened."

She swallowed. "Have you told anyone?"

He shook his head. "Then, it's true?"

Mara nodded, turning away as a tear slipped down her cheek. "I don't know what I'm going to do."

"Mara, don't cry! I didn't mean to—ah, gods." Finn pulled down his shirt, then he grabbed Mara's waist and hauled her onto the bed beside him.

"Don't pull your burn," she warned.

"Hush." He settled her in the crook of his arm, just like he'd done when they were confined to the carriage and she didn't feel well. "You've already seen to me. Let me see to you."

Mara rested her head on his shoulder. "You really haven't told anyone?"

"It's not my story to tell." He wiped her cheek with his thumb. "Have you told anyone? The father?"

"You and I are the only ones who know." Mara plucked at her skirt. "Kemen is the father. It was Madoc'na, and I wanted to attend, but I didn't have the courage to enter the hall. Then Kemen found me, and then he died, and here I am with his child."

"I'm so sorry, love." Finn pulled her closer, and pressed his face against her hair. "We're all here for you—your family, and mine, and me. I'm here for whatever you need."

"I don't even know what I need." Mara smoothed her dress over her belly. "I suppose I should look into some bigger clothing, for starters."

"I'll send for a seamstress," Finn said. "We'll have clothes made for you, and the baby, and we should probably look into a cradle, and, um, other things. Baby things."

"That's all very kind, but you don't need to take care of me."

"It's all right. I want to. Besides, you said yourself the rest of the palace is utter chaos. That's no place for a woman in your delicate condition. Better you stay here, where it's calm."

Mara looked up at Finn, the concern in his eyes warming her heart. "You have this all figured out, don't you?"

"Not all of it, but I'm working on the rest." He took her hand. "You are going to have to say something, eventually."

"I wish Mama and Wren weren't in Gannera," she said. "I was about to talk to Mama, when she announced she'd be going to the mortal realm to find my Auntie Sasha. I... I need her."

"What about Aeolmar?"

"He's wrapped up with my other aunts, and the queen, and, well, the rest of the chaos. He doesn't need me distracting him."

"Mara." Finn tilted up her chin, and glided his thumb across her jaw. "I don't know where you got the idea that you're a burden, or a distraction, but you are neither of those things. You are a kind, and beautiful, and intelligent woman, and many, many people love you."

Mara's cheeks warmed as she ducked her head. "I recall saying something similar to you when you worried you were a burden."

"Lies. You've never called me a woman."

She laughed. "You're right. I never have."

***

"I saw you at Madoc'na," Mara said. They'd sent for tea and bread, and moved out to Finn's balcony, which overlooked the palace square. Finn had taken Mara's advice and not put on his trousers, but he had covered his lap with a blanket.

"Did you?" Finn asked. "So that's why you weren't shy about lifting up my shirt earlier."

"Finlay Torim," Mara began, then the *saffira* arrived with their meal. Mara noted that there was no soup, but she had brought an assortment of fresh fruit with the bread.

"Thank you," Finn said, as the food and tea was laid out. "How is Neela?"

"She's all right," the *saffira* replied. "She'll be happy to hear you're doing well, my lord."

"As I am happy to hear she's well," Finn said. "She was mortified when I dropped the soup."

The *saffira* gave Finn a coy smile, and Mara wondered if all the palace girls flirted with him. She'd never noticed. "I will tell her. My lady, is the tea to your liking?"

"Yes," Mara said. "Thank you." With that, the *saffira* curtsied and left the balcony.

"You dropped the soup?" Mara asked. "I thought it was dropped on you."

"It was, but Neela was nervous," Finn said. "It was her first time serving me, and she somehow got this idea that princes are scary beasts. Then I had a lap full of hot soup and bellowed in her face, and proved her right." He gave her a sheepish grin. "Honestly, it was just a simple mistake."

"You're good to look out for her."

"Why, thank you. You were saying you saw me at Madoc'na?"

Mara cleared her throat. "I did, and that makes you officially braver than me." She eyed him over the rim of her bowl. "Can I ask what it was like?"

"You can ask me anything, dearest Mara," Finn began, "but please don't think me brave. Leran talked to me about it during dinner. He's the one who convinced me to take part."

"Really? What did he say?"

"As it turned out, I had the wrong idea about the whole event. I imagined it would be chaotic, with bodies everywhere frantically coupling and uncoupling. Leran explained that it was a much calmer, more relaxed celebration." Finn picked through the bowl of fruit, hunting for the brambleberries. "I almost didn't attend either, even after Leran's explanation. But then I figured we were leaving for battle the next morning, and I might not make it, so I might as well join in with the rest. As it was, I almost didn't survive my time at The Seat."

Mara shuddered, the memory of Finn's bloody, broken body still too fresh in her mind. "And was Madoc'na enough? If you hadn't survived, would you have died content?"

"No." He passed her a plate of brambleberries. "Here. I know the berries are your favorite."

"Thank you. What would have made you content?"

"Being with the one I love, but she wasn't at Madoc'na." He glanced at her, then away. "I thought she might attend, but she didn't."

The tart berry turned to stone on Mara's tongue. She swallowed it, and said, "My entire purpose for going there was to get over Kemen. I thought if I found someone else for the night, I could put him behind me." She patted her belly. "And now he's gone, yet part of him will always be with me."

"Do you regret it?"

"No, I don't," Mara said, her voice betraying that she herself wasn't sure of the answer until she said the words out loud. "Kemen was always good to me, and while I don't think we were meant to be together, I will miss him. And now I have my baby. This may sound strange, but I already love him so much."

"That doesn't sound strange at all," Finn said softly. "You'll be a wonderful mother, Mara."

"Do you really think so?"

"I do." Finn held out his arm, and Mara fit herself against him. "Do you remember when I told you I love you?"

Mara nodded, momentarily terrified Finn was about to recant what he said. "I think about it every day. I've often wondered if you meant it, or if you were delusional from your injuries."

"I meant it." Finn rested his head against hers, and said, "I swear to you I will be here for you, and the baby. For whatever you need today, and tomorrow, and until the end of time. You have my word."

"Thank you, Finn," she said. "You don't know what that means to me. With you by my side, things don't seem so scary."

"By your side as a friend, or something more?"

"More?"

He pushed her hair behind her ear, and caressed her neck. "Have you ever wondered what it would be like if we were together?"

Mara held her breath, unsure what to say or do or even if the moment was real. She had thought about what it would be like to be Finn's mate many, many times. The way he always knew what she needed, be it a kind word or plate of brambleberries, and the way he held her even now made Mara realize that whomever he took as a mate would be very happy. Mara never considered that she might be that happy, because he was the Prince of Parthalan, and she was carrying a dead man's child.

"Why didn't you ask me this in Tingu?" she asked, not yet ready to believe his offer was real. "Or on the way home when we were trapped in that carriage? Why wait until now?"

"As soon as I started feeling better, you started feeling worse," he began. "And we were always surrounded by people. I couldn't tell you such things with anyone else nearby who might overhear. What if... what if I told you how I felt, and you said no?"

She placed her palm against his cheek. "You really thought I would reject you?"

"I never thought that far ahead," he admitted. "It's taken me this long to garner the courage to talk to you." His black eyes held her gaze. "Tell me what happens next."

Mara closed her eyes, and wondered what it would be like to be with Finn. To have a family and a life with this kind man, to be content waking beside him every morning... But then, she'd already been waking beside him for almost four moons, beginning when she'd slept beside his sickbed at The Seat, and then during long the journey home. Almost as long as her baby had been growing inside her. She thought about how her nausea and exhaustion increased tenfold when she wasn't near Finn, and wondered if that was the baby's way of protesting being apart from him.

She wondered if the baby saw Finn as his father.

Mara wondered if she was the one he'd been looking for at Madoc'na. She hoped she was, but what if he'd been seeking someone else? What if Finn was settling for her, or worse, what if he only wanted to help her because of the baby? Before she could ask any of those questions, she heard two women calling her father's name.

"What's happening down there?" Mara craned her neck toward the square, and saw her aunts at one end of the space, waving and calling Aeolmar's name. In the center of the square was Aeolmar himself, who looked like he wished he could turn invisible.

"Those two are your aunts?" Finn asked.

"Yes, that's Auntie Elia and Auntie Jannei. Mama made the mistake of telling them she can speak to Papa mind to mind, and now they keep asking him to tell her things." Mara faced Finn, and shrugged. "I think if it were up to him, he would flee the palace to get away from them, but Ember's here. He wants to spend as much time with her as he can before she returns to Tingu."

Finn nodded. "Did you hear what I said?"

"I did. I heard all of it."

He grasped her hand, and said, "I mean it, Mara. Anything you want. Name it, and it's yours."

She laughed nervously. "I-I need a new clasp for my cloak, and I could do with more of those brambleberries, and—"

"Mara." He rubbed his thumb across her knuckles. "I'm not referring to cloaks or berries. Surely you know that."

"I know," she began, then she heard her aunts yelling for her father again. "I should help Papa." Mara said, relieved at finding an excuse to pause their conversation, and take some time to gather her thoughts. "Can we talk later? Please?"

Finn nodded, frowning. "If that's what you want."

"It is." Mara stood, then she caressed Finn's cheek. "And I want to talk to you, later when it's quiet. I'm not good at saying what I mean right away; I need time to consider my responses. I'm not trying to avoid you."

Finn smiled tightly. "I know you wouldn't do that. It's just a bit boring, being stuck in this room all day and night." He took her hand, and kissed her knuckles. "I look forward to talking to you tonight, at dinner."

"So do I. Wait, will you be wearing proper clothing?"

"I thought you preferred me this way."

"Finn!"

Chapter Eleven
Aeolmar Speaks

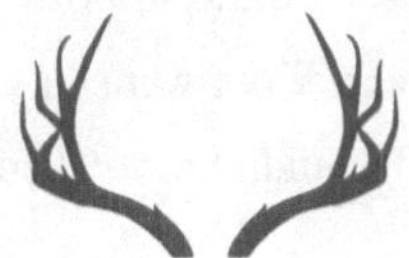

After a morning's worth of training in the *sola*, I crossed the palace square, intent on finding lunch before going on to the great hall. As I made my way across the space, movement from one of the royal balconies caught my eye. It was the easternmost balcony, which meant it was Finn's room. I hoped he was doing better since his fall, but I understood that when one's pride was bruised it was sometimes a long road back. As I got closer, I realized he was sitting with a red-haired woman. With Latera away, there were only two red-haired women in the palace. Since I knew Ember wasn't spending time with Finn, that meant Mara was sitting next to the Prince of Parthalan.

Mara, who'd spent nearly every waking moment with Finn since they'd been attacked at The Seat. I found that very, very interesting.

As far as I was aware, the only man Mara had ever been interested in was Kemen, and he had perished out on the Northern Waste. Mara had mourned him, and while I'd never approved of Kemen's interest in my daughter, neither had I stood in her way. Mara was a grown woman, and capable of handling her life without my interference. If whatever was happening between her and Finn turned out to be more than friendship, I wouldn't stand in her way now, either. At least Finn was an honorable man, unlike Kemen, who—

"Aeolmar! Aeolmar!"

The shrill shriek of my name splintered my thoughts. I sighed, and turned toward Latera's sisters. Now that I'd spent time with the adult versions of Elia and Jannei, I understood why Latera had left them in Teg'urnan while she and Wren went in search of their youngest sister, and the lodestone. I wouldn't have taken those two on a mission, either.

I waved at Elia, hoping that would quiet her down. Of course, it didn't. I glanced toward Finn's balcony, and saw he and Mara were also waving at me. "Need some help?" Mara called.

"A bit," I replied, then I continued on toward the sisters. "You were looking for me?" I asked, once I was close enough.

"Yes, yes," Elia said. "Have you had word from Latera?"

Why Latera told them we could speak to each other mind to mind was beyond me. Once she was home, we would have a long talk about keeping this aspect of our bond private. "A moment. I will ask how she is."

Beloved.

Mar? Mar! How are you? How are the children?

I smiled, despite my present company. While I had complete faith in Latera's ability to complete her mission, I also missed her terribly. *We're all well. Your sisters requested an update.*

Is that the only reason you reached out?

You know it isn't, nalla.

I could swear I felt her cheeks warm. *I love you, too. We've left Asherah's temple, and are on our way to Tarac. Apparently, that's where Sasha went. Wren and I are hopeful we will find her soon.*

I will let your sisters know. Stay safe, nalla.

You too, nall.

We ended our conversation, but I could still feel Latera in my mind. Her presence comforted me in a way nothing else ever could. Soon, she would be home, and I would tell her all about how much I'd missed her, and comfort her myself.

"Latera and Wren are well," I told the sisters, then I relayed to them what Latera had told me, save for the endearments. Whenever Latera referred to me as *nall,* which meant her beloved in *ahm'ri,* I kept that close to my heart.

"Tarac," Jannei said, after I'd told them everything. "I don't know how safe that will be."

"Why?" I demanded. "What's in Tarac?"

"Our mother's from Tarac," Elia replied. "Her entire family was exiled before we were born. It's how she ended up marrying the king of Gannera."

I grunted, because I had no love or respect for Latera's cruel, conniving father. "Will those in power know who Latera is?"

"Oh, most definitely," Elia said. "She looks exactly like our ancestor, the mighty Elvasla."

"Is that a good thing?"

Elia shrugged. "I suppose we'll find out soon enough."

I was a moment away from losing my temper with Latera's obtuse, infuriating, annoying siblings, when Mara approached us. "Hello, everyone," she greeted.

"Mara, how wonderful to see you," I said. "How is Finn?"

"Much better," she replied. "He is going to try to make it to the hall tonight."

"Wonderful news," I said, and it was. I'd been as worried about Finn as his parents were.

"Speaking of dinner, ladies, where will you be sitting?" Mara asked her aunts, then my gem of a daughter led them away from me. That threat dealt with, I continued on to my original destination, the great hall. Or, more specifically, the fortifications surrounding the great hall. My interlude with Elia and Jannei had destroyed my appetite for the moment.

We were re-fortifying the great hall because tomorrow was Reckoning Day, which was a holiday Asherah had created early in her reign. On Reckoning Day any citizen of Parthalan could come to Teg'urnan and have their grievances heard and judged by the queen and king. Since I'd been First Hunter, I'd witnessed land disputes, arguments about inheritances, and Asherah once heard a case about a chicken and its cursed eggs.

Reckoning Day was Asherah's favorite day of the year. As for Finlay, he loved Reckoning Day because Asherah adored it so, but I don't think he'd miss it if the tradition ended. As for me, I hated it, and every year it drove me to the edge of madness. Neither of Parthalan's rulers comprehended that letting everyone inside Teg'urnan meant that *everyone was inside of Teg'urnan,* including all of the thieves, murderers, and other ne'er do wells. Their naïveté with regard to who may find their way into the palace meant that I was tasked with reinforcing our defenses, posting extra guards, and ensuring that no one got too close to our royal family. If only I could convince Asherah to hold the event outside in the square, where I could keep everyone in view at all times. Or better yet, we could keep the masses outside the walls, and she and Finlay could hear cases while seated on the ramparts. Yes, that would work out quite well.

When I'd shared my ideas with Latera, she thought I was overreacting. I considered myself well-prepared.

I entered the hall and went directly to the dais. I liked to stand between the thrones and survey the hall while it was nearly empty, and try to ascertain where our weakest points were. Across the hall, I saw Elkin speaking to a group of guards. Next to him was my son, Tor. When he saw me, he said something to Elkin, then joined me on the dais.

"Are the preparations going well?" I asked Tor.

"Aye," Tor replied. "Elkin's got them all trained to perfection. He'd do well up in Tingu with Leran's men."

Tor had been greatly impressed by Tingu's legion, and truth be told, so had I. "That's good to hear. You will be on the dais tomorrow, next to Finn's chair." Finn's injuries made him more vulnerable than usual, and the added protection of Tor would greatly ease my and his parents' minds.

"I assume Mara will be sitting with him," Tor said.

"Why would she?" I asked. Mara hadn't attended a Reckoning Day in years.

"You haven't noticed?" Tor countered. "Those two are inseparable."

I recalled seeing the two of them on Finn's balcony, and the two moons they'd spent in a carriage together. This day was getting more interesting by the moment. "I'll have another chair brought out. Think you can watch over both of them?"

Tor grinned. "I can handle it. No one gets past me."

Latera has often said that Tor got none of my paranoia, and those gaps had been filled with confidence instead. Luckily, he also trained hard, so he could back up his wild claims. That didn't mean I couldn't tease him.

"No one?" I asked, then I called out, "Elkin! Tor claims no one can get past him."

"Is that so?" Elkin replied, as he approached the dais with his hand on his sword's hilt. "We'll see about that."

Chapter Twelve
Latera speaks

As luck would have it, many pilgrims visited Asherah's temple, and before long we met a few who were traveling on toward Tarac. Much as Sasha had, we offered one of them a few coins, and he allowed us to make room for ourselves in the back of his cart. Unlike Sasha, who was last seen riding off in a covered wagon, Wren and I rode along with some rather talkative chickens.

"I've never seen so many birds in one place," I said, as I picked feathers off of my lap. The birds were in cages stacked up so high Wren and I were hidden from view from anyone who passed by, which was the only benefit to this arrangement. "What madman first decided to transport them this way?"

"How did you think chickens got to market?" Wren asked, as I wrinkled my nose at the squawking beasts.

"I've never really thought about chickens at all." I knew they laid eggs, and that they made a good dinner, and that was the sum total of my knowledge. "I don't even know how to cook one."

"Hear that, girls?" Wren cooed to the birds. "You're quite safe with us."

"Glad you're enjoying yourself," I muttered, as I moved further away from the twig and twine cages.

"Now you're learning about some of the things you missed out on being raised as a princess," Wren said. "I've been around fowl my entire life. They can sense how uncomfortable you are," she added.

"I'm not uncomfortable. I'm getting pecked." I glared at one of the offenders. She lunged her feathered head at me again, but her cage was too far away and her beak landed in empty air. Ha. "And have you forgotten I was a stable hand for six winters? Horses, now those animals are worth your time."

"Don't listen to her," Wren said to her new friends. "By the end of this journey, she'll love you as I do."

***

Wren was wrong. By the time the farmer's cart rolled through the gates of Tarac's market I hated all birds, not just chickens.

"Here we are," the kindly farmer called back to us. "Are you certain you ladies will be all right if I let you off here?"

"We are. Thank you again for your help." Earlier, when we'd stopped for a rest, I'd offered him a few more pieces of gold for his trouble. The noble man had refused further payment, claiming he was doing good deeds in Asherah's name. I appreciated that, but I also dropped a few extra coins near his vicious birds. If nothing else, he'd need the coins for bandages after these beasts had their way with him.

I looked up at Tarac's castle, shielding my eyes against the sun. With any luck, we could gain entrance without too much fuss, and find a few people who may know of Sasha's whereabouts. However, neither Wren nor I had ever been to Tarac and thus had no relationships or other goodwill to draw upon, so entering the castle would require finesse. If there was anything I lacked, it was finesse.

As I examined the castle walls, and counted soldiers and entry points, I saw a man standing on the ramparts. He wore a green cloak, and even though his hood was pulled low over his face it was plain that he was watching us. After a moment, he turned and disappeared deeper into the castle, but not before I caught a flash of a distinctive shade of silver metal along his back.

"That man had a troll sword on his back," I murmured to Wren.

"Odd. Let's ask him where he got it."

"Excellent idea."

We meandered through the marketplace, trying and apparently failing to look like two human women running their daily errands. Even though she'd spent many years in Parthalan, Wren had maintained her mostly-human appearance, but the leather satchel she carried on her back with hay sticking out of the seams was unusual enough for others to notice. As for me, I'd left my hair loose to cover my ears and therefore my identity as an elf, but in my haste to find a clue about Sasha I'd forgotten that red hair is as uncommon in the mortal realm as it is everywhere else.

"Everyone is looking at you," Wren murmured.

"It's my hair," I said, but she shook her head.

"It's your swords," Wren whispered, and I wanted to kick myself. Mortal women didn't carry swords, or wear leather riding gear instead of dresses, or do most of the things that came as second nature to me. I may as well have shot a flaming arrow toward the portcullis and announced our presence that way.

I glanced at the crowd, and saw faces masked with confusion and fear; as a rule, mortals had never done well when presented with the strange or unusual. While I'd never shied away from a fight, there were dozens of them, and I also had Wren to look after. I swallowed, and hoped that most of these people were friendly.

The green cloaked man from the ramparts appeared at my elbow. "Come with me," he said, then he moved to grab my arm. My knife dropped into my hand and I took a step back from him.

"Don't touch me," I hissed, brandishing the blade.

He held up his hands, palms out. "I won't hurt you, but I believe I can help you. You're from Parthalan, are you not?"

"What makes you say that?" I demanded.

He lowered his hood, and I saw a fae man with short blond hair shot through with silver and wide blue eyes. It was as if a much older version of Caol'non was staring back at me. "Because I am, too."

"Tor," I said, because there was no one else this man could be. I'd found Caol'non's father, Aeolmar's grandsire, at a market in Tarac, of all places.

"How do you know that name?" he asked.

"My mate is Caol'nir's son."

"Your mate is the younger Tor?"

I blinked, since my first thought was of my own son called Tor, but I remembered that was also the name of Aeolmar's eldest brother. "No. My mate is one of Caol'nir's younger sons."

Tor grunted, the he beckoned Wren and me toward the castle. "Come inside. We have much to speak of."

The three of us entered through a small side door, and Tor led us down a narrow corridor. "Why are we taking the servants' passage?" Wren asked.

When Tor remained silent, I replied, "Discretion, most likely." There were so many things I wanted to ask Tor—how did he come to be in the mortal realm, did he know Nyshanti was hiding in a temple in Gannera, did he have any insight into what we should do about Olluhm—but I held my tongue. I knew very little about Tarac, but my mother's family had been exiled from this land while she was still a child. For all I knew, those in power had been waiting to get their hands on me and exact their revenge.

We came upon a heavy wood door. Tor pushed it open, and we entered a storage room. It was murky and cluttered inside, and I instinctively walked toward the light filtering in from the windows on the far side of the room.

"Stay away from the windows," he warned, as he shut the door and placed himself between us and the exit.

"Why?" I asked. "Do you have enemies here?"

"No, but you might." Tor crossed his arms over his chest and widened his stance, and in the darkness I could have mistaken him for Aeolmar. "Do you?"

"Not that I'm aware of." Every one of my instincts was telling me to flee, but this was Aeolmar's grandsire. Surely he wouldn't hurt us, would he? I touched the swords on my back, and silently thanked Grelk for his gift of excellent weaponry. Thus heartened, I asked, "Why are you in Tarac?"

"I could ask the same of you," he countered.

"That's fair," I conceded. "We're looking for our sister."

"Is she from Parthalan?"

"No. Gannera."

Tor grunted. "Who rules in Parthalan?"

"Asherah," I replied. "She has a king now. He's called Finlay."

"That's good," Tor said. "Asherah is both kind and just. I worried Lormac's death would haunt her forever, but I'm glad it hasn't." He looked toward the window, as if waiting for a signal. "I fear you have me at a disadvantage, since you already know my name."

"I'm called Latera, and this is my sister, Wren." I paused, and added, "My mate's name is Aeolmar."

Tor laughed through his nose. "That sounds like a name Alluria came up with."

"She did. She saw a hawk the morning she bore him." Aeolmar's name meant bird of prey on the wind. Mara's name meant little bird of prey.

"Did she tell you that story?"

"No. She died long before I met Aeolmar." Tor's jaw tightened, but he didn't ask what had happened to his son. If Alluria was gone, he already knew that Caol'nir was, as well. "My son—my and Aeolmar's son—is named Tor. We have two daughters, too."

"Is that so?" Tor asked, a hint of pride in his voice. He approached a set of shelves, and retrieved a lamp. "It is dark in here. Let me find a flint, so we can at least see each other."

I flicked my hand and muttered the words to call fire, and the wick caught. "Alluria taught that charm to Aeolmar, and he taught it to me," I explained. I hoped that these bits of information would reinforce my claim of knowing his family, and foster trust between us.

Tor nodded. "I remember her tossing fire about like a toy."

"She threw fire?" Wren asked. "That doesn't sound very safe."

"It wasn't." Tor adjusted the flame on the lamp. "I assume you're here for Sasha."

"You know Sasha?" Wren asked, while I demanded, "She's here?"

"Yes. She's with Priya."

"Priya," I repeated. "Elvasla's daughter?"

Tor blew out a breath. "How is it that we've never met yet we have so many people in common?"

"Perhaps we were destined to meet." Since I saw no reason to be less than forthright with him, I continued, "Finding our sister is only part of our mission. We've also been tasked with retrieving the lodestone from Gannera Castle."

"What in the nine realms are you going to do with the lodestone?"

I shrugged. "Free Cydia, remove Olluhm from the sky, and restore The Deliverer."

Tor sighed again, the lamplight deepening the lines on his face. "I don't know how Priya will feel about any of this."

"It doesn't matter how she feels," I said. "I have a duty to Parthalan and to Thurnda, and I will see my mission complete. Neither you nor Priya need concern yourselves with the outcome."

"You sound like Alluria," Tor said. "If Aeolmar's like my son, it's no wonder he's with you."

I was about to bite off a reply, when the heavy door creaked open. Framed in the doorway, with the lamplight turning her pale hair to gold, was Sasha.

"Latera," Sasha said. "I've been waiting for you."

Chapter Thirteen

Finn entered the great hall through one of the side entrances instead of the main door, just in case he felt unsteady. He didn't, but he hadn't felt unsteady before he'd fallen on the steps in front of the entire palace, either. At least this time, he'd brought his cane with him for added support.

Luckily Teg'urnan's hall was all on the same level, unlike The Seat's massive gathering place with its many raised platforms and other random steps. The hall's floor, while polished smooth as ice, wasn't slippery, and after a few test steps Finn was confident he could navigate the room all the way to his seat. As for what he'd manage to accomplish after tonight's festivities, that remained to be seen.

He didn't have any special duties for the night, nor would he tomorrow on Reckoning Day. It was a day his mother had established early in her reign, when any citizen of Parthalan was allowed to petition the royal seat for any matter that they wished to discuss, be it as complex as a land dispute or as mundane as a missing goat. Asherah loved her people, and she made sure that all of them had access to her.

Finn smiled, and realized that his mother's intense devotion to her people was yet another aspect of her role as The Deliverer.

He moved further into the hall, and saw Mara on the opposite side of the room, sitting with her aunts and Ember. He patted the pouch on his belt, which contained a gift he'd secured for her only a short time ago, and he couldn't wait to present it to her. Before he could approach Mara, Leran strode across the hall to greet him.

"Brother," Leran said, as he joined him. "How's the leg?"

"Much better," Finn replied. "Burnt my cock on some soup, though."

Leran regarded the younger man. "You and I eat soup very differently."

"Can't argue that." Finn beckoned a *saffira*, who gave them each mugs of ale. "How are you liking Teg'urnan? This is what, the third time you've been here?"

"Yes, the third time," Leran replied. "The first time was when Latera felled the *mordeth-gall*, and the second was Asherah's jubilee." Leran looked across the hall and smiled. "But this by far is the best trip, because now my mate is here with me."

Finn followed Leran's gaze, and saw Ember speaking with her aunts. When Ember felt her mate's eyes on her, she turned to him and smiled. "I can only imagine how wonderful this must be for both of you," Finn said.

"How goes it with Mara?" Leran asked; he was the only person Finn had ever confided to about his feelings for Mara, other than Mara herself. "Or is she the reason you got burnt?"

Finn leaned closer, and asked, "Who do you think put the salve on me?" Leran laughed and clapped Finn's shoulder. Before he could say anything further, a party arrived through the main entrance.

"Who's that lot?" Finn wondered. The party was made up of five people dressed in black clothes with red boots and gloves, and one carried a gold banner emblazoned with a black cat. When they got closer, Finn saw that the cat's jaws were bloody.

"I don't know that standard," Leran said, then Finlay approached them.

"That is Krylle, the High Priest of the old gods from the east," Finlay informed them. He glanced at Finn, and added, "Kemen's father."

Finn was suddenly very glad of his cane. "Why is he here, now?"

His father the king shook his head. "I can't imagine."

Finn searched the gathering, and saw Mara remained on the other side of the hall with her family. She'd also spotted Krylle, and based on the look on her face, she recognized his standard all too well. He moved to approach Mara, but Leran halted him.

"Don't draw attention to her," Leran said, without looking at Mara or mentioning her name. While Leran didn't know about Mara's baby, Finn knew he would remember her relationship with Kemen. "If he doesn't know who she is, let's keep it that way."

Finn nodded, and stood his ground. Krylle reached the center of the hall, and the standard bearer struck the bottom of the pole against the stone floor three times, to get the gathering's attention.

"I seek an audience with the queen," Krylle announced, once the hall was quiet.

"Who seeks an audience with me?" Asherah asked. She stood in front of the head table with a goblet dangling from her hand. Beside her, Innetha leaned against the table. Anyone who didn't know the queen and her huntress, and hadn't witnessed their speed first hand, would have dismissed them as nonthreatening. They would also be wrong.

"Reckoning Day doesn't begin until tomorrow, but I have time now," Asherah continued. "Please. State your business."

"I am Krylle, priest of Those Who Went Before," he replied. "I received your message about my son, Kemen. You told me about his death."

Asherah bowed her head. "You have my deepest condolences. Kemen will be remembered as a hero."

"That is all well and good, but what about his son?"

Finn went still. Heeding Leran's advice he refrained from looking toward Mara, but it was difficult.

"Kemen had a child?" Asherah asked. "I did not know."

"The child is not yet born," Krylle continued. "But Kemen sent me many, many letters telling me all about his beautiful mate. He said she was an elf, with red hair and blue eyes, and that she carried his boy."

Aeolmar moved to stand next to Asherah, his stance wide and his arms crossed over his chest. Leran clenched Finn's arm, keeping him immobile. Caol'non and Elkin took positions behind Krylle's party, blocking their exit.

"Again, Krylle, I don't know whom you are referring to," Asherah said. "Kemen never once mentioned having a mate, at least not to me. Perhaps these missives he wrote to you were a bit of fantasy on his part?"

"Now you deal in lies?" Krylle demanded. "The Ish h'ra of old would have cut out her tongue before telling an untruth."

"My name is Asherah," the queen snapped. "You may address me as Your Majesty. Call me anything else and you risk losing your own tongue."

"Apologies, Your Majesty," Krylle said with a bow. When he straightened, his gaze alighted on Ember. "You, your hair is red. Do you carry my grandson?"

Ember made a show of looking to either side. "Oh, you mean me?" she asked unnecessarily. Behind her, Elia and Jannei stood, thus hiding Mara from Krylle's view. "I carry no child. If you don't believe me, ask my mate." Ember crossed the room to Leran, drawing Krylle's gaze farther from Mara. Undeterred, Krylle shook his head.

"You all seek to distract me, but I know the truth," the priest said. "My agent in Thurnda saw my son together with his mate, and they have assured me he got her with child. They did not know how he died," Krylle added, with a pointed look at Asherah.

"He fell battling orcs in the Northern Waste," Asherah said. "Would you like me to repeat that in *ahm'ri*?" she added, naming the magical language that made one unable to tell a lie.

"Of course, I believe you, Your Majesty," Krylle said, with another bow. "Please, forgive me for my rudeness. We have traveled far, and Kemen was my only son. I grieve him still."

"Again, Krylle, you have my deepest condolences." Asherah beckoned a *saffira* and whispered a few instructions. "We will have rooms prepared for you and your party. Please, avail yourselves of all Teg'ur-nan has to offer. In the morning, after we are all rested, we will speak again."

"Many thanks, Your Majesty," Krylle said, then he and his party followed the *saffira* out the door through which they entered. Finlay made a sharp gesture, and six soldiers followed the priests to their rooms. Asherah looked at Finlay and nodded, then she retreated to the smaller chamber at the rear of the hall used for informal meetings. The king and others of their inner circle followed, as did Finn. Out of the corner of his eye, he saw Mara leave the hall with her aunts.

Finn and the king were the last to enter the room. Once the door closed behind them, Asherah faced the group, and demanded, "What in the nine realms just happened?"

"Krylle seems to think he has a legacy of sorts," Innetha said. "Does anyone know something about him having a mate, or a child?" When no one spoke, she nodded. "Good. We'll all keep not knowing."

"Why did he mention how Kemen died?" Finlay asked. "Was there something significant about his demise?"

Asherah opened her mouth, but Caol'non said, "I should tell them." Asherah gestured for him to continue. Caol'non faced the rest, and said, "I killed Kemen."

"Why did you murder one of my hunters?" Aeolmar ground out.

"It was during the battle, directly after Asherah summoned the light that destroyed many of the orcs," Caol'non replied. "Once she had revealed herself, Kemen approached her with a dagger intending to kill her. That's what Krylle preaches, that the old gods should be released in death," he explained. "It's why many of the old ones retreated to Ysr or the mortal realm, in order to hide themselves from those zealots. Regardless, Kemen approached the queen with a naked blade, and I stopped him before she was harmed."

"Why didn't you mention this before?" Aeolmar asked.

"I ordered his silence," Asherah said. "But everything Caol'non said is true. Kemen advanced upon me with his dagger drawn, and Caol'non stopped him. While I am grateful to you," she said to Caol'non, "I'm more interested in Krylle's claim that he has an agent in Thurnda."

"That's obviously Cerillia," Finn said. "Other than us, she was the only new person in the palace."

"And you don't think one of Thurnda's people, or one of our own, could be this agent?" Asherah asked.

Finn shook his head. "Elves don't involve themselves in fae business or with gods. As for us Parthians, to report on Kemen's activities to an outside party, even to Kemen's own father, would be a betrayal. Our people are loyal."

"Agreed," Leran said. "Both Sibeal and Latera have their doubts about Cerillia's true motives, as well."

Asherah nodded to her sons, and looked to the rest of the group. "Finn and Leran are correct," she said. "To give an outsider information on Kemen would be a betrayal of both lands."

The rest murmured their agreement, and Finn heard what everyone left unsaid: not only would such spying on Kemen be a betrayal of Asherah's hunters, but also Aeolmar's daughter. The First Hunter inspired as much loyalty as the king and queen did.

"By your leave, Ember and I will leave for Thurnda at first dawn," Leran said. "If this agent of Krylle's is indeed Cerillia, we need to alert Sibeal."

"Agreed," Asherah said. "We will watch Krylle, and find out what he has to say for himself tomorrow. Until then, be vigilant, all of you."

With that, Asherah dismissed them. Finn watched as the hunters filed out of the room in twos and threes while he remained rooted in place. When the room was almost empty, Asherah approached him.

"Where is Mara?" she asked Finn.

"I saw her leave with her aunts," he replied. Asherah nodded, then she placed her hand on Finn's arm.

"Do you need anything from me?" she asked. "Either of you?" Finn glanced at Leran, but Asherah shook her head. "I mean you, or Mara."

Finn sucked in a breath, shocked that she would ask him anything about Mara. "I can ask her if she needs anything."

Asherah patted his arm. "See that you do. I'll have guards posted at either end of the corridor that leads to her rooms, as well. We will keep her safe." As Finn's mind was still reeling with the implications that at least one of his parents knew how he felt about Mara, Asherah turned to Leran. "I'm sorry you'll be leaving so soon."

"As am I," Leran said. "Care to map out the route with Ember and I?"

"Of course." Asherah smiled at Leran and squeezed Finn's arm, then she returned to the hall.

Finn looked up at his brother. "She asked about Mara and I as if we're a couple."

Leran smiled. "Get used to it. Would you like to sit with us as we plan our route to Thurnda?"

"Perhaps later. For now, I'm going to check on Mara."

Chapter Fourteen

Mara Speaks

After Krylle and his men were escorted from the hall by a company of soldiers, Elia and Jannei each took one of my arms and walked me out of the side exit. We moved quickly and quietly down the corridors, and none of us said a word until we were inside my chamber with the door shut behind us.

"What an awful man that priest was," Jannei said. "Here, Mara, sit near the fire." I did, and Elia appeared at my elbow with a goblet of cold water.

"Thank you," I said. After I'd had some water, I asked, "How did you know to hide me?"

Elia shrugged. "A man dressed in black bearing a banner of a bloody toothed cat came into the hall, unannounced, looking for a red haired woman. We don't know what he's about, but it doesn't look good. And, you're family," she added, with a warm smile that reminded me of my mother. "That foul priest will have to go through us to get to you."

"Thank you," I said again, my hands trembling as I held the goblet.

"Deep breaths, now," Jannei said, as she took the goblet from me. "A woman with child must remain calm for the baby's sake."

I stilled. "You knew?"

Jannei smiled. "Of course we did."

"It's rather obvious," Elia added. "This child is from the priest's son, I gather?"

I opened my mouth to reply, but there was a knock at the door. Jannei opened it, and after a moment she announced, "There's a Caol'non here, looking to speak with Mara. Should I admit him?"

"Yes, please. He's also family," I called back. Caol'non strode inside the room, and knelt at my feet.

"Mara, I must speak to you about Kemen," he began, then he told me how Kemen had tried to murder Asherah during the battle out on the Northern Waste. Luckily, Caol'non saw what was happening, and killed Kemen in time to save the queen.

"I did not know he was special to you," he concluded. "I am deeply sorry for any pain my actions have caused you."

"If you'd known about him and I, would you have still killed him?" I asked.

"Yes," Caol'non replied. "I took an oath to defend Parthian royalty long ago. No matter that my oath was sworn to a different ruler, as long as I'm alive my oath still holds."

I nodded. "I appreciate your honesty, Caol'non. If Kemen was close to harming Asherah, I am glad you were there to protect her."

"I still have his dagger," he said. "Would you like it?"

"No, no," I said. "I've got my own dagger, and his will be put to better use in your hands. Thank you, for telling me what happened."

Caol'non smiled, but it didn't reach his eyes. Even though he'd done the right thing, Kemen's death weighed hard on him. "You are very kind. I will do what I can to keep Krylle at a distance from you. Your father has posted guards in the corridor, as well."

"Do you really think that's necessary?" I asked.

"Aeolmar does, and I agree with him," Caol'non said as he stood. "Better to have too much protection rather than not enough."

"All right," I said. "Thank you." A curt nod, and Caol'non was gone. No sooner had the door closed, than there was another knock.

"Mara, you've another visitor," Jannei said, and Finn entered the room.

Until the moment I saw Finn I didn't realize how much I needed him, but once I set eyes on him I felt a weight lift off my shoulders. No matter what Krylle was about, as long as Finn was with me I could handle it. We could handle it.

Well, we could handle it if Elia and Jannei stopped glowering at Finn as if he was their sworn enemy.

"Um, hello everyone," Finn said, as he set his cane against the wall. Elia looked him over. "You're the prince?"

"I am," he replied, with his wide smile that made everyone love him. Everyone except my Aunt Elia, that is. "I was hoping to speak with Mara. Privately, that is."

"Mara, will you be safe alone with this man?" Elia asked, keeping her sharp gaze on Finn. "We can remain, if you'd like."

"I'm safer with Finn than with anyone else in the realm," I replied. "He's a good man, Auntie. Really."

"You mustn't let Elia bother you," Jannei said to Finn. "We've recently had some trouble with a prince, so she's a bit wary."

"That sounds awful," Finn said. "Is there anything I can help with?"

Jannei patted his arm. "Latera and Wren are handling it, but thank you for the offer. Come along, Elia."

Elia gave Finn a long look, then she followed Jannei out of my rooms, leaving me with a prince of my own. Once they were gone, Finn watched me for a moment, then he gathered his nerves and approached me.

"I hope I'm not disturbing you," he began, but I took his hands.

"You know you're not." I held his hands for a moment; they were so warm against my icy fingers. "What happened after I left?"

"Ma called us into the council room she keeps behind the thrones," he began. "Leran and I think that Cerillia must be the agent in Thurnda Krylle mentioned. Leran and Ember are leaving for Thurnda at first dawn to warn Sibeal."

"How could Cerillia be working with Krylle?" I wondered, the chill in my hands creeping up my arms. "He said his agent saw Kemen and me. How could Cerillia have seen us... H-How could she know..." My trembling became rampant shaking, and I covered my face with my hands. Finn sat beside me, and put his arms around me.

"He was probably lying," Finn said, his lips against my hair. "Or, he knew that you and Kemen once had something, and is clinging to that shred of truth."

"But he's right. He's right about all of it." I clung to Finn, my every fear and worry I'd had since I knew about the baby vying for attention. "Is there any way Krylle could take my baby?"

"No." Finn moved so he was holding my shoulders, his face a hair's breadth from mine. "No. There is no way Krylle is taking you or the baby. No matter who he is or Kemen was, he has no claim." His hands moved up to cup my face. "I swear it, Mara. I won't let him have you, either of you."

"Do you promise?"

"I do," he said, then he kissed me to seal the vow. It was the first time we'd kissed since that day in Tingu, which was so long ago I'd begun to wonder if that single perfect kiss had been a dream. As Finn held me, swearing to protect me and my baby, I knew it wasn't.

"Can you stay with me tonight?" I asked when we parted. "I don't want to be alone."

"I'll stay, for as long as you want."

***

Some time later, I woke with Finn's arms still wrapped around me. We'd fallen asleep on the bench near the hearth, and the fire had burned itself down to coals, not that it mattered to me. I was so warm and content with Finn beside me I thought I might never be cold again.

I thought about my time with Kemen, and how I'd never once woken up in his arms. Even during that night we shared he'd left afterward, and I'd ended up sleeping alone. I'd thought he needed to ready himself for the march north, but now I wondered. Had he gone off to report to Cerillia that the deed was done? Could he have done something to me, or given me something to eat or drink that would have made me more likely to get with child?

Gods, I wished Wren were here. She would have known if such a thing were possible. Even as I replayed the events of that night over in my mind, I dismissed this latest fear as something far-fetched. The most likely explanation was that we had gotten the child the same way all other children were gotten, but that did not explain how Krylle seemed to know about it, when I hadn't breathed a word of it to anyone.

But Finn, he'd divined the truth on his own. So had Elia, and Jannei. If they had figured it out, others could, as well. Who else might know?

"Finn? Finn," I said, shaking him slightly. When he opened his eyes, I asked, "When you all were discussing Krylle, did anyone mention me?"

"No," he replied. "Innetha asked if anyone knew something about Kemen having a mate or a child, and no one said a word." His brow pinched, and he asked, "Have you been up all night worrying about that?"

"Not all night," I replied, then I looked toward the windows. The horizon was illuminated by the barest smudge of light. "It will be dawn soon. I want to see Ember off."

"I'll go with you," he said, then he winced as he stretched his leg.

"Are you all right?" I asked, as I called for the fire to relight.

"I'm not an invalid," Finn bit off, then he stood and took a few steps, leaning heavily on the side of the bench. "You don't need to take care of me."

"You don't need to take care of me either, but you do." I stood, and grabbed my cloak from its peg; since Krylle was on the hunt for red haired women, I wanted to be sure I covered my head. The broken clasp clinked at the movement, and I made a face at it. "I have got to replace this," I muttered to the bent hook.

"We can fix it now, if you like," Finn said, then he held out something wrapped in white silk. "I got this for you. I was going to give it to you last night, but then so many things happened, it didn't seem important."

I took the bundle from him, and unwrapped the item. Laying on the silk was a golden songbird made of metal, with winking blue gems for eyes. "A bird?"

"It's a clasp," Finn said. "You said you needed one for your cloak, and if you poke around long enough in the treasury you can find all sorts of items. I picked this one, because the sapphires reminded me of your eyes." I opened my mouth, but he continued, "And before you say it's too much, it's not. You need a cloak, and the cloak needs a clasp, and therefore this is just right."

I stood on my toes and kissed his jaw. "You're right. It's perfect, and I love it. I'll send for a seamstress to have it put on after we say goodbye to Ember and Leran. One thing I do not do is sew," I added.

Finn rubbed the back of his neck. "I can sew it on, if you'd like."

That, I hadn't expected. "The Prince of Parthalan knows how to sew?"

"My father taught me," he replied. "He was adamant I learn how to take care of myself, instead of relying on the *saffira* for everything."

"What else did he teach you?" I asked. There was a sewing basket on the mantle, long unused and gathering dust. I reached for it, and saw a bit of gold glinting on the mantle. It was Kemen's amulet. Asherah had given it to me after he died.

I picked up the amulet, turning it over in my hands. It didn't seem enchanted, just an ordinary gold disc on an ordinary cord, but what if it had somehow drawn Krylle to me?

Now I'm as paranoid as Papa. I tossed the amulet into the fire, because I didn't want to spend my life mourning a man who might not have seen me as anything more than a mission to complete. Finn watched me discard the amulet, but didn't ask about it. I grabbed the sewing kit as Finn reclaimed his seat on the bench, then I set the basket beside him.

"You were saying your father taught you things," I prompted, to get my mind out of the past and into the present. "What else did you learn about?"

"Oh, many things. After writing and arithmetic, he taught me Parthian law, how to keep a ledger and record figures, and more mundane things like how to sharpen knives, and even how to cook."

I brought Finn my cloak. He laid it across his lap and began examining the old, broken clasp. "Does that mean you'll make our supper?"

He flashed me a grin. "If you'd like I'll cook for you every night." I returned his smile, then Finn bent over my cloak and picked away at the old stitching. "How are your aunts liking Parthalan?"

"Well enough," I replied. "Mostly, they're worried."

"About your missing aunt?"

"Yes, and now about Mama and Wren."

Finn glanced up from his work. "If anyone can rescue a missing aunt and grab an ancient relic from a statue, it's Latera."

I smiled at Finn's assessment of my mother. She did have a habit of accomplishing the impossible. "I suppose you're right about that."

"And, it's finished," he declared, holding my cloak aloft so I could see the new clasp.

"That was fast." The stitching was a bit crooked, but far better than anything I could have done.

"It was a simple repair. Have you a mirror?"

"Yes. It's over here."

Finn followed me to the mirror mounted on the wall near my dressing area. He stood behind me and settled the cloak on my shoulders, lastly sliding the clasp into place.

"It's beautiful," I said, as I leaned back against his chest. The songbird was beautifully detailed, and the sapphires matched my eyes almost perfectly. "Thank you, Finn."

"You are very welcome, my dearest Mara." He put his arm around my waist, smoothing my dress over my ever-growing belly. "We look good together."

"We do." I reached back and touched Finn's hair. He kissed my temple, and in that moment I was happier than I'd ever been. Finn made me happy, and I realized that I did want to be with him, and it had nothing to do with Krylle's sudden and unwanted presence. I wanted to be with Finn because I loved him, and he loved me in return. "We look like a family."

Finn stilled behind me. "Is that what you want? To be a family, with me?"

Instead of answering, I faced Finn and slid my arms around his neck, tugging his head lower so I could kiss him. He hesitated, but only for a moment, then one of his hands tangled in my hair while the other went to the small of my back.

When we parted, I said, "Would you still like to talk, after we say goodbye to Ember and Leran?"After Krylle and his men were escorted from the hall by a company of soldiers, Elia and Jannei each took one of my arms and walked me out of the side exit. We moved quickly and quietly down the corridors, and none of us said a word until we were inside my chamber with the door shut behind us.

"What an awful man that priest was," Jannei said. "Here, Mara, sit near the fire." I did, and Elia appeared at my elbow with a goblet of cold water.

"Thank you," I said. After I'd had some water, I asked, "How did you know to hide me?"

Elia shrugged. "A man dressed in black bearing a banner of a bloody toothed cat came into the hall, unannounced, looking for a red-haired woman. We don't know what he's about, but it doesn't look good. And, you're family," she added, with a warm smile that reminded me of my mother. "That foul priest will have to go through us to get to you."

"Thank you," I said again, my hands trembling as I held the goblet.

"Deep breaths, now," Jannei said, as she took the goblet from me. "A woman with child must remain calm for the baby's sake."

I stilled. "You knew?"

Jannei smiled. "Of course we did."

"It's rather obvious," Elia added. "This child is from the priest's son, I gather?"

I opened my mouth to reply, but there was a knock at the door. Jannei opened it, and after a moment she announced, "There's a Caol'non here, looking to speak with Mara. Should I admit him?"

"Yes, please. He's also family," I called back. Caol'non strode inside the room and knelt at my feet.

"Mara, I must speak to you about Kemen," he began, then he told me how Kemen had tried to murder Asherah during the battle out on the Northern Waste. Luckily, Caol'non saw what was happening, and killed Kemen in time to save the queen.

"I did not know he was special to you," he concluded. "I am deeply sorry for any pain my actions have caused you."

"If you'd known about him and I, would you have still killed him?" I asked.

"Yes," Caol'non replied. "I took an oath to defend Parthian royalty long ago. No matter that my oath was sworn to a different ruler, as long as I'm alive, my oath still holds."

I nodded. "I appreciate your honesty, Caol'non. If Kemen was close to harming Asherah, I am glad you were there to protect her."

"I still have his dagger," he said. "Would you like it?"

"No, no," I said. "I've got my own dagger, and his will be put to better use in your hands. Thank you, for telling me what happened."

Caol'non smiled, but it didn't reach his eyes. Even though he'd done the right thing, Kemen's death weighed hard on him. "You are very kind. I will do what I can to keep Krylle at a distance from you. Your father has posted guards in the corridor, as well."

"Do you really think that's necessary?" I asked.

"Aeolmar does, and I agree with him," Caol'non said as he stood. "Better to have too much protection rather than not enough."

"All right," I said. "Thank you." A curt nod, and Caol'non was gone. No sooner had the door closed, than there was another knock.

"Mara, you've another visitor," Jannei said, and Finn entered the room.

Until the moment I saw Finn, I didn't realize how much I needed him, but once I set eyes on him I felt a weight lift off my shoulders. No matter what Krylle was about, as long as Finn was with me, I could handle it. We could handle it.

Well, we could handle it if Elia and Jannei stopped glowering at Finn as if he was their sworn enemy.

"Um, hello everyone," Finn said, as he set his cane against the wall. Elia looked him over. "You're the prince?"

"I am," he replied, with his wide smile that made everyone love him. Everyone except my Aunt Elia, that is. "I was hoping to speak with Mara. Privately, that is."

"Mara, will you be safe alone with this man?" Elia asked, keeping her sharp gaze on Finn. "We can remain, if you'd like."

"I'm safer with Finn than with anyone else in the realm," I replied. "He's a good man, Auntie. Really."

"You mustn't let Elia bother you," Jannei said to Finn. "We've recently had some trouble with a prince, so she's a bit wary."

"That sounds awful," Finn said. "Is there anything I can help with?"

Jannei patted his arm. "Latera and Wren are handling it, but thank you for the offer. Come along, Elia."

Elia gave Finn a long look, then she followed Jannei out of my rooms, leaving me with a prince of my own. Once they were gone, Finn watched me for a moment, then he gathered his nerves and approached me.

"I hope I'm not disturbing you," he began, but I took his hands.

"You know you're not." I held his hands for a moment; they were so warm against my icy fingers. "What happened after I left?"

"Ma called us into the council room she keeps behind the thrones," he began. "Leran and I think that Cerillia must be the agent in Thurnda Krylle mentioned. Leran and Ember are leaving for Thurnda at first dawn to warn Sibeal."

"How could Cerillia be working with Krylle?" I wondered, the chill in my hands creeping up my arms. "He said his agent saw Kemen and me. How could Cerillia have seen us... H-How could she know..." My trembling became rampant shaking, and I covered my face with my hands. Finn sat beside me, and put his arms around me.

"He was probably lying," Finn said, his lips against my hair. "Or, he knew that you and Kemen once had something, and is clinging to that shred of truth."

"But he's right. He's right about all of it." I clung to Finn, my every fear and worry I'd had since I knew about the baby vying for attention. "Is there any way Krylle could take my baby?"

"No." Finn moved so he was holding my shoulders, his face a hair's breadth from mine. "No. There is no way Krylle is taking you or the baby. No matter who he is or Kemen was, he has no claim." His hands moved up to cup my face. "I swear it, Mara. I won't let him have you, either of you."

"Do you promise?"

"I do," he said, then he kissed me to seal the vow. It was the first time we'd kissed since that day in Tingu, which was so long ago I'd begun to wonder if that single perfect kiss had been a dream. As Finn held me, swearing to protect me and my baby, I knew it wasn't.

"Can you stay with me tonight?" I asked when we parted. "I don't want to be alone."

"I'll stay, for as long as you want."

***

Some time later, I woke with Finn's arms still wrapped around me. We'd fallen asleep on the bench near the hearth, and the fire had burned itself down to coals, not that it mattered to me. I was so warm and content with Finn beside me, I thought I might never be cold again.

I thought about my time with Kemen, and how I'd never once woken up in his arms. Even during that night we shared he'd left afterward, and I'd ended up sleeping alone. I'd thought he needed to ready himself for the march north, but now I wondered. Had he gone off to report to Cerillia that the deed was done? Could he have done something to me, or given me something to eat or drink that would have made me more likely to get with child?

Gods, I wished Wren were here. She would have known if such a thing were possible. Even as I replayed the events of that night over in my mind, I dismissed this latest fear as something far-fetched. The most likely explanation was that we had gotten the child the same way all other children were gotten, but that did not explain how Krylle seemed to know about it, when I hadn't breathed a word of it to anyone.

But Finn, he'd divined the truth on his own. So had Elia, and Jannei. If they had figured it out, others could, as well. Who else might know?

"Finn? Finn," I said, shaking him slightly. When he opened his eyes, I asked, "When you all were discussing Krylle, did anyone mention me?"

"No," he replied. "Innetha asked if anyone knew something about Kemen having a mate or a child, and no one said a word." His brow pinched, and he asked, "Have you been up all night worrying about that?"

"Not all night," I replied, then I looked toward the windows. The horizon was illuminated by the barest smudge of light. "It will be dawn soon. I want to see Ember off."

"I'll go with you," he said, then he winced as he stretched his leg.

"Are you all right?" I asked, as I called for the fire to relight.

"I'm not an invalid," Finn bit off, then he stood and took a few steps, leaning heavily on the side of the bench. "You don't need to take care of me."

"You don't need to take care of me either, but you do." I stood, and grabbed my cloak from its peg; since Krylle was on the hunt for red-haired women, I wanted to be sure I covered my head. The broken clasp clinked at the movement, and I made a face at it. "I have got to replace this," I muttered to the bent hook.

"We can fix it now, if you like," Finn said, then he held out something wrapped in white silk. "I got this for you. I was going to give it to you last night, but then so many things happened, it didn't seem important."

I took the bundle from him, and unwrapped the item. Laying on the silk was a golden songbird made of metal, with winking blue gems for eyes. "A bird?"

"It's a clasp," Finn said. "You said you needed one for your cloak, and if you poke around long enough in the treasury you can find all sorts of items. I picked this one, because the sapphires reminded me of your eyes." I opened my mouth, but he continued, "And before you say it's too much, it's not. You need a cloak, and the cloak needs a clasp, and therefore this is just right."

I stood on my toes and kissed his jaw. "You're right. It's perfect, and I love it. I'll send for a seamstress to have it put on after we say goodbye to Ember and Leran. One thing I do not do is sew," I added.

Finn rubbed the back of his neck. "I can sew it on, if you'd like."

That, I hadn't expected. "The Prince of Parthalan knows how to sew?"

"My father taught me," he replied. "He was adamant I learn how to take care of myself, instead of relying on the saffira for everything."

"What else did he teach you?" I asked. There was a sewing basket on the mantle, long unused and gathering dust. I reached for it, and saw a bit of gold glinting on the mantle. It was Kemen's amulet. Asherah had given it to me after he died.

I picked up the amulet, turning it over in my hands. It didn't seem enchanted, just an ordinary gold disc on an ordinary cord, but what if it had somehow drawn Krylle to me?

Now I'm as paranoid as Papa. I tossed the amulet into the fire, because I didn't want to spend my life mourning a man who might not have seen me as anything more than a mission to complete. Finn watched me discard the amulet, but didn't ask about it. I grabbed the sewing kit as Finn reclaimed his seat on the bench, then I set the basket beside him.

"You were saying your father taught you things," I prompted, to get my mind out of the past and into the present. "What else did you learn about?"

"Oh, many things. After writing and arithmetic, he taught me Parthian law, how to keep a ledger and record figures, and more mundane things like how to sharpen knives, and even how to cook."

I brought Finn my cloak. He laid it across his lap and began examining the old, broken clasp. "Does that mean you'll make our supper?"

He flashed me a grin. "If you'd like, I'll cook for you every night." I returned his smile, then Finn bent over my cloak and picked away at the old stitching. "How are your aunts liking Parthalan?"

"Well enough," I replied. "Mostly, they're worried."

"About your missing aunt?"

"Yes, and now about Mama and Wren."

Finn glanced up from his work. "If anyone can rescue a missing aunt and grab an ancient relic from a statue, it's Latera."

I smiled at Finn's assessment of my mother. She did have a habit of accomplishing the impossible. "I suppose you're right about that."

"And, it's finished," he declared, holding my cloak aloft so I could see the new clasp.

"That was fast." The stitching was a bit crooked, but far better than anything I could have done.

"It was a simple repair. Have you a mirror?"

"Yes. It's over here."

Finn followed me to the mirror mounted on the wall near my dressing area. As I faced the mirror he stood behind me and settled the cloak on my shoulders, lastly sliding the clasp into place.

"It's beautiful," I said, as I leaned back against his chest. The songbird was beautifully detailed, and the sapphires matched my eyes almost perfectly. "Thank you, Finn."

"You are very welcome, my dearest Mara." He put his arm around my waist, smoothing my dress over my ever-growing belly. "We look good together," he said, as he watched our reflections.

"We do." I reached back and touched Finn's hair. He kissed my temple, and in that moment I was happier than I'd ever been. Finn made me happy, and I realized that I did want to be with him, and it had nothing to do with Krylle's sudden and unwanted presence. I wanted to be with Finn because I loved him, and he loved me in return. "We look like a family."

Finn stilled behind me. "Is that what you want? To be a family, with me?"

Instead of answering, I faced Finn and slid my arms around his neck, tugging his head lower so I could kiss him. He hesitated, but only for a moment, then one of his hands tangled in my hair while the other went to the small of my back.

When we parted, I said, "Would you still like to talk, after we say goodbye to Ember and Leran?"

"I'd like to." Finn kissed my forehead, then he drew the cloak's hood up and over my hair. "Let's bid them farewell."

Hand in hand, we left my chamber as if we were walking out of our old lives and ready to confront whatever came next, together.

"I'd like to." Finn kissed my forehead, then he drew the cloak's hood up and over my hair. "Let's bid them farewell."

Hand in hand, we left my chamber as if we were walking out of our old lives ready to confront whatever came next, together.

Chapter Fifteen
Ember speaks

The elder sun sent his brightness into our chamber, rousing me from a perfectly lovely dream. At this point, after all we had learned about how Teg'urnan was built, and of Asherah's dealings with the solar orb, I considered those sunbeams an act of war. "Go away," I mumbled, as I pulled the fur up and over my head.

"Who? Me?" Leran asked, as he got closer to me under the fur.

"You can stay," I said. "I don't want it to be first dawn just yet."

Leran slid his arms around me and kissed my shoulder. "You don't want to leave."

I rolled over, and laid my cheek on his chest. "I don't. I like living where it's warm, so we can sleep with the windows open, and run through the grasses barefoot. But, I'm Lady of Tingu now. I can't very well handle my responsibilities from the middle of Parthalan."

"You couldn't. What if The Seat was attacked again?" he asked, referring to the single time in history The Seat was besieged. That one time just happened to be when I was there, and Leran wasn't.

"Let's hope that never happens," I said, burrowing further into his arms. "Despite how much I like it here, I do want to make The Seat our home. We belong there, together."

Leran sighed, and even though I couldn't see his face I knew he was smiling. "You make me so very happy, love. Besides, we can visit Teg'urnan whenever you'd like."

I propped myself up on my elbows and regarded my mate. "Wouldn't that put us in a constant state of travel?"

"Perhaps not. Have you ever heard of a portal?"

"A portal?" I repeated. "Like what my mother uses to go to the mortal realm?"

"Yes, exactly. I've been thinking about them ever since Latera and Wren set off to find their sister. They were once used quite extensively throughout Parthalan and Tingu, but Asherah banned them after she became queen."

"Since she's still the queen, I imagine they remain banned."

"I believe she would make an exception, for you."

I snorted. "If Asherah's of a mind to bend the rules for anyone, it would be you. Where would we even get a portal, if they've been outlawed all this time?"

"Mmm. What if, upon our return to The Seat, we make some inquiries, and find out if any sorcerers know how to create such things. If we find one, then we can ask her."

"How exactly do you plan on asking Asherah? By portaling directly into her chamber?"

He laughed, and since I loved him more than anything I laughed with him. "Absolutely not. She'd probably stab me."

"You're probably right." I stroked my fingertip down the center of his chest. "Are you in a mood to tell me what's happening between my sister and Finn?" I'd asked him the same question last night, which he responded to by kissing me until I forgot about everyone else in the world but him. "Or are you planning to distract me again?"

"I do enjoy distracting you." Leran smoothed my hair behind my shoulder. "What makes you think I know anything about them?"

"I know that Finn confides in you," I replied. "You two are very much alike."

"Are we?"

I thought about Finn's loneliness at being an only child, and how he masked his pain with wide smiles and kind gestures. Leran had also grown up isolated from those around him, though he dealt with his traumas by stabbing things. "Yes, in many ways," I replied. "Is Mara having a baby?"

"She's your sister. Ask her yourself."

"She's not in bed with me," I said, then Leran grabbed my waist and flipped me onto my back while he kissed my neck. I squealed, and grabbed a handful of his hair. "Stop distracting me!"

"Never," he said, as his mouth traveled from my neck to my breast. "You're mine, and I get to kiss you whenever I want."

"You're mine, too," I said. "And I like more than just kisses." Leran grinned, then he fit his cock against me and pushed. Our lovemaking was hard and fast, and it was exactly what I needed to clear my head.

Afterward, we lounged among the furs, enjoying our last few moments of solitude. "So you're not going to tell me anything about Finn and Mara?"

"I have got to find more effective ways of distracting you," he said. "Most of what Finn told me was in confidence. I can tell you that he cares for Mara very, very deeply."

"That's good." I laid my head on Leran's chest, so I could hear his heartbeat. "Mara deserves to have someone who loves her, especially after all she's been through."

"Kemen didn't love her?"

"I don't think Kemen knew how to love her. Not all men are as wonderful as you are, my beloved."

Leran made a sound somewhere between a sigh and a groan. "Keep saying things like that and we're never getting out of this bed."

"Would that be so bad?"

We laughed and joked and kissed for a time, but the brightening sky meant we needed to leave our bed and prepare for our journey north. Krylle's sudden appearance, and his claim of having an agent in Thurnda, meant that neither Mara nor Sibeal were safe. While Mara had plenty of protection here in Teg'urnan, we needed to warn Sibeal that there was an enemy close to her.

Leran and I led our horses into the great square shortly after second dawn. In stark contrast to the elaborate means we'd utilized to travel to Teg'urnan, we were only taking a few essentials with us to Thurnda. The two of us alone would travel much faster, and time was of the essence. A side benefit of this journey would be me having Leran all to myself for a few days.

Waiting for us near the gate were Papa and Tor, the king and queen, and Mara and Finn. I wondered where my aunts had gotten to. Since Asherah was a queen and a goddess, I thought it only fitting to say goodbye to her first.

"My lady," I began, then Asherah had me in her arms.

"Ember, dearest Ember, I will miss you," she murmured. "Don't let Leran brood too much. If he does, threaten him with stories from his childhood. I'll write a few down and send them on, and I'm sure Aldo remembers some horrifying tales as well."

"I'll watch out for him. Promise." King Finlay similarly embraced me, then I approached my father.

"I wish we didn't have to go so soon," I said.

"Me, too." He embraced me, and for a moment I was a little girl who had fallen and skinned her knee, and the only thing that would make my hurts better was being squeezed by his massive arms.

"I won't ask if you'll be safe, or happy, because I know you will be," he murmured against my hair. "I will say that I love you; I'm very, very proud of you; and if you ever need anything, I'm here for you."

"I'm going to miss you so much." I snuffled against his shirt. "I love you, too, Papa."

He kissed the top of my head. "You're the finest Lady of Tingu there's ever been."

"Finer than Asherah?"

"She didn't defend The Seat against a host of orcs. You did."

"I did, didn't I?" I drew back and smiled, then I wiped my eyes and faced my brother. "Stay out of trouble."

"Same to you, pest," Tor said, then he squashed me in an awkward sibling hug. After he was done squeezing the life out of me, I turned to Mara.

"I don't suppose you want to come live with me in Tingu?" I asked, hopefully.

She laughed. "You'll be so busy you will hardly have a chance to miss me."

"You are very wrong about that." I embraced my sister, but there was something between us. Something round. Suspecting I knew what, I set my hand on her swollen belly. Absolutely delighted, I drew back and smiled.

"It's true," I said, unable to keep from grinning.

"Don't you dare say another word," Mara warned.

Undeterred, I asked, "When are you coming to visit me in Tingu?" I patted her belly. She smacked my hand away. "A year, perhaps? Or sooner? Say yes to sooner."

Mara sighed. "If I say yes will you stop harassing me?"

"Perhaps, but I need you to write often." I leaned closer, and said, "I want to know everything." I glanced at Finn. Mara gasped. I felt like I now understood what had been going on in that carriage for two moons.

"Get all of those thoughts out of your head, now," Mara ordered.

"Too late."

I was so elated at the thought of becoming an aunt all of my nascent homesickness melted away. I grabbed Leran's hand, and smiled. "To Thurnda?" I asked, my mood joyous with hope for the future.

He kissed my inner wrist. "To Thurnda, beloved."

Chapter Sixteen
Asherah speaks

I watched as Leran and Ember rode away from the palace down the royal road, their obvious happiness making my own heart light. Less than a year ago Leran and I had an uneasy truce between us that amounted to each of us treading on eggshells whenever we were near each other. Now, Leran had embraced me before he said farewell, and left for Thurnda with his mate.

"Our lives are good, aren't they?" I asked my own mate. Finlay took my hand and smiled.I watched as Leran and Ember rode away from the palace down the royal road, their obvious happiness making my own heart light. Less than a year ago Leran and I had an uneasy truce between us that amounted to each of us treading on eggshells whenever we were near each other. Now, Leran had embraced me before he said farewell, and left for Thurnda with his mate.

"Our lives are good, aren't they?" I asked my own mate. Finlay took my hand and smiled.

"They are," he said. "What shall we do next?"

What he really meant was, what should we do about our most unwelcome guest, Krylle. I didn't want to think about him just yet, so I jerked my chin toward the gate. "Perhaps we should look into updating these statues," I said, referring to the stag and doe leaping toward each other, which, as we now knew, wasn't what happened between Olluhm and Cydia.

"It will take a lot of effort to dismantle the gates," Finlay said, his merchant's mind already calculating hours of labor and what supplies would be needed. "We can repurpose the iron, but into what?"

I shrugged. "Anything we'd like, I suppose. If I'm a goddess, why can't I have a gate that represents me? For that matter, why am I scarred? Why is my eye still clouded? Shouldn't I be able to heal myself, at the very least?" I caught myself, and glanced toward Finn, where he stood with Aeolmar and Mara. "Shouldn't I have been able to heal Finn?"

"Perhaps you can do all of those things, but first you need to learn how. Finn," Finlay called, beckoning our son over to us.

"Please don't tell him I was considering myself a healer," I said. "Finn already thinks I'm mad."

"He does not. Finn adores you," he said, then Finn was standing before us. "We're thinking about removing these tired old statues. What do you think the new gate should look like?"

"We're getting a new gate?" Finn asked, then he pivoted to take in the black iron monstrosity I'd been staring at for far too long. His cane crunched on the gravel path, and my heart clenched for my poor, wounded boy.

"Oh, yes, I can see why you'd want to change these," Finn continued. "Perhaps we don't need a formal gate, and we can leave it open, the way things are at The Seat. Or, we could add a few of your symbols."

"Symbols?" I asked.

"Yes, your symbols," Finn repeated, then his brow pinched. "All gods have symbols, don't they? If you don't have anything yet, I'm sure we could come up with something. Stars, perhaps?"

"Why do you say stars?"

He shrugged. "Your hair's pale like starlight. Here comes Attia now."

I followed Finn's gaze, and saw my saffira-nell approaching us. Before we'd left to see Leran and Ember off, I'd sent Attia to the temple so she could set up a meeting with Krylle. Based on her sour face, the priest had not been agreeable to my suggestions.

"No meeting?" I asked, when she was close enough.

"I didn't even see him," Attia replied. "According to Atreynha he and his men entered the temple at first dawn and begged the use of one of the meditation rooms. Atreynha, kind soul that she is, granted their request."

"Which means he will be in that room all day," I finished, and Attia nodded. "At least I won't have to deal with him during Reckoning Day." Reckoning Day was by far my favorite day of the year, and I refused to let Krylle's presence ruin it. It was early yet, and the event wouldn't begin until noon, but my Parthians were already passing through the gates in twos and threes.

"Then we should all have our morning meal together, and not think about that fool for one moment," my brilliant Finlay said. "Aeolmar, would you and Mara and Tor like to join us for breakfast?"

"I love breakfast," Tor said, while Mara's eyes widened and she glanced at Finn. I wondered if the two of them thought they were fooling anyone. If anything, they were being more obvious about their blatant attraction for one another than Leran and Ember had been when they chased each other across Thurnda and Tingu.

"All of you are welcome," I said. "Aren't they, Attia?"

"Of course they are," Attia said, then she looped her arm with Mara's. "Walk with me, and tell me all about those aunts of yours."

"What would you like to know?" Mara asked.

Attia grinned. "Everything."

"They are," he said. "What shall we do next?"

What he really meant was, what should we do about our most unwelcome guest, Krylle. I didn't want to think about him just yet, so I jerked my chin toward the gate. "Perhaps we should look into updating these statues," I said, referring to the stag and doe leaping toward each other, which, as we now knew, wasn't what happened between Olluhm and Cydia.

"It will take a lot of effort to dismantle the gates," Finlay said, his merchant's mind already calculating hours of labor and what supplies would be needed. "We can repurpose the iron, but into what?"

I shrugged. "Anything we'd like, I suppose. If I'm a goddess, why can't I have a gate that represents me? For that matter, why am I scarred? Why is my eye still clouded? Shouldn't I be able to heal myself, at the very least?" I caught myself, and glanced toward Finn, where he stood with Aeolmar and Mara. "Shouldn't I have been able to heal Finn?"

"Perhaps you can do all of those things, but first you need to learn how. Finn," Finlay called, beckoning our son over to us.

"Please don't tell him I was considering myself a healer," I said. "Finn already thinks I'm mad."

"He does not. Finn adores you," he said, then Finn was standing before us. "We're thinking about removing these tired old statues. What do you think the new gate should look like?"

"We're getting a new gate?" Finn asked, then he pivoted to take in the black iron monstrosity I'd been staring at for far too long. His cane crunched on the gravel path, and my heart clenched for my poor, wounded boy.

"Oh, yes, I can see why you'd want to change these," Finn continued. "Perhaps we don't need a formal gate, and we can leave it open, the way things are at The Seat. Or, we could add a few of your symbols."

"Symbols?" I asked.

"Yes, your symbols," Finn repeated, then his brow pinched. "All gods have symbols, don't they? If you don't have anything yet, I'm sure we could come up with something. Stars, perhaps?"

"Why do you say stars?"

He shrugged. "Your hair's pale like starlight. Here comes Attia now."

I followed Finn's gaze, and saw my *saffira-nell* approaching us. Before we'd left to see Leran and Ember off, I'd sent Attia to the temple so she could set up a meeting with Krylle. Based on her sour face, the priest had not been agreeable to my suggestions.

"No meeting?" I asked, when she was close enough.

"I didn't even see him," Attia replied. "According to Atreynha he and his men entered the temple at first dawn and begged the use of one of the meditation rooms. Atreynha, kind soul that she is, granted their request."

"Which means he will be in that room all day," I finished, and Attia nodded. "At least I won't have to deal with him during Reckoning Day." Reckoning Day was by far my favorite day of the year, and it had been too long since one had been held. It was early yet, and the event wouldn't begin until noon, but my Parthians were already passing through the gates in twos and threes.

"Then we should all have our morning meal together, and not think about that fool for one moment," my brilliant Finlay said. "Aeolmar, would you and Mara and Tor like to join us for breakfast?"

"I love breakfast," Tor said, while Mara's eyes widened and she glanced at Finn. I wondered if the two of them thought they were fooling anyone. If anything, they were being more obvious about their blatant attraction for one another than Leran and Ember had been when they chased each other across Thurnda and Tingu.

"All of you are welcome," I said. "Aren't they, Attia?"

"Of course they are," Attia said, then she looped her arm with Mara's. "Walk with me, and tell me all about those aunts of yours."

"What would you like to know?" Mara asked.

Attia grinned. "Everything."

Chapter Seventeen
Latera Speaks

After Sasha found Tor, Wren, and myself hiding in a storeroom, the three of us followed her through Tarac's castle and ultimately to a set of rooms worthy of a king. Only, the way I understood it Tarac hadn't had a king in some time, and was now ruled by a council of lords. Whoever these lords were, they were certainly generous.

"You turned up on Tarac's doorstep as a refugee hiding from her new husband, and these are the rooms you were given?" I asked, gazing at the opulent chamber. "Tarac is a wealthier land than I'd realized. What did this council have to say about your arrival?"

"This isn't a particularly rich land, but Priya considers me family." Sasha moved gracefully around the room, lighting incense and lamps. "She'll consider you family, too. The council does whatever she asks of them, so it won't be a problem."

"She does realize that this is the same council that exiled our mother when she was still a child?"

"Priya wasn't here then," Sasha replied. "She takes these long stretches of time away from the castle, calls them going for a walk.

Sometimes she's away from Tarac for years, even decades. She was on one of her walks when our grandmother attempted to kill Asgeloth, and for everything that happened with Mother's family afterward."

"Yes, well, I suppose Mother being exiled turned out to be a good thing, since it led to all of us being born." I glanced at Wren, who was studying the far wall; we didn't have the same mother, being that hers was a scullery maid our father had taken up with prior to his marriage, and she always felt like the odd one out. I hated that, and I always went out of my way to include her. "If our parents hadn't met, poor Wren would have had to face Asgeloth."

Wren laughed. "Gods, then we'd all be demon fodder."

Tor blinked, then he said to me, "You're the one who killed Asgeloth."

I nodded. "I am."

Then ensuing silence was heavy, and I wished Tor hadn't made that connection. Reliving that awful day wasn't my purpose in Tarac. "Sasha, I... I don't even know how to begin. Are you all right? Did Gannok hurt you?"

She scoffed. "If anything, I hurt him. Come, let's have some wine."

Sasha led us to a table, and she poured wine as Wren and I sat. Tor planted himself between us and the door with his arms crossed over his chest.

"He's quite a bit like Aeolmar, isn't he," Wren said.

"Am I?" Tor asked. "In what way?"

"Aeolmar?" Sasha interjected. "Why would Tor in any way resemble your husband?"

I sighed. "Tor is Aeolmar's grandsire."

Sahsa's eyes went wide as saucers, then she regarded the older man. "Oh, yes, I see it now," she said. "The way he pretends he's big and scary, but in truth has the heart of a kitten."

The three of us burst into laughter while Tor stood there scowling, further proof he was Aeolmar's grandsire. When we quieted down, he asked Sasha, "Why didn't you ever tell me you knew him?"

"I had no idea you were in any way affiliated with him," Sasha replied. "You look nothing alike. Your behaviors, though, that's where the similarities lie."

Wren and I agreed with Sasha, and Tor stalked off to scowl out the windows. I put my hand on Sasha's, and said, "Tell me what happened with Gannok."

"There's not much to tell," she began. "After you refused to cow to him, our father decided to punish all of us by forbidding Elia and Jannei to have any suitors, and by keeping me a veritable prisoner until he deemed me old enough to marry Gannok. But Father's arrogance ultimately led to my escape, because all those years alone gave me time to plan a way out of this mess."

"You told Gannok he had to bring you to The Highlands to consummate the marriage," I said, and Sasha nodded.

"I did, and the soft headed sot believed me. Even better, I convinced him that he couldn't touch me in any way until we crossed his country's border, or it would invalidate the union. And he fell for it."

"And he left you alone?" I pressed. "He didn't hurt you?"

She shook her head. "He held my hand at the wedding, and kissed my cheek but once. That was it." She shuddered. "That was enough."

I closed my eyes and exhaled, grateful beyond words that slimy man hadn't touched my sister. "How did you escape?"

"It wasn't easy," Sasha said. "He put me under the watch of his sister, and she attached herself to me like a festering boil, unwanted and impossible to ignore. She even slept beside me! Then, one day when The Highlands were in sight, I knew I had to do something or I'd be trapped there forever. I did the only thing I could think of, and convinced Gannok that we could finally be together." She made a face. "I nearly retched saying the words, but his face lit up and he immediately had his tent set up for us. I told him I wanted a bit of time and privacy to bathe and prepare myself for him, and while I was alone in the tent I took every weapon and coin I could find, and slipped out the back. Then I went to the pack horses, got a spare set of man's clothing from the soldiers' supplies, and hid in the forest."

"Brilliant," I said, my heart swelling with pride. "You must have been terrified."

"I was, but I was more terrified of spending my life with him," she replied. "The way his sister was acting, I would have been more a prisoner than a wife, or a queen."

"I never knew Gannok had a sister," I murmured. "Odd, that she was never mentioned when he was pursuing me, yet she had such a presence with you."

"Count yourself lucky you never met Cerillia," Sasha said, and my blood went cold.

"Cerillia," I repeated. "She was a slight woman, wore an atrocious golden collar like a shackle?"

"Yes," Sasha replied. "Do you know her?"

I looked at Wren, and frowned. "Unfortunately, yes. She's been causing trouble in Thurnda, where Priya's from."

"This can't be a coincidence," Wren said.

"I'm sure it isn't." I rose, and approached Tor. "You heard all of that?" I asked, and he nodded. "We must speak to Priya."

Tor jerked his chin toward the open window. I looked across the courtyard to a room that mirrored ours, and saw a woman facing us. She was obviously an elf, and while her cropped hair wasn't as bright as mine it was Thurndian red.

"Priya," I breathed; there was no one else she could be. "We must speak to her."

Tor made a few motions with his hands. Priya completed a few gestures of her own, then she disappeared from view. "I've already told her." He faced me, and added, "Priya lost much of her hearing some time ago. We talk to each other with our hands."

"I don't really think she's deaf at all," Sasha said. "She knows everything that happens within this castle. She's like Halse, only sneakier."

"No one is sneakier than Halse," Wren said, her love for Gannera's royal nursemaid apparent, then the chamber door swung open and a person stood in the entrance. Priya.

CHAPTER EIGHTEEN

Priya stood in the doorway of Sasha's chamber and watched the room's occupants stare back at her. What Sasha said was true; her hearing wasn't as bad as most thought it was, but she liked being thought of as deaf when in truth she heard everything, although she couldn't always make sense of it. Sometimes, the sounds that swirled around her were muddled as if she was underwater, and straining to hear what was happening on land. It had been that way ever since her second trip through the underworld—the trip that had very nearly killed her—and one of the main reasons she'd left Thurnda and returned to the mortal realm; it was hard to be a hero's daughter when you couldn't even hear the tales being told about said hero. That, and because she couldn't imagine living in Thurnda without her mother.

She shook off the memory and regarded the two newcomers seated at the table. Ever the hostess, Sasha had lit the lamps and burned incense, and offered her guests wine. It was unfortunate that Sasha's father had married her off to a terrible prince in a remote kingdom out of spite, since she would have made a wonderful queen. Then again, King Harold's loss was now Tarac's, and Priya's, gain.

The woman seated next to Sasha looked like most of the human women in Tarac, with her long straw colored hair and large blue eyes. She bore a passing resemblance to Sasha, but she didn't interest Priya. The woman standing with Tor, with her fire bright hair and pointed ears, that was who Priya wanted to learn more about.

"You look like my mother," Priya said, her voice rusty with disuse. The strangers glanced at each other; Tor must have told them she conversed with her hands, and they assumed she couldn't speak, either. As if being deaf and being mute went hand in hand.

The red-haired woman nodded, then she asked Tor something. Her face was turned to the side, so Priya couldn't read her lips, which irritated her. Then she saw Tor make a few gestures, and the woman repeated them. After Tor nodded his approval, the woman faced her.

"My name is Latera," she said as she also signed the words, spelling out her name slowly. She pointed at the other stranger, and said, "My sister—"

Wren, Tor signed, when Latera didn't know the proper letters. *Her sister's name is Wren.*

"I appreciate the effort, but you don't need to sign everything," Priya said. "If you face me, I can read your words as you speak. Also, despite what Tor says, I am not as deaf as a stone."

You don't hear much more than a stone, either, Tor signed, and she smiled. For all that he called her stone deaf, it was Tor who was her rock, the one who made her feel like maybe she could actually rule Tarac this time, and not squander what was left of her family's legacy as her brothers had. Then again, this Latera appeared to be part of her family.

"You're Sasha's sisters, yet you're Thurndian?" Priya asked.

"I'm not," Wren replied, being sure to turn toward Priya, and speak slowly. "Only Latera and Sasha are descended from Elvasla. Their mother is from Tarac."

Priya's sharp gaze moved back to Latera, who nodded. "Our mother, Ladyslava, was exiled from Tarac some time ago. Apparently, our family is directly descended from yours."

Priya's breath caught, and the world swam before her. Of course, this Latera looked like her mother, Elvasla, she who'd saved all the realms when she felled Ehkron, the *mordeth-gall* they'd tracked as a family from Thurnda to the mortal realm. A few years ago, news had reached Tarac of a new warrior, an elfin woman called Demon-killer who'd killed Ehkron's whelp, Asgeloth, and had managed to not lose her own life in the process.

That woman was apparently standing before her.

"*Deva'shi*," Priya rasped, and Latera nodded. "Why do you want the lodestone?"

"Why is it in Gannera?" Latera countered. "Did they steal it from you?"

Priya snorted. "Gannelo, steal something? He could barely wipe his own arse. My brother needed funding for one of his building projects, and spun a tale of how the lodestone was a priceless relic that would keep Gannelo's precious palace safe for eternity. He traded it to Gannelo for six chests of gold."

Latera's brows lowered. "You traded such an important item for gold?"

"I did not," Priya shot back, then she was taken over by coughs. Sasha approached her with a goblet, but Priya pushed it away.

"Wine makes it worse," she tried to say, then sign, but the coughing was so intense she couldn't do either. Humiliated to show such weakness in front of these strangers, she barely resisted Wren's hands as she guided her to a chair and pressed a cup into her hand.

"She needs water, not wine," Wren said. "Wine will only burn her throat. Have you any honey? That will help soothe whatever's irritated her."

"I fear I'm what irritated her," Latera said, then she crouched in front of Priya. "I'm sorry. I did not mean to overstep, or upset you. I only wish to understand."

Priya nodded, and squeezed Latera's shoulder. She wasn't ready to talk just yet, so she looked at Wren and cocked an eyebrow.

"She wants to know how you knew what to do," Tor said.

"Don't you two have a strong connection," Wren observed. "I'm an herbalist, and a healer. If you're feeling up to it later, we can discuss your hearing and see what we can do to improve it a bit. After we take care of your cough, that is."

***

Wren sent Tor off with a list of items she needed to make a sore throat tonic, and while he fetched ingredients, she rearranged Sasha's bedchamber into her own private still room. Priya watched in mingled fascination and amusement as Wren gave instructions, and the princess and the warrior carried out every gentle command.

Everyone should listen to the healers, Priya mused. *This is as it should be.*

The door banged open and Tor strode into the chamber, his arms laden with Wren's supplies. Priya smiled, because Wren had commandeered not only Sasha and Latera to do her bidding, but also the former Prelate of Parthalan.

"What's so funny?" Tor demanded. Priya directed her gaze toward the pot of honey and assortment of herbs he'd retrieved for Wren's tonic. He set the items on the table, and signed, *I only fetch such things for you.*

Priya's smile widened, then she watched as Wren picked over the herbs and added various amounts to a pot of water she'd set up over the fire. After she'd deemed them steeped enough, and had added a measure of warmed honey, she portioned some of the elixir out for Priya. Wren had also made regular tea for the rest, and soon enough Priya and Latera were sitting near the windows with their mugs, and watched as the sun lower itself toward the horizon.

"Even though I lived in Gannera as a child, after all my time in Parthalan I find it so odd to only have the one sun in the sky," Latera said. "I suppose it's the same for you."

Priya shrugged; she'd never thought much about the suns in either realm. She was just glad they were there, unlike the cold, sooty darkness of the underworld. "Your sister is a marvel," Priya said instead of commenting on the sun. Wren's concoction had made her throat feel better than it had in years.

"She is," Latera replied. "I don't think there's anything Wren can't accomplish." Latera drank from her own mug; she'd happily switched from wine to plain tea, claiming that too much wine made her head throb. Priya also disliked wine, mostly because she didn't want to indulge in anything that dulled what was left of her senses.

After a time, Latera asked, "Are we—Sasha and I—descended from you?"

"Wondering if I'm your grandmother?" Priya countered; since they were sitting very close to one another, she could make out the bulk of Latera's words with her hearing alone. It was nice to pretend to be a normal person, even if only for a short time. "I've never had any children, so at best I'm your elderly aunt." She watched the setting sun, deliberately not looking at Latera as she continued.

"After Mama... after my mother killed Ehkron, I went back to Thurnda to tell Sibeal what happened," she said. "It was the last thing Mama asked of me, and I had to complete the task. I needed to complete it, to honor her. I returned the way I came, with the lodestone guiding me through the underworld... I made it to Thurnda, eventually, but I didn't want to stay."

Latera put her hand on Priya's arm. "Was it too much?"

Priya nodded. "It was." She ran a hand through her hair and frowned; she still wasn't used to having it so short. It had been cut moons ago, and still barely reached her shoulders. "By the time I returned to Tarac, Papa was gone, and my brothers had wives and families of their own. Since I wasn't needed here, I left the lodestone with them, and went out for a walk. I was gone for," she paused, calculating those years from so long ago. "Ten winters, perhaps? Thirty? No matter, by the time I returned, Ric had sold the lodestone to Gannelo, this castle was almost complete, and it was like everyone had forgotten why we came here in the first place."

Latera shook her head. "Not true. Elvasla is still honored in Thurnda, and in all the elflands. Sibeal remains the Lady of Thurnda."

"Does she?" Priya smiled as she remembered her aunt. "Who rules Tingu? I thought Lormac would rule forever, but Tor told me of his death."

"His son, Leran, is the Lord of Tingu."

"Leran," Priya repeated. "I remember him as a baby, so bright and happy."

"He's my daughter's mate," Latera said, her voice prideful.

"Fitting, to keep the lines of Thurnda and Tingu close," Priya said. "What do you mean to accomplish with the lodestone? Tell me truly, not just some 'I want to stop the sun god' tale. Those puffed up stories are for fae like Tor."

Latera wrinkled her nose. "You sound like Leran." She drank some tea, then continued, "This is a very long, very complicated story, and I promise I will tell you all of it. Well, I will tell you the parts that I know, as they have been told to me, but for the entire story, we're going to have to ask for help with the details."

"Skip the details, for now. Tell me the crux of the matter."

"Very well. You know of the old gods?" Latera asked. "The ones who came before Olluhm?" Priya nodded. "Olluhm's greatest foe was Ish h'ra, The Deliverer. Olluhm couldn't defeat her, so he destroyed her memory and hid her in flesh and blood. Now, she's gotten her memory back, and she wishes to resume her fight against Olluhm."

"Then you need the lodestone to reopen the old temple in Dremmsvard," Priya concluded.

"We do," Latera affirmed. She glanced at Tor, and added, "There's something else. The Deliverer is the current queen of Parthalan."

"Asherah?" Tor repeated. "Gods, that makes it complicated."

"Complicated or no, we need to get to that temple, and the shrine within it," Latera said.

"It's only a legend that the doors were sealed with the lodestone," Priya said. "Even if we retrieve the stone, and manage to get ourselves to Dremmsvard, there's no guarantee the temple will open for the stone. It may not open at all."

"We?" Latera repeated. "Then you'll come with us?"

Priya shrugged, and finished off Wren's concoction. She wondered if she could convince Wren to make up a pot of this sweet elixir every morning, because she hadn't felt this good since before the first time she'd set foot in the underworld. "I've been home for too long. Time to take another walk."

Chapter Nineteen

Aeolmar looked around the table as his and Asherah's families and ate their morning meal, and remarked to himself that his inner circle kept shrinking. What with Latera and Wren away in Gannera, and now Ember going off to begin her life in Tingu, he allowed himself a moment of melancholy. After spending so much of his adult life alone, he was proud of the family he'd created with Latera. He'd also grown used to having them near, and didn't like that his children were beginning to move away.

His gaze fell upon Mara, his eldest child. He noted how she picked at her food, and only drank plain water, and knew that Krylle's wild claims had been correct. Aeolmar mentally reviewed the palace's defenses, taking into account where each soldier and hunter was stationed. Only when he was certain Mara was safe did he let himself wonder when the newest member of his family would arrive.

Mara set down her spoon and pushed her plate away. Aeolmar wasn't sure what she'd been trying to eat, but he did recall Latera's eating habits from when she was with child. He waved over Attia, and asked her if there was any milk available.

"Of course," Attia replied, and a few moments later, she set a mug of fresh, cold milk next to Mara's plate. Mara, who hadn't drunk milk since she was a babe, thanked Attia and finished every drop.

After the meal was over, everyone rose to prepare for Reckoning Day. Aeolmar waited for Mara to stand, then he approached his daughter.

"Walk with me?" he asked.

"Of course," she replied, smiling. "I can hardly remember the last time I attended a Reckoning Day. Do you think there will be a flock of geese this time?"

"I hope not," he replied, remembering the time a disgruntled farmer brought all of his fowl to Teg'urnan. The children had loved it, but Aeolmar had spent the next two days scraping goose dung off his boots. "In fact, I hope no livestock make their way into the hall today or any other day."

"Agreed," Mara said, laughing, then she dropped her gaze. "Do you think Krylle will make an appearance?"

"Supposedly, he's in the vaults below the temple until sun rest. We have time." Aeolmar put his hand on Mara's shoulder. "You could have told me."

"I know. I haven't told anyone, except Finn, although he figured it out on his own." She looked up at Aeolmar. "Does Mama know?"

"If she does, she kept it to herself," he replied. "But I don't think she would have left for Gannera if she'd known. Would you like me to tell her?"

"No. I will, when she returns."

Aeolmar put his arm around Mara, and kissed the top of her head. "Finn knew first?"

"He might have known before I did. Well, I knew, but I didn't want to admit it to myself. Admitting it makes it real, you know? And now

Krylle is here, and everyone knows, and I'm still here just trying to put one foot in front of the other."

"Don't worry about Krylle," Aeolmar said. "He's nothing but a sack of wind."

"But, he said—"

"But, nothing," Aeolmar said over her. "Krylle has no claim on you, or the baby, and there is no way—*no way*—I will allow him to harm one hair on your head."

"Thank you, Papa." Mara squeezed herself against Aeolmar's side, and now that his suspicions had been confirmed, and he'd reassured her that she was safe, he let his heart swell with pride. His baby, his firstborn, was having a baby! He had no idea how he would keep the news from Latera, being that she felt everything he did through their bond. Hopefully, she would just assume he was unusually happy.

"You know, Mama didn't tell anyone when she was carrying you," he said.

"But you knew, didn't you?"

"Not at first. There was the business with Asgeloth, then we were tasked with rebuilding Teg'urnan. One day, we were walking back from the stables, and she finally told me. We were very happy, but Mama wanted to have a secret for a time, and of course I agreed. So, you ended up being our secret baby." Mara giggled, then Aeolmar asked, "You and Finn are happy?"

"I suppose we are," Mara replied. "Finn's got all these grand ideas."

"Do these grand ideas involve you?"

"Some of them, yes."

They reached the greater hall, where Aeolmar would stand on the dais with Asherah and Finlay while they heard petitions from their people. Aeolmar noticed three chairs had been set to the side of the dais, for Mara, Finn, and Tor, and felt another surge of relief. With

Mara seated between her mate and her brother, she would be the safest woman in Parthalan.

"I must be First Hunter for a time," he said. "I'd like to talk some more later, if you're up for it."

Mara hugged her father. "I would very much like that, Papa."

Chapter Twenty

Finn used to love Reckoning Day. This year, it was more of an annoyance.

When he was a boy, he would sit on his father's lap while Parthian citizens came from all across the land to present their cases to the court. No grievance was too large or too small to be heard, and Finn listened in rapt attention while his mother ruled on the cases, and his father quietly explained to him which laws and rules were in play. How Finn had cherished those days.

Now, he sat off to the side with his cane balanced across his knees, feeling like a bit of furniture while his parents dealt with the greater matter of the land. It wasn't that he minded not being the center of attention; Finn had long ago come to terms with the fact that as a prince he was important, but not *that* important while his parents still reigned. Since he has no designs on the throne, and definitely didn't want anything to incapacitate the king or queen, he was content with his not too important status. What did bother him was the unusual amount of eyes he felt watching him, and the whispers that flowed about the hall.

"What's wrong?" Mara asked. He debated saying nothing was amiss, but Mara knew him better than anyone else ever had. Perhaps she knew him better than he knew himself.

"I feel like everyone's staring at me," Finn replied.

"Of course they are," Mara said. "You're the prince."

"It's probably the first time they've seen you since your little fall," Tor said. Mara whispered at her brother to be quiet, but he continued undeterred, "They probably want to know if you've recovered, or if they'll be needing a new heir soon."

Finn clenched his fist and ignored Tor. He also did his best to ignore the crush of people in the hall. No matter where Finn turned, he caught sight of people straining to get a look at him, the crippled prince with his cane at the ready lest he fall again.

After a short eternity, Asherah declared that the court would take a break, and that the hearing of cases would resume in one hour. Finn rose without speaking, and made his way out of the hall without a backward glance. He pushed himself to walk faster than was comfortable down the corridor and away from the crowds. When he turned onto the long passage that led to the royal apartments, he felt a hand on his arm.

"Finn, wait," Mara said, out of breath.

"You shouldn't be running," he said, over his shoulder. "Think of the baby."

"Finlay Torim," Mara began.

"Stop calling me that," Finn snapped, as he spun around to face her. "I've gone by Finn for most of my life. No one's called me Finlay Torim since I was a child." Finn took a few halting steps away from her, cursing his stiff leg and the cane he needed far too much. "Except you. You still see me as a child to be looked after."

"I don't," Mara said. She cleared her throat, and continued, "After Sarelle took me, and did those things…" She paused, then cleared her throat again. "Papa rescued me, and Wren healed my burns and bruises, but I wasn't the same. Not inside. And everyone knew I wasn't the same, could see my pain on me like a brand, and they treated me differently… And I hated that. I withdrew into myself for a long time, but when I was ready to get back to the business of living, everyone still treated me as if I was a different person. Everyone, except you."

Finn glanced up at her, saw her smiling. "You weren't any different. You'd been hurt, but you were still Mara. My Mara."

"And you were the only one who really saw me," she said. "You've always treated me the same, so I've always thought of you as just the same. That's why I still call you by that old name. You're still my Finlay Torim, my stalwart—"

Finn crossed the distance between them in two long strides, trapping Mara between himself and the wall as he kissed her. One of his hands cradled the back of her head, protecting her from the hard stone, while he braced his other arm above her. He felt Mara's hands on either side of his waist, grasping the fabric of his shirt.

When they parted, Finn rested his forehead against hers. "Please tell me you weren't going to finish that sentence by calling me your stalwart friend."

Mara laughed, the light notes making his heart and his belly flutter. "What, we can't be friends any longer?"

He laughed shortly, but her answer hadn't reassured him. "Is that all we'll ever be?"

"Finn, you're the best friend I've ever had, and I'm so lucky to have fallen in love with my best friend." Mara moved her hands from his waist to behind his neck. "I'm sorry it's taken me so long to understand how much I need you. If I'd understood sooner, maybe this would be our baby," she added, placing his hand on her belly.

"That hardly matters," Finn said. "Under Parthian law, if a man claims a woman while she's with child, the baby becomes his and his mate's."

Mara drew back, blinked. "What?"

An explosion shook Teg'urnan. Finn threw himself on top of Mara, shielding her from the stones that fell around them. Despite his efforts to protect her, soon they were buried in rubble.

Chapter Twenty-One

Aeolmar had walked almost all the way from the great hall to the *sola* when the first explosion rumbled deep below ground. At first, he thought it was an earthquake. Then he heard screams, and saw people fleeing from the palace covered in dust and blood.

By the time the second explosion rocked Teg'urnan, he'd run halfway across the palace square. Then the third hit and knocked him off his feet.

The first two explosions had come from deep in the palace. The third had crumbled an entire exterior wall, exposing the rooms within.

He recognized one of those rooms as Mara's.

"Father!"

Aeolmar looked up, saw his son running toward him from... somewhere. His sense of direction had gotten skewed after the third explosion. "Tor!"

Tor pulled Aeolmar to his feet. "What's happening?"

As if to answer Tor's inquiry, a fourth explosion shook the palace, this one directly across the square from the last. Aeolmar watched in horror as the royal balcony Asherah and Finlay had stood on earlier that morning came free of the palace walls and shattered in the square below.

"We need to find Mara, and then get to the royal wing," Aeolmar said. "After we find Asherah and Finlay, we'll go to the temple."

"Why the temple?" Tor asked.

"The first explosions happened inside the palace, near the center," Aeolmar replied. "Krylle and his men were last known to be in the meditation rooms near the temple's southern doors."

"He brought four men, and we've had four explosions," Tor said, and Aeolmar nodded. "Why would Krylle do this? I thought he wanted to take Mara, not take down the entire palace."

Aeolmar headed toward the collapsed section where his daughter's rooms once were. "Perhaps he decided if he couldn't have her, no one could."

Chapter Twenty-Two
Asherah Speaks

I blinked myself to consciousness, then I tried to remember why we'd gone to sleep on the floor. We hadn't done that in ages, not since...

We? I'm all alone here. Where's Finlay?

"Finlay?" I called.

Silence answered me.

My hands swept across the floor and came away full of dust and shards of stone. Instead of the smooth floor I'd been walking across for ages, I was lying atop heaps of shattered stones and broken glass, with their sharp, newly broken edges poking into me. I looked up, and saw the sky. Where was the ceiling?

Where was Finlay? Where was our son?

Leaping to my feet, I ran through my chambers, calling their names. Something had happened to the palace, something horrible, but before I could deal with any of that, I needed to find my mate and my son. Every fear I'd had since Lormac's death bubbled up in my throat, threatening to choke me.

I'd always known my enemies would target those I loved. I never thought they would destroy the palace to get to them.

"Finlay!"

I stumbled through my chambers, which were devoid of all living things save me. That was good, since I didn't have time to sift through the rubble for survivors. I needed to find my family. When I got to the balcony that overlooked the square, I nearly fell to my death.

The entire façade of the palace had slid off from the rest as cleanly as if it had been sliced through with a knife. Frantic, I looked across the square and saw other gaping holes in my home. My people's home.

I looked into the sky, saw cursed Olluhm driving his stolen chariot past the clouds, and screamed.

FINLAY

Sher?

I heard his voice, not with my ears, but inside my mind. I tugged on the—the what? The string, the tether that bound me to him?—as I ran toward him, all the while screaming his name.

Sher, I'm here.

I spun around, and saw my mate, my man from the desert, my Finlay, half buried in rubble. Dust had turned his dark hair a pale gray, and there was blood on his sleeve. I fell to my knees as I flung the pieces of wall and ceiling away from him. I wasn't nearly done digging him out when he grabbed my hands.

Sher. I'm all right.

"What?" I demanded, then I realized. He'd spoken inside my head. I touched his cheek. "How?"

"I don't know," he began. "I've always been able to feel you, just a bit, but I could never feel very much of you. It was like you were holding yourself back. Now, I can feel all of you."

All of me. I felt around the inside of my mind, reached into my memories—and found them. All of them.

My mind was whole.

Once again, I was The Deliverer.

"I remember everything," I said. "Finlay, I'm me again!"

He pressed his forehead against my cheek. "You've always been you. You just couldn't see it for a time."

While Finlay brushed off the rest of the dust and rubble, I reached out with my mind and found those who mattered most to me. Finn. Attia. Aeolmar. Mara. Leran. Ember. Tor. My mate, my sons, and all of my hunters were accounted for, and I dared to hope that those I couldn't locate were either asleep or temporarily stunned.

No. I didn't dare to hope. I finally had hope—real hope—more of it than I'd had in a long time.

"Come, beloved." I held out my hand and pulled Finlay to his feet next to me. "We need to find the rest of our people, and set this to rights."

CHAPTER TWENTY-THREE

Mara coughed as she woke. A thick layer of dust had settled onto her, making her eyes and skin gritty, and breathing was difficult. Once she'd gotten most of the dust off her face, she opened her eyes and gasped.

Wracked with a second bout of coughs, she took in the destruction that surrounded her. The corridor had all but collapsed, and the outer wall was open to the sky. When Mara looked toward the ceiling, she saw the upper floors. She tried to move her legs and found that between her and the layer of rubble was Finn.

"Finn? Finn!" Mara patted his cheek as she tried to tamp down her panic. This scene was all too similar to when he'd been dragged out of the battle at The Seat, broken and close to death. "Finn, please. Wake up, for me."

"What happened?" Finn coughed, then he looked up at Mara. "Are you all right?" he asked, his hand on her belly.

"I am." She covered his hand with her own. "We both are, thanks to you."

"I didn't do much, just fell on you," he said with that grin of his. "Let's get you up off the floor. What's left of it, anyway." By the time they got to their feet, Aeolmar and Tor burst into the corridor, shouting Mara's name.

"Here," she called.

Aeolmar appeared out of the dust clouds and pulled Mara into his arms. "Thank Cydia you weren't in your rooms," he said.

"Why? What happened to my rooms?" she asked.

"They're gone," Tor replied. "That side of the palace has fallen clear off the walls and into the square."

"What did this?" Finn demanded, then he stilled. After a moment, he glanced at the other three, and said, "I may have taken another blow to the head. I could have sworn my mother was speaking to me in my thoughts."

"Me too," Tor said, as Mara nodded. "Is that how you talk to Ma?"

"It is," Aeolmar confirmed. "I suspect another aspect of the goddess has returned to Asherah." He assessed the crumbling walls and ceiling of the corridor. "I'm not sure how stable the walls are. Let's go back the way we came and get out from under all of this stone. Mara, cover your hair."

Mara frowned, but did as she was told and pulled up her hood. The four of them picked their way through the rubble. It was slow going, and Mara worried the ceiling would collapse at any moment. Her fears proved unfounded, and soon enough they emerged from the ruined palace into the great square.

"Gods," Mara murmured, turning in a slow circle as she took in the devastation. The area where her rooms had been was indeed gone; she could see the inside of her chamber door, and her dressing area where she'd stood with Finn a short time ago. Everything else was gone. Across the square, the royal balcony was also gone.

"I felt four distinct explosions," Finn said. "Yet I only see evidence of two. Where were the others?"

"Near Teg'urnan's center," Aeolmar replied. "I fear the temple may be destroyed."

Aeolmar had no sooner said the words when Caol'non emerged from the center of Teg'urnan, carrying Atreynha in his arms. He brought the unconscious priestess to Aeolmar, and laid her on the ground.

"I don't know how badly she's injured," Caol'non said as he straightened. "I couldn't find the rest of the priestesses either."

Aeolmar nodded. "Tor, Caol'non, with me. Finn." Aeolmar unbuckled his sword and handed it to Finn. "Protect Mara and Atreynha."

Finn nodded. "I shall."

Aeolmar, Tor, and Caol'non jogged toward the gaping hole in the palace wall that would lead them to the temple. Mara knelt beside Atreynha, and used the corner of her cloak to wipe the dirt from her face.

"Of all the times for Wren to be away," she lamented.

Chapter Twenty-Four
Latera Speaks

"Wren," I hissed. "What are you doing?"

"Signaling Gilson," she replied.

"You're going to alert the entire castle!" Wren's signal was a small polished silver mirror, which she was using to reflect a very bright, very noticeable light toward Gannera Castle's main guard tower.

"Don't worry," Wren said, as she continued angling her mirror in the sun. "Only Gilson looks for such flashing lights."

"Yes, I'm sure the rest will think it's nothing but a very shiny groundhog," I grumbled. Wren, Sasha, Priya, Tor, and I had returned to Gannera, again riding in the back of a cart, though this one had been devoid of chickens. Wonderful, that. Now we were crouched atop a rise just outside the castle wall. Apparently, when Wren sent the letter Gilson from the inn, it had included this elaborate plan of signals and flashes to alert him of our presence. She'd been flashing the mirror at the castle for the better part of an hour, with no results. If this kept up much longer, all of Gannera would know our location.

"Wren's correct," Sasha said, when I glared at Wren's mirror. "Father looks for loyalty in his guards, not intelligence. Gilson's the smartest of the lot of them."

"A king guarded by fools," Tor said. "Sahlgren once attempted that."

"This Sahlgren was a king in Parthalan?" Sasha asked, and Tor grunted an affirmation. "What happened to him?"

"Asherah cut off his head," Tor replied, and Sasha fell silent.

"You were there, weren't you?" I asked Tor. "You saw everything."

He faced me, his eyes filled with sadness and memories. "I was. I saw Sahlgren's execution, helped build Lormac's pyre, all of it." He laughed shortly. "Asherah may not want to see me again, for fear of what memories my presence dredges up."

"She may not want to deal with a few memories, but she needs you," I replied. "We all do. Besides, you need to catch up with Caol'non, and meet Aeolmar and your namesake."

Tor smiled, and bowed his head. "I only hope they want to meet me."

"They will be thrilled," I said, then a burst of light from the guard tower caught my eye. "Was that Gilson?"

"It was." Wren stashed her mirror and got to her feet. "Come along. He'll meet us at the guard's entrance."

The rest of us followed Wren as she made her way down the hillside and skirted the castle wall. Opposite the main entrance was a smaller door, one used almost exclusively by the perimeter patrolmen. As soon as we emerged from the trees, Gilson himself opened the door.

"Wren," he said, then his smile faded as he saw the rest of us behind her. "Oh, there's five of you instead of three? No matter, get inside," he said, as he waved us along. "Quickly, now."

Once inside, Gilson closed and barred the door, then we followed him up a narrow flight of stairs and into a small room. He pulled down the canvas window coverings, then he faced us.

"Sorry it took so long for me to get you inside," he began. "It took a bit of time to get everyone else assigned away from where we need to be."

"You reassigned them?" I asked.

"I'm captain of the entire guard now," Gilson replied.

"That's wonderful," Wren said, with a wide grin that told me she was absolutely delighted to be in Gilson's presence. Now I understood why she and Bron were no more than friends. She'd been in love with another man all this time. As for Gilson, he beamed at Wren.

"Wonderful, yes, but about what we mean to accomplish here." Gilson rubbed the back of his neck. "If I help you steal the lodestone, that's treason. I'll be hung."

"Then don't help us," I said. "You've already done more than enough. Get as far away from us as you can, and set up an alibi. We don't want you to suffer the consequences of our actions."

"Actually, I had a different idea," he said. "What if I were to go to Parthalan with you?" When we all merely stared at him, he continued, "Gannera isn't the same as it was when you and Wren were small. The king's grown sour in his old age, and he lashes out at those close to him. He's become more of a tyrant than he ever was. Surely you can attest to that, Princess."

"It's true," Sasha said. "Father's only joy is making people suffer, including himself."

"What of Mother?" I asked.

Sasha's head drooped. "He makes her suffer most of all."

I wondered why I ever bothered making plans. We'd never once followed them. "I'm not in charge of who goes to Parthalan, but if you'd like to come with us, I'm sure we can put you to work at Teg'urnan. The palace always needs soldiers. Isn't that right, Tor?"

"Very true," he replied. "Think Asherah will give me my old position back, or is Harek still Prelate?"

"He was beheaded some time ago," I replied.

"A lot of people seem to lose their heads in this fae realm," Sasha said.

I shrugged. "Believe me, Harek deserved his fate. As for how we should proceed," I paused, and faced Priya. "Do you have any insight about the lodestone?"

"I do," she replied, with her now-smoother voice. "Since the stone knows me, I should go with the group tasked to retrieve it."

"We're splitting up?" I asked, since that had certainly not been part of the plan none of us were following.

"Aren't you going to get your mother?" Priya countered, nodding toward myself and Sasha.

I looked toward my youngest sister, saw the hope in her eyes. "Yes, I suppose we should."

***

After much debate, it was decided that Tor, Priya, and Wren would secure the lodestone, while Sasha, Gilson, and I would retrieve the queen. Our reasons were practical; Priya claimed the lodestone knew her, and would willingly go with her. I'd never known a stone to be particular about who carried it, but anything's possible. Tor would serve as their protection, and Wren could lead them stealthily through the palace. As for the rest of us, since Gilson was the captain of the guard, he could lead us to where the queen was imprisoned without being stopped or having to answer questions from anyone we might encounter.

And yes, my mother was now a prisoner.

"How long has she been in the tower?" I asked, as we ascended a damp, windowless stairwell.

"Not long," Gilson replied. "After we got word that Princess Sasha escaped from Gannok's retinue, there were a few rather loud arguments heard in the royal wing. Then your other sisters disappeared without a word, and the king sentenced the queen to confinement in the tower."

"For how long? When will this punishment end?"

"It's not a standard sentence," Gilson replied. "It won't end until all of his children are home again."

"Has he hurt her?" I demanded of Gilson, but it was Sasha who laid her hand on my arm.

"Tera, he hurts everyone," she said.

I clenched my fist. Even though we'd never seen eye to eye, I also never thought my father would one day become my enemy.

We reached the top of the stairwell. "Here's what will happen," Gilson began. "I'll walk ahead, and you two fall in behind me. Keep your eyes on the floor, like you're just servants accompanying me through the tower. With any luck, this corridor will be all but deserted, and anyone who is present won't recognize you."

"And if someone does recognize us?" I prompted.

Gilson grinned. "You've got those swords. Stab them."

With that, Gilson thrust open the door and strode down the center of the corridor. Sasha and I followed close behind, but fortune was with us and the corridor was empty. When we reached the end, Gilson withdrew a set of keys and unlocked a heavy wooden door. He pushed it open, and I saw my mother, Queen Ladyslava, sitting in a rocking chair in front of the window.

"Mama," Sasha said, as she ran across the room and knelt at our mother's feet. "I'm so sorry he's done this to you!"

"There, there," Mother said, seemingly unsurprised to see Sasha or me burst into her cell. "It's not your fault. Your father lost what few shreds of goodness remained in him a long, long time ago."

"Have you been mistreated?" I asked.

"Not in the slightest," Mother replied. "I am still queen, and the guards treat me as such. I must say, it's much nicer up here, far from Harold's screams and tantrums. The guards are very good to me."

"I'm glad you approve of your current accommodations, but we need to get moving," I said. "Elia and Jannei are in Parthalan, and I'm bringing Sasha there as well. You can come with us, and be free of Father."

"I can't," Mother replied. "My place is here."

"Mama," I said, crouching before her. "We are about to steal the spear from King Latera's statue. Father will know I'm involved, and he will punish you. You can't stay here."

Mother caressed my cheek. "My Latera, my oldest, bravest girl. Actually, you're all brave, far more so than I ever was." She pushed back a stray piece of my hair, and ran her fingertip along the pointed edge of my ear. "If I stay here, Harold has a focus for his rage. If I leave as well, he will search for a way to find me and all of you in Parthalan. By remaining here, I can keep all of my girls safe."

"Mama," Sasha began, but Mother shook her head.

"My mind is made up," she said. "It is my desire to remain in this tower until your father is no longer king, be it by old age or politics. Once he's gone, I'll resume my life without him."

"You can't just sit here waiting for him to die," I said.

"You forget, he's more than two decades my elder, and I've always been patient. Now come here." Mother embraced us, and whispered, "Go, get the lodestone, and get out of here before Harold suspects you."

"When you're free, go to the temple," I began, intending to give her directions to Parthalan, when I realized what she'd said. "You know about the lodestone?"

"Yes," she replied, "and I can see Priya looking at it right now."

Chapter Twenty-Five

When their small group split in two, Priya assumed that Wren would lead them toward the castle square, and the statue of King Latera. After all, that was where the lodestone was, and obtaining the lodestone was the entire reason they were attempting this heist. Instead, Wren led her and Tor into the bowels of the castle, past the kitchens and into the servants' wing.

"Why are we going deeper into the castle?" Tor asked, after they'd passed yet another store room.

"Gilson may have reassigned the guards, but if we're to get the lodestone, we will still need a distraction," Wren replied. "I'm going to ask the castle's servants for help."

Tor grunted. "You're certain they'll help a princess?"

"I'm the king's daughter, but I'm not a princess," Wren replied, then they reached an arched doorway. "I was raised with the servants. Ah, here we are." Wren knocked three times on the door frame. A moment passed, and three answering knocks came from inside the room. Wren beckoned them forward, and they entered a sewing room. Large windows near the ceiling let in plenty of light, and the opposite side of the room was taken up by shelves packed with bolts of fabric in every color and weave imaginable. The main area of the room held long tables where a dozen women worked on various projects. Sitting in the center of the room was one of the oldest humans Priya had ever seen, her snow white hair stark against her lined, leathery skin. Though aged, her sharp eyes missed nothing, and they monitored every cut and stitch that took place at the tables. Wren ran to the elderly woman, who stood and embraced her.

"Halse, I'm so glad to see you," Wren said. "I've missed you!"

"As I've missed you, child." Halse regarded Priya and Tor, and asked, "What sort of trouble are you and your new friends up to?"

"We're going to steal the spearhead off King Latera's statue," Wren replied, to Priya's shock. She hadn't thought of Wren as a fool, but she'd just advised a room full of strangers they were about to steal from the king. "I probably won't be able to come back and visit afterward."

"No, I imagine Harold will truly be out for blood after that," Halse agreed. "Where are the other girls?"

"Latera and Sasha are here," Wren replied. "Elia and Jannei are already in Parthalan."

"Then Sasha evaded the prince?"

"She did."

Halse nodded. "Good. I imagine Gilson's also sticking his neck out for you?"

Wren blushed, and said, "Yes. He's going to come to Parthalan with us. You can too, if you'd like."

"Perhaps I will one day, but I've got some things I'm still working on here," Halse replied. "Let's see about arranging a suitable disaster that will keep everyone away from the square. Lady Priya, I assume you're here to grab the stone?"

Priya blinked. "You know me?"

"I do," Halse replied. "My mother, Halessey, cared for Lord Gedric's brood. I came here from Tarac with Lady Ladyslava."

Priya nodded, at last seeing the resemblance between the ancient woman before her, and the memory of the kindly nursemaid who cared for her brother's children. "Thank you, for helping my family once again."

"It's nothing," Halse said, with a wave of her hand.

"She likes causing trouble," Wren added. Halse didn't argue.

"We'd better get moving," Tor said, with a glance toward the windows. "The longer we linger, the sooner our luck will run out."

"No need to worry," Halse said. "I've got the perfect catastrophe in mind."

***

After Halse assured them that she would take care of everything, Wren led Priya and Tor out of the servants' wing and to an arcade on the far side of the castle square. In the center of the square was the statue, and upon the statue was the lodestone.

"I still can't believe Ric traded the stone away," Priya muttered.

"Building his own castle must have meant a great deal to him," Wren said.

"It did," Priya admitted. "He'd always wanted a family of his own, and he dreamed of a large home filled with children. My brother thought with his heart rather than his head, but it was a big, beautiful heart."

"What of you?" Wren asked. "Did you also desire a large family home, or were you the ever practical sister?" When Priya hesitated,

Wren added, "I fear I'm the practical one, always talking Latera down from her lofty goals."

"I don't know if I'm practical, but for a long time I felt out of place," Priya replied. Tor slid his hand against hers, and she continued, "It took me a long time to realize that people are what make a place a home, not a castle or palace or even a hut."

"You're right about that," Wren said, then she jerked her chin toward a tower across the square. "The queen is being held in that tower, which means Gilson and the rest will exit that door." She indicated a door at the tower's base. "Once Halse has everything in motion, we should hurry toward the statue. Priya, you get the stone while I watch for threats."

"And me?" Tor prompted.

"If I call out a threat, eliminate it," Wren replied. "But try not to hurt anyone too badly. They're only humans."

"Tor is the gentlest warrior I've ever known," Priya began, then there was a shout, followed by a crash. The few guards stationed around the square craned their necks toward the noise. Suddenly, Gilson burst out of the tower door.

"Guards, to the throne room," he bellowed, and every guard abandoned their post and rushed inside the castle. Priya didn't want for them to be out of sight before she ran to the statue and climbed onto the pedestal, and came face to face with the lodestone.

"Hello, old friend," she said, as she ran her fingertips along where it was fixed to the spear. "Want to go on another adventure with me?"

"How is it attached?" Tor asked.

"Not sure," Priya replied. Out of the corner of her eye, she saw Gilson embrace Wren, and Latera and Sasha join them. "Some form of cement, I believe."

"Can you chip it out?"

"Latera," a man screamed. Priya looked up from the lodestone, and saw a scowling, red-faced man standing on the upper arcade walkway. Since he was wearing a crown and white fur cape, Priya assumed he was the king.

"Father," Latera yelled back. "How dare you betray your family! How dare you imprison the queen!"

"The queen's tainted blood is what turned the lot of you against me," the king seethed, then he raised his arm. Priya heard the crossbow's release and knew the bolt was aimed at Latera's heart.

Latera, *deva'shi* that she was, drew her sword and knocked the bolt aside faster than Priya's eyes could track. "Fire at me or my sisters again, and I'll send these bolts back your way," Latera warned.

"You dare threaten me?" the king yelled. "Treason! My daughter commits treason!"

"Make haste, love," Tor urged, as the guards filed back into the square. Since there was no longer a reason to be stealthy, Priya withdrew her dagger and cracked the hilt onto the seam where the lodestone was attached to the statue. Another crack, and the stone fell into her hands.

"Got it," Priya said, as she jumped down from the pedestal. "Time to go."

Lodestone secured, they ran toward the gate. The watchman called for the gate's closure, and the portcullis began lowering.

"Wait," Wren yelled, as she held Sasha back. "We'll be crushed!"

"I have it," Tor yelled, then he caught the bottom edge of the portcullis and lifted it up over his head. Ganneran guards mustered behind them, but Gilson ordered them to stand down. Tor groaned under the portcullis's massive weight, but his grip never faltered. After the rest had scrambled underneath the spiked bottom edge, Tor let it go and dove outside the castle walls, amid shouts from the guards to raise the contraption back up again.

"They'll be on us in a trice," Tor said, as he got to his feet.

"Not if they can't get through," Wren said, and she opened up her sack of hay and threw it against the gate. "Latera, fire!" Latera waved her hand, and the hay caught, then Wren tossed a vial onto the sack that emitted a thick white smoke.

"Let's move," Priya ordered, and they fled into the surrounding forest.

"This way," Gilson called, and he led them into a cave. Once they were inside, he pulled a lever, and a net woven to resemble a tangle of vines obscured the entrance. "This is one of the old escape routes," Gilson said, as he grabbed a waiting torch from a wall bracket and ignited it. "We can follow this straight through to the other side of the mountain."

"And when we emerge, what then?" Tor asked. "It's only a matter of time before we're found."

"And we set our entire supply of meadow hay on fire, meaning we can't cast the return spell unless we find more," Wren added.

"What about the temple?" Sasha asked. "The priestesses would help us."

"Father will know to look there," Latera said. "We can't risk endangering them. We will have to find more meadow hay, and then cast the spell."

"We don't need to cast a spell," Priya said. "I can lead us to Parthalan with the lodestone."

"You can?" Latera asked. "How?"

"Through the underworld."

Chapter Twenty-Six

Mara sat on the ground in the center of the Great Square with the High Priestess's head resting in her lap, while Finn stood next to them, sword in hand. Others ran through the square, screaming for help and shouting for their loved ones. Some stopped to talk to Finn, hoping that the prince would have an idea of what was happening. Finn listened to each person, and gave them a few words of encouragement before he sent them on their way, but he never budged from his place. He was tasked with guarding Mara and Atreynha, and nothing could make him move from his post.

"Please, wake up," Mara said, as she stroked Atreynha's forehead. The priestess had no visible injuries save for a few cuts and bruises, but Mara had learned both from Wren's teachings, and from caring for Finn during his convalescence, that many wounds sat deep inside the body. It was those hidden wounds that often caused the most damage.

Mara looked up, and watched Finn as he stood over them. He was strong now, but not that long ago she'd feared he would pass at any moment. When he was first pulled from the battle at The Seat, they'd thought he was no more than a corpse. It was Ember that saw him breathing, and she hauled him into the healers' ward herself. At first Mara had only wanted to stop his many wounds from bleeding, and splint his broken leg so the long bone would heal. Later, talk turned to a possible head wound, and other things that might incapacitate him for several moons, or perhaps the rest of his life. Mara had been terrified of what could lie ahead for Finn, but he'd proven time and again that he was stronger than anyone realized.

She reached up and touched her fingers to the palm of his free hand. Finn smiled at Mara, then he crouched down beside her.

"How is Atreynha?" he asked, wincing.

"No different," Mara replied. "Your leg?"

"It doesn't like being bent," Finn said, as he stood. "It's either standing or lying down, nothing in between." He bent at the waist and kissed Mara's forehead. "How are you feeling, beloved?"

She grasped his hand, pressed it against her cheek. "I'm fine, as long as you're with me."

Finn kissed her again, then he saw something in the distance and straightened. Mara followed his gaze, and saw Finn's parents coming toward them. Asherah knelt beside Mara, while the king went to his son.

"You're both well?" Asherah asked, and Mara nodded. "What of Atreynha?"

"Caol'non pulled her out of the temple," Mara replied. "She hasn't stirred since, but her breathing is steady."

Asherah nodded, and felt Atreynha's forehead. "Wren has taught you well. You're certain you're all right? Is the baby well?"

Mara's voice caught in her throat; she wasn't used to speaking openly about her child. "I-I think so."

"If you think anything is amiss, please tell me at once," Asherah said. "I won't have this madman hurting any more of my people, no matter if they aren't yet born."

"Thank you, my lady."

"I'll have no formalities between us," Asherah said. "Finlay and I have always considered you part of our family. Now, with the baby coming, even more so."

"Is that why you could speak to me in my mind?"

"I am not sure," Asherah admitted. "While many of my memories have returned, I'm still relearning much about myself." She looked at the unconscious priestess. "I feel like I should be able to heal both myself and others, but I can't figure out how to do it."

"It will come to you," Mara said. "Mama always says that it's easiest to learn the skill you need at the time you need it. When you need to heal, you will know how."

Asherah squeezed Mara's hand. "Thank you, dear one. Here comes your father, now."

Mara glanced over her shoulder, and saw her father, Tor, and Caol'non emerge from the depths of Teg'urnan. Behind them walked eight of the twelve temple priestesses.

"Where are the rest?" King Finlay asked, as Asherah went to speak with the priestesses.

"They weren't in the temple when the explosion hit," Aeolmar replied, as he reclaimed his sword from Finn. "As for where they are now, that's anyone's guess."

"Krylle is also unaccounted for," Caol'non said. Mara gasped, and felt the blood drain from her face. Her brother sat on the ground beside her and patted her shoulder.

"Don't worry, Mara," Tor said. "We're not going to let that creepy old priest near you. You're my sister, which means only I get to torment you. Everyone else needs to treat you with respect or they'll feel the edge of my blade."

Tor grinned, and Mara remembered when he was much younger, and smaller, yet still fancied himself her and Ember's protector. "Does this everyone else include Finn?"

Tor leaned closer, and asked, "Has he been bothering you?"

"No, Tor. He's very good to me."

Tor shook his head. "Ember has much better taste in mates than you do."

"Tor," Mara exclaimed. "Take that back!"

"Won't!"

"Children," Aeolmar admonished, and they both fell silent. "We need to get Atreynha and the rest of the wounded out of the open, and somewhere safe. Finlay, are any parts of the palace undamaged?"

While Aeolmar and the king discussed where they could relocate the wounded, Caol'non reclaimed Atreynha. "I'll take her," he told Mara, as he lifted her up from the ground. "It's my duty as *con'dehr* to look after her."

Caol'non strode toward the tents being erected on the opposite side of the square into a makeshift healers' ward with Atreynha in his arms, and Asherah returned to help Mara to her feet. "Should I help with the wounded?" Mara asked.

"Perhaps," Asherah replied. "Wait here a moment?"

Mara nodded, and watched as Asherah spoke in hushed tones to Aeolmar and the king. Finn approached Mara, and slid his arm around her waist. "I don't know what I should be doing. I hardly even know what to think."

"What are we going to do about the palace?" she asked. The entire royal wing was destroyed, and the center of the palace, where the Great

Temple was located, had caved in down to the vaults. "Our home is gone."

Finn rested his forehead against her hair. "I will build you a home. Anywhere you like, as big or as small as you want." Mara pressed her cheek against Finn's throat, concentrating on the sensation of his arms around her and the warmth of his skin, instead of the carnage that surrounded them.

"Can I come live with you, too?" Tor asked. "I don't think my room made it, either."

Mara laughed against Finn's chest. "Yes, Tor, you may live with us," Finn said, then the king approached them.

"I must see to the legion," Finlay began, then he pulled a chain over his head and put it in Finn's hand. "This is the king's seal," he explained. "It can get you anywhere money can't. Be well, both of you."

With that, Finlay embraced his son and Mara, then he left toward the *sola*. "What was that all about?" Mara asked.

"I've no idea," Finn said, then he grasped the chain and examined the seal. It was a gold pendant etched with a stag. "Why would he give me this?"

"Finn," Asherah said, as she took her son's hand. "I don't fully understand how to use my abilities, but you've always been able to figure things out better and faster than I ever could. Therefore, I give you this, trusting that you will use it well." A ball of light grew on Asherah's palm. When it was about the size of an egg, she pressed it into Finn's hand, where it disappeared into his skin.

"Was that some of your... your power?" Finn asked. "As in, your power as The Deliverer?"

"Yes, it was. Take care of yourself, and you as well, Mara," Asherah said, embracing them both. "I can't wait to meet my grandson."

Asherah released them as quickly as Finlay had, and followed the king toward the *sola*. "What is happening?" Mara asked her father.

"Follow me," Aeolmar said. "You too, Tor. We need to go to the stable."

Mara, Finn, and Tor followed Aeolmar across the square, and around to the far end of the palace complex where the stables were situated. "Tor, make sure we're not disturbed," Aeolmar ordered, as they entered the stable. Tor took up his position at the entrance and drew his sword.

"Aye, Father," Tor said. "No one gets past me."

"What is going on?" Mara demanded. "We should be out there helping people, not skulking around the quite undamaged stable!"

"Patience," Aeolmar said, then he turned a corner and led them to the stalls that housed his and Latera's horses, Myrnnhe and Enna. Some time ago, Latera had charmed the stable master, and asked him to build two spacious stalls onto the already large structure. Of course, the stable master had gone along with Latera's whims, and as a result, their horses had nicer accommodations than many of those who lived inside the palace. None of that explained what they were doing in the stable now, instead of out in the palace proper.

"Finn, how's your leg?" Aeolmar asked. "Can you ride?"

"I believe so," Finn replied. "Are we going somewhere?"

"We're not. You two are." Aeolmar swung himself up to the loft above the stalls. "Get the horses ready. I'll explain in a moment."

Finn glanced at Mara, then he grabbed Myrnnhe's saddle. Mara went to Enna, and soon enough both of the horses were ready to be ridden. Aeolmar tossed a few bundles down from the loft, then he jumped down and rejoined them.

"Good job," Aeolmar said, looking over Enna's gear. "Mama taught you well."

"Mama also taught me to ask questions," Mara said.

"We can't locate Krylle," Aeolmar said, not bothering to ask his daughter for clarification. He knew what she wanted to hear, and he wasn't one to play games with the truth. "As long as he's unaccounted for, you're in danger. Therefore, you need to be someplace other than Teg'urnan."

"You're sending me away? How is that a good idea?" Mara asked, her voice going shrill. "What if he follows me?"

"He won't," Aeolmar replied. "As soon as the first explosion went off, Merrick sealed the gate, and it hasn't been reopened since then. After you leave, the gate will be sealed again, and it will remain so until I or the queen say otherwise. We'll search the palace, and either locate where Krylle's been hiding, or where his corpse is lying."

Mara blinked away tears. "And you really think that sending me away is the best course of action?"

Aeolmar pulled her into his arms. "It's the best way to keep you safe," he said. "Mara, we don't know what else Krylle is capable of. He's already destroyed half of the palace, and likely murdered his men in the process. Who knows how far he'll go? But we do know that he wants you, and that's why you need to be somewhere else." He held her face close to his. "The day you were born, I promised you I would always protect you. Right now, I can best protect you by sending you away, so I'm certain he can't reach you. Then I can search for this madman and put an end to this."

"Will you kill him?" Mara asked.

"If I have to, yes." Aeolmar drew back, and wiped Mara's cheek with his thumb. "Do you understand?"

"I do, Papa," she said, nodding. "I take it Finn's going with me?"

"Yes," Aeolmar said. "If he agrees to, that is."

"I do," Finn said. "I'll protect Mara with my life. No one in the realm's safer than her."

"Good," Aeolmar said, then he turned toward the bundles he'd tossed down from the loft. "I have supplies for you."

"Is this why Mama had these stalls built?" Mara asked. "So you could leave your caches of weapons all across the palace, and keep them out of our chambers?"

"It's good to be prepared," Aeolmar said, instead of answering her question. "There's two bedrolls, a tent, five days' worth of rations, and a map."

"Are there provisions for the horses, too?" Mara asked.

"Of course. Your mother would never allow a horse to go hungry. Here, Finn. I remember your skill with a bow." Aeolmar handed Finn a crossbow and quiver. "I made the bolts myself."

"Thank you," Finn said, as he slung the weapon across his chest. "If we have a moment, I'd like to get some coin from the treasury."

"No need." Aeolmar went to the far corner of the stall and opened a hidden panel in the floor, revealing more bundles. He withdrew two, and tossed them to Finn. "There's enough gold in there to see both of you all the way to Tingu."

"You really think of everything," Finn said, as he passed a pouch of coins to Mara.

"Once, there was a time when I was helpless to save my family. After I became First Hunter, and I had the means to plan for my future, I swore that I would never let that happen again." Aeolmar and Finn set about lashing the supplies to the horses' saddles.

"What route should we take?" Mara asked.

"Ember and Leran are less than a day ahead of you," Aeolmar replied. "They took the royal road, and just after Vilja's estate, they veered west toward Thurnda. Meet up with them, and the four of you will be safe in Thurnda within a few days' time. As soon as we know what's happening here, I'll send word."

"Will you follow us?" Mara asked.

"Perhaps, but not until after Latera returns," Aeolmar replied, as he offered Mara a hand. "Here, I'll help you mount."

"Are you sure you want us to take your horses?" Finn asked.

"Absolutely," Aeolmar replied. "Enna will look after both of you as if you're her own foals. If you need to rest, she'll make sure you do. As for Myrnnhe, he's been in his share of battles. If you run into trouble, he'll fight with you."

"Hopefully it won't come to that," Mara said, as she adjuster herself in Enna's saddle. "Papa, thank you."

"You can thank me by staying safe," he said. "Mara, I'm very proud of you."

Mara ducked her head. "I'm only doing what you've taught me to do." She set her hand on her belly. "What if he comes before we see each other again?"

"He?" Aeolmar asked. "You know, Mama could see each one of you before you were born." He grasped Mara's hand. "You're so like her. Brave, intelligent, and now this."

Shouts rang out from beyond the stable. "You need to get moving," Aeolmar said. He took Enna's reins, and they walked out of the stall toward the main aisle. "Keep them safe, Finn. I'm counting on you."

"I will," Finn said. "I swear it."

Chapter Twenty-Seven
Asherah speaks

I stood on what was left of the palace steps as I directed the chaos around me. Chandra and the rest of the healers had set up tents and cots along the eastern side of the square, and the kitchens were set up on the western side. Attia oversaw the cooks and *saffira*, while half of the legion had been tasked with removing the necessary supplies from the healers' ward and relocating everything to the outdoor infirmary. The rest of my soldiers were searching the rubble for any sign of Krylle and his men, under command of the king.

I glanced at the ground, and tried to remember how many tunnels ran beneath the square. What I wouldn't give for my map table that had easy access to such information. Sadly, it had been destroyed along with the rest of my chamber. I reached out with my mind, and asked Finlay how the search was going.

We've cleared the north and south wings, he replied. *Rubble is still falling around the temple, so we can't get too close until we shore up the walls. My guess is that anyone who was inside that part of the temple is now entombed there.*

What of the tunnels?

I've got two teams working from the outer edges inward. Don't worry, beloved. We will find them.

I know you will. I looked again at the healers' tents, and added, *Please have them check the tunnels below the square as soon as possible. I don't want the last safe space in Teg'urnan to collapse under our feet.*

It will be done, Sher.

With that, Finlay redirected his attention back to the search, and I took a moment to savor the feeling of him inside my mind. I'd frequently wondered why we couldn't speak mind to mind, as other bound mates did, and assumed I was the problem. Wasn't I always? But now I knew that wasn't the case. When Olluhm buried my memories, he also buried the truest part of myself, the inner me that would only ever be shared with a mate.

I turned my face skyward and scowled at the elder sun. "You will pay for this and for everything else you've done to me, and those I love."

Movement at the perimeter wall caught my eye. The gates were being dragged ever so slightly open so Finn and Mara could flee the palace. I didn't like the idea of sending my injured son away at such a time, but Finn had proven time and again that he was strong. Hells, when The Seat was attacked, he single-handedly held off the invading orcs while the rest scrambled for weapons. Without Finn, The Seat may have fallen that day. Thanks to his bravery, the orcs were defeated and nearly every one of Tingu's soldiers survived.

Be safe, I said, from my mind to his. Finn glanced over his shoulder, and waved at me. *I can't wait to meet your child.*

Me too, Ma. We'll all be together soon.

Then they slipped through the gate and were gone. After Aeolmar gave the gatekeeper a few orders, he jogged toward me. "Where's Tor?" I asked, once he was close enough to hear me.

"In the tower, keeping watch and making sure they're not followed," he replied. "Did our children really fall in love with each other under our noses? Again?"

I smiled, recalling how Leran had really thought no one noticed how he watched Ember's every move from the moment he first laid eyes on her. "I suppose now you want me to have another child so you can pair that one off with Tor?"

"If it's not too much trouble." Shouting near the gates attracted Aeolmar's attention. It was the gatekeeper, Merrick, issuing orders as the entrance was sealed.

"Merrick assures me that no one has left since long before the first explosion," Aeolmar said. "Krylle is here, somewhere."

"Hopefully, he martyred himself," I said. "It would be like him and his followers to die for the glory of their gods."

"Do you think Kemen coming at you with a dagger was his form of suicide?"

"Perhaps." I thought about how he'd approached me, one hand clutching his dagger while he tried to convince me how much my followers couldn't wait for me to rise again. "Why is all of this happening now? And why is Mara's child so precious to Krylle?"

"Perhaps it's because of me," Aeolmar replied. "Sarelle took Mara because of my blood link to Olluhm. Maybe Krylle also thought Mara's blood could somehow assist him. The fabled heir to the sun, and that nonsense."

I shook my head. "That doesn't make sense. Krylle was against Olluhm, and wanted to see him replaced. There must be a different reason."

Aeolmar shrugged. "What if it's exactly what Krylle said, and he's a grieving father who wants to meet his grandson?"

"Maybe. Or maybe his interest lies not in you, but Latera. Mara's not just your child. She's also the daughter of the *deva'shi*."

"And, she's strong like Latera." Aeolmar frowned, and looked toward the Hill of Torim. "I want to go after Latera, and bring her home."

"What happened to you trusting her to complete her mission?"

"I do trust her, but something isn't right. Something's changed." Aeolmar glanced at me, then away. "She needs me."

"What of her quest to find her sister?"

"I'll bring Sasha and Wren home, too." Aeolmar would have said more, but Elkin picked that moment to emerge from the depths of the collapsed temple. He was covered in dust and debris, and blood darkened the side of his head near his brow.

"You're hurt," I began, but Elkin waved it away.

"It's not my blood. I found one of Krylle's," Elkin said, once he joined us on the steps. "Or rather, what was left of him. Based on the burn marks on the floor, and that there was only part of his lower legs remaining, I'm thinking they must have strapped the bombs to their bodies."

"If there were only legs remaining how do you know it was one of Krylle's men?" I asked.

"Many ways," he replied. "Firstly, they all wore red leather boots, which is what these legs had on. Bomb proof leather, perhaps? Also, the corpse in question was found inside one of the meditation rooms Krylle's men requested."

"Any chance it was Krylle himself?" Aeolmar asked.

Elkin blew out a breath. "I don't know if we would get that lucky. No, based on how this is going, Krylle has a vendetta, and he seems like the type to sacrifice his men to obtain his goal."

"He won't win," Aeolmar ground out.

"We'll find him," I said. "You know we will."

"Mara's safe?" Elkin asked.

"She is," I replied. "She might be the safest of us all."

"Good." Elkin surveyed the square. "What now?"

"What now, indeed." I followed Elkin's gaze, saw the tents filled with wounded, the kitchen staff setting up tables and handing out soup and bread, and the weary, dusty soldiers emerging from the depths of Teg'urnan. Suddenly, I realized something.

This all seemed familiar.

"I've done this before," I said.

"Done what, exactly?" Aeolmar asked.

I spun around and regarded the ruined palace. "Had my home destroyed. Rallied my people. Marched to destroy a god." I faced Aeolmar and Elkin, and tried to ignore the concern on their faces.

"Do you remember my shrine in the north?" I asked. "The one with the gold roof?"

"Are you referring to the time you and the king left our caravan with nary a whisper as to where you were going, just to visit a ruined shrine?" Aeolmar countered. "Is that the location you're referring to?"

"Are you ever going to accept that you are not in charge of when or where I go places?" I demanded. As for Elkin, he laughed so hard he leaned on his knees for support.

"Aeolmar must have been in a state," Elkin wheezed. "All red faced, charging around the caravan like a bull trying to find you."

Aeolmar glared at his second. I suppressed my smile, barely. "Yes, well, when Olluhm destroyed my shrine, I was forced to rally my people so we could march on Dremmsvard. Now that Teg'urnan is destroyed, I believe that's what we should do next."

"Dremmsvard," Elkin repeated. "If memory serves, that's so far north even Innetha's never been there."

"It's where Nyshanti's only shrine is located," Aeolmar said. "Dawn's abode, near where the elder sun rises every day."

"All right," Elkin said. "Consider this. Even if we assemble the proper supplies out of all this wreckage, and manage to leave immediately, Dremmsvard is farther north that The Seat. It will take us a moon to get there, maybe longer, and that time could be better spent here."

I frowned, but Elkin was right. I needed to see to my people's safety and well-being before I could entertain thoughts of marching to Dremmsvard or anywhere. My war against Olluhm had been paused long ago, and it could wait a bit longer.

Aeolmar backed down a few steps, shielding his eyes as he gazed at the southern tower. He once kept a room up there, before he began his life with Latera. "If I can get into my tower store room, I have the means to get us to Dremmsvard."

"What? How?" I asked, assuming he had another one of his weapons caches in his old room, and wondering what a few dusty swords would do for us.

"With a portal."

Chapter Twenty-Eight

P riya stood at the entrance of the cave that would lead them to the underworld, lodestone in hand, with the rest of their small party fanned out behind her. She'd sworn—multiple times—that she would never set foot in the dark, deathly realm ever again. She had yet to keep that promise to herself.

"Is this a good idea?" Wren asked, loud enough for Priya to hear.

"No," Tor replied, before Priya could even turn around. "It is a very, very bad idea, and we'd do well to find another way to Parthalan."

"Actually, the lodestone will bring us to the northern lands near Thurnda, not Parthalan," Priya said. "Don't you recall?"

"Did you meet each other in the underworld?" Latera asked.

"I'll tell the story," Tor said, over Priya's response; she frowned at him, but understood he was only trying to take the burden of speaking from her. "I was tracking a demon through the underworld, and got lost. Priya found me, and brought me back to Thurnda for healing. Once I was well, she set out for Tarac, and I followed her."

"How long were you lost?" Latera asked, eyeing the dark cave in front of them.

"I'm not sure," he admitted. "I was nearly dead when she stumbled across me. As it was, I'm not quite sure how I made it."

"You're too stubborn to die," Priya said. "You'll outlive us all, and complain about it the entire time."

Latera burst into laughter. "You're so much like Aeolmar. I can't wait for the two of you to meet."

"Being that I'm his elder, he is like me," Tor said, "but the fact remains that traveling this way is dangerous."

"How else do you propose we leave this realm?" Priya countered. "Gannera is a wealthy land. Harold has the means to not only send messengers far and wide to look for us, but to keep sorcerers and the like from helping us cross magically. It's either venture below, or wander the countryside looking for patches of meadow hay."

"Why do we need meadow hay, again?" Gilson asked.

"Meadow hay is the catalyst for the spell to cross the veil," Wren replied. "The herb thins the veil, then the dagger pierces through it."

"We won't find any meadow hay in Gannera," Sasha said. "Father's ordered all of it destroyed."

Priya nodded. "Then this is our best option." She regarded Tor, and said, "You don't have to come with us."

"If you think I'm letting you go below without me, you're mad." Tor pulled up his hood, and adjusted the flame on his lantern. "Let's go. The sooner we go down, the sooner we'll come back out."

They entered the cave, Priya with her lodestone and Tor with his lantern leading the way, while Latera brought up the rear. She kept a puff of flame dancing on her palm, which afforded enough light for them to not lose their footing. It wasn't enough to illuminate the majority of the cavern, and that was for the best. No one needed to see what they were really walking through.

Priya thought about the second time she'd ventured below, the time that had almost cost her life. She shouldn't have made the journey alone, but she had promised her mother she would return to Thurnda in the event of her death, and tell Sibeal what had happened. So Priya plunged into the darkness, already half-blind with grief over the loss of her parent, and fell into an ash pit.

She never knew what substance had been rendered down to ash, or why there was so much of it. What she did know was that even though ashes filled her mouth and nose, she never suffocated, and while she was trapped for hours or possible days, she hadn't felt hunger or thirst. The ash had wanted her to die, but not all at once. It wanted to bleed the life out of her, one sense at a time.

Eventually, Priya dug herself out of the pit, and after she'd gulped the stale cavern air as if it was the sweetest water she'd ever tasted, she counted her blessings and resumed her journey home. Foolishly, she'd thought she escaped the ash unscathed, but once she was back in Thurnda, others noticed how she was off. Wrong. She couldn't hear as well as she once did, her sense of smell was all but gone, and no matter what she ate or drank, it tasted like sawdust. What's more, her sense of touch was altered as well, with some parts of her skin being unusually, painfully sensitive, while other areas were thick and tough and felt nothing at all. The only sense that remained constant was her sight, and once Priya realized that she understood what had happened to her. She'd closed her eyes tight in the pit, and the ash hadn't gotten past her eyelids.

Now, she wondered if the ash remembered her, would try to claim what few shards of her former self were left.

Priya squared her shoulders. She would see herself and everyone in their party through to the other side, and someday she would find a way to wash away what the cursed ash had done to her. Someday.

"Watch where you step," Priya said. "There are pits in the floor."

"Who dug them?" Latera asked. "Are they traps?"

"Traps implies there's something down here with us," Gilson said.

"Yes, they're traps," Priya replied. "And no, we are not alone."

***

Latera had no idea of how long they slogged through the underworld. All she knew was that it was dark, and the stale air was settling in her lungs like two cold, wet boulders, dragging her down and sapping her strength. But she kept moving, because she needed to get back to Parthalan, and her family. She needed to reunite with all of her sisters, and with her children, and bring Tor to Aeolmar.

Aeolmar...

She reached out for him with her mind, concentrating on the sensation that was so uniquely him. Asherah had once asked her what it felt like to have another person in one's mind, and Latera replied that Aeolmar's presence was like a warm fur collar drawn about her neck, soft and comforting and safe. Only this time, she held her full presence back from Aeolmar; he didn't need to know she was in the underworld, and she saw no reason to worry him. Soon enough, she would be in his arms again, and she'd tell him all about her adventures.

Sasha stumbled, and Latera caught her elbow. "Thank you," Sasha murmured.

"Of course," Latera said. She didn't mention that the bone Sasha had tripped on was dark gray and horned; in other words, it looked demonic. "It seems this rescue has taken a turn for the worse."

"Believe me, I would rather be down here than with Gannok. I wish you'd stabbed him back when you were his betrothed."

"I considered it, but I thought his greasy hide would ruin my blade." Latera saw movement in the shadows, so quick she almost missed it. She drew her dagger, and passed it to Sasha. Then Tor dropped his hood and drew his sword, thus confirming her fears.

"Gilson," Latera snapped. "Eyes up."

"Aye, commander." Gilson passed Wren a knife much as Latera had passed her dagger to Sasha. Once they were all armed, Latera increased the intensity of the flames on her hand, and gasped.

They were surrounded by ghouls.

Chapter Twenty-Nine

Mara Speaks

Finn and I rode away from Teg'urnan, neither of us speaking or looking back while what was left of the palace remained in view. I rested my hand on my belly, and wondered what sort of madman would topple a palace jut to find a child he wasn't sure existed. I shuddered to think of what other mad plans Krylle was working on.

No matter what Krylle's true agenda was, Papa was right. Krylle hadn't followed us out of Teg'urnan., nor had anyone else. Even so, we didn't slow until we reached a crossroads, and Finn consulted the map Papa had given us.

"This way," Finn called, map in hand. "Leran and Ember would have taken this route."

And on we went, traveling past farms and larger estates as our home got smaller and smaller behind us. We were so focused on getting as far from Teg'urnan as possible that when the suns began to set, we were nowhere near an inn. Finn consulted his map again, and realized that we were indeed on our own.

"I'm sorry, Mara," he said. "I should have paid better attention to our surroundings."

"I'm sure we can find a good spot for the night," I said, then I spied a clearing up ahead. "What about over there?"

"All right, let's have a look," Finn said, as he urged his horse toward the tree line.

The clearing turned out to have everything one could need for a night's rest. The ground was relatively flat and devoid of stones, and there was a stream nearby. It was also set back from the road, so we had as much privacy as one could hope for while sleeping out. We quickly unpacked and saw to the horses, then set about getting ourselves settled.

"It was good of Aeolmar to provide us with this tent," Finn said, then he rubbed the back of his neck. "However, I have no idea of how to erect one of these."

I laughed, because I didn't know how to set up a tent, either. "It's warm. We'll just use the bedrolls, and sleep under the stars. The horses will guard us, won't you, Enna?" She snuffled into my hand. "Make sure you give Myrnnhe one of the dried carrots. He loves them."

"How did you know there were carrots?"

"Papa always packs the same food." I remembered his many caches of rations and weapons from when I was younger, and how I would follow him around the palace and stables as he methodically checked and replenished his supplies every moon or so. My father was paranoid, yes, but he was also well prepared. "I bet there are a few honey biscuits in the pack, too."

Finn rooted around until he found the biscuits. "There are. Does Enna like these?"

"She does, but he packs them for Mama." I picked a comfort-able-looking patch of ground, and arranged the bedrolls next to each other. "Sit with me?"

Finn smiled, only to wince and groan as he got down beside me. "Does it hurt a great deal?" I asked, nodding toward his leg.

"It's more stiff than painful," he replied. "I supposed that's as much as I could ask for." He handed me a honey biscuit. "When I said I'd make you dinner every night, I meant actual food."

"These are fine," I said, then I bit off the corner of the biscuit. They were very sweet, and hard as a rock. "They're better if you dunk them in tea."

"I'm sure." Finn set the pouch of biscuits aside. "You saw my moth-er give me a bit of her power?"

"I did." Asherah had passed Finn a glowing orb of light which had sunk directly into his skin. "What does it feel like?"

"It's not bad, but it is strange," he said. "It's like the power is banging around inside my skull, waiting for me to do something with it."

"What can it do?"

"Honestly, I've no idea."

"Well, then." I took one of his hands in mine. "What do you want to do with it?"

"I want to keep you safe," he said. "I want to use the power to heal, so you're never hurt or in pain. I want to protect you, and the baby, and give you both a home you'll be happy in."

"Just me and the baby? What about you?"

"If you want me to, I'll stay."

"Of course I want you to stay," I said, as I studied the lines on his palm. "Earlier, at the palace, you called me beloved."

Finn used his free hand to push back my hair. "I did."

"Well, you're not supposed to call me that yet. Only mates call each other beloved."

He laughed, a rumble deep in his chest that did things to me. "What are you going to do? Report me?"

"Perhaps I shall," I said, as I laughed with him. He moved to get closer to me, only to grimace when he stretched his leg. "Here, lay down. You need to rest your leg."

"Yes, beloved," he said, as he stretched out on the bedroll. "Lie down with me?"

I did, and for a moment we remained as separate as islands on our respective bedrolls. "This is so odd," I said. "We've slept next to each other so many times, yet now it feels strange, and new."

"Probably because when we shared a tent, you tended to have your back toward me." Finn moved onto his side, and I mirrored his pose so we faced one another. "Although, I remember one time when you came into my bed, and when I rolled over, you were facing me."

"And what was so interesting about that?" I asked, since Finn saw me all the time.

"You were so beautiful I couldn't look away," he said softly. "I stayed awake the rest of the night, watching you sleep." Finn caressed my cheek, then he brought my face close to his and kissed me. "Mara, my dearest Mara. I do love you so."

"Do you really," I whispered, then I shook my head. "I'm sorry. That sounded far more pathetic than I'd intended."

"It didn't." His hand glided down my neck and then my arm, then he studied my fingertips. "I'm sure you think it's odd, me claiming to have loved you for so long, yet never having said anything."

"Why did you go to Madoc'na?" I blurted out. "If you love me, why look for someone else to be with?"

"Mara, I went there looking for you."

I gasped, and covered my mouth with my hand. It was true that when I'd seen Finn from the balcony above the celebration he hadn't been with anyone. At the time I'd been glad I hadn't caught him in a compromising position, but now I recalled how he'd stood in the center of The Seat's great hall, alone in a sea of people.

But he hadn't been alone. He'd been waiting for me.

I threaded my fingers into the soft curls at the nape of his neck, and kissed him. "I wish you'd found me," I murmured against his lips. "Although, if you had, I don't know if I would have made love with you with all those other people around."

"There was no way I would have shared you on that night, or any other," he said, then he became quite serious. "I would never push you to do anything that made you uncomfortable."

I opened my mouth, intending to say that I was rather comfortable now if he'd like to do more than kiss, but before I could speak I felt a flutter in my belly and gasped. "What's wrong?" he demanded.

"The baby," I said, as I moved even closer to Finn. "I felt him move! Here, give me your hand." I pressed Finn's hand near where I felt the flutters. "Do you feel that?"

"That's him?" Finn asked, and the baby answered with a fresh round of kicks. "He's already so strong!"

I nestled myself in the crook of his arm, and asked, "What do you want to call him?"

"Call him? Oh, um, I've never once tried to come up with a name for someone. What names do you like?"

"I'm not sure." I bit my lip, and took the biggest gamble of my life. "We could name him after his father."

"Kemen?"

"No. Finlay."

Finn kissed me so hard tears pricked the corners of my eyes. He saw himself as my baby's father, too. "I love you so much," he said, his voice hoarse.

"I love you, too," I said. "What do you think about naming him after you?"

"I don't know about that," Finn said. "Having two of us named Finlay was confusing enough. Three just might be our undoing."

"I certainly don't want to be undone," I said, around a yawn. Finn reached past me and grabbed the blanket, then he pulled it up to our chins.

"Rest now, beloved," he murmured. "We'll talk more about names in the morning." He kissed my forehead, and I drifted off to sleep feeling happy and loved and most of all, content.

When I woke, my sister was standing over us, apparently unconcerned that she nearly scared the life out of a woman with child. "What in the nine realms are you doing here?" I demanded.

"I could ask you the same thing." Ember had found the pack of rations, and was sharing the honey biscuits with Enna while Myrnnhe munched on the rest of the carrots. "He sleeps like a rock, doesn't he?" she asked, jerking her chin toward Finn.

"He's still healing," I snapped, as I pushed myself upright. "I thought you and Leran would be closer to Thurnda by now."

"We would have been, but the earth told us when the blast happened at Teg'urnan," she replied; I remembered her explanations of the Sala, and how it connected her and Leran to the land around them. "When we turned around, the Sala told us you were near, so we came to find you."

"Where is Leran?"

"Scouting the area, to make sure we're alone." She sat next to me, and asked, "How are you? Was anyone badly hurt?"

"Many were," I replied, and I told her about the explosions that had caved in the center of the palace, and destroyed the Great Temple and the entire royal wing.

"Krylle must really want to meet this child," Ember said, jerking her chin toward my midsection. "You're sure you weren't hurt?"

"I'm fine, as is he," I replied, smoothing my skirt over my belly.

"A boy? Boys are fun. And Finn wasn't hurt, either?"

I glanced at Finn's sleeping form. "He seems well enough, but I worry about him. He's so determined to no longer be an invalid, I'm afraid he is ignoring any injuries he might have gotten."

"Can you blame him?" Ember asked. "The attack on The Seat was over five moons ago. I'm sure he wants to move on with his life."

"Five moons," I murmured. I was nearly halfway done carrying my baby. "I hadn't realized it has been that long."

"Yes, well, time moves quickly when you're hiding in a carriage," Ember said with a wink. "Best wake the prince."

I glared at my sister, then I gently shook Finn's shoulder. By the time he blinked himself awake, Leran had joined us, along with the news that we were indeed alone. While the horses finished their breakfast, we spent some time catching up, and discussing what we would do next.

"Thurnda has a garrison inside Parthalan's borders a day's ride due north," Leran said. "If we ride hard, we can be there before nightfall." His brow pinched, and he asked, "Mara, can you ride hard? I can go on alone, if needed."

"I can travel as well as ever," I replied. "Besides, until we understand more about what Krylle's after, we should probably stay together."

Leran nodded. "My thought, as well. Once we reach the garrison, I'll send a messenger on to Sibeal, and another to The Seat. Then we can take some time to rest. The garrison keeps an apartment ready for my use," he added.

"Being the Lord of Tingu certainly comes in handy," Finn said, then he withdrew the necklace the king had given him. "My father gave me this, as well. It's his seal."

"And Asherah gave him a bit of godhood," I added.

Leran blew out a breath as he regarded Finn. "This is good. We don't know what's happened in Thurnda with Cerillia, but we won't be going in blind or powerless. It's good to keep your enemy off guard."

"We think there might be enemies in Thurnda?" I asked.

"Nothing has been confirmed," Leran replied. "But it's best to be prepared."

Chapter Thirty

Asherah Speaks

"I cannot believe you've been hiding portals in my palace," I barked at Aeolmar's back. Thankfully, the southern tower and the spiral staircase had survived the blasts intact. Now, I followed Aeolmar up to his tower room, where he had been keeping a stash of illegal portals. "One of my first acts as queen was to outlaw them!"

He glanced at me over his shoulder. "Yes, you've told me as much. And I'm not hiding anything."

"Then why am I just now learning about them?"

"I hoped I would never need to use them."

We reached the top of the stairs, and Aeolmar pushed open the door to his storeroom. He'd moved into these damp, out of the way quarters after Latera had been stationed at the Eastern Border, and he was faced with spending the next two winters without her. It had hurt to watch him draw his depression around him like a cloak, and no matter what I or anyone did he remained in that dark place until he was reunited with Latera. Now, no one lived in the rooms, and they held an assortment of his family's mementos, old weapons, and other odds and ends.

And some of those odds and ends were an act of treason.

"Aeolmar, I do need more of an explanation than that." I granted my First Hunter a great deal of leniency, but my patience was limited.

"Do you remember when Latera was taken right before our eyes?" he asked.

"Of course I do." Unbeknownst to us at the time, Latera had been kidnapped from her childhood home by Sarelle, Harek, and his brother Sarfek—all of them traitors, and all of them now dead—and many winters later they spirited her back to the mortal realm. She'd been taken in broad daylight right from my receiving chamber, and none of us had any idea what had happened to her.

"I would have given anything to find her," he continued, "and I couldn't. No matter who I questioned, what scouts I sent, what maps I read, my mate was gone. I felt helpless, and I hated that."

"None of that was your fault," I said. "None of us realized that Latera had been taken to the mortal realm."

"That's the thing. No one knew where to look, but if I'd had a portal, I could have gotten to her in an instant." He picked up a metal casket, and held it between us. "If I'd had just one portal, I could have retrieved Latera, and maybe we could have ended that false war Harek engineered before it truly started."

"Perhaps," I conceded. "When and where did you get these?"

"When Latera first brought me to Gannera, I met a sorcerer who remembered how to make them." He paused, and added, "Latera doesn't know about the portals."

"Why didn't you tell her?"

"The same reason I never told you. I never wanted to use them." He opened the casket, and withdrew one of the small, shiny discs. "I swore to Latera that I would always protect her, and that I would always find her... Then she was kidnapped, and all of my promises were broken."

I put my hand on his forearm. "Aeolmar," I began, but he wasn't done yet.

"She made her way back to me, and I thought all would be well," he continued. "Then she was about to have our first child, and all I could think about was what if someone took her again? What if someone went after our child? I needed a way to protect them, so I returned to Gannera alone and secured the portals."

I reached toward the portals but didn't touch them, my hand hovering over the shiny silver discs. "Why didn't you use one when Sarelle took Mara?"

"I tried, but Mara was hidden behind magic." He withdrew a handful of portals, then he closed the casket and handed it to me. "I'm going to find Latera. There should be more than enough portals in here for you to take a force to Dremmsvard."

I accepted the box as Aeolmar stashed the portals in his belt pouch, then he retrieved a sword and strapped it to his back. I recognized that sword, and remembered when it was made so long ago. "You're taking Caol'nir's sword with you?"

"Something isn't right with Latera," he replied. "I'm not sure what it is. Maybe it's nothing, but maybe it's something I'll need to cut my way through. If it is, an extra sword will come in handy." He gathered a few more supplies and put on his cloak, then he faced me. "I am sorry for never telling you about the portals."

"But not for having them?"

He shrugged. "They've been sitting here for decades, not bothering anyone. I'd hoped they would remain here, unused, until long after I turned to dust."

Only my First Hunter could blatantly break my rules and somehow make me see his side of the issue. "Should you take someone with you?"

"If whatever's harrying Latera is powerful enough to defeat both her and I, best we keep it in Gannera and away from here," he replied. "Don't worry. I won't let any demons follow us home."

"We certainly have plenty here already." I tucked the casket under one arm, and placed my other hand on his cheek. "Be safe. I need both of you, and Wren."

"What about Latera's other sister?"

"Hopefully this Sasha is nicer than the other two." We smiled at each other, then Aeolmar covered my hand with his.

"I'll bring them all home. Watch over Tor?"

"As if he's my own son."

He released my hand, then he cast the portal and was gone. I stared at the empty space he'd left behind, then I went to find Finlay.

We had a legion to move.

CHAPTER THIRTY-ONE

Finn brought his horse to a halt next to Leran's, and shielded his eyes against the setting suns as he gazed toward the small yet imposing building. "That's it?" he asked.

"It is," Leran replied. Perched on the edge of a cliff was the Thurndian garrison Leran had mentioned earlier that day. Whomever had first built it had taken advantage of the area's natural features, since the structure sat on the highest point in the area with unobstructed views in all directions. Add to that the tall stone walls and single entrance by way of a bridge over a ravine, and the garrison seemed nigh on impregnable. "Ever since we fought the war against Nibika, Asherah has allowed Thurnda to keep garrisons inside Parthalan's border as part of a mutually beneficial agreement."

"Makes sense," Finn said. "Until recently, she was everyone's queen, so she might as well have all of her soldiers nearby and ready in case she needs them."

"She remains our queen," Leran began, then he frowned. "Ember is now the Lady of Tingu, but neither of us have any plans to supplant Asherah. We remain loyal."

"I know that, and so does Ma," Finn said, touched that the Lord of Tingu, the sovereign leader of the wealthiest and oldest land in the realm, had gotten tongue tied over their mother's queenship. "Besides, after what happened at Teg'urnan, and what's about to happen up at Dremmsvard, I've a feeling Parthalan is going to look quite different in the near future."

Leran glanced over his shoulder, where Ember and Mara were speaking in hushed tones. "What if you were called on to take the throne?"

Finn's eyes widened. "I suppose I would do it, if needed."

"Would Mara be your queen?"

"That depends on Mara," Finn said. "She knows how I feel. Everything else is up to her."

"May I offer some advice, brother?"

"Always."

"Instead of sleeping next to her, sleep with her."

Nervous laughter erupted from Finn. "She's with child, and we were traveling, and then we slept outdoors, and—" Mara looked toward Finn, no doubt wondering why he was going on like a madman. Finn gave her what he was sure was an atrocious smile, then he leaned closer to Leran. "It's complicated."

"Is it, or are you making it complicated?" Leran countered.

Finn narrowed his eyes at Leran. "As if you and Ember didn't make your courtship the most complicated event of the century."

"We had a rough start," Leran admitted, "but that was because I acted poorly. Be better than me, Finn."

Finn watched his hands where they clutched Myrnnhe's reins. "I don't know if I can."

"You can, and you will," Leran said. "Mara deserves nothing less."

With that, Leran extended his hand to Ember, and she brought his horse alongside his. Finn did the same, and soon he and Mara were riding abreast of one another.

"Did you have a good talk with Ember?" he asked.

"We did," Mara replied. "We've always been close, but you knew that."

Finn ducked his head. "I did. I was always so jealous of you and Ember and Tor. I've always wanted siblings."

"And now you have Leran," Mara said. "Everything works out as it's supposed to, doesn't it?"

Finn glanced forward at Leran's back, then he took Mara's hand. "I suppose it does."

The four of them passed through the garrison's gates just before full dark. While Leran spoke to the garrison's commanders—and introduced them to Ember—Finn and Mara waited off to the side.

"It's as if every elf adores Leran, no matter where they hail from," Mara said. "The other elflands may as well dissolve their borders, so all can remain under Tingu."

"It used to be that way," Finn said. "Well, the different lands existed, but they were all provinces of Tingu. After Leran's father died, they broke apart, and became independent."

"That must have been awful for Leran."

"I'm sure it was." Finn noticed how Mara's breathing was labored, and asked, "How are you feeling?"

"A bit tired," she replied. "This child takes much of my stamina. But soon enough he will be here, and then I'm sure I will be even more exhausted."

"No doubt," Finn murmured, wishing he had the slightest bit of advice to offer Mara. Sadly, he knew next to nothing about rearing children, but he did know he would do anything for her. "No matter what happens, I'll be there for you," he said, as he laced his fingers with hers.

Mara leaned against his shoulder. "You're very good to me."

"That's what you said to Tor, back at the palace," Finn began, then Ember joined them.

"Our rooms are being prepared now," Ember told them. "Leran's also sending off three messengers, rather than two. One will go to Thurnda, one to The Seat, and one to Teg'urnan. The commander here thinks we should wait until we have word back from Thurnda before moving on," she added.

"Why is that?" Finn asked. "Have the roads been bad?"

"He didn't elaborate," Ember said. "Leran doesn't like the idea of waiting, and neither do I. However, it's good to know they're willing to put us up for a time, if we need it." She glanced at Mara, and continued, "They also want to have a special dinner for us, but I would rather sleep."

"As would I," Mara said. "Perhaps the Lady of Tingu can convince them to prepare us a nice breakfast, instead."

"I can't wait to have some selka," Ember said, mentioning the dark, bitter brew favored by elves. As far as Finn was concerned, they could keep their selka, since he preferred tea. Before they could discuss any-thing further, a *saffira* arrived to show them to their rooms.

"I'm Luce, and I'll bring you upstairs," she said, as she curtsied. "My lady, our lord said you would prefer to have supper in your rooms?"

"Please," Ember said. "We appreciate your hospitality, but we have traveled very far."

Luce nodded, then she turned to Finn. "Would you also like supper in your rooms, my lord?"

"Y-Yes, please," Finn said; despite that he was a prince, he wasn't accustomed to anyone referring to him as such. Most of the *saffira* in Teg'urnan followed Attia's example and treated him like family. "Thank you."

"Of course," Luce said, then she turned to Mara. "As for you, my lady, I will send you up some broth. It will do wonders for you and the babe."

"It will?" Mara asked, her hand moving to her belly as her cheeks went scarlet.

"Oh, most definitely," Luce said. "I've six boys myself, and my special broth did all of them well."

"Six boys," Mara said. "I'm sure they're all wonderful."

"That they are. You're what, about halfway along?" Luce asked, and Mara nodded. "I'll make up some teas for you, as well. They'll help you sleep, and ease some of those aches. Ah, here we are."

They paused on the second floor landing, and Luce indicated the corridor to the right of the staircase. "That door leads to the Lord of Tingu's apartment," she said, then she pointed to the door across from it. "My lord, you and your lady will be across the way. If anything in the room isn't to your liking, please ring for me and I'll have it corrected at once."

"I'm sure the rooms are perfect," Ember said. "Many thanks, Luce, from myself and Leran." The *saffira* curtsied, and made her way back to the first floor. Ember stretched, and said, "I don't know about you two, but I'm going to take a nap before our supper arrives." She entered her room and shut the door, leaving Finn and Mara alone in the corridor.

"We should rest, as well," Finn said, and he opened the door for Mara. She entered the room first, and went directly to the hearth.

"I'm glad they lit the fire for us," she said, as she rubbed her arms. "Nothing worse for aches and bruises than sleeping in the cold."

"You're bruised?" Finn asked.

She peeked at him over her shoulder. "A palace did fall on us, and sleeping on the ground last night didn't help." She turned back to the fire. "Tell me about your leg."

"It's all right." Finn approached Mara, and encircled her with his arms. "While we were traveling earlier, I experimented with the power Ma gave me. I was right, and it does want to heal."

"Does it?" Mara leaned back against his chest. "Can you show it to me?"

Finn held his hands in front of Mara's torso, and willed the power to come forth. Just as it had when Asherah passed it to him, the power revealed itself as a ball of white light. "Have you an ache?"

Mara pushed up her sleeve, revealing a bruise. Finn frowned, mostly because she was hurt, partly because she hadn't told him about it. "May I?" he asked, as he gently grasped her forearm. After she nodded, Finn pressed the glowing orb against the bruise.

"Oh," Mara gasped. "It's cool, like water flowing over me. You tried this on your leg?"

"I did."

"And?"

"Feels like it did before everything at The Seat." For a moment he remembered falling from the ledge above The Seat's entrance and into the horde of orcs, how he'd tried to get up but the monsters had pushed him down, the massive feet above him as they stomped on his shoulder and leg again and again, the feeling of his bones splintering...

"Finn?"

"Mmm?"

"Are you all right? You got quiet."

"I'm fine," he said quickly. "Just concentrating." He removed his hand from her forearm, and saw the unmarred skin left behind. "How does it feel?"

"Better. Thank you."

He almost asked her if she had any other aches he could see to, but he didn't want to fall back into their familiar routine of invalid and caretaker. Finn was long since healed, and neither of them needed a caretaker. What he needed was a lover.

Instead of sleeping next to her, sleep with her.

Finn moved Mara's hair to the side, and kissed the nape of her neck. "Beloved," he murmured.

"Right before the palace fell, you said something about mates and claiming," Mara said in a rush. "You said that if a man claims a woman while she's with child, the child becomes his."

He rested his forehead against the back of her head. "Under the law, the man who claims the woman is recognized as the child's father. Of course, this would never change who actually got the woman with child, but it clears things up in matters of succession, or inheritance. I didn't mean it to come off as though you should have someone claim you. I just thought you should know the law."

"Someone?" Mara turned around. "You were thinking of some person other than you claiming me?"

He stared at her, slack jawed. "I didn't want to presume... It's not up to me who you choose."

"Perhaps you should stop being so polite and start presuming," she said, then she grabbed the front of his shirt and kissed him hard. "I want you, Finn. Not someone. Not anyone, but you."

Finn rested his forehead against hers. "You're certain?"

"I am."

"So am I." Finn lifted Mara against him, and as she wrapped her legs around him, he prayed for his newly mended bones to not buckle as he carried her to bed. His leg held strong, and he laid Mara among the cushions, then he pulled off his shirt. Bare to the waist he knelt between her knees, his elbows on either side of her head.

"Tell me what you like," he said, as he nuzzled her neck.

"I don't really know," she admitted, then he kissed her lips.

"Then we'll find out together." Finn tugged at the laces of her bodice. "I have no idea how to get this off you."

Mara took his hands. "Let me help," she said, then she wiggled out from under him and unfastened her dress. Finn helped her tug it down, past her hips and down off her legs.

"You're beautiful," he said, and she was. Mara's skin was velvety smooth, her limbs well-formed and elegant. Finn stood in order to shed the rest of his clothing, then he laid his body atop Mara's, careful of her belly. He kissed her neck, and murmured, "Beloved. Or would you like me to call you *nalla*?"

"You can call me whatever you want," she said, as she twined her arms around his neck. "The more I think about you and me, the more I realize something."

"What's that?"

Her deep blue eyes locked with his, and she said, "I've loved you for a long time, too. You've always been the person I looked for, to talk, or for help, or just to be with. Finn, you're my perfect mate. I choose you."

"Dearest Mara, my beloved," he replied. "If you hadn't chosen me, I would have spent my life alone. For me, it's always been you or no one."

"I'm sorry I didn't figure it out earlier," she said. "I wish I'd had the courage to discover how much you meant to me, before."

"It's all right. We're here now." Finn kissed her neck and felt her shiver, and pulled a blanket across them. "Let me tell you all the things I've always wanted to say."

CHAPTER THIRTY-TWO
MARA SPEAKS

Finn lowered his head and kissed the curve where my neck met my shoulder. The sensation of his lips on my skin made me shiver. Finn, loving man he is, misinterpreted those shivers as me being cold. He pulled a blanket across us, which was a shame. He had a beautiful body, and I enjoyed looking at him.

"Better?" he murmured. "I don't want you to be cold."

"I'm not," I began, then Finn took my breast into his mouth and I forgot how to speak. One of his hands moved lower, parting my thighs and massaging me in such a way I saw stars behind my eyes. I gasped and arched my back, writhing in pleasure, then I cried out and Finn covered my lips with his. When I opened my eyes, Finn was smiling at me.

"Already?" he asked. "We might as well go to sleep now."

"Don't you dare," I said. He kissed my lips again, then he fit himself against me. Gods, he'd already pleasured me more than anyone else ever had, and we weren't anywhere near completing the act. If Finn did anything more to me, I might lose my mind.

I felt the blunt head of Finn's cock against me, and I remembered how I'd thought that after Kemen and I were together, I would lie in his arms, and we'd talk about our future, perhaps plan a life together. Instead, he'd gotten up and left, and, since I didn't get a chance to see him before he marched out to the battle that killed him, I never spoke to him again.

If that happened between Finn and I...

I caught Finn's hand. "Don't leave me afterwards," I whispered.

"Why would I leave you?" he asked. "Mara, I never want to be apart from you. Never, not for one moment."

"I'm sorry." I bit the inside of my cheek, because I didn't want to say Kemen's name while I was in bed with Finn. "I just want things to be perfect."

"How is this not perfect? We're warm and safe, and alone, and we both know what we want." He pushed my hair back from my face, and smiled. "And the most beautiful woman in Parthalan has chosen me to be her mate. I only hope I can make you happy."

"You already do," I began, then he kissed me hard and pushed forward at the same time. I'd worried it would hurt, but it didn't. Finn was gentle when he needed to be, and more intense when I needed it, then he was mine and I was his, and Finn was right. Everything was perfect.

Chapter Thirty-Three
Latera Speaks

Deep in the underworld, we finally saw what was making the strange, scraping noises. Around us was a mass of gray skinned, silent ghouls that swayed to unheard music, and stared at us as if they were starved. Starved for what, I couldn't say. We formed a circle with myself, Tor, Priya, and Gilson on the outer edge, and Wren and Sasha—neither of whom were warriors—in the middle. The ghouls blocked our way forward and back, and I was rapidly losing my patience with these creatures. I glanced at Priya, and hoped she was a fighter like her mother.

Turning to face her so she could read my lips, I asked, "You've fought these creatures before?" The ghouls chose that moment to shuffle closer, then they retreated. So far they hadn't made contact with us, but they hadn't moved on or gotten out of our way, either.

"Fought? No," Priya replied. "Ghouls don't have much of a form. You can run straight through them."

"Then why aren't we running?" Wren demanded.

"They make you see things that aren't there," Priya said. "And, there's what tends to be on the other side."

"You mean something lurks beyond them?" I demanded, then I saw it. An arm encased in rotting flesh, a foot made more of bone than meat. "What are those creatures?"

"They're undead," Tor said, as if that wasn't the most outlandish concept. Something undead would be alive, wouldn't it? Then one of the creatures dragged its rotting form forward, and I understood.

They were corpses, yet they lived.

"How are they moving?" Wren shrieked.

"I've heard stories about this," Gilson said. "They're the bodies of the damned. Their gods won't admit them to the next world, so their souls remain in their bodies while they rot away to nothing."

"Stupid gods," I muttered, since everything an arrogant god tried to do invariably made my life more difficult. "All they do is make things worse."

"Aye, cousin," Priya said. "It's why we elves moved on from gods ages ago."

I nodded, agreeing wholeheartedly, and asked, "Gilson, how do we kill them?"

"Chop them up," he replied. "Small bits, so they can't come after you."

"Are you telling me that if I cut off a leg, it could still hop after me?"

"I only know what the stories say."

I dropped the magical fire in my hand to the ground, and drew my other sword. "Very well. Chopping it is."

One of the undead creatures advanced. I moved forward and swung my sword across its torso. By the time I'd stepped back to the group, its disembodied arm had crawled across the ashen ground and was grabbing at my ankle.

"What if we cut off the heads?" I yelled, as I stabbed at the arm. Sludgy black blood spurted from the undead wrist onto my boot. "Is this blood caustic?"

"Not like a demon's," Tor yelled. I glanced over my shoulder, saw him cleave a creature in two with a great arching blow that reminded me of Aeolmar. "Stinks, though."

Sasha screamed. I spun around, saw one of the creature's dragging her into the mass of ghouls by her hair. I flipped my sword around and bashed the hilt into its face. "Stay behind me," I yelled, as I cut off its hands.

"They're coming from behind you!" Sasha pulled the hands out of her hair and flung them at the ghouls, while I hacked apart the rest of the creature. My swords were troll forged and sharp enough to slice clean through sinew and bone, but they were smaller weapons made to match my frame. I needed a heavier weapon, like the sword I'd used to kill Asgeloth.

Aeolmar's sword.

Mar!

Beloved! I'm coming!

"What," I said out loud, because why would Aeolmar say that when we're in different realms? Then more undead were coming toward me, and I screamed.

A white light flashed in the darkness beyond the ghouls. Fearing the worst, I pushed Sasha behind me and raised my swords. When I saw the silver blade swinging above the ghouls and cutting through the undead, I hardly believed it was true. Another flash of light appeared, this one so bright it momentarily blinded me. Once my eyes readjusted to the underworld's dim glow, I saw him.

Aeolmar.

My mate had come for me.

"Aeolmar," I cried as I flung myself at him. He grabbed me with one arm, while his sword arm sliced an undead in two from its head straight through its torso. The threat dealt with, he wrapped both arms around me.

"*Nalla,*" he murmured.

"How are you here?" I touched his face, half terrified he was a mirage and would dissipate when I made contact. But no, he was real.

"You needed me." He turned his head and kissed my palm. "I sensed you were in danger. Something wasn't right in our bond."

I thought of a thousand things to say—how he should trust me, how I didn't need him to fight my battles for me—and didn't say any of them. Aeolmar was here, and I was so glad he'd come for me. *I love you.*

You know I'll always find you.

I stepped back, since we were still battling a horde of ghouls and undead... And realized that the monsters' numbers were greatly reduced. "Where have they gone?"

"I sent them off." Aeolmar withdrew a handful of shiny glass discs from his jerkin.

"Are those portals?" I asked, and he nodded. "Asherah will skin you for having those."

"She knows," he said. "I gave her most of them, so she could get to Dremmsvard." He stepped toward the remaining ghouls, and said, "Get behind me." Aeolmar stepped in front of Tor and Priya, and tossed a portal at the monsters. A moment and a third flash of light later, they were gone.

"Where did you send them?" I asked.

"The Southern Sea," he replied, as I rekindled the fire in my palm. Aeolmar finally got a good look at our party, which was three people larger than he'd anticipated. *Beloved, who are these people?*

"You remember Sasha," I began. "This is Gilson, captain of the Ganneran guard. He and Wren engineered our escape from the castle." Wren smiled as Gilson saluted Aeolmar, and I turned to my newly met aunt. "This is Priya."

"Elvasla's daughter?" Aeolmar asked, and Priya nodded, her face betraying her surprise at his recognition of her. "Then the lodestone is with you?"

"It is," she replied, and she showed him the stone. "We have a history, the stone and I."

Aeolmar scrutinized the stone in Priya's hand, then he turned toward the last member of our party. Tor. I opened my mouth to speak, but Aeolmar held up his hand. I paused, waiting to see what he would do or say. After they watched each other for a time, Aeolmar withdrew a sword from a sheath along his back. I saw the blue pommel stone and knew it was his father's sword, forged so long ago by Grelk himself. Tor's face crumpled when he saw the blade. He recognized it, too.

"You knew the owner of this sword," Aeolmar said.

"He was my boy, my youngest," Tor replied. "However, you look more like your mother." Aeolmar glanced at me, his face panicked.

It's him. Tor. He knows who you are.

Aeolmar refocused on Tor. "Have you been in Gannera all this time, while Caol'non was on Ysr?"

"Ysr?" Tor shook his head. "Caol'nir and Caol'non were obsessed with that island." Tor paused, and added, "Is Caol'non still there?"

"No. He's returned to Teg'urnan." Aeolmar re-sheathed the sword. "I've got a son named after my brother, who I'm told was named after you."

Tor smiled. "Your mate said as much," he said, then he pulled Aeolmar into his arms. "Grandson. I am so happy to meet you."

"Grandfather," Aeolmar said, and I could feel his happiness through our bond. "When I left Teg'urnan, Caol'non was looking after Atreynha, and what's left of the temple."

"What do you mean, what's left?" I demanded.

"Walk and talk," Priya said. "Aeolmar may have dealt with this batch of monsters, but there are more. Down here, there are always more."

"She's right," Tor said. He and Aeolmar stepped back from one another, and after everyone had sorted themselves out, we resumed following Priya and the lodestone.

"Can't we use a portal to get wherever we're going?" Sasha asked.

"Better to save them," Aeolmar replied. "This way leads to Thurnda?"

"Aye, Thurnda," Tor replied, since Priya probably hadn't heard him.

"It's good that we're headed toward Thurnda," Aeolmar said. "Ember and Leran left for Thurnda at first dawn, and I sent Mara and Finn after them. We suspect Cerillia is working against us."

"Mar, Cerillia is Gannok's sister," I said, and between Sasha and me, we explained what had occurred between my sister and the Highlanders.

"Years ago, I wanted to kill Gannok, but Latera wouldn't let me," Aeolmar said to Sasha.

"Tera's always been good-hearted," Sasha replied. "Next time you'd like to kill a Highlander, I give you full approval. Since Gannok named me their queen, I can even order you to kill one," she added.

I narrowed my eyes at Sasha, and said, "I understand why Ember and Leran left for Thurnda, but why did you send Mara and Finn after them?"

"Kemen's father, Krylle, came to the palace looking for Mara," Aeolmar replied, and he went on to detail the explosions that had destroyed Teg'urnan.

"Krylle, the mad priest?" Tor asked.

"Yes," Aeolmar replied, then he said to me, "Krylle sought out Mara because she's with child."

"Oh," I said, covering my mouth with my hand; my baby was with child. "That's what she wanted to talk about the day I left. Is she all right? Does she need me?"

"She's well, as is the baby. I sent her after Ember to keep her away from Krylle. We sealed the gates after the explosion, so he's in the palace, somewhere."

"I'm glad you sent Finn with her," I said. "He loves her so much he won't allow anything to harm her."

Aeolmar cocked his head to the side. "You knew?"

"Didn't you?" I countered, though I'd had no idea about a baby. "Is the child his, or Kemen's?"

"I didn't ask, but now it hardly matters," Aeolmar replied. "It's plain that she and Finn are committed to each other."

"That's good," I said, then Priya held up a hand.

"This is the way to Thurnda," she said, indicating a relatively flat expanse that led to a trail that steadily climbed higher and, presumably, to the surface world. "But that," she added, pointing toward a dark valley below us, "is the way to Dremmsvard."

"Dremmsvard," I repeated. "Asherah will need our help, won't she?"

"That she will," Tor said. "I vote for going on to Dremmsvard. It's been too long since I was in the northern reaches."

"What of Olluhm?" Aeolmar asked. "It's him we will be fighting."

"What, are you afraid of going up against a god?" Tor countered. "Come now, grandson, surely you've got bigger balls than that."

Wren gasped and Sasha giggled. As for me, I kept a straight face, but I felt Aeolmar's indignation through our bond. "Dremmsvard it is," Aeolmar declared. "I'll show you who's got the bigger balls."

Chapter Thirty-Four
Asherah Speaks

I rushed down the steps from the southern tower with the casket of portals tucked underneath my arm, and returned to the palace square. I found my mate standing in front of a cluster of tents. "What's happening?" I asked, as I caught my breath.

"We've gotten almost the entire healer's ward out here," Finlay replied. "The legion made it through all of the tunnels, and while we didn't find Krylle, we did establish that none of the tunnels collapsed. In fact, none of them were damaged in the slightest, which makes me think Krylle didn't know they existed."

"That's good," I said. "Where are we with casualties?"

Finlay withdrew a parchment, and read it over before continuing. "The only confirmed deaths are Krylle's men," he said. "However, many remain unaccounted for, including Krylle himself."

"And he could be anywhere." I looked toward the gate, which was still closed. "What if he left before the explosions were detonated?"

"That's a possibility," Finlay allowed. "However, if he did leave it wasn't through the gate. Merrick keeps a log of all who enter and leave, and Krylle hasn't left through that exit. Since he seemed to be unaware of the tunnels, the only other way out would be for him to scale the wall."

I stared at the wall that surrounded the palace. It was taller than five men, wider than three, and six watchtowers dotted the upper edge, in addition to Merrick's post above the gates. Krylle's cult was housed deep in the Eastern Mountains, so perhaps he was well versed in climbing. Although, even if he had scaled the walls like a goat, someone would have seen him and reported on the activity. "Whether he knew about the tunnels or not, the odds of him using them are low," I said. "They don't connect to the temple, and that's his last known location. He's in here, somewhere."

"We'll find him," Finlay assured me, then he tapped the metal box I held as if it was precious. "What's this?"

"Aeolmar had a stash of portals up in his old rooms." I opened the lid, saw Finlay's eyes widen when he saw the shiny silver discs. "Apparently, he was holding on to them in case he ever needed to find his family in another realm."

"Then I assume he's used a few, and gone after Latera?"

"That he has." I picked up one of the discs, and watched how the light shone through it. "He suggested that these would be an excellent way to reach Dremmsvard."

Finlay nodded, but he was frowning. "It would be, but can we really leave with so many wounded and unaccounted for? With Krylle still missing?"

"No." I dropped the portal back into the casket, and shut the lid on the portals, and my half-formed plan to reach the shrine. "We have much to do here before we can even consider leaving for Dremmsvard. Where's Atreynha? Has she awakened?"

"She hasn't. I'll take you to her," Finlay said, and I followed him through the maze of healers' tents until we reached a larger one bustling with activity. Tucked away in a quiet corner behind a screen, the High Priestess lay on a cot. Caol'non sat beside her while the remaining priestesses moved about the tent grinding herbs, and preparing simples and poultices for the rest of the wounded.

"How is she?" I asked.

"No worse," Caol'non replied. "Her breathing is steady, and her wounds have been seen to. She just needs to wake up." I noticed how Caol'non held Atreynha's hand, and realized that not only did he need something to distract him from the priestess's condition, he was one of the true *con'dehr*. Not the *con'dehr* as they had functioned under Harek, may his soul rot in hell, but the temple guards of old. Which meant he might be the key to finding Krylle.

"You know the temple well, yes?" I asked.

"I do," Caol'non replied. "I know the layout inside and out. Why? Have you a task for me?"

"Do you any idea of where Krylle could have gone after he set the bombs? Or where he could be hiding even now?"

"He's probably in your garden," Caol'non replied. "Behind the altar's platform is a passage that leads directly into the garden. In my day, both priestesses and *con'dehr* went there when we wanted to be alone."

I raised an eyebrow, but didn't comment on Caol'non's admission that the supposedly chaste priestesses were sneaking off with their guards. It's not like I hadn't suspected as much, especially since Aeolmar's parents had been a priestess and her own temple guard; Alluria and Caol'nir, how I miss them both. More, Olluhm was the biggest hypocrite that had ever drawn breath, and I couldn't fault anyone for not following his edicts.

Caol'non stroked Atreynha's forehead, then he looked up at me and said, "I promised Mara I would keep Krylle from harming her. By your leave, I will enter your garden, find him, and end him."

I nodded, then I withdrew a portal and pressed it into Caol'non's hand. "It's easy to get lost in the garden," I said. "If you can't find your way out, use that to return to me."

Caol'non slipped the portal inside his jerkin, then he left for the garden. I set the casket of portals on the chair he'd left empty, and faced Finlay.

"Now what?"

"Now, we see to our people."

Chapter Thirty-Five
Mara Speaks

I loved being in bed with Finn.

Granted, I'd slept next to him many times before, but this was different. Better. There wasn't anything I didn't love about lying beside him. Firstly, there was his body. His skin was a deep golden shade reminiscent of desert sands, but his body hair was the same white blond as the hair on his head, giving him the appearance of having been dusted with snow. The pale curls clustered above his heart were soft and thick, and I couldn't stop stroking them. What's more, my nose was pressed against his neck just underneath his jaw, and he smelled amazing. I didn't think I could ever get enough of him.

Aside from taking pleasure in his very pleasing form, Finn himself only got kinder and more loving the longer we were together. When our supper was delivered Finn leapt out of bed and threw on his clothes, then he collected the food and brought everything to me. After we ate, he climbed back into bed, took me into his arms, and proved yet again that choosing him was the best decision I'd ever made.

Now I lay on my side with my head on his shoulder, my belly pressed against him as I tugged at the curls on his chest. "How are we going to lay together once I'm as big as an elephant?" I asked. "If I get much bigger I won't be able to reach you."

"You won't get that big," he mumbled. "And even if you do, it's only temporary. Soon enough we'll have our boy with us, and then you will be regular sized again."

Our boy. Finn hadn't only claimed me, he'd also claimed the baby as his, and it made me so happy I thought my heart might burst. "We still need to pick a name," I said, but his only response was a few gentle snores. As I let myself drift off to sleep, I hoped I would dream about our son. Dream I did, but not in the way I'd hoped.

My dreams had been chaotic ever since the attack on The Seat. More often than not they were terrifying, and I often woke soaked in sweat. I'd never told anyone how bad they were; most didn't know anything about my dreams, and I wanted to keep it that way. Only Finn knew how awful they could be, and that was only due to all of the time we spent together on the journey back to Teg'urnan. That night, as I lay on a hard bed in a soldier's garrison, my dreams weren't bad, but they were some of the strangest dreams of my life.

The dream began pleasantly enough. Finn and I were sitting in a field. It was a cold day, but the sun was bright and the skies were clear. Finn looked at me and smiled, and I was happy.

I was also confused.

"Finn, why is there only one?" I asked. I shielded my eyes from the glare of the single sun, and wondered where the other had gotten to.

"There's two," he said, and jerked his chin toward the far side of the field. Running toward us were two children. One had pale blond hair, while the other's hair was bright auburn.

"Who are they?" I asked.

"They're ours."

My eyes snapped open, and I lay there listening to the blood pounding in my ears. After I got my breathing under control, I rolled onto my back and set my hands on my belly. It could have been my imagination, but it seemed bigger than it had been the day before. That wasn't so strange, since I would be steadily growing until I gave birth. As I recalled the children in my dream, I wondered if my belly was growing twice as fast, because it had two babies inside of it.

"Blessed Cydia, how could there be two," I murmured.

My speculation ended when I heard our main door open. I was about to wake Finn so he could deal with the intruder, then I remembered the nosy person in the room across the corridor who knew a charm to unlock doors. Our father had taught it to both of us.

"Hello, sister," Ember said as she entered our sleeping area. "I trust I'm not interrupting anything."

I reached for my chemise and awkwardly pulled it over my head. It's difficult to dress in a hurry when you feel like you're as big as an ox. "Hush. Finn's sleeping."

"He's always sleeping," Ember said. "You do wear him out, don't you?"

I narrowed my eyes at her. "Is there something I can help you with? Or did you wear out Leran, and now you're bored, so you've come to harass me?"

"Leran has more stamina than you can imagine," Ember said. "However, something about this place isn't right. Remember how Leran sent off three messengers, one each to Tingu, Thurnda, and Teg'urnan? A horse returned, riderless, about an hour ago. Leran went to investigate, and found the message he'd written for Sibeal still in the saddlebags."

"What happened to the messenger?"

"We don't know, and what's more interesting is that the stable master also doesn't seem to know, and neither does the garrison commander. They both acted as if messengers going missing was a common occurrence."

"Odd." I wrapped a shawl around my shoulders, and joined Ember in front of the hearth. She was picking through what was left from our supper and putting together quite the meal for herself. "Is someone trying to keep us away from Thurnda, or keep us here?"

"Or, perhaps Thurnda is a trap," Ember suggested. "Really, bad options abound."

I sat next to her, and put the kettle over the fire to warm. Since we were apparently staying awake for the rest of the night, I might as well make some tea. "Where is Leran now?"

"He's walking the garrison's perimeter, talking to the soldiers in the hopes he can figure out what's going on." She worried the edge of the table. "If anyone at this garrison purposefully harmed that messenger, and withholding knowledge from us, it's a direct betrayal of Leran."

"And you," I said, since Ember was the Lady of Tingu. "If you were betrayed, how will you handle it?"

"I believe the accepted punishment is death," she replied.

I shuddered. "Hopefully it won't come to that."

***

Ember and I shared some tea, then she left to locate Leran while I woke Finn and explained our new, worsened situation.

"And no one seems to know or care what happened to the messenger?" he asked, as he pulled on his boots.

"Apparently not." I went to the window, and scanned the darkened yard behind the stables. "Even if we can get to the horses, we need to get the gate open."

"Can't Leran order them to open the gate?" Finn asked. "He's their king."

"True, but if someone is making things difficult for him there could be complications." I sat next to Finn, and touched the golden chain around his neck. "What of the king's seal? What can that accomplish?"

"If Leran has no authority at a Thurndian garrison, I fear I'll have even less," Finn replied. "However, it might be something useful to mention, if the soldiers here seem inclined to keep us from moving on." Finn wrapped his arm around me. "Don't worry, Mara. I can protect you."

"I know you will," I said. "Just don't try any heroics like you did before, like charging off into the enemy by yourself. I nearly died of sadness when you were dragged out of the battle."

"I won't." Trembling, he kissed my hair. "Then, I had nothing to live for, aside from keeping everyone else alive long enough for Tingu's legion to return." He set his hand on my belly. "Now I have both of you to care for."

I set my hand on top of his. "We care for each other."

We heard the door across the corridor open and shut. A few minutes later, we heard it again, then Leran strode into our room.

"We're leaving," Leran announced. "The commander isn't pleased about it, but nor can he stop us. I've told him we're returning to Teg'urnan, but that's a ruse."

"What if they follow us?" Finn asked.

"Let them try," Leran replied, then he glanced at me. He probably wasn't used to evading the enemy while traveling with a pregnant woman. "If they follow us now, I suspect only one or two will be sent after us. We can easily evade them, or we can fight if it comes to it. However, I know a route that will take us in a loop around the garrison, and back northward to Thurnda. The odds of them finding us are small."

"You still think Thurnda's the best place for us to go?" I asked.

"We must warn Sibeal about Cerillia's possible treachery," Leran said. "Also, we can be inside Thurnda's walls by sun rest tomorrow. As strong as you are, Mara, I don't want to risk you riding straight through to Tingu at this time of year. We simply aren't prepared for such a long journey."

I nodded, grateful Leran wasn't planning on dragging me across the frozen tundra. "And when we reach Thurnda, what then?"

"Then, we will find out if Cerillia really is a traitor."

***

We waited for Ember to return to our rooms before leaving. She'd been charming the kitchen staff into packing us extra provisions, all the while listening to their chatter to try and determine what was really going on in the garrison. When she finally joined us, she had a basket full of food and news we didn't enjoy hearing.

"It's Thurnda they're trying to keep us from reaching," Ember said. "The cook was ready to put together enough rations for us to reach Tingu, and the captain of the guard promised us a carriage and an armed escort all the way to The Seat."

"Then they're not working against us?" Finn asked. "They're trying to protect us?"

Leran rubbed his chin. "But from what?"

"Cerillia," I said. "Whatever she's doing in Thurnda, they're aware and they want us far away from her."

Ember blew out a breath. "I don't like the idea of four of us walking into unknown danger in Thurnda. Perhaps we should go back to Teg'urnan, for reinforcements."

"We can't go back," I said. "The palace is destroyed, and who knows what else Krylle has done since then. Asherah needs to see to her people, and we're Sibeal's heirs now. We must go to Thurnda and set things right."

Ember nodded. "You're right. We must go on to Thurnda." She leaned against Leran, and added, "Of all the times for Mama to go to Gannera. We need her here."

"Do you think Papa's followed her there yet?" I asked.

"Aeolmar's planning on going to the mortal realm?" Finn asked.

"He hates being separated from Mama," I replied. "The moment he thinks she needs him, or when he can't take being away from her another moment, he'll go."

"That's good," Leran said. "With any luck, once they've both returned from the mortal lands, they'll seek us out. I don't know what's happening in Thurnda, but I fear we'll need them."

Chapter Thirty-Six

Latera Speaks

Our group of seven trudged in silence through the underworld, though the landscape around us was filled with sounds. My feet crunched on the thick layer of ash that carpeted the ground, and occasionally I kicked aside a bone. All of the remains we encountered were old and brittle, and I wondered how long ago we entered the underworld. Was it yesterday, or a sennight past? The dark, never-changing landscape made it impossible to gauge the passage of time.

I wondered how many had entered with the intent of crossing from one realm to another, and never made it to their destination.

It was well known that one could use the underworld to navigate to any of the nine realms, being that this land of ash and soot touched upon all of them. Priya and Tor claimed to have crossed through the dark realm many times, with varying degrees of success. While Priya hadn't said too much, I understood that injuries she sustained in the underworld had led to her hearing loss, and problems with her other senses and her skin. Tor also admitted to barely surviving his first trip through the realm, and I wondered yet again if we were mad for attempting this.

If Elvasla's daughter and the Prelate of Parthalan barely survived this realm, what hope do the rest of us have?

I wasn't worried for myself, or Aeolmar. We'd battled many awful creatures both together and alone, and as long as Aeolmar didn't run out of portals, I was confident we would make it to the other side. However, Sasha and Wren were no fighters, and while Gilson was a soldier, he'd lived his entire life in Gannera Castle. If we were attacked many more times by ghouls or undead, I feared one of them might not make it.

Aeolmar, sensing my discomfort, took my free hand with his and squeezed. In our other hands, we carried flames, illuminating the area around us so we could navigate around the many obstacles in our path, but not enough to be able to make out whatever made the shuffling, scratching noises in the distance. No one needed a better look at those monsters.

"Does Tor remind you of your father?" I asked.

"A bit," he replied. "He's got the same air about him, of someone who's always smiling and good natured, but confident they can deal with any threat they come upon."

"I suppose as Prelate he would have to be confident and capable," I said. "He was pleased to hear that Caol'non has returned to Teg'urnan." I thought about our son, who was in Teg'urnan without his parents or siblings. He was far from alone, but my heart still ached for my sweet, brave boy. "Do you think Caol'non will watch out for our Tor?"

"Absolutely, as will Elkin, and Asherah, and everyone else who remains at the palace," Aeolmar replied. "Tor is safe."

"Good. Once we're all together, he'll enjoy showing his grandsire his troll sword."

Up ahead, Priya stopped moving, then Tor snuffed out his lantern. I released Aeolmar's hand and drew one of my swords. *What is it?*

Wait here. Keep the fire low.

Aeolmar extinguished the magical flame on his palm and approached Tor, sword in hand. They exchanged a few low words, then Aeolmar backed up and raised his sword.

"What is it?" Sasha asked.

"Hush," I whispered.

"Whatever's out there already knows we're here," Sasha said. "Tell me what's happening."

"I'm not sure. Let me talk to Aeolmar and Tor."

Leaving Sasha standing with Wren and Gilson, I approached Aeolmar. I'd just reached him when Tor yelled and pointed behind us. Aeolmar dropped his sword and generated the largest fireball I'd ever seen him create, and threw it out into the darkness.

The fireball struck the cave wall and burst into a shower of sparks, illuminating the dozens if not hundreds of undead surrounding us.

"Swords up," I yelled. "Surrounded?"

"No," Aeolmar replied, as he kicked up his sword and caught it by the pommel. "They're all near the cliff side."

Instead of attacking, all the undead jumped in place. Then, they jumped again.

"What are they doing?" Tor asked, and I felt a tremor.

"They're trying to cause an avalanche," I said, and I looked toward the two members of our party that were the farthest away from me. They were our most vulnerable, and also standing dangerously close to the cliff's edge. "Sasha, Wren! Run!"

My sisters had no time to move. The ground gave way underneath them and they screamed as they slid down the black ash. Gilson lunged toward Wren but he was too late, and the three of them went over.

"No," I screamed, ready to leap after them when Aeolmar grabbed me. He dragged me away from the edge as he flung a portal down the slope. An instant and flash of light later, Wren, Sasha, and Gilson were gone.

"You portaled them?" Tor asked. "Perhaps we should have all portaled out of here at the beginning of this walk."

"That was my last portal," Aeolmar said. "It was either use it to get them out of the ravine, or jump off the cliff after them."

"Where did you send them?" I demanded.

"Teg'urnan," he replied. "They'll be safer there."

I stared at the empty space where my sisters had been a moment ago. I understood that Aeolmar had done what he thought was necessary, and that there was no way we could have scaled the collapsing cliff to rescue them. Despite these facts, my heart was in my throat.

I raised my gaze, and saw the undead clustered on the far side of the collapsed path. The only thing keeping them from us was over the rockslide they had created, but even if they could navigate the debris the slope was dangerously steep. Yes, Aeolmar had made the right choice.

"You're certain they made it?" I asked.

"The portals have never failed me," he replied. "Beloved, you will see your sisters again. All of your sisters."

"Latera, Aeolmar," Priya shouted. "That collapse will have weakened the entire cliff. We need to move before there's another avalanche."

I cast a final glance toward the bottom of the cliff, then I took Aeolmar's hand and we followed Priya and Tor through what I hoped was the final tunnel before we reached Dremmsvard.

CHAPTER THIRTY-SEVEN

The last thing Wren remembered was Gilson's panicked face as the ground fell out from under her. As she reached for him, a white light flashed so brightly she worried it would scorch her eyes, and the world dissipated around her.

In the next moment, she landed flat on her back as a new, different light stung her eyes.

Sunlight.

Wren sat up, and saw Sasha and Gilson lying on the ground alongside her. She ran her hand across the paved surface beneath her, and realized she was in the palace square. Aeolmar had sent them to Teg'urnan.

Wren crawled toward Gilson, and shook his shoulder. "Gilson," she said. "Wake up. We're in Parthalan."

Gilson's eyes blinked open, and he rubbed the remains of the underworld's ash from his face. "You're certain?" he asked. "I saw you—all of us—go over the cliff."

"I'm certain," Wren said, as she smoothed back his hair. "We're at Teg'urnan."

"I thought this was a ruin," Sasha said. Wren watched as Sasha sat up and gazed around the square. The normally pristine and crowded square was filled with heaps of rubble and debris, and the portion they were in was nearly deserted. "This is the fabled fae palace? I expected something a bit more finished."

Wren took in the destruction, and saw how the center of the palace was collapsed in on itself. "Aeolmar did say that four explosions had damaged the palace." Wren spied the tents on the far side of the square. "Let's find someone who can explain to us what's been going on here."

They got to their feet, and Wren led them across the square. "So this is where you live," Gilson said.

"I'm mad at you," Wren said. "What were you thinking, leaping off a cliff like that? You could have been killed!"

"I was thinking that you were falling, and I needed to catch you." Gilson grabbed her hand. "I couldn't just let you go over."

"Luckily Aeolmar was there," Sasha said. "I assume he used one of his portals to send us here?"

"I would say so." They reached the tents, and Wren saw where the healers were set up. "Chandra," she called.

"Wren!" Chandra rushed across the open area and embraced her. "I am so glad to see you!"

"I'm glad to be back," Wren said. "Do we have a lot of wounded?"

"Yes, but most of them are doing well. Your sisters have been a great help to us." Chandra looked past Wren, and asked, "Who are these two?"

"Chandra, this is Sasha, yet another sister to me and Latera," Wren replied. After Chandra and Sasha exchanged a greeting, Wren continued, "And this is Gilson."

"My lady," Gilson said with a bow. "I am Gilson Cadoret, captain of the Ganneran Guard. Please, how may I assist you?"

Chandra looked over Gilson, and said to Wren, "This is the human man you've been missing?"

"Yes, I greatly missed my childhood home," Wren said as her cheeks warmed, and Gilson grinned.

"I can see why," Chandra said. "Since I am Wren's assistant, you'll be tasked with doing whatever she says, but I suspect you're already used to that." She looked over her shoulder, and added, "The High Priestess currently needs the most care. She was near the center of the explosions, and has yet to wake."

"I'll see to her," Wren said. "Come along, you two."

"You missed me?" Gilson asked.

"Perhaps."

"I missed you, too."

Wren glanced at him. "I'm very glad you're here. Now, let's see how we can help Atreynha." Wren drew the tent flap aside, and saw the High Priestess lying on a cot. Standing next to her cot were Elia and Jannei.

"Sasha! Wren," they cried, as they ran to embrace their siblings.

"We were so worried," Jannei said to Sasha.

"You could have sent a message," Elia added. "The castle was in an uproar after you ran away from Gannok!"

"I was more concerned with evading the prince than sending messages," Sasha said, and they all murmured their disdain for the Highland prince. "How are you?" she asked. "Are you happy here?"

"We're well," Elia replied, "and these Parthians have been very good to us. Where's Latera?"

Sasha glanced at Wren, and replied, "Latera's still in the underworld, along with her mate, and our friends Priya and Tor."

"The underworld?" Jannei repeated, wide eyed.

"It was how we escaped Gannera," Sasha said. "I don't know if we'll ever see any of them again."

"We will," Wren said. "We will see to our wounded here, and if Latera and the rest haven't returned once our patients are well, we will set out to find them. Now, we have our friend to help." Wren approached Atreynha's cot, and felt the priestess's hands and forehead. "Elia, tell me everything you know about Atreynha's injuries."

Chapter Thirty-Eight

Caol'non accessed the royal chambers easily enough. The various bombs Krylle and his men had planted around the palace had collapsed the corridors that led to the royal wing, but Caol'non had navigated through devastation before. His entire life had been devastation in one form or another, from his mother's death, to the time he served at the Southern Border, to when he left Teg'urnan after Sahlgren's fall, and when he at last found himself standing on Ysr's shores.

Sailing to the island was the most bittersweet journey; his twin had long wanted to go to Ysr to learn more about the enigmatic land, and Caol'non had ended up going there without him. He almost left as soon as he'd arrived, to return to Caol'nir's side and tell him that yes, he'd finally made it. However, Caol'non had always had a curious mind, and he plunged into the jungle eager to learn more about the inhabitants. He'd never meant to spend half a lifetime with the monks under Dinnu's tutelage, but that was exactly what he'd done. If only he'd known that every oath and promise he swore would end up leading him right back to Teg'urnan, and Atreynha.

Back when he'd first joined the *con'dehr*, Caol'non and Atreynha hadn't been close. They'd been friendly, yes, but they weren't exactly friends. Then again, Caol'non had made a habit of not being too friendly with the priestesses, since his eldest brother had a long-standing relationship with one of the novices, and Caol'nir was still sneaking around with Alluria. Shortly after Caol'nir announced that he'd bound himself to Alluria, Caol'non found himself alone in the temple with Atreynha.

"What do you think of your brother's mate?" Atreynha had asked him.

"I think they belong together," he replied. "Are you disappointed that Alluria left the order?"

"Truly? No. A life in the temple was never her calling. She will be much happier with Caol'nir. We should all hope to find someone we can love with all whole being, and be loved in return."

"I thought priestesses only sought love from Olluhm."

"There's much you don't know about priestesses," Atreyhna replied, then she'd put her hand on Caol'non's arm. "I could teach you, if you'd like."

And so began their time together, which had been satisfying in a way none of Caol'non's relationships had been before or since. They only parted ways after the Battle for Teg'urnan, since he left the palace while Atreynha stayed on to become the High Priestess. Their separation was amicable, since both were on different paths, but he'd never stopped thinking about Atreynha's warm smile, or her gentle laugh. He often wondered if she still thought of him, or if she'd long ago forgotten about her besotted temple guard.

Then he returned to Teg'urnan, and after their brief reunion in the royal chamber he'd walked her not to the Great Temple, but to his own rooms. They came together as easily as if no time had passed, and Caol'non thanked whatever gods were watching over them.

Now Atreynha lay unresponsive in a healer's tent, and the man responsible was somewhere in the palace. For harming Atreynha, Caol'non would end Krylle just as he'd ended his son's life out on the Northern Waste. Not all lineages were meant to be preserved.

Caol'non crested the last mound of debris in the corridor, and found himself in the royal receiving chamber. He recalled following his father the Prelate in and out of this room often, back when Sahlgren was still their king, and not a traitor in league with demons. Of course, now he understood that the demons were the first Parthians, the ones that had been displaced by Olluhm when the false sun god began his reign of terror. Caol'non considered the Sahlgren he once knew, and wondered if the old king hadn't been trying to right an ancient wrong.

Then Caol'non recalled the *dojas* where Parthians had been sent as slaves to serve those same demons, and he shook his head. Sahlgren had been wrong, and he had earned his fate.

Carefully, he traced the black scars along the walls, evidence of the explosions that had damaged this portion of the palace. Many had spoken of four blasts, but Caol'non's trained eye detected evidence of at least five explosions in this area alone. Krylle had most likely rigged several bombs to detonate at once, and had placed many such devices near the royal chambers. Caol'non realized that Krylle had not come to Teg'urnan as a priest, or a grieving father seeking answers about his son's death.

Krylle had come as an assassin.

Caol'non drew his sword, and stepped over the piles of stone and plaster as he approached the queen's walled garden. The door hung limply off its hinges, the wood splintered and the glass shattered. The shards cracked and popped underneath his boots as he stepped out of the palace, and into the garden where some say Olluhm first met Cydia, but Caol'non had never believed that story. He'd been around Olluhm and his temples all his life, and whatever magic resided in the garden was older and kinder than the sun god. Caol'non wondered if this had once been The Deliverer's home, and the remnants of her magic had helped hide her from Olluhm as he rode across the sky.

A twig snapped. Caol'non knew the garden well enough to know that there was no dry or fallen wood present on that or any other day. That noise had been made intentionally. Slowly, Caol'non turned around and saw Krylle standing on a hillock with a heap of kindling at his feet.

"Planning on burning down the palace?" Caol'non called. "Is that how you seek to release the old gods in death? Kemen only used a dagger."

"That dagger was sacred," Krylle spat. "Give it to me, and I'll let you live."

"No." Caol'non strode toward Krylle. "I took an oath to defend the throne. I wouldn't let Kemen harm Asherah, and I won't allow you to harm her, either. Wasn't it enough that your men died for this foolish plan?"

"Enough?" Krylle threw back his head and laughed. "You, you who spent so much time on Ysr with Nu himself, you should know that nothing is enough."

"Nu," Caol'non repeated, then he remembered Dinnu, the kindly old monk who led the monasteries. Dinnu's name meant "of Nu"...

And it was Nu, the original sun god, who had been cast from the sky by Olluhm.

"It can't be," Caol'non said.

"It can, and it is," Krylle said. "The old gods walk among us still! Help me release them in death, and we shall join them when the new world rises!"

Caol'non raised his sword. "You're insane."

"What you call insanity is merely devotion to my gods," Krylle said, then there was fire in his hands and he dropped it onto the kindling. The dry sticks ignited, and in moments Krylle was consumed with a column of flame. Caol'non raised his arm to shield his face from the heat, wondering what Krylle had doused himself with to turn his body into a torch. He hadn't seen such a fire since he's served in the legion, and they used signal fires to alert far-flung camps.

Who is Krylle signaling?

Cold fear slid down Caol'non's spine, and he looked skyward. The elder sun—Olluhm himself—was descending to the ground. It wasn't nearly time for sunrest, but the god was so close to the garden Caol'non could see the wheels on his chariot.

"I struck a bargain," Krylle wheezed; somehow, his throat hadn't burned through. "Alert Olluhm to The Deliver's location, and he will ensure I sleep with the old gods."

Caol'non took a step back from Krylle, then he cast the portal and returned to Asherah's side. She was among the wounded, with the king at her side.

"Krylle is dead, but it was a trap," he began. "Olluhm is coming."

Asherah's head snapped toward the sky, and she too saw the sun as it fell toward the palace. "We must evacuate! Get the wounded loaded into carriages, saddle the horses!"

"We'll never make it," Finlay said. "Use the portals. Go to Dremmsvard. We will hold him off."

"I can't leave!"

"You can," Finlay said. "When Olluhm realizes you aren't here, he will move on. Once he's gone, I will begin the evacuation." Finlay took her hands, and pressed his forehead against hers. "Sher, you are the only one who can set things right, but you need to be in Dremmsvard to do it."

"But, our home," she murmured. "Where will you take everyone?"

"I will take them to you," he replied. "Our home can be anywhere. It's our people that matter."

She nodded, then she withdrew two portals from the casket. "Keep the rest of the portals on you," she said. "If you have to, portal our people as far away from that madman as you can. And please remember, I love you more than anything."

"Not half as much as I love you." Finlay kissed her, then Asherah stepped back and cast the portal. Once she was gone, Finlay turned to Caol'non.

"Please tell me you have some insight as to how to fight a god."

CHAPTER THIRTY-NINE
EMBER SPEAKS

Despite Leran's suspicions, no one tried to keep us from leaving the camp, and no one from the garrison followed us. Many told us that they would prefer it if we stayed safe inside the camp's walls, and Luce even tried to bribe us with a cake. That cake was positively exquisite, and very nearly won me over. Leran, however, was unswayed by sweets and dire warnings. He was certain that Thurnda was where we needed to be, and nothing in the nine realms was going to change his mind.

Once we were ready to depart, the garrison's commander took Leran and me aside and shared a few things he'd been keeping to himself.

"We don't know what's happening in Thurnda," he said, which was his first acknowledgement that something odd was going on up north. "Whenever we send messages to the palace, they come back returned and answered as they always have been. Our supplies are delivered without fail, and we've never been shorted."

"But," Leran prompted.

"But something is off," he replied. "All of the supply men are new. Not one of these new men can adequately answer my questions, and there's what happened with your messenger."

"Why didn't you mention any of this earlier?" I asked.

"I have no proof, and I see no reason to worry my people without having actual facts," he replied. "There may be nothing going on. I might have imagined it all, but I don't think that I did." He regarded us, and said, "I am glad you've decided to return to Teg'urnan, instead of going on to Thurnda. If we lost our Lord and our new Lady, I don't know what would become of us."

Leran reassured the commander instead of reprimanding him for withholding information—I doubt I would have been so understanding—then we joined Mara and Finn. We quickly sorted ourselves out, then we departed from the garrison and began the looping route south and west that would bring us back around to the road to Thurnda.

"Why didn't you tell him we would find out what was happening in Thurnda?" I asked Leran, after we were out of sight of the garrison. "He seemed genuine."

"He did," Leran said. "However, we don't know if anyone else at the garrison was compromised. And what about the new supply men he mentioned? They could be spies."

Leran was almost as paranoid as my father. "Spies for whom, exactly?"

"That, I do not know yet," he admitted. "We will learn more once we reach Thurnda. Didn't I tell you that life as Lady of Tingu would never be boring?"

"Life with you could never be anything but wonderful," I replied, and we spent the next hour or so talking about what we would do when we returned to The Seat, with each plan of ours more outlandish than the last. Mara and Finn remained behind us, where they were having their own conversation. I wanted them to join us, but I didn't press them. They had plenty to discuss about their own future, what with the baby coming.

The ruse of heading to Teg'urnan didn't cost us too much time, and two days after we left the garrison behind Thurnda's palace came into view. It was a grand structure, not nearly as big as Teg'urnan or as ostentatious as The Seat, but it had an undeniable elegance about it. If anything, the palace reminded me of Sibeal, with her quiet, dignified strength.

"I never thought I'd be back in Thurnda so soon," I said to Leran. "In fact, I never really thought I would be back at all."

A cloud passed across Leran's face. "I understand if you didn't enjoy your time here, what with how I acted toward you," he began, and I grabbed his hand to stop that sort of talk.

"It's not that," I said. "I've never been very good at imagining what fortune will bring me. When we left Thurnda the last time, I assumed it would be for good. And, I did enjoy my time here with you. Most of it, anyway."

Leran grinned, a simple twitch of the mouth that transformed him from the Lord of Tingu into the beautiful man who'd won my heart. "Even when you remind me of things I'd rather not think on, you still manage to make me happy. I love you to no end, little flame."

I squeezed his hand. "I love you, too." I glanced at the palace, and asked, "Should we use the Sala out here, and see what the earth and stones have to tell us?"

He shook his head. "Sometimes, the images are confusing, and I want to enter with a clear head."

"Clear heads it is." I glanced back at my sister and Finn. "Are you two ready?"

"We are," Finn replied, and the four of us approached the palace walls.

The gates were wide open, which wasn't unusual. What was strange was the lack of a gatekeeper, or any watchmen or soldiers stationed along the ramparts. In fact, the four of us were the only living souls in the area. "Is the palace abandoned?" I asked.

"Not entirely," Leran said, and he pointed toward one of the towers. Smoke steadily rose from the chimney. "If at least one fire remains lit, that means it warms at least one person. Let's find them, and have them explain what's happening here."

We went to the stables first, and got our horses settled and fed. While Mara and I brushed Enna—that mare was a warhorse through and through, but she did love to be fussed over—a stable hand found us, dropped what he was carrying, and fled. A few minutes later, the stable master himself appeared, and apologized for us having to care for the horses ourselves.

"Truly, it's no bother," I said, and it wasn't. I adored Enna, and was slightly jealous that Mara got to ride her instead of me. "But I must ask, where is everyone?"

His face darkened. "Many things have changed since you were last here," he replied. "It's not my place to discuss the operations of the palace, but please be careful, my lady."

Since he seemed unwilling to speak further, Mara and I left the stable master in the stalls and went to find our mates. They were standing in the courtyard behind the stables, watching the back of the palace.

"What's so interesting about the rear courtyard?" I asked.

"The *saffira*," Finn replied. "For a palace of this size, you would expect the kitchens to have ten, maybe twenty cooks working at all times, along with those responsible for hauling supplies, washing up, and what of the laundry? So far, we've only seen two people come and go."

"Perhaps they're all inside," I began, but Finn shook his head.

"When we were last here, this space was packed with those who made the palace run smoothly," he said. "Now, it's as if no one lives here."

Finn's words chilled me to the bone. "Where did everyone go?"

"I am going to find out," Leran declared, then he strode past the kitchens and around to the main doors, with Finn following him. I remarked to myself that I hadn't seen Finn move so quickly in ages, and realized he wasn't using his cane.

"How did Finn's leg improve so quickly?" I asked Mara.

"He used some of the power Asherah gave him to strengthen his bones," she replied. "He said the power wants to heal, and something about preserving life."

I nodded, wondering what it must feel like to have a god's power suddenly inside of you, even just a small portion. Perhaps it was similar to working with the Sala. "Has he healed anything else?"

"A few of my bruises. I don't think he's attempted anything beyond that." Mara absently stroked her belly. "He should apprentice with Wren."

"If he's healing bruises and bones with a thought, he's beyond anything Wren could teach him," I said. "How do you feel?"

"Good," she replied. "Nervous, and my back is a bit sore, but over-all, I am good."

I eyed her belly. "Please forgive my blunt question, but how are you so much bigger than you were less than a sennight ago?"

Mara looked down at her belly, and swallowed hard. "You noticed."

"I did." I looped my arm with hers, and whispered, "Tell me what's happening. I can get you a healer, or a midwife, or anything you need.

Say the word and I'll send a messenger to Aldo, and he'll relocate the entire Seat here to take care of you, if that's what we need to do."

Mara smiled tightly. "Thank you, Ember, but honestly I don't know if I need anything. No, that's not true. I wish Mama was here."

"She'll be back soon," I promised. "You know she and Papa will both be here as soon as they can be. They won't be able to resist their first grandchild."

"I know. I just miss them so much." Mara glanced at Finn, then she leaned close to me, and whispered, "I think there might be two."

"Two? Two what?" She looked pointedly at her belly. "Oh! You mean twins!"

"Hush," she said. "I don't want to say anything to Finn unless I'm sure." She frowned, and asked, "Is it odd for you, seeing me with Finn after what happened between the two of you?"

"Honestly, no, and no one's more surprised about that than I am," I replied. "I held onto my bad feelings for far too long, so long that they festered inside me. They nearly ruined my chance to be with Leran."

"Luckily, Leran is as stubborn as you are, and he refused to give up on you."

I looked ahead, and briefly admired Leran's form as he strode toward the palace's main entrance. "You're right. I am lucky, just as you and Finn are lucky to have found each other. Will you name one of the babies after me?"

Mara narrowed her eyes. "If one is a redheaded trouble maker, then yes. We shall call that one Ember."

I smiled. "Wonderful. I've always wanted a namesake."

Leran and Finn had reached the palace's steps, and waited for us to catch up. The main courtyard was as deserted as the stables had been when we arrived, with not even a single guard watching the entrance.

"Beloved," Leran said, as he held out his arm. "The Lord and Lady of Tingu enter together."

I squeezed Mara's hand, then I took Leran's and we ascended the steps. Since there was no one there to assist us, Leran and I dragged the doors open, and we stepped into the dark, cold antechamber.

"Wherever that fire's lit, it's not near the doors." I muttered the words to call fire, and the candles in the wall sconces burst into light.

"You must teach me that trick," Leran said.

"Asking to learn my secrets, now?" I teased, but I was in anything but a teasing mood. This vacant palace was had gone from mysterious to terrifying in a very short time, and the candlelight was doing little to alleviate my fears.

Leran, however, was as fearless as ever, and he moved with purpose down the wide corridors, the sound of our footsteps echoing off the stone walls the only sounds we heard. When we reached the main hall, the doors were wide open, and inside we saw firelight reflected on the walls.

"Finally," I breathed. "People."

There was no one at the smaller hearth, so we crossed the hall and approached the one where Sibeal normally sat. When we got closer, I saw a large chair in front of the fire. It was turned so the occupant faced the fire, and it reminded me of a throne. Only, Sibeal never used a throne.

"Sibeal," Leran said. "My Lady and I have come with news from Teg'urnan."

"Oh?" said a voice I'd hoped to never hear again. "What sort of news?"

I put my hand on Leran's arm. "That's not Sibeal."

"Sibeal isn't here." Cerillia stood and came around her throne, that golden collar of hers reflecting yellow in the firelight. "There's only me, now."

Chapter Forty

Finlay stared at the empty space his mate had been standing in a moment before. He was certain that sending Asherah on to Dremmsvard was the right thing to do. She had work to do, his goddess did, and by keeping Olluhm occupied they would give her a better chance to succeed, and survive. More than anything, he needed Asherah to come back to him.

Now he only needed to mount an offensive against a god, and keep himself and his people from dying in the attempt.

"The smartest thing we can do is run," Caol'non said, as he kept his gaze on the sky. "Olluhm has destroyed pantheons of gods and laid entire civilizations to waste. His fury is legendary."

"We should run, but we can't," Finlay said as he turned toward the tents that housed the wounded—and he saw Wren walking toward the supply tables. "Wren!"

The king jogged toward the healer. Wren halted, and faced him. "My lord!"

"When did you return?" he asked, while looking behind her for a tall, surly man and a woman with fire bright hair. "Where are Aeolmar and Latera?"

"In the underworld," she replied.

Finlay assumed he'd misheard her. "They are where, exactly?"

"The underworld," Wren repeated. "We were crossing through from Gannera to Dremmsvard when we were attacked. The ground collapsed under Sasha, Gilson, and me, and Aeolmar used one of his portals to send us here. He saved us."

Finlay blew out a breath; he would have preferred having the First Hunter and Huntress with him, but at least Wren would be able to help the wounded. "Sasha was your missing sister?"

"Yes. We found her unharmed, in Tarac."

"I'm glad you found her." Finlay looked toward the sky, and saw Olluhm hurtling toward Teg'urnan. "We're about to be attacked by the sun god. Please do what you can to secure the wounded."

Wren spun around and followed his gaze. "How much time do we have?"

"Very little," he replied. "Ready everyone for evacuation. Perhaps if we distract him, the rest of you can escape." Wren nodded and rushed toward the tents. Finlay saw Innetha, and called her over.

"Where's Elkin?" he demanded. With Aeolmar and Latera in the underworld and Asherah in Dremmsvard, the Second Hunter and Caol'non were their best defenders.

"On his way," she replied, then she cocked her head skyward. "That who I think it is?"

"Yes. Suggestions?"

"Meet him in the open, and get him to talk," she replied. "And make him get out of the chariot. The longer he's on the ground, the weaker he gets."

"Weaker?" Finlay repeated. "Why would being on the ground weaken him?"

"He's not a true god," Innetha replied. "He gets his power through what he's stolen from others."

"She's right," Caol'non said, as he joined them. "The bulk of his ability comes from Nu's chariot, but it only generates power while it's in motion, like a water wheel at a mill. Halt the wheels, halt the power."

Finlay nodded. "I'll keep him talking. Caol'non, find Tor, then I'll need both of you to help Wren with the wounded. Innetha, you and Elkin will oversee getting the rest to safety."

"Do you really think I'm going to let you face Olluhm without me?" Innetha asked. "Absolutely not."

"Innetha, I am not asking," Finlay said.

"And we're ignoring you," Caol'non said as he drew his sword. "Forgive me, my lord, but if Asherah knew we abandoned you to face Olluhm alone you she'd have our hide."

"Face it, she's much scarier than you'll ever be," Innetha added, then a gust of hot wind silenced all three of them.

Olluhm the Elder Sun landed his chariot on the broken pavement of Teg'urnan's great square. Having never met a god before, save his mate, Finlay took a moment to note his appearance. Olluhm's chariot was magnificent, made of gilded wood and encrusted in a rainbow of gems. When Finlay looked closer, since his sharp eyes always caught details that most overlooked, he realized that the gilding was flaking off the front of the chariot, and the gems looked like they hadn't been polished in an age. Olluhm's continued use of Nu's chariot seemed to be destroying it.

As for Olluhm himself, Finlay noted that he didn't appear all that godlike. He was unnaturally tall and long-limbed, with shining chestnut hair and the most intense blue eyes Finlay had ever seen, but more than anything he looked like an ordinary man.

They could defeat an ordinary man.

"Gods, he looks like Aeolmar," Innetha muttered. "A too clean, too perfect version of him."

"Aeolmar takes after his mother, who took after her own father," Caol'non said, jerking his chin toward the god. "Fear not, Alluria didn't have her father's temperament."

"Let's hope that's a good thing," Finlay said, then he walked toward their unwelcome guest, and said, "Welcome to Teg'urnan, Lord Olluhm. Or do you prefer to be addressed as Elder Sun?"

Olluhm ignored Finlay's question. Instead, he surveyed the damaged pavement and ruined walls, and curled his lip in disdain. "What has befallen my home?"

"Krylle, the High Priest of Those Who Went Before, is what happened," Finlay replied. "He and his men brought bombs into the palace, and destroyed the Great Temple. I'm told you built that temple with your own hands."

Olluhm's eyes flashed the colors of sunset. "Where is this Krylle now?"

"The signal fire that brought you here? That was Krylle himself going up in flames," Caol'non replied. "By now there will be nothing left of him but ash."

Olluhm cocked his head to the side, and regarded Caol'non. "You resemble my firstborn."

"I am directly descended from Solon and the first Parthian king's daughter," Caol'non replied.

"Then you and yours have defended Teg'urnan for many generations," Olluhm said. "To my side now, son. We shall seek my newest heirs together."

"I'm afraid I cannot do that." Caol'non widened his stance. "I took an oath to serve the king of Parthalan. Only he may direct me."

"Where is this king?" Olluhm demanded.

Finlay stepped forward. "That would be me."

Olluhm looked over Finlay as one would a stray dog. "You stink of troll."

"Yes, well, it's been a stressful day," Finlay said. "How may I help you, my lord?"

"You know what I want," Olluhm said, his voice like cracking glass. "The Deliverer has returned. I mean to gather my heirs, and end her."

Finlay's ears went hot, but he kept his voice calm. His many years as a merchant meant he could keep even the most disagreeable person talking for hours. "She isn't here."

"Lies," Olluhm shrieked, his fury heating the air around him. "You will take me to her, now."

"She went to the mortal realm to find the lodestone," Wren said; she'd come up behind the sun god, and was standing perilously close to the gilded chariot. "She won't return until she has it."

"The lodestone has been missing for an eon," Olluhm seethed. "Ish h'ra will never find it."

"It's in a land called Gannera," Wren said. "The king's name is Harold. He can help you find it."

"Very well. Son," Olluhm said to Caol'non, "you will accompany me to the mortal realm."

"No," Caol'non said, as he raised his sword. Olluhm twisted around in his chariot, and Finlay felt the god's fury heat the stones below their feet.

"Twice you have refused me," Olluhm seethed. "To my side, now."

"He said no," Finlay said, as he drew his own weapon. "And you'll have to go through me to get him."

Olluhm's eyes narrowed. "That is not a problem," he said, then he opened his mouth and hot winds rushed across Teg'urnan's square. While they were disoriented, Olluhm struck at Finlay with a fiery sword. Finlay blocked the flaming blade with his own sword, while Olluhm stared at the locked weapons in disbelief.

"It's troll forged," Finlay explained. "I suppose our stink is what makes the metal so strong." Finlay twisted Olluhm's sword up and out of his hands and it clattered to the ground, smoldering. "Leave my home, and my people. Now."

"You will not defy me," Olluhm seethed. "I built this palace!"

"And yet you don't seem to have any power here," Finlay said. "Go, before I extinguish your stolen flames permanently."

Olluhm screamed, and unleashed a fiery wind directly onto Finlay and Caol'non. Innetha ran toward the chariot from the opposite side, and flung her knife into Olluhm's face. He screamed and clutched his eye with one hand while he grabbed Innetha's arm with the other, then he was gone.

Finlay dropped to his knees, the pain in his sword arm dulling his senses. He looked at Caol'non, and saw the red, angry burns across his chest. Realization dawning, he held his charred hand in front of him.

"My lord? My lord!"

Hands bracketed Finlay's head, and Wren turned his face toward her. "Finlay! Can you walk?"

"I..." He glanced at his legs. They were present, and unburnt. "Yes, I think so. Why?"

"I need to get you to the healers' tent." Wren put herself under Finlay's good arm, and got him upright. "We need to treat those burns as soon as possible."

"I can't be incapacitated." Finlay watched as the human soldier, Gilson, carefully lifted Caol'non and carried him toward the healers. "I must lead."

"Right now you're in no condition to lead," Wren said. "Let us help you get back to it." They'd almost made it to the tents when Finlay remembered Innetha.

Olluhm had grabbed her, then they both disappeared.

"Wren, you must find Elkin," Finlay said. "Olluhm took Innetha."

She nodded, and sent a *saffira* to locate the Second Hunter. As Wren cut away the remains of Finlay's jerkin, he saw Gilson lay Caol'non on the cot next to Atreynha. Elkin arrived as Wren began spreading salve across Finlay's burns.

"Where's Innetha?" Elkin demanded.

"She disappeared with Olluhm." Finlay reached into his belt pouch and withdrew a handful of portals. "Do you know how to use these?"

"Yes."

"Go. Find Innetha."

"I will, then we'll come straight back here."

"No," Finlay said. "Go to Asherah. She's gone on to Dremmsvard, and she's alone."

Elkin nodded. "We'll go to the queen," he said, then he cast the portal and disappeared. Finlay closed his eyes and gritted his teeth as he tried to will away the pain from his burns, and hoped Elkin and Innetha would find Asherah soon. She would need all the help she could get against Olluhm.

Chapter Forty-One

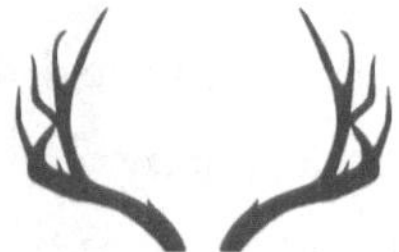

The pain was what woke him.

He took a breath, and almost cried out. Caol'non remembered Olluhm opening his mouth wider than any being should be able, wide enough to swallow a man whole, and unleashing the hot, searing wind onto him and the king. He'd tried to shield Finlay with his body, and as a result Caol'non had borne the brunt of the sun god's fury. Now, pain seared his skin across his chest and upper arms. He only hoped he'd kept the king safe.

Caol'non attempted to raise his head, and felt a new circle of pain lash itself around his throat. He swore as he let his head fall back, then he felt cool fingers on his face. Knowing that touch as well as he knew his own name, he opened his eyes and saw Atreynha watching him.

"You were hurt," he rasped.

"As you can see, I have recovered, and now you're hurt." Her mouth was pressed into a thin line, and her brows were pinched in concern. "Olluhm did this to you?"

Caol'non gave the barest nod. "Finlay?"

"His sword arm is burnt to a crisp, and awful though it is, that's his only wound." Atreynha's gaze tracked over Caol'non's chest. "You shielded him?"

"I did." Caol'non moved his hand toward Atreynha, trying to touch her without also moving his shoulder. He felt her silken robes, and curled his fingers into the fabric. "Is he going to be all right?"

"He's better off than you are." She nodded, then she turned away. A moment later, she had a cool wet cloth in her hand, and dabbed at his face. "We've already cut you out of your tunic and jerkin. What was left of them, anyway. With any luck, the salve Wren put together for you and Finlay will do the bulk of the healing. I haven't seen anyone as talented with herbs and simples since Alluria was with us."

"You only cut away my shirt?" Caol'non asked, his eyes twinkling. "Nothing lower?"

"You're in no condition for that," Atreynha said. "Now stay still, and let the salve do its work."

Caol'non found her hand, and squeezed her fingers. "Can you stay with me, or do others need you?"

"I will stay with you." She stroked his cheek with her free hand. "If you think I waited all this time for you to come back to me only to lose you to a silly burn, you're mad."

He tightened his fingers against hers. "I'm sorry it took me so long to return."

"You're here now." Atreynha kissed his forehead. "I'm going to get you some cooled broth. We need to build up your strength now more than ever. Try to rest, and I will come right back to you."

She kissed his forehead again, then she rose to get that bowl of broth. Caol'non watched her walk away, and even though he was lying on a cot with half of his body covered in painfully deep burns, he felt like the luckiest man in Parthalan.

Chapter Forty-Two

Asherah Speaks

The portal enveloped me in a searing white light so intense I thought it might scorch me. Despite my fears, the light proved to be warm, and gentle. When the light faded, I was alone, and shivering at the base of a mountain. As I rubbed my arms for warmth, I looked toward the mountain's peak, but it was far too tall for me to glimpse the small shrine at the summit. Fires had always burned brightly inside the temple, as evidenced by the warm orange glow that illuminated the windows, and I wondered if those fires were still lit. Despite the frigid air, this had always been a place of light, and of love.

I'd done it. After all this time, I got myself back to Dremmsvard.

I'd never lived here, not really, but I had spent a great deal of time on this mountain, especially in the shrine and in the village nestled not far below it. Back when the land was young Nyshanti and her father Nu, the true sun god, lived in that temple. Every morning Nyshanti would rise in a shower of colors and chase back the darkness, then Nu's chariot thundered forth, and he rode across the sky. While Nu was illuminating the land, I kept Nyshanti company in the shrine, and we thought our happiness would last forever.

And it would have, if not for Olluhm's jealous gaze. He wanted everything that wasn't his; first he stole the sun's chariot, then he claimed the moon against her will and the night sky was forever cast in red. Soon after Cydia's capture, Olluhm began murdering other gods, then he claimed the land as his. Nu and his mate, the sky goddess Clea, fled south, but Nyshanti and I remained in Dremmsvard. Honestly, if we'd had a shred of sense, we would have gone with them, but I stayed to defend my people from Olluhm, and Nyshanti stayed for me.

Nyshanti... She who I loved more than anything, she who stayed by my side even when Olluhm at last captured me. How the false sun had tortured me in every cruel manner imaginable, but in the end, even he couldn't end me. I was too strong, my worshippers too numerous; back then, Olluhm had few if any followers. So he did what he thought was his worst, and trapped Nyshanti and me in bodies of flesh and blood.

We became Torim and Hillel, and we worked a croft together. The days were long and the labor backbreaking, but we had each other. As long as we were together, we were happy.

Our happiness ended when we were captured by demons, and I lost what was left of my memories. But I didn't lose my warrior's soul, and I organized a revolt to save not my own life, but Torim's. I had no memory of the time I'd loved her as Nyshanti; indeed, I'd lost all but my most recent memories. Still, I couldn't let her come to harm, not as long as there was breath in my body. For Nyshanti, I would beat back the demons.

I've been a goddess, a peasant, a slave, a queen, and now I'm a goddess again... But why had Nyshanti never returned to me? It felt wrong being in Dremmsvard without her. Would she always be a spirit trapped in the mortal realm? Would she finally come back to me, now when I needed her most?

Again, I rubbed my arms for warmth. Despite all the challenges I've faced, I met each and every one of them head on, but as my gaze tracked the path that led up the side of the mountain, I knew I did not want to walk this route by myself. For all my strength, I needed more than just myself in order to defeat Olluhm. I needed allies, yet here I stood alone.

"Asherah!"

Startled, I turned around. Who was living in this barren and frigid land, and how would they know my name? When I saw the source of the voice, I almost collapsed from joy.

Aeolmar and Latera were running toward me.

"You're here," I said as Latera embraced me.

"We're here," she said, then Aeolmar was standing over us, scowling and smiling at the same time in a way only he could manage. "You didn't think we'd let you do this by yourself, did you?"

"How did you get here?" I demanded, then I got a nose full of her hair. "And why do you smell like ashes? Where's Wren, and your other sister?"

"We came through the underworld," Latera replied, as she released me. "As if that wasn't bad enough, we were attacked by undead. There was a landslide and Mar sent Wren, Sasha, and Gilson to Teg'urnan with one of the portals he's not supposed to have."

I had no idea who Gilson was, and I'd already stopped caring about the portals, but I had more pressing questions. "How did you survive traveling across the underworld?"

"Priya led us, with the lodestone."

My breath caught in my chest. "You have it?"

Latera grinned. "We do."

"Well, where is this Priya," I began, then I looked past Latera and saw two people, a man and a woman, coming toward us. The woman—Priya, I assumed—bore such a strong resemblance to Latera she could have been her mother. Before I could ask if that was the case, the man lowered his hood, and I was shocked yet again.

"Tor?" I stepped toward him, fearful he would disappear if I got too close. But he was real, just as me being in Dremmsvard again was real, and he embraced me as Latera had.

"Asherah, it is so good to set eyes on you again," he said.

"You have no idea how much I've needed to see you," I said, for the Prelate of Parthalan was one of the strongest allies I'd ever had. "Caol'non is at Teg'urnan."

"So my grandson tells me." He released me, and I noticed something different about him.

"Where's your braid?" I asked, since Tor and his sons had always worn their hair long.

"I, ah, had to cut it off," he replied, and Priya laughed.

"He got tar in his hair, is what happened," she said. "After all this is done, we'll sit with a bit of wine and I'll tell you the whole story."

"Don't you dare," Tor warned, but he was smiling as he said it. He looked just like Caol'non when he smiled, and I remembered the mess I'd left behind.

"Much had happened since you left," I said.

Aeolmar folded his arms across his chest. "Tell us everything."

"Teg'urnan was severely damaged by Krylle and his men," I began, relating the earlier events for the benefit of Latera and Tor. Priya, too, though I didn't know if she even knew where Teg'urnan was. "The whole of the temple collapsed in on itself, possibly down to the vaults. Caol'non found Krylle in my garden, where he set himself alight as a signal for Olluhm to descend. Finlay... Finlay sent me here, so they can hold off Olluhm while I—we—try to enter the shrine." I bit the inside of my cheek and looked away. "I can't believe I left him."

"Finlay made the right call," Aeolmar said. "If you remained at the palace, who knows if you would have ever made it back to the shrine. This is where you need to be."

"Caol'non won't let anyone harm the king, be they god or man," Tor said. "My boys are the strongest fighters in the realm," he added, with a nod toward Aeolmar.

"They're right," Latera said. "Finlay and the rest can handle a single puny god."

"Puny?" I repeated. "My, you elves are arrogant."

"We're arrogant because we know our worth," Priya said. "Now, let's get moving. The lodestone wants to go to the shrine. It's practically pulling me up the path."

"Very well," I said, heartened by my four companions. "Lead the way."

Chapter Forty-Three

Olluhm ripped through the sky of the mortal realm, his hand still clenched around Innetha's arm just below her shoulder. At any other time Innetha would have marveled at his great strength, since he was holding her aloft one handed. But Olluhm had just dragged her from one realm to another, and they were still airborne, which meant Innetha had other concerns—such as when she looked down, and saw the ground rushing at them.

"Keep flying, you bastard," she hissed. Olluhm realized they were descending too fast, and dropped Innetha into the base of the chariot. Innetha braced herself for the coming impact, and noticed the panicked look on Olluhm's face. "Why can't you skate across the sky the way you normally do?"

He didn't answer her, and instead glared at the mortal sun. Innetha knew they were in the mortal realm, because Olluhm had told her exactly where he was taking her, right before he dissolved her reality and plunged her into a new world. If these first few moments were any indication, coming here had been a bad idea.

The mortal sun wheeled her chariot toward Olluhm, and held up her hand. Innetha felt the chariot drop, and heard the mortal sun ordering Olluhm to remain on the ground and out of her domain.

Ah, there's not room for two suns in the sky. The chariot crashed, but Olluhm pulled up on the reins. There were no horses attached to his conveyance, but he managed to get it under control, and it skidded to a halt in a meadow. Innetha peeked over the edge of the chariot, saw the massive ruts it had dug into the ground.

I wonder if Latera's still in this realm. Perhaps I can make my way to Gannera, and find her. Innetha watched Olluhm as he steadied himself after their near-crash landing, and wondered what he would do next. To her surprise, he stepped off the chariot and smiled.

"This is a new realm for me," he said. "It's been a long time since I've conquered a new people."

"Have at it," Innetha said, as she winced in pain. Her arm and shoulder were charred where he'd held onto her, and thanks to the hot winds he generated as he flew, even her lungs felt singed. "I'm sure the mortals will keep you occupied for the next few centuries."

Olluhm grasped her by the throat and lifted her off her feet. "Careful, witch," he seethed. "Respect your betters."

"I'm not a witch," Innetha said as she put her hands on top of his. Innetha had been cursed long ago by a jilted landowner, but the curse had gone awry and gave her the ability to heal herself and others. The catch was that she needed skin to skin contact with another in order to heal, and in order to save herself she would drain every drop of life from Olluhm she had to. "I'm a nymph."

"Nymphs," Olluhm growled. "Do you know what I've done to nymphs?"

"Yes." Innetha healed her lungs first, then she pushed her power, and her injuries, toward Olluhm. Moving an injury from one body to another was a talent few knew she possessed. Before her eyes, blisters bloomed on the sun god's skin. "We all do."

His arm, weakened by the burns, trembled and he dropped Innetha. Her back struck the chariot's hard wooden floor, but she wasn't concerned. She'd already healed the bulk of her injuries. "Where is the lodestone?" he demanded.

"Gannera Castle," she replied, as she rolled out of the chariot and onto the ground.

"Take me there. Now."

"I don't know the way. Can't you ascend to the sky, and fly around until you see it?" Innetha glanced at the mortal sun. "Oh, is she in your way?"

Olluhm's nostrils flared, then he caused earthen shackles to erupt from the meadow and bind Innetha's ankles to the ground. Without another word, he rose into the air. As Olluhm hurtled toward the mortal sun, all the while screaming at her to surrender the sky, Innetha withdrew the smaller dagger she kept in her boot and began chipping at the shackles. She heard shouts from above, and saw the two suns circling each other among the clouds.

"That madman is going to destroy every realm he enters," she muttered, then there was a flash of light and her mate, Elkin, appeared next to her.

"Beloved," Elkin said as he dropped to his knees beside her. He looked over her charred jerkin and frowned. "What did he do to you?"

"Mostly, he annoyed me. Help me with these shackles." Elkin used brute force to break apart what was left of the shackles, then he helped Innetha to her feet. "How are you here?" she asked, as she fell into his arms.

"Portal," he said, and showed her the rest of the discs Finlay had given him. "I didn't ask where they came from, but they're probably from the stash Aeolmar thinks no one knows about."

Innetha nodded; the First Hunter wasn't nearly as sneaky as he imagined himself to be. "What happened at Teg'urnan?"

"Finlay's started an evacuation," he replied. "He and Caol'non got burned pretty badly. Wren's back, along with another one of her sisters, and a mortal soldier."

Innetha nodded. "Good. They'll need Wren for help with the burns."

A terrible scream rent the air. They looked up, and watched as the mortal sun struck down Olluhm. The fae sun plummeted toward the earth, and landed in a shower of sparks.

"Interesting," Innetha said. "The mortal sun is too powerful for him. Olluhm can't harm her." She glanced at Elkin, then back toward the warring suns. "I hurt him."

"Did you?" Elkin wrapped an arm around his mate, and kissed the side of her head. "How?"

"He burned me, inside and out," she began, her voice catching as she remembered her the pain on her skin and in her lungs. "When he put his hands on my skin, I started absorbing his life force in order to heal myself. Then I sent my injuries back to him."

"I hope he suffered," Elkin bit off. "I felt it when he burned you. Brought me to my knees." He kissed her again. "Thought I might have lost you."

"You think I'd let a little burn take me from you," she began, then a flurry in the sky caught her attention.

The mortal sun was racing toward them. She was beautiful, with shining gold skin and long honey colored hair streaming behind her, and she was wearing a gown of clouds. Based on her scowl, she was also furious.

"Why have you brought that villain to this realm?" the sun demanded.

"We did no such thing," Innetha said. "He's searching for an arti-fact, and dragged me with him to this realm. We are not his allies. We only want to be done with him."

The sun looked toward where Olluhm had fallen, and curled her lip. "I do not know what happens in your realm, but here we do not take kindly to men who play at being gods."

"Even though he drives the chariot, Olluhm isn't a god?" Elkin asked.

"No," the sun replied. "All he is, is a fool."

With that, the mortal sun wheeled her chariot around and returned to the sky. "Did you hear what she said?" Innetha murmured. "Ol-luhm is but a man, and none of the true gods care for him. He is without allies." She watched the mortal sun's ascent, then she faced Elkin. "We need to go to Dremmsvard, and tell Asherah what we've learned."

Elkin withdrew a portal and grinned. "I can have us there in the blink of an eye."

Chapter Forty-Four

Finn observed as Cerillia stood and walked around her throne. He stepped in front of Mara, shielding his mate with his body. *Let her face off against Leran and me,* Finn thought. *I only need to keep her away from Mara.*

"What do you mean, only you're here?" Leran demanded. "Where are Senan and the rest? Where is Sibeal?"

"Where she belongs," Cerillia snapped.

"And where is that?" Ember asked. Cerillia bared her teeth and lunged at Ember, but Leran drew his sword and barred her from approaching his mate.

"You," Cerillia hissed at Ember. "You never wanted me to be Lady of Thurnda! You made things so, so... difficult!"

"What did she make difficult?" Finn asked. "You were never going to be Lady. That title will be passed to Sibeal's female heirs. You must have known that."

"I am her heir, and now I am Lady," Cerillia shrieked.

Leran glanced over his shoulder. "Finn, Mara. Find Sibeal. We'll deal with this one."

Finn nodded, then he took Mara's hand and led her out of the hall. Once they were in the corridor, he cupped her face with his hands.

"Are you all right?" he asked.

"I'm fine," she replied. He rested his forehead against Mara's, and took a breath. "How are you?"

"As long as I'm with you, nothing can stop me."

"We should find Sibeal, and the rest," Mara said.

"I don't know if we can." Finn stepped back from Mara, and continued, "I can't really explain this, but there aren't very many living souls here. I... I feel them, and there aren't many."

"Is this from the power Asherah gave you?"

Finn shrugged. "Perhaps. It can heal, so perhaps sensing others is a facet of that?"

"And this power is now telling you that very few are here... Can you tell where they are?"

"Mostly near the kitchens, and the stables." Finn swallowed, and continued, "What if Cerillia killed everyone else?"

"How could she? She's but one woman, and Thurnda has an entire legion." Mara pursed her lips, and looked away.

"What is it?"

"What if she really is Krylle's agent?" Mara asked. "What if he gave her some sort of ability, much as Asherah gave one to you?"

"If that's the case, then everyone in Thurnda could be in danger. Where would Sibeal normally be?"

Mara began walking toward the stairs. "This way. There's a solarium she enjoyed spending time in after completing her morning duties. We will probably find her and Senan there."

***

"Is this about the lodestone?" Ember asked.

"What do you know about the lodestone?" Cerillia countered.

"Very little," Ember replied. "I'm trying to put together why you wanted to be in Thurnda in the first place. You're from Dremmsvard, no?"

"Senan and I met in Dremmsvard, but that is not where I'm from," she replied. "Had you ever bothered to pay attention to me, you would know that I hail from a place called the Highlands. My brother was betrothed to your mother, but she humiliated him, then your aunt did the same."

"Your brother is Gannok?" Ember blurted out, then she turned to Leran. "She's from the mortal realm."

"Finally, the idiot understands," Cerillia said, clapping like a child at a puppet show. "I could forgive your family for humiliating mine once, but twice? No, I could not let that pass."

"But Sasha left Gannok after you met Senan," Ember began.

"Time moves differently on either side of the veil," Leran said. "She could have crossed in such a manner that made her arrival here years prior to what happened with her brother." Leran leveled his sword at Cerillia's throat, the tip scratching against her golden collar. "Why come here at all? And why Dremmsvard?"

"When I learned that Latera had family in Thurnda, I decided that they should be the ones to suffer for her misdeeds," she replied. "It's only fair, after what she did to mine. But, I needed help. I needed someone with power, and it took some doing, but I found him. A man so obsessed with dead gods, he wanted to find a living one to help him join his idols in the grave."

"Who?" Leran bellowed.

"Krylle," Ember whispered. "You spied on my sister for him!"

"I spied on no one," she shot back. "Krylle wanted a way to persuade Olluhm to give him what he wanted. I told Krylle the tale of the lodestone Elvasla used to track demons to the mortal realm, and together we went to Dremmsvard and found one who convinced Olluhm that we could help him find and destroy the lodestone, and thus keep his prisoner locked away forever."

"Let me guess, that someone was Iruna," Ember said. "Yet another who feels slighted by fate. Has it ever occurred to any of you that you can make your own destiny? That you can move on from your past?" She turned to Leran, and said, "What Iruna lacks in morals and sense, she more than makes up for in wealth, as evidenced by this fool's gaudy necklace."

Leran pressed his sword against Cerillia's collar, the edge now denting the delicate gold flowers. "You didn't do this solely to avenge your brother's wounded pride. You also did this for yourself. You desire wealth, and prestige."

"Things that were denied to my family by yours," Cerillia said, then she lunged toward Leran. Ember gasped as smoky black tendrils emanated from Cerillia's fingers and coiled around her mate's arms and throat.

"Leran," she yelled, as he fell to his knees, then his eyes slipped shut. "Leran!"

Chapter Forty-Five
Asherah Speaks

The region surrounding Dremmsvard was a lot bigger than I remembered.

The village itself sat about a third of the way up the mountain, and it was both larger and more ancient than the city surrounding Teg'urnan. Not surprising, since these northern towns had existed long before Olluhm had designs on godhood. The village wasn't necessarily a hindrance to us, but it did mean we had quite a bit farther to go than I'd anticipated.

"A portal would certainly come in handy right about now," Tor said.

"I've only got one left," I said, trying to keep my voice even as I recalled that Tor and the rest had already crossed the underworld to reach me. They must be exhausted, and hungry, and I had no way to provide for them. Although...

"The village has an inn," I said. "We should rest tonight, and climb the rest of the mountain tomorrow. However, I left the palace in such a hurry I don't have any way to pay for a room."

"I have gold," Aeolmar and Tor said in unison. Yes, they were certainly related.

"Of course you do," Latera teased.

"And Tor's always up for a nap," Priya added.

"There's nothing wrong with being prepared," Aeolmar said. "Asherah, please lead the way to the inn."

Onward we went, into the village proper. The inn was exactly where I remembered it being, which gave me hope for the coming battle. If I could find my way through a village I hadn't set foot in for an entire lifetime, perhaps I could open the shrine and free Cydia. Perhaps I could hold Olluhm accountable for his crimes, and restore Nyshanti's father as the true sun.

Perhaps I wouldn't die in the attempt, and would live to see my mate and son again.

The innkeeper—who thankfully had no idea who I was—set us up with three small yet clean rooms. I ended up with a room all to myself; not only did I not want to intrude on Aeolmar and Latera's time together, I had no idea of what sort of relationship Tor and Priya had between them, nor was I looking to find out. As soon as I was alone in my room, I sat in the center of the bed and reached out with my mind toward Finlay.

Beloved.

Sher! Where are you?

Dremmsvard. Aeolmar and Latera are here, along with two others. We're staying in an inn tonight, and will head to the shrine tomorrow.

I felt his pain through our bond, and asked, *Did Olluhm hurt you?*

Yes, he replied, then he told me of his encounter with the sun god. By the time he was done describing his injuries to me, I had tears streaming down my face.

Gods, Finlay, I never should have left you.

Yes, you should have. Finlay paused, and I sensed he was interacting with someone at Teg'urnan. Hopefully, a healer; he'd told me of Wren's arrival at the palace, and she was truly gifted with herbs and salves. *Olluhm took Innetha. I gave Elkin some portals, and sent him to find her.*

I would hate to be the one standing between Elkin and Innetha. They would tear the realm apart to reunite with one another.

Sher, Caol'non told me something about Olluhm. His power comes from the chariot, but the chariot only makes power while it's in motion. Caol'non said it's like a mill's wheel.

That's good to know. I wish I was with you.

So do I. We'll be together soon, he promised, his fatigue evident in his mind.

Soon. Since he obviously needed to rest, I said, *I'm going to check on Finn. I love you.*

I love you too, Sher.

Finlay faded from my mind, and I took a moment to appreciate my man from the desert. He was intelligent, and capable, and fearless, and if anyone could keep our people safe while I ran off to fight gods and monsters, it was him. I will never understand his devotion to me, but I will be forever grateful we met that day in Cadogan. With Finlay at my side, I could accomplish anything.

My mate seen to, I reached out to our son. *Finn?*

Ma? Gods, warn me before you pop into my head!

Sorry! Are you well? How is Mara?

We're with Leran and Ember in Thurnda, he replied, which wasn't exactly answering my question. *Where are you? Do you have time for a question?*

Of course I do. What do you need?

Explain the power you gave me.

I sighed, because I didn't understand it myself. *I'm not sure I can answer that. It's a form of protection, I believe.*

Would it be life?

I blinked, because that was so obvious even with all the time in the world I never would have figured it out. *Yes, I suppose it is. What brought you to that conclusion?*

I used it to heal my leg and a few of Mara's bruises, but it's more than healing. I can sense things... people. He paused, and asked, *When you were with child, how fast did your belly grow?*

I carried you for nearly a year, I said, then I realized there was only one reason he would ask such a thing. *What's wrong with Mara?*

Nothing. She's perfect. She also looks about ready to give birth.

Chapter Forty-Six

Latera Speaks

This little inn in Dremmsvard was my new favorite place in the world.

One thing that elves had always done far better than the fae was bathing. The northern lands had many hot springs and pools bubbling just below the surface, and wherever you found a town or village of some size, it meant it was built around one or more of these oases. Dremmsvard was no exception, and Aeolmar had taken the innkeeper aside and paid him who knows how much gold in order to secure us a room directly above the spring, which came with our own private corner of the bathhouse.

"I told him you were modest, and wanted to bathe privately," Aeolmar said as we sank into the steaming water. I laughed; I'd never thought of myself as particularly shy, but I did enjoy having this portion of the bathhouse all to ourselves.

"Or did you want to keep me all to yourself?" I countered. "I'm surprised Tor didn't acquire this area for Priya."

"I'm certainly not sharing you." Aeolmar positioned himself behind me, then he poured a bowl of water over my hair and began washing the ash out of it. "And Tor and Priya can figure out their own baths."

"Tell me about Mara," I said, as I faced him. "She seemed well? Happy?"

Aeolmar raised an eyebrow, probably because he'd already told me everything he knew about our daughter and her coming baby. "Mara is happy," he replied. "Finn, too."

"Good. I hope the baby isn't giving her too much trouble."

"She's drinking milk," he said. "Other foods don't seem to sit well with her."

"I imagine not." I remembered how queasy I'd been when I carried her, and how milk was one of the few foods that hadn't made me ill. "She said it will be a boy?"

"She did. Rinse." I ducked my head under the water. When I emerged Aeolmar extended his arm, and I nestled myself against him. "Face it, *nalla*. We made a perfect girl, and now she will have a perfect child of her own."

"We had a perfect girl, then another, and then a perfect boy." I grabbed the soap and started on Aeolmar's shoulders. I'd always enjoyed bathing with him, especially after we had our children. It was a quiet ritual for just the two of us, when we could talk and touch and relearn all the little details about one another. "What do you think will happen at the shrine?"

"I've no idea. If the legends are true, and the lodestone opens the doors, what next? What will Cydia do after we free her?" He stroked my hair. "What if she doesn't want to be free?"

"Why wouldn't she?" I countered. "Although, I suppose it's rather presumptuous of me to assume I know what she does or doesn't want. Hopefully, us barging into her home won't upset her too much."

"There's so much we don't know, and much of what we did know has turned out to be lies," he continued. "I don't like going into this with so little information. It's not a good way to meet the enemy."

"Cydia isn't the enemy," I began, then I glanced at my mate. "Is she?"

Aeolmar kissed my temple. "We'll know the answer to that soon enough." He tightened his arms around me. "Whatever happens, please don't enter the underworld again."

"Taking that route was not my idea," I said. "But we burned all the meadow hay to cover our escape from the castle, and we knew it was only a matter of time before my father's guards found us. It was a bad option, but at the time it seemed like the only one we had."

Aeolmar pulled me closer, getting soap and ash on my newly clean hair. No matter, I could wash it again. "When you concealed your location from me—"

"I did not!"

"You did," he said quietly, and I questioned myself. I had pulled back from our bond, but it was because I didn't want to worry him, not in order to conceal the truth.

"Mar, I would never lie to you," I began, but he kissed me to quiet me.

"That's not what I meant. I know you concealed your location to keep me from, as you call it, charging in to rescue you. But you were wrong." Aeolmar held my face close to his, and said, "I will always come for you. No matter what realm you're in, no matter how many foes stand between you and me. I will always find you."

I smiled at this man who held my heart. "Then no hiding place is safe? No matter where I go, you'll follow?"

"That's correct."

"What if I go back up to our room?" I asked, as I raised myself out of the water.

Aeolmar hauled me into his arms, and I squealed so loudly I hoped no one in the inn heard us. "I will definitely follow you there."

CHAPTER FORTY-SEVEN

Priya stood in front of her room's window, staring at the mountain they would begin scaling at first light. It was vast, but not particularly steep, and she hoped the climb wouldn't be too strenuous. After this latest journey through the underworld, Priya wasn't sure how much more physical exertion she could take. What she needed was a long, restful sleep, followed by a moon's worth of relaxing. But when had she ever gotten what she wanted?

As he always did, Tor knew when she needed him. He stood behind her and wrapped his arms around her waist, then he pressed his cheek against her temple, and Priya smiled. She already had everything she would ever want, because she had Tor.

"Every time we say no more adventures, we get wrapped up in something new." He spoke with his mouth against her skin, enabling her to feel his words as well as hear him.

"My brothers often looked away from the problems of the world, but I never could." Priya turned her head so her cheek was against Tor's throat. "I wish I could feel you the way I was meant to."

"I've always thought you feel more than most." Tor placed his hand over Priya's heart. "You feel everything."

"I meant with my body."

"I know what you meant. We've always managed just fine," he added, and that was true. Tor knew where the underworld's ash pits had made her skin as thick and stiff as old leather, and where she was so sensitive the barest touch could send her into convulsions. Priya's former partners had complained when she didn't respond to their touch the way they expected her to, but not Tor. He was patient, and attentive, and in time he learned how to play her as if he was a bard, and her body a harp.

"What will our next adventure be?" she asked.

"You're already planning something after this?" he asked. "I haven't thought beyond getting you into bed."

"I don't believe you," she said, as she turned around and embraced him. "I think you've already planned a route up the mountain, and a secondary route if the first proves impassable, and you'll have a third option worked out before dawn."

Tor laughed. "You know me well." He rubbed the back of her neck, which was one of her sensitive areas. "Two of Aeolmar's children are in Thurnda. After this is done, we could go there, visit them and with Sibeal."

"We could." Priya stretched her neck, nearly purring under Tor's touch. "Or we could go somewhere new."

"New? Who wants new?" Tor slid his hands down her back and underneath her thighs, then in one smooth motion he lifted Priya off her feet and deposited her on the bed. "I have everything I need right here."

Chapter Forty-Eight

"I've just spoken to Ma," Finn said. He and Mara were walking through the palace's empty corridors and vacant rooms as they searched for the residents. So far, they'd encountered no one.

"Oh, the way she spoke to us before, in your thoughts?" Mara asked.

"Yes. She's in Dremmsvard, with your parents and two others." The corridor they were in branched off in either direction. Finn looked down each darkened hall, then beckoned Mara to follow him into the one on the right. The corridors appeared identical, and Finn chose the one he did based on instinct alone.

"I'm glad Mama's back from Gannera," Mara said. "I'm sure my father went to get her. I wonder who else is with them."

"I didn't ask." The corridor emptied into the gallery behind the ramparts. Finn pushed open the doors, and he and Mara stood on the same walkway the palace's residents had stood upon almost six moons ago, as they watched for the warriors to return from their battle against the mountain trolls. It had been Finn's first battle, and he'd only joined in because Leran encouraged him. That was the beginning of his close relationship with his brother in all but blood.

"I remember standing here when you all went out to fight the trolls," Mara said, as she set her hands on the railing. "I was so worried for everyone. And it was so cold; I wanted to go back inside, but I couldn't look away until everyone returned."

"Were you even worried about me?" Finn asked. He remembered how he'd seen her waiting on the rampart when they returned, and how she'd plunged into the crowd searching for Kemen.

Mara turned around, and touched Finn's hand. "Even you." She stroked the back of his hand. "When I ran out to greet Kemen, and he treated me like I was nothing to him..." She frowned, and turned toward the plain.

"When he brushed off my concern and acted as if I was bothering him, that was when I knew once and for all that he and I weren't meant to be," she continued. "I was still too scared to consider being with anyone else, but I knew he would never be my mate."

"Funny, when I saw you run to him, I assumed we would never be together," Finn said. "Glad I was wrong about that."

"Me, too. Remember how we sat together at the celebration that night?"

"I do." He took Mara's hands in his, and pulled her closer. "Beloved. About the baby."

"I know," she whispered, nodding vigorously. "I've gotten too big, too fast, and you're worried, but I think it's all right. All of us are all right."

Finn stilled. "All?"

Mara raised her head, and met his gaze. "There's two. I don't know how, because there was only one, but we were together and now there are two."

Finn's mind went blank. "Two?"

"Two." She traced circles onto his inner wrist, and gasped as a white light emanated from his flesh and met her fingers. "Is that Asherah's power?"

"It's reaching toward you," Finn said. "When I talked to Ma, she confirmed that the power doesn't just heal. It's how she protects people. It's life."

"Life." Mara set her hand on the swell of her belly, then she saw movement on the path that led to the practice yard behind the stables. "There," she said, pointing. "I saw something. Something, or someone."

"Are you all right to go on?" Finn asked.

"I am. We are," she amended. "Let's find Sibeal."

Hand in hand, they approached the stables. The first thing they did was check on Myrnnhe and Enna, and found them and the rest of the horses safe in their stalls. Mara tugged Finn toward the practice yard behind the stables, and he remembered how nervous he'd been following Leran out to battle, but his brother was confident he'd do well. Being that Leran had been in hundreds if not thousands of battles, Finn believed him.

"Two children," Finn said. "It's like we've already got a complete family. I like that."

"I'm sure you do," Mara said, smiling at him over her shoulder. When she turned toward the yard, she screamed.

The practice yard was packed with corpses.

Chapter Forty-Nine

Ember Speaks

I fell to my knees beside Leran and tried to push the black tendrils Cerillia had manifested away from him. They slithered around his nose and into his mouth as if they were tiny evil snakes stealing his breath. While this substance had a definite effect on Leran, my hands passed through the tendrils as if they were so much smoke.

"You can't wipe away death," Cerillia cooed. "Not even the Lord of Tingu is immune to the inevitable."

"Shut up," I snapped. Leran's skin had gone gray and cold, but I refused to believe he was gone. He was strong, and virile, and damn all the gods I did not want to live without him.

"Leran, Leran, Leran," I whispered. When he remained still, I tamped down my fear and pushed my thoughts toward his mind.

Beloved!

He didn't respond, but I felt him. His soul was weak, and was very nearly detached from his body. I squeezed my eyes shut, and willed his soul to stay with him. With me.

Leran, please don't leave me!

I glared at Cerillia, and wondered if she really did hold power over death, or if it was more of her arrogance speaking. "If I kill you, will Leran live?" I demanded.

Cerillia laughed. "Can one kill death? Doubtful, little elfling."

"Why are you doing this?" I wailed, as tears streamed down my face. "Because my mother didn't want to be with your brother? Perhaps take your fury out on your brother, not us!"

"Your family ruined mine," Cerillia said. "Now, I will end yours, one death after another, leaving your mother for last."

I brushed Leran's hair back from his forehead. His face had gone cold, and clammy. "No," I whispered. "I've just found you. I can't lose you."

Cerillia laughed again, a high-pitched cackle that frayed my resolved right down to my last nerve. I grabbed Leran's dagger from his belt and flung it at the screeching lunatic, then I took off the Sala and set it on Leran's chest, right over his heart.

"Ancestors, don't let Leran move on," I yelled. "Keep him here! We're not done yet! We can't be done."

I whispered the last bit as I bent over Leran's body and pressed my forehead against his chest. All my life I'd wanted to be mated, to have a special person who understood me and loved me and would go along with my schemes and mad plans. That person was Leran, and I loved him so much at times I thought my heart would swell up with so much affection it would no longer fit inside my breast. He was my perfect mate, and he loved me for me, imperfections and all. If he died now, when we hadn't even been together for a full turn of the seasons, I didn't know if I could go on.

Leran's chest wasn't moving. No heartbeats, no breath.

"Lormac," I wailed, calling out to Leran's father for aid. "Please, Lormac. Send Leran back to me."

Something moved along my back. I couldn't care less if it was a rat or Cerillia or a stinking orc crawling across me. My mate was gone, and I wept for the loss of him, and our life together.

The life we would never have.

"Lormac, help me," I whispered. Silence was the only reply.

My mate was gone.

Everything was over.

"Beloved?"

I blinked, not believing my ears. That must have been Finn speaking to Mara. I hoped they had found Sibeal, and the rest of the palace's residents.

"Beloved, why are you calling out for Da?"

Fingers—Leran's fingers—moved up my back and sank into my hair. I pushed myself up and saw him watching me.

Breathing again.

Living.

"Leran!" I gasped and cried his name as I held his face close to mine. "You were dead!"

"Do you really think I'd leave you?" He kissed me, and even though his skin was still as cold as a corpse I kissed him back. I didn't care if I slept next to a cold man for the rest of my life, as long as it was him. "I'll never leave you."

"But, you were gone." I searched his pebble gray eyes, terrified I would find a shade or a demon lurking in my mate's form. I only found Leran. "Your heart. It stopped."

One of my tears splashed onto his cheek. I wiped it away, then he took my hand and kissed my fingers. "Da and the rest heard your call. They piled on me, and wouldn't let my soul leave my body."

I squeezed my eyes shut. "Thank you, Lormac," I whispered. Leran moved to sit up, and went still when he saw something behind me. "What's wrong?"

"Nothing, nothing at all," he murmured, as he pressed his lips against my hair. "Did you... Little flame, Cerillia is dead."

"Is she?" I glanced over my shoulder, and saw Leran's dagger protruding from Cerillia's eye. "I threw the dagger at her to shut her up. You were dying, and she laughed about it. I didn't mean to kill her, but I can't say I'm sad about it."

Leran pulled my face close to his. "You saved me," he said, and kissed me until I was breathless.

"What has she done to the rest?" he asked when we parted. "Where are Finn and Mara?"

I got to my feet, and pulled Leran up beside me. "Let's find them."

Chapter Fifty
Asherah Speaks

The morning after we arrived in Dremmsvard, only one sun ascended into the sky. Even more interesting, I was certain that single orb was Solon, the child sun. It seemed that my archenemy had better things to do than illuminate the world.

"Where are you?" I murmured to the sky. As far as I knew, Olluhm had never failed to make his daily journey through the clouds, not even when he and I were at war. There were times when he descended to the ground, but he always resumed his journey when his earthbound business was concluded. I recalled my conversation with Finlay from the day prior, when he told me Olluhm had gone to the mortal realm in search of the lodestone. Perhaps he was still there.

I briefly entertained the notion of Olluhm being permanently trapped in another realm. While that would certainly make my life much easier, it wasn't very likely. Olluhm was as slippery as an eel, and had foiled every trap I'd ever laid for him. Therefore, the mortal realm would probably not prove to be his undoing. Pity.

After I got myself as ready as I was going to get, I went down to the inn's common room to see what they were going to put out for breakfast. Northmen tended toward hearty fare, but a piece of bread or bowl of gruel was plenty to satisfy me. Imagine my surprise when I entered the main room and saw Innetha and Elkin sitting at the main table.

When Innetha saw me she stood, and said, "I hurt him."

I stopped moving, shocked and terrified and just the smallest bit hopeful. "You did?"

She nodded, and I noticed her red jerkin was blackened and charred near her shoulder. "Badly."

While Elkin arranged for our breakfast to be brought over, Innetha told me everything that had happened between her and Olluhm at Teg'urnan, and later in the mortal realm. It seemed that Innetha's talent for absorbing wounds, and being able to move them from one body to another, was how she'd managed to weaken Olluhm. She'd always referred to this ability as a curse, but now I wondered if it, and she, was our greatest gift.

I was also most interested in the mortal sun's reaction to Olluhm's attempts at invading her sky.

"She was not pleased with his presence," Innetha said. "She didn't say where she was going when she left us, but I imagine she was in pursuit of Olluhm."

"For a moment I worried she'd take out her wrath on us," Elkin said, as he set out seven clay bowls on the table. The innkeeper was at his side a moment later with a steaming pitcher of selka. "Getting stared down by an angry goddess is not a pleasant feeling. No offense, Asherah."

When the innkeeper heard my name, he paused, glancing between Elkin and me. Since the last thing I needed was the innkeeper genuflecting when he could be bringing out more food, I demurred, "Now, Elkin, when have I ever been angry with you?"

"True, true," Elkin said, as he reclaimed his seat and poured the selka. "It's usually Aeolmar you're yelling at."

"Why am I getting yelled at?" Aeolmar asked, as he and Latera entered the common room. Priya and Tor followed them a moment later. "Not about the portals again."

"The portals have proven somewhat useful," I allowed.

"Innetha," Latera said, moving around the table to greet the huntress. "Elkin! How did you two get here?"

"More of those portals," Elkin said. "At this rate, we'll all be hung."

"Tor, Priya, meet Innetha and Elkin," I said, ignoring Elkin's attempt at humor. "They followed Olluhm to Gannera and back."

"Why was Olluhm in Gannera?" Latera asked.

"He's looking for the lodestone," Innetha replied. "Wren told him it was at Gannera Castle."

"It was, but we've already stolen it," Priya said, as she set the lodestone on the table for all to see.

"Wren spoke to Olluhm?" Latera demanded. "How?"

"Olluhm attacked Teg'urnan—"

"Wren was at Teg'urnan?" Latera interrupted. "Was my sister Sasha there, too?"

"Yes," Innetha said. "And a human man came along with them."

Latera leaned against Aeolmar's shoulder. "I'm so glad they're all right."

"Portals never fail," Aeolmar said, with a pointed look at me.

"Possessing them is also treason," I said, then I tore off a piece of bread. "But I am glad you had them, Aeolmar. Yet again, your foresight has helped us in unusual and unexpected ways." He dipped his chin toward me in a graceful acknowledgement that he'd done well.

"Now that we're seven, I feel better about scaling the mountain," I continued. "We may even survive this mission."

"If we survived the Battle for Teg'urnan, we can survive anything," Tor said.

I tore at my bread until it was reduced to crumbs. "I hope you're right about that."

***

After breakfast, we paid the innkeeper for our rooms and headed to the market. Those of us who came to Dremmsvard by way of the underworld were dressed for travel, but Innetha, Elkin, and I had all departed Teg'urnan with only the clothes on our backs. We needed gear appropriate for the much colder mountain air, and I didn't even have a weapon, save whatever offenses my newly remembered abilities could mount.

"There must be a seamstress here, somewhere," Latera said as she scanned the tents and stalls that lined the market. "Even if we can't find proper cloaks, blankets would do."

"They would be better than nothing," I agreed. Even though I'd spent a great deal of time in the norther reaches, I absolutely despised the cold. "Do you think Olluhm made it all the way to Gannera Castle?"

"I'm trying not to think about it at all," she replied. "No one in Gannera has the means to fight a god, and when he realizes the lodestone isn't there, he'll be furious. I fear for what he could do to them."

"Hopefully, when he realizes the lodestone isn't there he'll move on," I said, remembering how Olluhm had razed villages and murdered my people over the smallest affront. He had always been jealous of my followers' devotion to me, but he never understood that I was also devoted to them. For a man who had redefined himself as a god of love, he understood nothing about the emotion. "At least your sisters are safe."

"Yes, there is that." Latera nodded toward the far side of the market. "Tor and Aeolmar are at the blacksmith."

"They are so much alike," I murmured. "What was it like when they met?"

"It was wonderful." Latera would have said more, but something else caught her eye. "Asherah, do you see that symbol? It's a grape leaf with a melon flower."

"Iruna's symbol," I muttered. The decoration was carved above the blacksmith's entrance. "Markham's last estate is nearby. Perhaps he was once a patron of the smith's."

"Did he own the village?" Latera turned in a slow circle, and examined the rest of the village square. "That symbol is everywhere." I followed her gaze, and saw the elegant floral symbol carved into nearly all the shop doors, and painted above the windows. It was even incorporated into the central fountain in the form of a mosaic around the base. "Look, it's even on the inn."

I turned and saw the front of the inn, and the heavily decorated walls. Twining around the door and windows were painted grape vines, punctuated by gilded melon blossoms. "We must not have noticed them last night, in the dark," Latera said, then she grabbed my arm. "The third window on the upper floor."

I follower her gaze, and standing in the window was the innkeeper. When he noticed us watching him, he closed the shutters. A moment later next set of shutters was closed, and then the next, until the warm, welcoming inn we'd slept in the night before appeared ready to wait out a siege.

And I remembered the innkeeper's thoughtful face when he heard my name.

"We need to move," I said, and we hurried across the square toward the blacksmith. There we found Tor and Aeolmar picking through a rack of swords while our other three companions looked on.

"Tor, what do you know about King Markham?" I demanded.

"Not much, I'm afraid," he replied. "He was king before Sahlgren, but most of his family was murdered by the usurper. Only his two youngest children survived." Tor paused, and added, "He kept an estate near Dremmsvard."

"Iruna's symbol is everywhere," Latera said, as she scanned the crowd. "And these people know who we are."

"Iruna was Markham's daughter," Tor said. "She's an enemy?"

"She funded Sarelle," I said.

"You should have let me kill her," Latera bit off.

"Perhaps we'll accomplish that today," I said, and gestured toward the village. One by one, the shops closed their doors. Behind us, the blacksmith banked his forge and retreated out the back without a word. "Whatever's happening, it's starting now."

Aeolmar handed me his sword, then he withdrew his father's blade from the sheath on his back. "Elkin, flank left. Tor, right. Priya, can you fight?"

Priya stowed the lodestone and drew her sword. "Like a tigress."

"There." Latera pointed toward the far side of the market with one of her swords. "They're coming."

"What's coming?" I demanded.

"Demons."

Chapter Fifty-One

Mara Speaks

I dropped to my knees when I saw the corpses scattered throughout the practice yard, despondent and repulsed and so, so scared.
What had killed all of these people? Surely, it couldn't have been only
Cerillia. She was but one person, and there were scores of bodies on
the ground.

Scores.

Finn knelt beside me and wrapped his arms around my shoulders.
"I wish I could have kept this sight from you."

I nodded as I clutched his arm. "Are they all gone?"

"Wait here. I'll walk among them, and check for survivors."

"I'll go with you." When he protested, I added, "Where you go, I
go." Finn sighed, but he helped me to my feet, and we ventured into
the field of corpses.

"Odd," he said, as we picked our way among the bodies. "None of
the bodies seem to have any wounds. It's as if they all fell over, dead."

"It was Cerillia," Leran said as he strode into the yard with Ember
close behind. "She had some sort of ability that drains one's life away

without leaving a mark." Leran stopped in front of me, and asked, "Mara, we heard you scream. Are you all right?"

"I'm as good as I can be while standing here," I replied. "Where's Cerillia now?"

"I killed her," Ember said. "It was either her or Leran."

"An easy choice, then." Near the back of the yard was a weapons shed. I remembered my father and Caol'non standing out there, with my uncle trying and failing to convince Papa to trust him when they'd first met. Luckily, Papa had gotten over the shock of their unexpected meeting, especially since Caol'non went on to save Asherah from certain death.

Certain death at Kemen's hand, that is.

Unsure what emotions might be playing across my face, I turned away from Finn. The more I thought about my time with Kemen, the more apparent it became that he had never loved me. He'd only sought to get this fabled heir to the sun on me to somehow appease his father. Well, he failed, because the father of my children was my mate Finlay Torim, the Prince of Parthalan, and no one else. Heartened by the good turns my life had taken, I moved closer to the weapons shed, and gasped.

"What is it?" Finn demanded, as he rushed to my side.

"There," I said, as I pointed against the side of the shed. Propped up against it was Senan's body. By the haggard look of him, he must have been one of the first to die. "She even killed her own mate."

"But, why?" Finn asked. "Why did she do any of this?"

"Revenge on our family," Ember replied. "Cerillia is Gannok's sister."

"Gannok?" Finn asked. "Who is that?"

"My mother was betrothed to Gannok against her will, by her father," I replied.

"As was Auntie Sasha," Ember added. "Sasha ran away from Gan-nok. She's the reason why Mama went back to Gannera."

I thought about Cerillia's golden collar, and how it so closely matched Iruna's symbol of grape leaves and melon blossoms. "Didn't we speculate that Cerillia might be working with Iruna? And now all of our parents—except for the king—are going to Dremmsvard, where Iruna's last estate stands."

Leran swore. "They're walking into a trap."

***

We left the field of death and returned inside, our footsteps echoing in the vacant corridor. "Where is everyone?" Ember muttered. "There's no way that field contained an entire palace's worth of residents."

"They're probably hiding," I replied. "And terrified."

"We must find Sibeal," Leran said. "Her rooms are this way."

Leran strode through the palace with Ember at his side while I lagged behind, struggling to keep up. "Beloved," Finn said, as set his hand on the small of my back. "Let them rush. We can take our time."

"I suppose we can," I conceded, as I slowed my pace. "I just want to get as far away from those bodies as possible." Finn reached for me and I went to him, and soaked up all the comfort he could spare me. "How could she have killed so many?"

"Leran said she had an ability to take life," Finn murmured, his lips against my forehead. "But to take so many lives..." Finn tightened his arms around me. "I'll admit, I never cared much for Cerillia, but I never thought she could do something so awful."

"What if she wasn't taking lives, so much as collecting them?" I asked. "What if she was collecting them for something?"

"Something, or someone." Finn released me, and we resumed walking toward Sibeal's rooms. "This stinks of Iruna, and her madness."

I shuddered, because Iruna had been the force behind Sarelle, the crazed former priestess who'd kidnapped and tortured me in an insane attempt to regain Olluhm's favor. Even after all this time, it was hard for me to hear her name, or think about what had happened while she held me in a remote cottage concealed behind a wall of magic. "You know, I never even met Iruna," I said. "She arranged for all of those awful things to be done to me, and yet she never once gave me the courtesy of looking me in the eye."

"I met her, and her brother, Avinor, and believe me, you are better off staying away from her," Finn said. "She invited my parents and me to their western estate. The Golden Knoll, they called it."

"What was it like?"

"It was very nice," Finn allowed. "Easily as luxurious as Teg'urnan, but I didn't like it there. Iruna clearly hated my mother and antagonized her at every turn, and all Avinor was interested in was gambling, and Iruna."

"Why was he interested in Iruna?" Finn gave me a look that made his meaning clear. "But they're brother and sister!"

"Yes. They are. Needless to say, we only remained at their home for a short time. But, while we were there, Iruna showed us their private temple dedicated to Olluhm, and Ma recognized it as one of The Deliverer's old shrines. That might have been the beginning of her realizing who she truly is." Finn looped his arm through mine. "If I'd had any idea she was about to send Sarelle after you, I'd have slit her throat while she slept."

"Thank you, beloved," I said, understanding for the first time why my parents occasionally made such violent declarations of love toward each other. It was oddly satisfying to know your mate would kill for you. "Why would Iruna need the living energy of others?"

"Not for anything good," Finn replied. "I assumed she would need them for a spell, though of what sort of a spell I couldn't say."

We reached Sibeal's rooms. Finn entered first, which was fine with me. I didn't mind exploring the palace, but I had my babies' welfare to think of, and Finn wouldn't let anything harmful near us. There didn't seem to be anything interesting in the outer room, then Ember exited Sibeal's sleeping chamber and shook her head.

"She's gone," Ember said. "Leran found something."

Ember beckoned us inside the bedchamber. I noticed that someone, probably Ember, had drawn the curtains around Sibeal's bed, and my heart clenched. While I hadn't known Sibeal very well, she had always been kind to me, and she was very close with my mother. I wished her spirit safe passage.

Beyond the bedchamber was a sitting room; I remembered Mama and Sibeal sitting there together for hours, laughing and gossiping as they went through their books and scrolls. Now there was nothing on the scratched old desk except a red sphere suspended in a golden metal frame.

"What's that?" I asked. The sphere appeared to be made of glass, and glowed as if lit from within.

"It's an enthrallment sphere," Leran replied. "The question is, who's being enthralled?"

"Look." Ember pointed to the metalwork along the stand. "Grapevines and melon blossoms. Iruna's behind this, all right."

"And our parents are her targets," I said. "Not that we know what she's set in motion."

"Maybe we don't need to know how it started." Finn kissed my cheek and squeezed my hand, then he stepped forward and placed his hands on the sphere. "Maybe we only need to put a stop to it."

Chapter Fifty-Two
Latera Speaks

"At least it's only demons," Innetha said, as she watched the stinking horde swarm across the field toward Dremmsvard. "I'd rather face them than a man with delusions of godhood."

I glanced at her jerkin. Olluhm's handprint was burned onto her shoulder. "Did he hurt you very badly?"

"Not half as badly as I hurt him," she replied. "His ego was rather delicate."

"Soft as a demon's underbelly, I assume." I assessed the village's layout. There were three main entry points to the village's center, all of them narrow alleyways. Aeolmar called out for Elkin to flank left, and Innetha went to join her mate.

"Mar, I'll take center," I called.

Aeolmar nodded. "Priya, watch Latera's back."

"Always," Priya said, and we strode toward the enemy. There was no point in being stealthy, since the demons obviously knew we were here.

I faced Priya, and asked, "How many do you think there are?"

"Thirty, maybe fifty," she replied. "You're like my mother. She was always the first one in the fight."

"I always take point," I said, but my words lost to the screams of the horde. Whenever demons were in the mix, I was the first warrior on the field, and the last to retreat. Asherah may be a goddess, but I am the *deva'shi*. I am what demons fear.

"How long ago was your last kill?" Priya asked, as she took a position beside me.

"A few moons ago. You?"

"Longer than that. We don't get many demons in the mortal realm." She raised her sword. "How many *mordeth-galls* have you felled?"

"Just the one."

Priya pointed toward the advancing demons with her sword. "Here comes the second."

I followed the line of her blade, and saw the biggest demon I'd ever encountered lumbering toward us. It was so tall and wide it towered above the surrounding beasts, and its footfalls shook the ground like so many little earthquakes. This latest *mordeth-gall* to stomp across my life was enormous and terrifying, so much so it made my memory of Asgeloth seem like I'd gone after an angry bull, not a demon warlord.

"How big was Ehkron?" I asked, referencing the *mordeth-gall* Priya's mother had killed all those years ago.

"Not that big." She raised her sword, and grinned. "Good thing we're both here."

"That monster doesn't stand a chance against us," I said, then Priya and I ran toward the ranks of demons.

Chapter Fifty-Three

Aeolmar Speaks

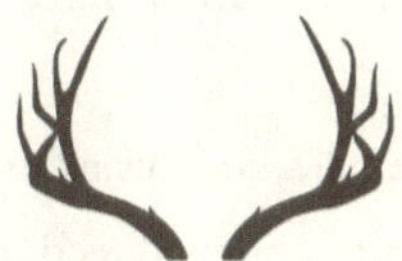

"Your mate is amazing," Tor said.

"She is," I replied, pride evident in my voice. "As is yours."

The demons had appeared on the plain just north of the village, and were spilling into the market square through three narrow streets. Latera and Priya had taken positions at the mouth of the central alley, Elkin and Innetha were at the western point of ingress, and Tor and I were standing at the easternmost alley. Asherah was behind Tor and me, and unpleased about being so far removed from the fight. That was too bad, because I hadn't come all this way to watch her get injured by a demon before we even got to this shrine. More importantly, Latera and Priya were already decimating the beasts. At this rate, the battle would be over before my sword got wet.

"Thurndian women are a true marvel," Tor began, then he indicated the felled demons. "Why are the demons wearing gold? I've never seen that before." He was right; the demons were wearing gold bands around their upper arms.

"Neither have I," I began, then I saw one of the demon corpses move. Before my eyes, the corpse stood, even though its guts were hanging out and dragging in the dirt.

"Olluhm's Balls, they're like the undead from below," I muttered. "Latera! Behind you!"

Latera spun around, her swords flashing as she struck at the demons she'd already killed. "Elkin!" I yelled to my second. "How many portals do you have?"

"Two," he yelled, then he ran toward me. When he was close enough, he tossed the portals in my direction. I caught them in one hand and sheathed my sword with the other.

"I'm going to send as many of these beasts to the Southern Sea as I can," I said to Tor. "Guard the queen!"

"I shall, grandson."

I dropped my cloak and climbed up the blacksmith shop's wall. Once I was on the roof, I leapt to the next, and then the next, until I was standing directly above the onslaught.

Beloved! I'm going portal them to the sea!

Make me a path to the mordeth-gall!

You don't need to fight him! I can send him away!

If you do, he'll just come back. Latera pushed an image of her and I surrounded by our children into my mind. *Let me make the world safer for our family.*

I'll be right behind you. I tossed one portal into the fray, pleased when scores of demons disappeared. I aimed the second toward the group right in front of the *mordeth-gall.*

Gods, that beast is huge.

All the more reason to kill him now!

She was right, but then my mate was always right. I sent off the second batch of demons, then I jumped down from the smithy's roof and into what was left of the morass and followed my mate as she ran toward her quarry. We would make the world safer for our family, together.

Chapter Fifty-Four

Asherah Speaks

I watched as Aeolmar jumped off the roof of the smithy, and into the demon choked field. A quick glance behind me told me that the villagers had either retreated inside their homes or abandoned us altogether. Since there were no innocents to protect, I raised my borrowed sword and let out a whooping yell.

"Push them back," I cried. Latera and Priya had stoppered the flow in one of the alleyways, and there wasn't enough room in the one Tor and I were in to swing a sword without one of us striking the other. "I'm going up!" I announced.

"Yell if you need me," Tor replied, as he cut a demon in two.

"I shall!"

I climbed up the wall of the nearest structure, wanting the advantage of height so I would know where I was needed most. The wall I'd chosen was crumbling brick, and by the time I fought my way to the roof, my knuckles and palms were bloody. As I surveyed the plain below, I saw Elkin and Innetha fighting together as they often did, back to back. Momentarily worried for Tor, I ran to the other side of the building to check on him, and laughed.

The jovial man I'd eaten breakfast with was gone. In his place, the mighty Prelate of Parthalan cut a swath through the demons, his massive sword cleaving several foes apart with each stroke. I noticed that unlike the demons felled by everyone else, the ones Tor cut through didn't get back up.

Hm. His sword must be enchanted. I must remember to ask him about that.

I returned to the front of the building, and reached deep within myself as I called for my light. When I'd been surrounded by orcs on the Northern Waste, I'd summoned dawn's light and killed scores of the beasts with a single flash. Now I will use the light again, and save the village and my people from this demonic attack. I extended my hand, and willed the light to come forth.

It didn't.

I extended my other hand. "Light," I yelled. Nothing.

"Torim, help me," I shrieked. "Nyshanti!"

Movement caught my eye. Latera had leapt on top of the *mordeth-gall's* back while Priya stabbed at his legs. Aeolmar was moving toward them, but he was slowed by the horde.

They needed me, and I had nothing to offer them.

"Nyshanti," I whispered. "Why have you abandoned me now?"

The *mordeth-gall* bellowed, and Latera fell behind him. I couldn't stand here waiting for help that may never arrive while my people were still fighting, light or no. I leapt off the roof and rolled to my feet, and began fighting my way through the mass.

These demons and their *mordeth-gall* would fall, as would anything else that stood between me and the shrine.

Chapter Fifty-Five
Latera Speaks

The *mordeth-gall* reared up, and I lost my grip on its neck. I grabbed a handful of the stinking, greasy fur on its back, which was disgusting but kept me from hitting the ground and being trampled by the beast's massive hooves. In fact, this beast was so massive I wondered if it was older than Asgeloth, or even Ehkron. It certainly smelled like it hadn't bathed in a thousand years.

"Latera," Priya yelled.

"I'm all right!"

I grabbed more handfuls of fur and climbed up the beast's back as if I was scaling a sheer cliff. When I got to its neck, I balanced myself on its shoulders, wrapped an arm around one of its horns, and with the other I plunged my sword into the back of its head. The blade sliced through flesh and the beast roared, but my sword slid right off his skull. Stupid, hard headed demon. Still clutching its horn, I stabbed my sword into its head and neck, cutting off chunks of skin and muscle that would have instantly killed anything else.

Did the *mordeth-gall* go down? No. If anything, I'd made it angrier.

I kept hacking at its head, then it bucked and I had to grab onto both horns so I wouldn't be flung to the ground. My chest was pressed against its raw flesh and the demon's black blood soaked me, burning my skin and making me worried for Priya down below.

"Beloved!"

Aeolmar yelled with both his voice and inside my mind as he ran toward the *mordeth-gall*. At the last moment, he dropped to his knees and skidded underneath the beast's legs, his sword flashing silver as he sliced open the demon's thigh. The *mordeth-gall* bellowed and fell forward onto its arms. I hung onto the horn, but barely.

The beast tried to push itself up. Aeolmar set on its legs and Priya stabbed at its arms, then the lesser demons rushed to save their master. My mate and aunt peeled off the beast to face the rest, leaving me alone with the *mordeth-gall*.

It succeeded in pushing itself upward, and I slipped off its blood-slick back and landed in the mud. In the next moment, the beast was above me, growling and spitting and ranting about all of the things he would do to me both while I was alive, and later to my corpse. I shoved my sword straight up into his throat, and rolled away from the blood that gushed onto the ground. While it clutched at the gaping wound, I flung myself onto its torso and climbed up to its head, and beat the pommel of my sword against its exposed skull. I kept hitting the monster's skull until the bone cracked and it fell forward, its head split in two.

A sane woman would have taken a moment to rest. But I'm not sane, I'm the *deva'shi*, and as the thrill of battle coursed through my veins I broke off one of the *mordeth-gall's* horns. I climbed on top of the dead demon's chest and brandished my grisly trophy to the lessers, baring my teeth as I dared them to attack.

Then they all fell over, dead.

"Olluhm's Balls!"

Chapter Fifty-Six

Finn set his hands on the red enthrallment sphere they had found in Sibeal's chamber, and winced as the glass sizzled against his flesh.

"What's wrong?" Mara demanded. "What is it doing to you?"

"It feels like... like lightning," he replied, not having the proper words to explain how the sphere felt, or the magic gathered within it. "This is how Cerillia was collecting souls. She kept them in here, and now they're trapped."

"Collecting?" Leran repeated. "How do you know this?"

"Ma's power?" Finn shrugged. "I'm not really sure."

"Can you stop it?" Leran asked. "Whatever Cerillia's done here was intended to harm Asherah, and anyone standing with her. We can't get to Dremmsvard in time to help them face the enemy, but if we can undo whatever Cerillia's done, I'm certain it will aid their quest."

Finn nodded absently, his focus on the enthrallment sphere. If he concentrated on the swirling colors within, he could make out faces. He squinted as he tried to recognize some from his time in Thurnda, maybe even find Sibeal herself...

"Finn!"

He blinked, and faced Mara. "What?"

"You're scaring me." She put her hand on his forearm. "It was like you were getting lost in there with the rest."

Finn put his hand on top of his mate's, then he stepped back from the sphere. He had been getting lost among the other trapped souls, and he felt he now knew how Cerillia had captured many of her victims: after she'd imprisoned the first few souls, the rest went willingly to try and free them.

"I don't know if all of Cerillia's victims are within the sphere, but many of them are," Finn said. "Maybe... Maybe I can restore them to their bodies."

"No," Ember said. "Many of them have been dead for days, perhaps longer. If you send them back to their bodies, you'll be dooming them to live in their corpses."

"Gods," Finn muttered, then he replaced his hands on the sphere. "Stand back. I'm going to push Ma's power at it and see what happens."

"What if it explodes?" Mara asked.

"That's why I want you to stand back." Finn closed his eyes, and visualized his mother's power. It was white like starlight, and he wrapped it around the sphere, much like one would wrap a scarf around one's neck. The red sludge within the sphere recoiled from the bright light, but the souls flocked to it. To him. The souls understood that Finn was there to help them.

The glass cracked, and a bit of the red, corrupt magic leaked out. Finn ignored the sludge dripping onto his foot, and worried at the crack. As soon as he'd widened it, he pushed more of the white light inside the sphere, and felt those trapped within move toward it. Finn pulled the light back, taking the souls with him, then his vision changed and he saw his mother fighting in a field of demons. He screamed as the souls were set free, then his world went black.

***

When Finn came back to himself, he was lying in an unfamiliar bed and momentarily thought he was once again an invalid in Tingu's infirmary. But this bed was far more comfortable than those cots had ever been, and the silk hangings around the bedframe spoke to a luxury not usually wasted on those who might soon expire. Finn rolled onto his side, and saw Mara lying next to him.

"Hello, my magical mate," she said.

"What happened?" he asked, as he pushed himself up to a sitting position. "The last thing I remember is the sphere cracking, then I saw a field packed full of demons." He glanced about the quiet room. "Were we attacked?"

"We weren't, but our parents were in Dremmsvard," she replied. "Leran's been in contact with Asherah. Apparently, a horde of demons wearing golden grapevines and melon blossoms around their arms appeared out of nowhere. When you broke the sphere, they all died."

"Then Cerillia was using those souls to fuel a demon army," he said. "That's awful."

"It was, but you stopped it." Mara moved so she was sitting beside Finn, nestled in the crook of his arm. "They're all safe, and it's all because of you."

"I expect they'll be on their way to the shrine soon," Finn said, and Mara nodded. "What should we do next?"

"For the moment, we will be staying here. Leran's sent a messenger to The Seat asking for some of the staff to relocate here for the time being. We cannot leave the palace or Thurnda in such a state."

"No, we cannot," Finn murmured. "Where are Leran and Ember?"

"They're walking the corridors and assessing how many remain here," she replied. "Once that's sorted out, we need to build pyres for Sibeal, and Senan, and all the rest." Mara's voice trailed off at the end. Finn grasped her hand and kissed her knuckles.

"None of this we," he said. "You are not building or burning anything."

"I need to help," she began.

"You can help by letting me take care of you," Finn said over her. "How are you feeling? You weren't hurt, were you? And, um, whose bed is this?"

"We're in Leran's rooms," she replied. "He and Ember graciously gave us the use of their bedchamber. Since the rooms remain sealed while Leran isn't here, we knew they'd be free of Cerillia's influence. And, I'm fine," she added. "I was worried when you passed out, but your breathing and heartbeat were strong. I knew you'd come back to me."

"Always, beloved." He kissed the top of her head. "Is your mother the Lady of Thurnda now?"

"Yes, I think she might be."

Chapter Fifty-Seven

Asherah Speaks

After the battle ended in such an abrupt manner, I spoke with Leran mind to mind. Thanks to him, I learned that Finn's use of the magic I'd given him was the reason why the demons had all collapsed at once, and that Cerillia was indeed Iruna's and therefore Krylle's agent in Thurnda. Armed with such knowledge, we regrouped and retreated to the village inn. Latera lugged the *mordeth-gall's* massive horn with her the entire way.

"That horn must weigh almost as much as you do," I observed.

"It's no feather," she replied. "But I killed it, and I'm going to mount it over the inn's door as a reminder of what betrayal gets you in the end."

"You're a true Lady of Thurnda," Tor said. "It always falls to the Lady to dispatch the *mordeth-gall.*"

Latera frowned. "If anything, Priya's the new Lady," she said, then she fell silent. Latera had been very close to Sibeal, and she was taking news of her death hard.

"We will avenge Sibeal," I said. "Ember's already done away with Cerillia. Iruna will fall next, as will anyone else with a hand in this treachery."

"She will fall," Latera agreed, as she held the *mordeth-gall's* horn in a white-knuckled grip. "I will make Iruna regret the day she was born."

When we reached the inn, Aeolmar went to the kitchens to make up a poultice to alleviate the many blood burns we'd sustained, and I sent Tor and Elkin to deal with the innkeeper. The rest of us retreated to the subterranean baths, where we peeled away our filthy gear and began washing away the blood and gore.

Innetha immediately began assessing Latera's burns; the blood of a *mordeth* is more caustic than that of a lesser demon, which meant getting a *mordeth-gall's* blood on you was like getting doused in liquid fire. Since those two were on the other side of the baths near the pool of cold water, that meant I was standing behind Priya when she removed her jerkin and then her tunic, and I saw her bare back.

It was covered in scars.

Being that Priya's hair only brushed the tops of her shoulders, I had a full view of the marks that covered her. I'd never seen anyone with so many scars, save myself. Priya felt my gaze on her skin, and turned around to face me.

"I'm so sorry," I blurted out before she could speak.

"Sorry about what, now?" she asked.

"Your scars," I began, my face going hot with shame. "I saw them, and I shouldn't stare, but." I pulled off my own tunic and turned around, thus showing her the red, raised marks across my own back. "They remind me of my own."

I felt the heat from Priya's fingers as they hovered above my skin. "Why are they red?"

I turned around so she could watch me speak, and replied, "They're from a *mordeth's* blood." I left off how the monsters would score my skin, then laugh as they purposefully bled into my wounds in some sort of sick game. They weren't laughing when I killed them, and I did kill every last one of my captors. "Before, all of my scars were red, but Lormac used the Sala to heal the ones on the front of me." Priya glanced down, and saw the silvery spider webs that covered my breasts and abdomen, all the way down to my legs.

"Lormac was amazing in so many ways," Priya murmured. "Come, let's get in the water." We did, sinking into the steaming water while Latera and Innetha remained in the colder bath. The hot water felt amazing, and I did not envy Latera her burns.

"Unlike you, I don't have an interesting story about these marks," Priya began. She raised an arm in front of her, and showed me how some of her skin was pale, and thicker than the rest.

"You don't have to tell me." Sometimes, the mere sight of my scars reduced me to tears, and I didn't want Priya to suffer for my curiosity.

"Telling others what happened releases some of the power the memories have over me," she said. "I'm the one in charge, not a bit of leathery flesh."

I nodded. "All right, then. If you want to talk, I'd be honored to listen."

"I fell into an ash pit," she said; it took me a moment to realize that was how she'd been injured. "I was crossing the underworld alone, which was foolish enough, and in the dark I stumbled right into the pit. As you can see, I got myself out of the pit, but wherever the ash had been against me for a time, my skin got thick and stiff like old leather. The underworld very nearly turned me into a boot."

I smiled. "You're very brave, what with how many times you've crossed the underworld."

Priya shook her head. "Bravery's got nothing to do with it. The first time I went below I was following my family as we tracked Ehkron, and the second time I went back the way I came so I could relate what happened to Sibeal. She needed to know of my mother's—her sister's—death, and that she was the new Lady." She wiped her cheek. "I will miss Sibeal."

"I will, too." Sibeal was one of the strongest people I'd ever met, and had successfully led Thurnda for longer than I'd ruled Parthalan. "Will you be the next Lady?"

"Let's leave that decision for another day," Priya replied. "After I'd given Sibeal news of my mother and Ehkron's demises, I couldn't find a place for myself in Thurnda or Tarac, so I started going for walks. Some of those walks led me below, and I ended up crossing the underworld several more times. Now here we are."

"Here we are indeed. Is your hair short to keep it off the scars on your back?" I asked. I'd always deliberately kept my hair long in order to hide as much of my body as possible.

"The scarred bits feel nearly nothing. I can even poke myself with a knife's point using a fair bit of pressure and my skin won't break. I cut my hair off when Tor lost his braid. Poor man was despondent, but it's only hair."

"His sons wore their hair the same way," I said. "Caol'non still does."

"You've met all of his children?"

I shook my head. "The eldest was killed before I arrived at Teg'ur-nan, but the twins are much like Tor. Big-hearted, honorable men. Sadly, only Caol'non still lives."

"I would like to meet this Caol'non," Priya murmured, then she continued, "Tor loves his sons very much, and he loves tradition even more—but there was no saving the braid. It was soaked in tar, and no amount of brushing or oil could remove it. So after I cut off his hair, I cut off my own and laid it next to his. We burned all that useless hair, and we've kept it short ever since."

"You're brave and beautiful," I said, and she smiled.

"That's very kind of you," she said. "I've never been complimented by a goddess before."

"Perhaps, once all of this is behind us, you and Tor will consider staying on with me for a time. I'll need a Prelate, and someone not afraid to travel the realm when I need her to."

Priya leaned back so the waters reached her chin. "Perhaps we shall."

"You still need to tell me how this tar got into Tor's hair in the first place."

"I will, but only with Tor present. Every time I tell the story, he goes as red as a ripe berry!"

I smiled. "I can't wait to hear it."

Chapter Fifty-Eight

Aeolmar Speaks

I stood in the empty kitchens mixing honey and dried oats into a pail of milk I'd found in the larder, while the thrill of battle subsided in me. The inn's entire staff appeared to have fled, which was probably for the best. Fewer people meant fewer chances of betrayal. Not to mention, I was in no mood to deal with anyone of questionable loyalties.

Tor entered the kitchen, and looked into the pail. "Are you making sweet cakes?"

"It's a poultice for the blood burns. Here." I grabbed a bowl and scooped up some of the mixture. "Put that on the burn on your hand."

He spread the poultice across the angry red mark. "It already feels better. Did Alluria teach you how to make this?"

"She did." I resumed stirring. "She taught us many things about herbs and healing."

Tor laughed softly. "I remember when your father would dress her up as a *saffira* and sneak her out of the palace, all so she could pick her own herbs. The ones he brought her were never good enough," he added.

"I'm sure they weren't," I said, my mind conjuring up images of my mother hunched over her herb table and sifting through petals and leaves. "Did they sneak out together often?"

"Yes, and they went on that way for seasons," Tor replied. "Once I discovered what was happening, I ordered the gatekeeper to let them pass without question. For them to take such a risk, they obviously meant a great deal to each other."

"You didn't consider punishing them for breaking the temple's rules?"

"Would they have listened?" Tor countered. "Besides, they were in love. Who was I to stand in their way?"

"I wonder why they didn't just leave the palace altogether," I mumbled. "They obviously weren't happy in Teg'urnan."

"The reason they stayed is that Caol'nir was the most honorable man to ever live," Tor replied. "He'd sworn an oath to guard the priestesses and keep them chaste, and nothing in this realm or any other could have made him break it. If Alluria hadn't left the order, they'd probably still be in the Great Temple today, exchanging looks and pining for one another."

"Not now, they wouldn't." I deemed the poultice thoroughly mixed, and began portioning it out. "Krylle and his men destroyed it with their bombs, along with much of the rest of the palace. I don't know if we'll ever go back to Teg'urnan."

"Do you want to?" Tor asked. "Continue living in the palace, that is."

"I'm not sure," I admitted. "I've never felt as if I belonged there. If it wasn't for Latera, I would have left long ago."

"Does she like it there?"

"She's a princess. She's used to living in a palace." I glanced at Tor's thoughtful face, and decided I liked having a grandfather to talk to.

"Although, when I met her, she slept in a stable. Latera makes her home wherever she finds it."

"It sounds like home for you is wherever your mate is."

I reached out with my mind, and felt the comfort that was so uniquely Latera. "You're not wrong. Let's bring these poultices to the bathhouse."

***

After the rest of us had bathed and treated our burns, Elkin decided to join us. He'd found the innkeeper and most of the other villagers to a pub across the square; according to Elkin, they'd been cowering in a root cellar wondering if they'd be murdered by demons, or executed for treason by the queen. My second persuaded them to leave the cellar and return to their usual positions, though he didn't promise them leniency.

"I told them that any punishment they were due would be decided by you," Elkin said, with a nod toward Asherah, "but I also let them know that a hot meal and warm room would go far toward softening your heart."

"If they were enthralled along with the demons, none of this was their fault," Innetha said. "Olwynn told me what enthrallment was like. If they were under thrall, they wouldn't have been in control of their bodies, not even for the most basic acts."

"A very good point, Innetha," Asherah said. "I would rather fall on the side of leniency than punish a village full of victims. Good work, Elkin."

"Did you negotiate anything beyond a meal?" I asked.

"The tailor's putting together clothes and other gear for our walk up the mountain, and I've got the blacksmith working on weaponry," he replied. "Stable master's also gearing up some horses for us. We'll be ready to go by sunrise."

I smiled. "I'm impressed."

"You should be," Elkin said. "Now, I'm off to visit these baths."

"I'll go with you," Innetha said, and the two of them disappeared down the rock cut stairs to the hot springs.

"He's your second?" Tor asked.

"He is."

"I saw him fight earlier. Excellent technique."

"My father was his first teacher," I said. "Elkin's father was a cobbler, and he did anything he could to avoid going into that trade."

"Good thing he did." Tor clapped me on the back. "Let's find out what's for dinner. I'd like to talk to a few people, and try to find out if they truly were enthralled. Though I haven't heard of anyone using an enthrallment sphere since before Asherah took the throne."

"Speaking of enthrallment," Asherah said, as she joined us, "Tor, is your sword enchanted? I noticed that none of the demons you felled got up again."

"It's warded against demons," Tor replied. "The blade kills them with a single cut."

"Interesting," Asherah said. "Who enchanted it?"

"Rahlle himself," Tor replied, smiling as Asherah's eyes widened at the mention of the legendary sorcerer. "He did it as a gift when I was named Prelate."

"We have got to find Rahlle," Asherah muttered.

"Why didn't the sword's enchantment work on the undead?" I asked, since the monsters we'd battled in the underworld had kept getting up no matter how often we stabbed them.

Tor shrugged. "They must not have been demons before they died."

"Whatever they were, I hope they stay below," I said. "We'll have enough to deal with tomorrow without having a group corpses following us up the mountain."

We entered the common room and claimed our seats at the long table. Mugs and a pitcher of ale had already been set out, and Asherah began pouring for us. Latera and Priya were sitting at the bar with their own mugs and a platter of food set between them, and were charming the villagers into telling them their life stories. Sometimes, I wished I was a genial as Latera, but I preferred being her scowling shadow. That way, not only did I get to keep her safe, if the person in question turned out to be less than forthright and Latera unleashed her fury on them, their shock was quite amusing.

"If only life could stay like this," I murmured. "A hot meal in a warm inn, surrounded by family. And Innetha," I added.

"When do times like this ever last?" Asherah said. "But I understand how you feel. I only wish Finlay, and Finn, were here with me."

"And my namesake," Tor said. "Tell me more about this boy."

"He's strong and honorable, much like his father," Asherah said, smiling at me over the rim of her mug.

"He's all that and more, which makes me think he takes after Latera more than me," I said. "And soon, my queen, Finn and Mara will have one of their own."

"More children is a sign for more ale." Tor smiled, and reached across the table for the pitcher and started topping up our mugs. "Aye, grandson, I agree. If only times like this would last."

Chapter Fifty-Nine

Asherah Speaks

The morning after we fought Iruna's demon army, I was woken by a loud and obnoxious pounding. I went to the ground floor of the inn to investigate, and found Aeolmar mounting the *mordeth-gall's* horn over the front door.

"What in the nine realms are you doing?" I demanded.

"Latera wants this trophy left in the village as a reminder, and she wants it someplace everyone can see it whether they want to or not," he replied. "Hand me another nail, please?"

I did, and asked, "What exactly are we reminding people of? The *mordeth-gall's* mighty stench?"

"That, and if anyone betrays you again, Latera herself will return to deal with the traitors." He fixed the last nail in place, then Aeolmar climbed down and admired his handiwork. "Who would risk having someone who can kill a *mordeth-gall* coming after them?"

"No one in their right mind," I said. "We're certain the villagers were enthralled?"

"Tor believes them."

"And you?"

He jerked his chin toward the mounted horn. "I believe Tor, but as Latera says, a reminder won't hurt."

"Agreed." I rubbed my arms. The morning air was frigid. "Has the tailor come through with cloaks for us?"

"About that." Aeolmar opened the door for me. "Come inside."

"Has something happened?" I asked. "Did the tailor renege?"

"The tailor delivered his wares before sunrise, as promised," Aeolmar replied. Remembering something, I went to the window.

"Again, a single sun," I murmured. "Where is Olluhm?"

"No one knows, and people are beginning to panic." He crossed his arms over his chest, and stood behind me as he gazed out of the window over the top of my head. I had always felt small around Aeolmar, but never unsafe. He had a way of comforting people with his presence, even if he did loom over everyone like a living, scowling mountain. "Tor believes that the lack of Olluhm's presence in the sky made people more susceptible to whatever spell Cerillia, or perhaps Iruna herself, cast over the village."

"You think the lack of Olluhm in the sky made them want to kill me?"

"No, I think the lack of Olluhm's presence terrified them, and it's easier to sway a scared man to do something he normally wouldn't," Aeolmar replied. "These people have been watching two suns travel across the sky for their entire lives. For the elder sun to suddenly disappear is nothing short of apocalyptic."

I nodded, since that did make sense. "What are you saying? We shouldn't go on to the shrine?"

"You need to go on," Innetha said from behind me. I turned around, and saw her and Elkin standing in the entrance to the common room. "Elkin and I will stay here, and quell the local's fears."

"I don't know," I said, shaking my head. "I need both of you with me."

"It's a good plan," Innetha said. "What if the villagers are enthralled again, and go after you? Elkin and I can either stop them, or get to you with a warning."

"And if something happens you need to know about, 'Neth will be able to track you down," Elkin added. "And if you need backup, you'll have us waiting here, and you can contact us mind to mind if need be. We can get a message to the king, or The Seat, or Thurnda, or anywhere else you need one sent."

"This is a good idea." I glanced at Aeolmar. "You approve of this plan?"

"I do," he replied. "As do the rest of us."

"Why am I always the last to know things?" I griped. "As queen, I should be the first."

"You're the last to know because you slept the latest," Aeolmar replied. "We worked all of this out over breakfast."

"Did you? I don't suppose there's any food left for me."

"There's a bit," Innetha replied. "Elkin ate all of the sausages, though."

***

After we'd all finished eating, we loaded up our gear on our borrowed horses, said farewell to Elkin and Innetha, and headed toward the mountain's peak. It was a beautiful, clear day, perfect for travel. I suppose having only one sun didn't affect the weather much, and for that I was glad.

"Is the shrine far from here?" Latera asked, as we left the village behind and ascended the trail.

"It's at the very top of the mountain," I replied. "Nyshanti would rise from it every morning and decorate the sky with her colored lights."

"It must have been a beautiful sight," Latera said.

"It was," I said. "If only my own light would return. Out on the Northern Waste I decimated the orcs with little more than a thought, but when I tried to summon it yesterday against the demons, nothing happened. Why would my light return to assist me against the orcs, only to abandon me when I needed it again?"

"I don't think your light has abandoned you at all," Latera said. "You're still healing after how many years of not truly knowing who and what you are? You had a lifetime to forget, so it stands to reason you will need time to fully remember. Be gentle with yourself, and your abilities. The light will return when you need it."

"You always make me feel better," I said.

"I only speak the truth," Latera said. "How does it feel to be returning home after all this time?"

"Exciting," I replied. "Before I was in Dremmsvard, I was so nervous. I kept wondering if I was wrong, and I wouldn't be able to defeat Olluhm this time, either. And if I failed again—"

"You will not fail," Latera said as she squeezed my forearm.

I placed my hand on hers. I loved my *deva'shi* so much more that I could ever properly express. "My fear was that if I failed, he would take out his anger on my people again. All of these thoughts coursed through my head, but they fell silent as soon as I arrived here." I smiled at my huntress. "But, you're correct. I won't fail. This is what I'm meant to do, and where I'm meant to be."

"If we don't enact a final defeat against Olluhm here, we may need to follow him to the mortal realm," Latera said. "The single sun up there makes me worry for Gannera."

"That is a concern," I said. "Aeolmar said the one sun overhead was apocalyptic. While I do think he was being a bit dramatic, I don't want my people consumed by fear."

"We'll just have to handle things one thing at a time," Latera said. "We cannot reassure all of Parthalan at once. We will deal with Olluhm, and with whatever comes next, until things are as they should be. Only then will we be able to show your Parthians that you're their true god, and not that madman in a stolen chariot."

I squeezed Latera's hand. "I don't know what I ever did to inspire such confidence in you, but I am glad I did."

"As am I," she said, her pale blue eyes twinkling. "There's something I've been meaning to ask you."

"Please. Ask me anything."

"What were—are—you the god of, exactly?"

"I... Well, that is a very good question." I cast my memory back several lifetimes ago, and considered how my people once saw me. "I was the people's protector. I stood between my people and anything that might harm them, be it an earthquake, or blizzard, or war with a neighboring realm. I was their first and last defender."

"Sounds much like what you do as queen," Latera said. "What was the hierarchy like? Did you lead the pantheon?"

"No. If anyone was considered a leader, it was Clea and Nu, the sky and sun. They're Nyshanti's parents."

"Then Nyshanti is a princess," Latera said. "Your temple in the mortal realm looks just like Teg'urnan, albeit much smaller, and Nyshanti is a princess in her own castle."

"Why does it look like Teg'urnan," I wondered out loud.

"Rahlle purposefully built it that way," Tor said, as he brought his horse up next to mine. "After Torim—Nyshanti's—mortal body was destroyed, her spirit needed a place to rest, so Rahlle created the temple."

"Rahlle," I repeated. He was one of Olluhm and Cydia's original twelve children, and one of the most powerful sorcerers that had ever lived. "Why did he build the temple in the mortal realm, and not here?"

"I really don't know," Tor said.

"I do," Latera said. "When Wren and I spoke to Nyshanti a few days ago, she said there's no place for her in Parthalan because her shrine is occupied. She cannot return until Cydia is freed."

"I had no idea." All this time I'd thought Nyshanti had abandoned me, but she'd really been waiting for a chance to return. I turned to Tor, and asked, "Is Rahlle still in the mortal realm?"

"I haven't seen or heard of Rahlle in a donkey's age, but the priestesses at your temple would know where he is," Tor replied. "They're all his and Alyon's children."

"I may need to visit this temple," I said, then a feature up ahead caught my eye. It was a deep valley that ran next to our trail, and along the width of the mountain like an emerald collar. Within the valley I could see crops, and a vineyard, and in the center was a lake so still and blue it was like a perfect piece of sky had fallen to the ground. Situated on the lakeshore was a castle worthy of a king, or a deceased monarch's two upstart children.

"Markham's last estate," Tor said, thus confirming who owned the castle.

I glanced at Latera. "We've found Iruna."

Chapter Sixty
Latera Speaks

I runa.

My hands tightened on the reins. Iruna and her lay about brother, Avinor, had been the forces behind Sarelle, the former High Priestess of Teg'urnan. Through her they'd arranged for my kidnapping from the mortal realm, and a second abduction that ripped me out of Aeolmar's arms and sent me back to Gannera. Years later, they had Mara kidnapped and tortured. Now we knew that Iruna had been behind Cerillia, and Krylle, and perhaps even Kemen's actions, and all of their machinations and murder had been nothing but a lame attempt at regaining Olluhm's favor.

I was sick of evil gods and their sycophantic followers, but more than anything, Iruna had harmed my children. For that fact alone, retribution was mine to give.

"Permission to cut off her head?" I asked.

Asherah blew out a breath. "We can't just walk in and behead her," she said. "We must first find her doing something wrong, then punish her."

"She strung Mara up like a pig and tried to bleed her dry!"

"I can kill her," Tor said. "Rahlle dissolved my oath to the throne long ago. If Iruna harmed my granddaughter, I claim vengeance."

"I'm not saying she doesn't deserve to die," Asherah said, "but we must be careful. She's proven more than once that she's wily, and not to be underestimated."

"Perhaps she shouldn't underestimate me," I muttered. Asherah pursed her lips, so I let it drop for the time being. Everyone knew I had a claim against Iruna, and no one would stand in my way if I barged into Iruna's home and killed her and Avinor where they stood. But Asherah was correct. There were rules to be followed, and if I went running off to dole out my revenge without considering the consequences of my actions, who knew what additional problems I might create.

"You're right," I said. "We have more important matters to deal with than her. I can wait."

"Thank you," Asherah said. "Believe me, I want to hold her accountable for many things, and I will. Many want retribution against Iruna, and we will all have it."

I nodded, and kept the rest of my grumblings to myself. Asherah's current mission far outweighed any claim of vengeance I had on Iruna or anyone; even Aeolmar would agree with that. Besides, part of Iruna's problem was her misguided self-importance. If we all rode past her home without a glance in her direction and thus proving she didn't matter to Parthalan any longer, that would be what she truly deserved.

Asherah and Tor resumed discussing Rahlle, and I took point on the trail. They had a lot to talk about, being that they hadn't seen each other for such a long time, and I got the impression that they'd once been quite close. While they reminisced, Priya brought her horse alongside mine.

"What's that?" Priya asked, nodding toward the valley.

"Iruna's estate," I grumbled. "She deserves punishment, but apparently we'll deal with her later."

"She's coming to deal with us now."

I followed Priya's gaze. Coming up from the valley below were a dozen men, all of them wearing gray uniforms decorated with gold vines and melon blossoms. Their skin was dark, but not in the way of southerners like Finlay. Their skin looked like it had been pickled, and their slow, jerking movements reminded me of the monsters we'd fought below.

They were also filing onto the path ahead of us and blocking our way up the mountain.

"Mar," I yelled, since he was behind Asherah and Tor. "Undead!"

Aeolmar let out a string of curses that made Asherah scowl and Tor laugh out loud. "I agree wholeheartedly," Tor said.

"Asherah, these are Iruna's undead," I yelled, as I pointed at this latest problem. "We cannot let her go unpunished!"

"Fine," Asherah said. "Latera, you can cut off Iruna's head, but do it later! For now, just clear the way so we can continue on the path."

I dismounted and drew my swords. "As you wish, my queen."

Priya joined me. "Why did this Iruna build a fancy farm in the middle of a cold mountain?"

"It's warmer in the valley," Tor replied. "You can grow anything down there, and with very little effort. It's as mild as Teg'urnan near the lake."

"Good. That means Iruna's corpse will rot quickly." I eyed the approaching warriors. "Why does she mark everything with gold?"

"Probably just showing off," Aeolmar said as he stood beside me. "Asherah, stay with the horses. Everyone, we need to keep these corpses away from the queen. Our priority is making sure Asherah can finish her mission."

I saw Asherah scowling, but she didn't argue with Aeolmar. As for me, I raised my swords. "There's three undead for each of us. Practically nothing after what we dealt with below."

"I bet I kill more than you," Aeolmar said, with a sidelong glance at me.

"I'll take that bet," I said, then we ran to meet the walking corpses.

***

Neither Aeolmar nor I killed the most undead. That honor went to Tor.

Unlike the undead we'd encountered in the underworld, and the demons in Dremmsvard, these monsters didn't require repeated stabbings to stay down, and none of their parts dragged themselves after us. That meant this skirmish was short, and sweet.

It was also too easy. That meant more was coming, and we had no idea what Iruna would unleash next. Would it be more undead, or demons, or something entirely new? Uncertainty in battle led to death, and all of Parthalan needed Asherah to succeed.

After I shared my concerns with Aeolmar, and he and I decided on a course of action, I approached the queen. "The way up the mountain's clear," I began. "The three of you should have no problems."

"Three?" she repeated, arching a delicate silver brow. "We are five."

"Aeolmar and I will stay here," I said. "It's unlikely that Iruna will give up after sending only a dozen monsters after you. We have enough provisions for a few days, and we don't mind sleeping out. Mar and I will guard the path for you."

Asherah drew in a breath. "I don't like leaving my two best fighters behind."

"Are we the best? You still have Tor, and Priya."

"You will be too exposed here. What if there's a storm?"

"We can descend into the valley for shelter. Hells, we can take Iruna's estate and live like royalty, if we need to." I took Asherah's hands. "If you spend all your time looking over your shoulder, you'll never make it to the shrine. Let us guard the way for you."

"Are you doing this so you can flush out Iruna and murder her?"

"I'm doing this for you," I said, "but you already gave me permission to kill her. If I see her, I will. For Mara, and Sibeal, and me, and everyone else she's hurt."

"If you see her, or when?" Asherah asked.

"She hurt you too," I said, "and she's trying to hurt you even now. I am First Huntress, and I guard the queen from all enemies, no matter if they're demons or a king's daughter."

She pursed her lips, then she embraced me. "You are stubborn and insufferable, as is your mate. Very well, my huntress. Remain here and guard the trail, but I'm coming back for you as soon as this is done."

"I wouldn't want it any other way."

CHAPTER SIXTY-ONE

Aeolmar watched as Asherah, Tor, and Priya made their way farther up the trail. He'd been confident in his and Latera's plan to stay behind and guard the way for Asherah in order to give her the best chance to reach her goal, until the moment when their small party broke into two. Now, he worried he was sending them off to face untold dangers with two fewer people to protect them.

"I hope we're doing the right thing."

Latera slid her arm around his waist. "So do I."

Aeolmar kissed the top of his mate's head; she was so much smaller than him, yet she was easily as fierce. *Perhaps she's the fiercer of the two of us,* he thought, remembering how she'd killed the *mordeth-gall* and taken his horn. His mate was a true warrior, and he loved that about her.

"Should we wait on the trail, or descend into the valley?" he asked.

Latera looked toward the sky. "Clouds are gathering. We might have rain soon, so finding shelter is a good idea. Also, if there are more undead in the area I'd rather find them before they find us."

"Agreed." Aeolmar grabbed his horse's reins, and followed Latera down the trail that led deeper into the valley. It soon became apparent that the valley was larger than either of them had realized.

"This valley is enormous," Latera said. "It goes on all the way to the horizon."

"And look at the crops." From their vantage point Aeolmar could see vineyards, and fields of grain, and what looked to be several orchards filled with fruit trees. Coupled with the large lake and densely forested areas, one would hardly ever need to leave the valley.

"This valley has everything one could want to live a comfortable life," Aeolmar said. "No wonder Markham petitioned the Lord of Tingu for this land."

"Iruna has all of this, yet instead of enjoying her life in peace she seeks to make others miserable," Latera said. "If I had an estate like this for our family, I would never leave it."

"There are many homes like this in the westlands," Aeolmar said, smiling as he remembered the land he'd be born in. "Large homes surrounded by fresh water and farmland. Some families lived on and worked the same land for generations."

"Is that what your home was like?"

His jaw tensed, the only outward signal that his memories brought him pain and happiness in equal measure. "Yes, and no. We had a farm, but it wasn't an estate like this. Our house was small, and our family was one of the poorest in the area."

"But you were happy?"

"Yes. We were happy." Aeolmar reached for his mate, and wrapped an arm around her shoulders. "I wish you could have met them."

"Me, too." They walked together for a time, hand in hand, while scanning the valley for threats. They, and their horses, were the only ones about. "Would you like to go back to the west and set up another farm?"

He almost asked why they would want to do that, then he recalled the state of Teg'urnan. "Our next home doesn't have to be the west. As long as I'm with you, and close to our children, I'll be happy."

***

They completed their walk into the valley without incident, and were soon standing in front of the main estate. There was no gate or perimeter wall, but Aeolmar had noticed several watchtowers scattered throughout the valley. No one had attempted to hinder their descent, though he felt many sets of eyes watching them.

Latera jerked her chin toward the estate's doors. "Should we knock?"

Before Aeolmar could reply, the doors opened just enough for a woman to exit. Aeolmar couldn't tell if she was fae or elfin, but the way her eyes darted about told him she was nervous. She hurried toward the hunters, and curtsied.

"I am Graellyn, *saffira-nell* of this estate," she said in a rush. "Please, are you here to help us?"

Aeolmar glanced at Latera, who shrugged. Of all the things they'd expected, a plea for help was not one of them. "Why are you in need of assistance?" he asked.

"It's been a year and more since we've been left on our own," Graellyn, replied. "No messages, no instructions, nothing. Then earlier today, that terrible company she kept marched up to the trail, and ever since, we've been dreading what might happen next." Graellyn paused, and asked, "You didn't see them, did you?"

"We stopped them," Aeolmar replied. Graellyn gasped, and clasped her hands over her heart. "You're safe now."

"When you say she, do you mean Iruna?" Latera asked.

"Yes, yes, this is the Lady Iruna's estate," Graellyn replied. "She came here after all her other lands were seized, and we've never been the same since."

"Is she here now?" Latera asked.

"No, my lady. She left without a word as to where she was going, and we've been waiting on her return."

Waiting for her return and what else, I wonder. Out loud, Aeolmar said, "We are the First Hunter and Huntress of Parthalan, here on behalf of the king and queen. May we beg your hospitality?"

"Oh, yes, my lord," Graellyn said as she hurried them inside. "Let me call for a stable hand and we'll get your horses seen to, and I'll have rooms prepared for your stay."

"Just one room will do," Latera said. "We don't mean to impose on you."

Graellyn spun around so fast Aeolmar's hand went to his sword, but the *saffira-nell* only grabbed Latera's hands. "This is no imposition, my lady. We've needed help for quite some time."

"Call me Latera," she began, "and we are here to help. Please, tell us what you need."

"We need to know what's happened to us!"

***

Aeolmar had been prepared to deal with many situations at Iruna's estate. He hadn't expected to feel sympathy for the people Iruna had left behind.

Even though Graellyn insisted they needed help, the estate's staff appeared to be quite capable. Once they reached the main hall, Graellyn practically ordered that he and Latera rest and take some refreshment before they explored the rest of the property. And so the First Hunter and Huntress sat at the head of the table while Graellyn served them wine and bread, and the rest of the *saffira* peeked at them through the doorway.

"We don't bite," Latera said to a group of quiet, wide-eyed children who watched them from the far end of the hall. "Would you like to sit with us, and have something to eat? We've plenty to share."

Soon enough, all of the children crowded around Latera, laughing and talking as she passed them slices of fruit and bits of bread. Aeolmar loved watching her surrounded by children; as much as his mate was a warrior, she was also a caretaker, and it appeared that these children had been abandoned some time ago.

"Why are there so many children at the estate?" Aeolmar asked, when Graellyn stopped to refill his wine. "Do they belong to the *saffira*?"

"Would that they did," Graellyn replied. "They're all of them orphans from the villages."

"From down in Dremmsvard?"

Graellyn shook her head. "Not there. Our villages. Come, I'll show you."

Beloved. I'm going to see where the children are from.

Latera glanced at him, and smiled. *Be safe.*

Aeolmar returned her smile, then he followed Graellyn through the estate and out to a portico at the rear of the building. "There," she said, sweeping her arm toward a second, larger valley. "That's the smallest of the villages, Medla."

"Smallest?" Aeolmar repeated. This Medla was as large as some of the cities in the elflands. "How many more are there?"

"There are three villages of comparable size, and some farms scattered in between," Graellyn replied. "Many of these families were here long before King Markham set up his estate here, and he was good to all of us. When he died, he was mourned, but we were able to continue our way of life. Everything changed when she returned."

"Iruna was alone when she came back?"

"Not at first. Her brother accompanied her here, but they quarreled and he moved on. I don't know what became of him, but I believe that his departure drove Iruna truly mad."

"My mate would argue that she was always mad," Aeolmar said.

Graellyn nodded. "I suspect that to be true. Such madness and anger take time to fester in one's heart, and the Lady Iruna was as heartless as the come."

"Did she hurt you?" Latera asked, as she joined them. "Or the children?"

"She drove us out of our minds, then she drove us out of our bodies," Graellyn replied. "Somehow, she made us all compliant with every request she made. Of course we were beholden to follower her regardless, but the things... the things..." Graellyn covered her mouth and turned away. Latera took her into her arms, and the *saffira-nell* sobbed against Latera's shoulder.

Mar, what happened to them?

I don't know, but we will make things right.

***

After Graellyn got herself under control, she explained how Iruna enthralled first the people living in the estate and then the entire valley to do her bidding. No task was too difficult or too dangerous for them to undertake in order to please their lady, and soon the villagers began dying while carrying out Iruna's whims.

"And that's when she truly began tormenting us," Graellyn said. She had led them from the portico to a rock cut cellar many levels below the main floor. "This is where she kept the bodies, and where she made them walk again."

Frowning, Aeolmar examined what was inside the room. It held several wooden vats similar to those used in winemaking. He recalled the undeads' skin, and how it had appeared leathery and pickled, and realized that Iruna had been preserving corpses in these vats. Preserving them with what, he couldn't guess.

"Iruna was creating undead." Latera moved to go further into the room, but Aeolmar caught her arm. He didn't want his mate anywhere near whatever foul magic Iruna had subjected on the villagers. "How did she learn to do such a thing?"

"She may have hired a sorcerer," Aeolmar replied. "Graellyn, we will need to seal off this room. I don't know how to counteract such magics, and until we have a sorcerer nearby, we can trust I don't want to risk anyone else getting hurt."

"Yes, my lord," Graellyn said as she curtsied. "I'll arrange for a few masons to begin at once."

"Before you go," Aeolmar added, "have you any idea where Iruna's gone?"

"I'm afraid not," she replied. "She disappeared some time ago, though her walking corpses were still here, scaring us half to death."

"The corpses are gone, and I swear to you they'll never return," Aeolmar declared.

Graellyn curtsied again. "I've no doubt, my lord. Your arrival here gives us hope that The Deliverer will shine again." As Graellyn left, Aeolmar turned to his mate.

"These are Asherah's people," he said. "When Graellyn was showing me the villages, she told me that many of these families had been here since long before Markham."

"Then these are the people Asherah sought to protect from Olluhm." Latera ignited a puff of flame on her hand, and looked around the cellar. "For all that Iruna did evil things here, there is still room for good, and the people need a leader. Perhaps it now falls to us to protect them."

"What of your vengeance against Iruna?"

Latera shrugged. "Let someone else cut off her head. My days would be better spent caring for the children she orphaned."

Chapter Sixty-Two
Asherah Speaks

The three of us continued on up the mountain; at the rate I was hemorrhaging people I would be alone before long. That was my biggest fear about this mission, because me being alone likely meant I would not be strong enough to defeat Olluhm. I'd lost to him before, and that was when I understood and had access to all of my abilities. Now, with my barely remembered powers appearing and disappearing for unknown reasons, who knew what would happen.

Soon after we left Latera and Aeolmar behind, the weather took a turn for the worse. The temperature plummeted, and it began raining. We pushed on through the deluge, but I was worried about the horses. Near sun rest we came upon a pilgrim's hostel. It was empty, but the walls and roof were sound, and there was clean straw in the barn. Since we probably wouldn't find a better location, we settled in for the night.

In the morning, the sky was clear and I could see the shrine at the mountain's peak. It was a small structure made of bluish gray stone, with iron latticework over the windows. Right now the windows glowed an orange red, but I remember when Nyshanti had illuminated them with more colors than I could name.

"We're so close," I said. "We can make it there by noon, I'm sure of it."

"Best leave the horses here," Priya said. "That rocky terrain's no good for their hooves. We'll be better off without them, and they'll be happier here."

"I've just fed and watered them," Tor said as he exited the barn. "They'll be all right for a day, perhaps two."

I nodded. If we weren't able to make it back here in two days, we would probably be dead and the horses would need to fend for themselves. "Gear up. I want to get to that shrine as soon as possible."

Priya was right. The trail beyond the hostel was rocky and, thanks to yesterday's rain, slick. Tor fashioned us walking sticks from a few scraggly trees he found growing alongside the trail, and we trudged on.

And on.

The last leg of the trail wasn't long, but it was more difficult than the lower portion; by the end, we were all but scaling the mountainside like a pack of goats. I was also as stubborn and ornery as a goat, and nothing was going to keep me from reaching the shrine. We reached the plateau at the mountain's peak just as the child sun soared overhead. Olluhm was absent from the sky yet again.

"Look," Priya said, pointing upward. We were so far up the mountainside we could almost touch the sky. We could also see Solon's face as he passed over us.

"He looks like Caol'non," I murmured, not that I was surprised. The Prelates of Parthalan were directly descended from Solon. From all accounts, their strengths of both body and character were inherited from him.

Solon looked down, and frowned when he saw us standing at the edge of the plateau. "That doesn't bode well," Tor said. "I hope he doesn't think we've come to harm Cydia."

"He's probably wondering where his father's gotten to." I turned toward the shrine, and that was all it was now. The temple that once surrounded it was gone, whether due to it being exposed to the elements at the mountain's peak for all this time or Olluhm's fury, I didn't know. Two slabs of granite comprised the doors, and that was all that stood between me and my goal. "According to the legends, only the lodestone will open the doors."

Priya pressed the stone into my hand. "Go. It's your task, Deliverer. We'll guard your back."

I stared at the stone in my hand, then I spun on my heel and climbed the length of rocky steps that led to the shrine's door. For a moment, I stared at the closed doors, wondering why there weren't any handles, and if my journey ended there. Then I noticed a notch carved into one of the doors. On a whim, I set the lodestone in the notch.

It fit perfectly.

"The lodestone is the key," I murmured. I pushed open the doors, and gasped.

Standing in the center of the shrine was Olluhm.

Chapter Sixty-Three

Asherah Speaks

"Why are you here?" I demanded. "How did you get in?"

He pointed toward the ceiling, and I swore. The shrine had an oculus, which was how Nyshanti and Nu would ascend to the sky every day. I should have remembered that, but I'd only recently started remembering anything, and my recollections were jumbled.

"Where's Cydia?" I asked. Olluhm stepped aside, and I saw the moon goddess on the opposite side of the room, reclined on a cushioned bench. Her tawny hair and wide blue eyes remained unchanged, as did the pale gray gown she wore. Her ankles were shackled to the bench, much like they had once been shackled to the altar in Teg'urnan.

"Ish h'ra," Cydia spat. "You said you would come for me!"

"I'm here, aren't I," I replied; I understood that Cydia had been waiting for an age, but so had I. We could complain about how long we'd both waited for retribution once all of this was behind us. I turned to Olluhm, and said, "I've heard that you're on the hunt for the heir to the sun. Are you looking for the true heir, or all of your progeny?"

Olluhm smiled tightly, and I saw a hint of injury on his neck. Innetha had indeed hurt him, and I hoped it was very, very painful. "Ish h'ra, what do you mean to accomplish here?" he asked.

"My mission remains unchanged," I replied. "I am going to remove you from the sky and send you back to where you came from."

"What of Solon?" Cydia demanded. Olluhm glanced at her, irritated, and I noted his slow, jerking movements. Was that Innetha's doing, or a result of him clashing with the mortal sun?

"I have no quarrel with your boy," I replied, then I asked my enemy, "What's wrong with you?" Olluhm turned his glare toward me. "Did the mortal sun wound you so badly? Or was it my huntress?"

"Your huntress led me to the mortal realm for nothing," he seethed. "I went to the tiny human castle, and nothing magical was there."

"What did you do to them?" I demanded, fearful for Latera's people. "Does the castle still stand?"

"Humans are beneath me," he said with a pained shrug, and I remembered what Finlay had told me, about the chariot only generating power while it was in the sky, and how Innetha had described Olluhm's shock at not being able to share the sky with the mortal sun.

"You were too weak to harm them," I said, as his eyes widened. "You're still weak."

"The lodestone can kill him," Cydia said. Olluhm rounded on her, but she continued, "It's why he hid it with the elves. Like you, it was too powerful for him to destroy."

"Always hiding your failures instead of learning from them," I said, then to goad him further, I added, "Will you never learn, Ollie?"

Olluhm spun around and roared. I braced myself for the hot winds he'd assaulted me with in the past... and felt nothing. All he did was yell about how he was so much better than me.

While he ranted, I loosened my dagger and tossed it to Cydia. "Free yourself," I yelled, then I sprinted toward the door. I retrieved the lodestone from the keyhole as Olluhm's hand closed on the back of my neck.

"No, Ish h'ra," he growled, as his hand slid around to my throat. "Your time has ended. Your worshippers are no more. I am the true power here." He closed his fingers over my neck. I grabbed at his hands, but my vision was already going dark.

Light flashed from deep within me, and Olluhm screamed.

Olluhm flung me aside as he stepped back. Gasping, I looked toward him, and saw the skin on his hand was red and steaming.

"You burned him," Cydia said, as she ran past him to me. "Now, while he's wounded."

"Now what?" I rasped.

"Give me the lodestone," she said. "I will kill him, and avenge us all."

I didn't want to give Cydia the stone, but she snatched it from my hand and lunged toward Olluhm. He felled her with a single strike to the breast. Cydia's head struck the stone floor with a sickening crack.

"What have you done?" I shrieked, as I fell to my knees. Cydia's blood darkened her hair as her eyes stared blankly at the oculus above her. "How many times has she bled for you? You professed to love her, yet you hurt her most of all."

"No," Olluhm said, as he got to his feet. "I will hurt you most of all." He held his hand aloft, clutching the lodestone. Before my eyes, he crushed it to dust.

"Ish h'ra," he sneered. "The mighty Deliverer. Here you are, weeping on the floor yet again. You couldn't defeat me when thousands of Parthians chanted your name. What made you think you could defeat me now, when you have nothing?"

I wailed as my gaze darted to the open doors, wondering if I could get a warning to Tor and Priya in time for them to flee. Olluhm was right; I was weak, and alone.

Sher?

Finlay? I reached toward my mate with my mind. *Where are you?*

Where are you? he countered. *What's wrong?*

It's Olluhm. I can't—

You can. I believe in you. We all believe in you.

Finlay nudged my awareness beyond his mind, and I felt our son, my hunters, my soldiers... My people. All Parthians were my people, and it wasn't the cold, bitter elder sun they looked to in times of need.

It was me.

Ish h'ra, Hillel, Asherah. I have had many names, but I've always been The Deliverer.

I have always been stronger than Olluhm.

"Olluhm." I rose to my feet. "This ends here."

His lip curled. "As you wish," he said, then he opened his jaw and loosed his scorching winds toward me.

I raised a hand, and stopped them.

"No more," I said, while he stared, dumbfounded. "Your reign of terror is over. Parthalan is mine. It always has been."

My light came to the surface of my skin, and the rays struck Olluhm like so many golden darts. He screamed as they burned through his clothes, then flesh and bone. In a matter of moments, the man who'd tormented for so long me was nothing more than a pile of ash.

"What happened?" came a man's voice from behind me. Solon, the child sun and Olluhm and Cydia's eldest child, stood in the doorway. Unlike his father, he looked like a true solar god, what with his iridescent golden skin and shock of yellow hair, and eyes as blue and clear as the sky.

"Olluhm killed Cydia, and I killed him," I replied. Solon strode into the shrine without a glance toward his father's remains. Instead, he knelt at his mother's side, and took her hand.

"Do you know why I became the child sun, Ish h'ra?" he asked.

I knelt across from him, and took Cydia's other hand. "I don't."

"It was so I could keep him above, and away from the people. Away from my mother." A thick, golden tear slipped down his cheek and splashed onto Cydia's arm. "I couldn't stop him, and now she's gone."

"You did everything you could," I said. "Every Parthian knows what a good and noble man you are. Cydia taught you well."

He nodded, as more golden tears flowed down his cheeks. "Mother knew you'd stop him someday. She knew."

"She is the wisest woman I've ever known." I set her hand on her breast. "I will help you build her pyre."

"No need." He gathered her in his arms and stood. "I will take her where she needs to go. Goodbye, Ish h'ra."

I bowed my head, and watched the child sun carry his dead mother away. After he cleared the doorway, I saw someone else waiting for me.

Nyshanti.

CHAPTER SIXTY-FOUR

Priya wasn't a fan of waiting, yet it seemed like it was all she ever did. Now she stood at the bottom of the steps that led to the shrine alongside Tor, hoping Asherah knew what she was doing as she fought a god.

"She's been in there too long," Priya grumbled. "We should help."

"Patience, love," Tor said. He was always espousing the virtues of patience and careful, methodical planning when Priya would rather charge ahead and do something. It was maddening, mostly because he was always right.

"How patient were you when you regularly fought demons?" she asked. "Or did you wait so long they all wandered off out of boredom?"

"I killed thousands of foes in my day," he replied, unruffled. "However, my greatest conquest remains your sweet heart."

Tor always could disarm her, which was also maddening. "Who's to say I didn't conquer you first?" she countered, as he pulled her into his arms. Before he could make good on his intentions, a white-hot light burned behind her eyes, and Priya fell to the ground.

When she opened her eyes, she felt Asherah inside her mind. The fae goddess was smiling and happy, which made Priya assume she'd won her fight in the shrine. She rolled to her side, which was painful due to her having landing on the stone steps. Tor was sprawled out beside her, his breathing ragged.

"Tor? Tor," she said, her heart in her throat as she shook him awake. "Tor!"

"I'm here, I'm here," he said, then he swore as he felt his back. "Why are we on the ground?"

"Asherah was in my mind again." She wrapped her arms around him, and laid her cheek on his chest. "Wake faster, next time."

"Worried for me?" he said, as he smoothed her hair. He went rigid underneath her, and moved to rise. "Eyes up."

Priya scrambled to her feet, and saw what had alerted Tor. Solon, the child sun, was directly overhead and hurtling toward the shrine.

"What should we do?" she asked. "Have you ever met him before?"

"I've no idea what to do, other than to be respectful. And no, we've never met."

Solon's chariot landed soundlessly in the small courtyard between the shrine and the steps. He disembarked from his chariot, and fixed his gaze on Priya and Tor.

"Are you here with him?" Solon demanded.

"We're with Ish h'ra," Tor replied. "The Deliverer holds our loyalty."

Solon nodded, then he entered the shrine. Relieved, Priya slumped against Tor.

"Glad he didn't kill us," she murmured.

"That's not Solon's way. He's the best of the fae." He pulled Priya close and kissed her hair. They held each other for a time, and Priya hoped Tor's assessment of Solon was correct.

"It's not dark," Priya said, after a time. "There are no suns in the sky, yet it's still light out."

"We don't need to be aloft for the light to shine," Solon said, startling Priya as he exited the shrine with a woman's body in his arms. Priya lurched forward, but Tor held her back.

"That's not Asherah," Tor murmured against her skin. Louder, he said, "My condolences, my lord."

Solon acknowledged him with a graceful nod. "Thank you. My father will trouble you no longer." He turned to leave, and paused.

"I will share a secret with you," Solon continued. "Neither I nor my father have ever turned night into day. We don't need to be in the sky for daylight to exist."

"Thank you," Priya said, not knowing how else to reply. Solon dipped his chin toward her, then he stepped onto the chariot and departed. Before Priya could appreciate that a god had just shared a few facts with her, a woman ascended the steps to the courtyard. She was beautiful, with dark skin and deep golden hair, and eyes that flashed in the rosy shades of dawn and twilight. And, Tor knew her.

"Torim?" he asked, disbelief plain in his voice. "Or would you prefer I call you Nyshanti?"

"You may call me whatever you'd like, my friend," Nyshanti replied. "It is good to see you again."

"I never hoped to lay eyes on you again, yet here you are," Tor said.

"I've been waiting," Nyshanti replied. "Is she inside?"

"She is."

Nyshanti smiled shyly, and entered the shrine. Priya watched her disappear, then she hugged Tor a bit tighter. "It's like we're here to bear witness to the gods."

"An elf, talking about gods," he said. "And the Lady of Thurnda, at that."

"I will never be the Lady," she said. "I'm nothing like Sibeal. Let Latera or one of her girls be the next Lady. If we want to rule a land, we can go home to Tarac."

"What about staying on with Asherah?"

Priya rested her head against his shoulder. "We could do that, too."

Chapter Sixty-Five
Asherah Speaks

"Torim! Nyshanti," I said, as both a cry and a wail. She was standing in front of me, alive and solid and here. My first love was standing right in front of me. "You're here!"

"I'm here," she replied, and I fell into her arms as I had so many times before. "I've missed you so much, Hillel."

"I didn't know you were trapped in another realm," I said, tears blurring my vision. "If I'd known, I would have come for you."

"You don't need to say such things," Nyshanti said. "I know your heart, and how you long to keep everyone safe within it. I was content to wait for you."

Of course she was content, because she was gentle, and kind, and everything that was good in the world. Nyshanti had always been patient where I was rash, and level-headed when I would have rushed straight into danger. She balanced me, and completed me. Only now, thanks to her long absence from my life, someone else had taken on that role.

"I have a mate now, and a son," I told her. "They're both called Finlay."

She smoothed back my hair and kissed my forehead. "Your huntress told me. Do I get to meet them?"

"Of course you do." I pressed my face against her warm, real, solid shoulder. "Of course you do."

As much as I would have preferred spending the rest of the day in Nyshanti's arms, there was work to be done. Between the two of us, we incinerated Olluhm's remains with our light. Now nothing would remain of the cruel man who so desperately wanted to be a god. When that awful task was done, we exited the shrine, and found Tor and Priya anxiously waiting for us.

"Everything's good?" Tor asked.

"Olluhm is no more," I replied. "But not before he murdered Cydia."

Tor nodded. "We saw Solon take her body. Should we return to the valley, and inform Aeolmar and Latera of what happened?"

"We should." I faced Nyshanti. "How far can you go from the shrine?"

"I'm not sure," she replied. "Before, I could go as far as I needed to, but now things are different."

I smiled tightly, because she was right. Many, many things were different. "Can you go as far as the valley? Or down to Dremmsvard?"

Nyshanti returned my smile, and it was as if the sun rose in her eyes. "Yes. I believe I can."

We began our descent down the mountain, and stopped at the pilgrim's waystation to collect our bored horses. Of course, we were now four riders and therefore a horse short, but before I could speak, Tor handed his reins to Nyshanti, and mounted up behind Priya. Our traveling arrangements thus sorted, we continued on to Iruna's estate.

When we arrived there, we found the First Hunter and Huntress waiting for us on the trail, and the estate's owners were still nowhere to be found.

"She's not here, and neither is her brother," Latera said, before we even had a chance to dismount. "Mar and I have scoured the estate and talked to dozens of her *saffira*. Iruna fled about a year ago, and Avinor left long before that. Coincidentally, Senan met Cerillia a little more than a year ago." I dismounted as Latera stopped for breath. "We saw Solon fly down to the temple. What happened?"

"He's gone, as is Cydia. She tried to save me, but Olluhm killed her, then I killed him." Latera's brow pinched, and she pulled me into her arms.

"I'm so sorry you had to do that," she said, as she held me tightly. "For all that you're Asherah the Ruthless, I know how heavily each death weighs on you." I nodded and stepped back, wiping my eyes.

"And Nyshanti," I began, then Latera rushed forward to embrace my oldest, dearest friend. Latera had interacted with Nyshanti many times when she was confined to the temple in the mortal realm, and was almost as pleased to see her in solid form as I was.

"Hello, huntress," Nyshanti said, as she patted Latera's back.

"You're real." Latera held her at arm's length, marveling at Nyshanti's tangible form. "How is this possible?"

Nyshanti smiled, and dawn's colors flashed across the sky. "With The Deliverer, all things are possible."

After we'd all caught up and shared news, we descended to the valley's estate. We still weren't sure how far Nyshanti could travel from her shrine, and we decided to spend the night at the estate and continue on to Dremmsvard in the morning. The home itself was a veritable castle set in the middle of verdant farmland. One could relocate to such an estate and live a very good life while needing little from the outside world.

"And you believe the *saffira*?" I asked Aeolmar. Over supper he'd relayed how the people had been treated by Iruna. According to him and Latera, they had been unaware of their lady's true agenda.

"I do," Aeolmar replied. "Based on what they've told us, Iruna and Avinor relocated here after they were stripped of their titles. Soon after their arrival all of the *saffira* went into a docile, non-questioning state. Their bodies did whatever she asked of them, regardless of how they felt about her requests."

"More enthrallment," Tor said. "It seems we have a rogue sorcerer loose."

"There's more," Aeolmar said, and I sighed. When isn't there more? When I motioned for him to continue, he said, "They've also told us about visitors from Krylle's temple, and the mortal realm. We now have absolute confirmation that Iruna was behind Krylle and Cerillia."

I blew out a breath, and drank some wine. "My biggest mistake may be not letting Latera execute Iruna all those years ago."

"I disagree," Latera said. "Iruna is the cause of many, many problems, but you did the right thing. She twisted your mercy into vengeance, but that's on her. And now Tor, Priya, and Nyshanti are returned to us. Iruna is a villain, but by following your heart, you have always been on the side of goodness, and good things came of your actions."

Nyshanti leaned close to me, and said, "I like your huntress."

"I do, too," I agreed, then I asked Latera, "You see the best in everything, don't you?"

Aeolmar wrapped his arm around Latera, and kissed her hair. "She does."

"About this estate," I continued. "What should we do with it?"

Latera shrugged. "We could live in it."

"Here?"

"Teg'urnan's a pile of rubble," Aeolmar said, "and we now know it was built by a madman in order to keep a woman hostage. Perhaps it's time to start over somewhere new."

"More like somewhere old," Nyshanti said. "We were always in the north, before the wars began. It was Olluhm who wanted the southern lands, and you only went there to stand against him. Before he fought you, the Northern Wasteland was as green and fertile as this valley."

"It was," I said, memories of green meadows and dark, quiet forests filling my mind's eye. "Back when the trolls lived above ground."

"Grelk, in the sunlight?" Latera shook her head. "I don't believe it."

"Believe it," Nyshanti said, and we spent the rest of the day sharing stories about the halcyon days before Olluhm set his sights on Parthalan. By the time we retired for the evening, I thought Latera might be right, and the north would be a wonderful place for all of my people.

The next morning we left our warm valley, and made the descent to Dremmsvard. We found Innetha and Elkin holding court at the inn as competently as any landowners I'd ever known. Remaining in the north was looking like a better option by the moment.

The eight of us settled into our new and unexpected lives in Dremmsvard, and began running Parthalan from the inn's common room. Our first order of business was to send messages across the land, informing the people of my location and reassuring them that even though the elder sun and the moon had vanished from the skies, all was well. Solon had returned to his daily trek across the sky as the single sun, but I did wonder if he would bring up one of his own children to keep him company.

As for the lack of the moon, at least we had the stars to light our nights.

A moon passed in the blink of an eye, then one day a scout ran to the inn seeking me. There was a party of four on the trail; two men and two women, though one of the men had pale hair like mine. Excitement dancing upon my skin, I ran out to the courtyard and met my boys and their mates.

"Finn," I cried, and he smiled at me from on horseback. Then Leran dismounted, and I was in his arms, and we were smiling and weeping and had I ever been so happy?

"How are things in Thurnda?" I asked, once I'd gotten myself under control. I still wasn't used to these happy reunions with Leran, and I wanted to savor each one for as long as possible. "Who's overseeing it?"

"For now, I am," Leran replied. "Aldo sent many of his advisors from The Seat. Once a new Lady is named, we will have a better idea of how things will look."

"Who will be the new Lady?" I asked, as I craned my neck to the side. "What is taking Finn so long to get off his horse? Is it his leg?"

"His leg is fine." I glanced up and saw Leran's face split by the widest grin I'd ever seen him wear, then he stepped aside. Behind him, Ember was helping both Finn and Mara dismount, and there was much shuffling between the three of them concerning two tiny bundles. The Finn turned around, and I saw the two babies he held.

His babies.

"They're here," I gasped, amazingly even happier than I'd been a moment ago. Then Finn placed them in my arms, and it was a wonder my heart didn't burst. One baby had pale blond curls like Finn, while the other was auburn-haired like Mara. "I didn't think it had been long enough."

"It hasn't," Mara said, coming to stand beside Finn. "Whatever power you gave Finn somehow affected them. They started growing faster and faster, as if they couldn't wait to see the world."

"They're perfect," I said, gazing at their tiny sleeping faces. "What are their names?"

Mara glanced sidelong at Finn, and said, "We're working on that. Your son wants to call them Walnut and Snowflake."

"For their hair," Finn said.

"No," Mara said.

"Not Walnut," Ember said. "We're calling that one Ember."

"No," Mara said again, this time making a cutting motion with her hand. "No more repeated names. It's too confusing."

"What's too confusing?" Aeolmar asked, as he and Latera joined us. I passed the babies to him, and watched as the stoic First Hunter melted over his grandchildren. Then they were with Latera, and then Mara, and by then everyone else had come out to see what all the commotion was about. Before long each and every one of us had held the babies, some for a mere moment like Innetha, others for much, much longer. It was safe to say that the twins were already well loved by all of us.

Later that evening, we gathered in the common room as we usually did for our evening meal. The twins were sleeping contentedly on Tor's chest, even through the roaring chaos that was typical of one of our meals. As I looked around the room at family and friends that I loved so dearly, I only had one thought.

I wished Finlay was with me.

"We've also had word that the moon crashed into the sea," Leran told us, as he relayed the news from the rest of the realm.

"Did it," I murmured. "That must have happened shortly after Cydia died."

"Apparently it caused a catastrophic wave near Ysr," Ember said, continuing the story. They complemented each other so well, and I was glad they'd found each other. "Reports from the south indicate Nu has evacuated the island's population to the mainland."

"Interesting." I wondered if Nu would bring his people back to Dremmsvard, and reclaim his place in the sky.

"We should discuss Thurnda," Aeolmar said, because it was like him to ruin a perfectly happy mood with talk of work.

"By rights, you are the next Lady," Leran said, with a nod toward Priya.

"True, but I worry I cannot lead the land as well as my mother or Sibeal ever did," Priya said. "I get itchy feet, and need to go on walks. The Lady needs to be in Thurnda, for her people."

"Why can't Tingu oversee Thurnda?" Finn asked. "Ember is also Sibeal's heir, and she's already the Lady of Tingu. It could work."

"It could," I said. "All the elflands were once as one, with the hereditary titles no more than names on a scroll. What do you say, Priya? Will you be the Lady in name only?"

She bowed her head. "I can do that. If Leran approves, of course."

"You know I will," he added. "I'll send a message to Aldo in the morning."

"I'll let you all in on a secret," I said. "Aldo is the real power in the elflands. No one would dare to defy him."

Leran laughed. "That is true."

***

Four months to the day after we met our grandchildren, Latera and I stood at the bottom of the mountain in the center of the road that led to the village.

"I can't believe they're almost here," Latera said. I squeezed her hand, too excited to speak. She was excited, too, but for a slightly different reason. Our Parthians were almost here. Latera would be reunited with her son and sisters, as I would finally be with my mate again.

"I see them," Latera said, then she ran down the road toward the approaching people. I should have done the same, but part of me was too terrified to move. What if they weren't really here, and were only a mirage? A trick of the light? Iruna's last spell?

Then Finlay was there, cresting the last rise in the road with our people fanned out behind him; some were in carriages, and some were on horseback, but not him. The King of Parthalan walked at the head of the procession as he led our people away from their ruined home, and toward a better life.

As he approached me, I made out the details of his appearance. His hair was the same deep black curls, though it was longer than usual, and the warm golden skin on his neck was scarred from the burns Olluhm had inflicted upon him. But his summer blue eyes hadn't changed at all, and neither had his smile.

My king, my mate, my man from the desert. He was here.

"We would have been here sooner, but we had quite far to go," Finlay began once we were close enough to speak, then I closed the distance between us and ran into his arms.

"I missed you so much," I said with my face pressed against his neck.

"I missed you too, Sher." He drew back, and tucked a length of hair behind my ear. "We're all here, just as you wanted. What do we do next?"

"I... don't know." I hadn't thought one moment beyond my reunion with Finlay. "I suppose we can do anything we want."

"As long as we're together," he added.

"Yes, beloved," I said. "Together we can do anything."

Epilogue

The first few days after Finlay brought the remaining residents of Teg'urnan to Dremmsvard were filled with reunions and chaos and a few less than ideal sleeping arrangements. Aeolmar loved every moment of it.

Leran and Ember had returned from The Seat to assist with moving Parthalan's capital to Dremmsvard. Through Grelk and his endless resources, Leran had found a sorcerer who remembered how to construct portals, which meant Ember could visit her family whenever she liked. So far, a sennight hadn't passed without her coming by. As for his other children, they had taken up residence near him and Latera in Iruna's repurposed estate. Mara, along with Finn and their children, had chosen rooms near the garden, and Tor picked an apartment close to the stables. As for the elder Tor, he and Priya had set themselves up in rooms near Aeolmar's on the upper floor.

"You have five generations of your family in this home," Latera said, as she slid her arms around his waist. They were standing in the walled courtyard, where the estate's orphans were playing a game that involved them running from one side to the other. Aeolmar didn't think there were any rules to this game, but based on the amount of laughter he heard they didn't need any.

"And you have all of us, and all your sisters." Aeolmar wrapped his arm around her shoulders. "Although Caol'non will be going to the temple with Atreynha soon, along with the rest of the priestesses."

"I think it's wonderful that Atreynha will return the temple to its original purpose as a place dedicated to The Deliverer," Latera said. "And Caol'non can train a new generation of *con'dehr*."

"Tor's already expressed an interest in helping him," Aeolmar said, his voice flush with pride. His son was proud to be a descendant of Solon, and wanted to take up the family legacy as a temple guard. As for how they were also descended from Olluhm, they didn't talk about that much.

"What about you?" Latera asked. "Are you content to remain First Hunter, or would you also like to embrace your legacy?"

"For now I'm content to stay here with you, and help you raise the estate's children," he replied. "However, they won't be children forever."

"I know. They'll grow quickly, as all children do." She tightened her arms around him, proving that she understood what he'd left unsaid. "And Iruna's still out there, hurting who knows how many people. When the children are grown, we'll go after Iruna, and stop her."

Aeolmar kissed Latera's forehead. "We will, and in doing so we'll make the world safer for all of our children."

***

Asherah and Finlay stood in the small courtyard in front of the shrine, watching as Nyshanti ascended to the sky by way of the oculus. "She's always gone straight up like that?" Finlay asked, shielding his eyes against the bright sunlight as he watched her climb higher.

"Always," Asherah replied. On this day, Nyshanti was going to speak with her mother, Clea, who had come back to Dremmsvard after Olluhm's demise. Asherah was hopeful that Nu and the others would soon return, as well. "I once did, as well."

"And now?"

She gave him a sheepish grin. "I can't remember how to fly."

"Do you miss it?"

"A bit," she admitted. "But to be honest, there's more for me on the ground."

Finlay laced his fingers with hers. "What, you think I wouldn't fly with you?"

Asherah laughed, because she knew Finlay would do anything for her, just as she would do anything for him. "We still need to decide where we want to live."

"Down in Dremmsvard would be the most convenient," he began, "although Elkin and Innetha have effectively taken over. Would you have ever pictured those two as town administrators?"

"Never," she replied. "And I wouldn't want to get in their way."

"Then we could stay here, in your temple," Finlay continued, "or in the valley with Aeolmar and Latera."

"Neither of those options seem right," Asherah said. "I feel like we should go somewhere new. Not someplace far, because our people need us, but a new place that's only ours. After all, this is a new chapter of our lives."

Finlay kissed the back of her hand, then he pulled her into his arms. "All right, then. Tomorrow, we'll start looking."

Asherah laid her head on Finlay's shoulder. She had no idea where their search would take them, or what they would find along the way, but for the first time in many years she knew who she was, and where she was supposed to be. She was The Deliverer, and Parthalan was hers to protect. It always had been.

***

Author's Note

Well, here we are at the end of book six! It's been a wild ride since Asherah escaped the *doja* way back in Heir to the Sun, and it looks like she finally has her happy ending.

But is this the end?

No, not by a long shot.

There's still a lot left to do. Mara and Finn need to raise the twins, Atreynha needs to reestablish The Deliverer's temple with Caol'non at her side, and Innetha and Elkin are running an entire village. Add to that Ember and Leran taking on rulership of all the elflands, Latera's sisters acclimating to life in Parthalan, and Wren and Gilson navigating a new life together, and the struggles our heroes have yet to face seem almost endless.

And there's the biggest unanswered question of them all: Iruna.

What I'm saying, friends, is that Parthalan has many more stories to tell. Thank you for coming on the journey with me this far, and I hope you'll join me for the rest.

For now, if you haven't already picked up *Pieces of Parthalan*, now is a great time to do it. It features six all-new stories ranging from what

Caol'nir and Alluria's lives were like before they met, to Aeolmar's legendary (in his opinion) stand against the orcs. One of those stories, Fettered, begins on the next page. You can get the entire collection in print or ebook here: https://books2read.com/PiecesOfParthalan

Happy reading!

FETTERED

OR, HOW
INNETHA AND ELKIN
LEARNED TO BE TOGETHER

Fettered, Part One

These events take place during Book Two, The Virgin Queen. Innetha is one of my very favorite characters, and I enjoyed delving deeper into her past. As for Elkin, he was supposed to be a one-off bit character, but he wouldn't stop talking. I'm glad he didn't.

***

Elkin lifted a bale of straw onto his shoulder and headed toward the stable. Even though he commanded the Northern Contingent of hunters, he reckoned only a poor leader would refuse to do the same work as his men, and Elkin always did his fair share. His father had taught him that a good man puts in a good day's work each and every day, and Elkin followed him to the letter.

That was where the similarities between Elkin and the man who sired him ended. For all that he respected his father, he refused to spend his life as a cobbler, surrounded by piles of worn boots and slippers while hunched over a workbench. Elkin wanted to spend his days in sunlight, and he wanted more adventure than his home village of Savey could offer. When Elkin declined to learn the family trade, his father turned him out and told him not to come back until he changed his mind. That had been many winters ago, and Elkin had only occasionally returned to Savey, and then only to visit his mother. His father preferred it that way, too.

He was still reminiscing about his last visit home when he felt it, the tickle at the back of his mind that told him she was near. The bale slid off Elkin's shoulder as he turned and watched her approach.

Innetha.

She was riding a horse he didn't recognize, not the one she'd ridden when he brought her to Teg'urnan eight winters past to help the queen track a *mordeth*. As for the huntress herself, even from a distance, Elkin noticed her pale skin, her disheveled clothes. The feeling in his mind was of her sadness, and exhaustion. When Innetha saw him, it changed to relief.

Innetha reined in her horse, slid off the saddle and ran across the clearing and into his arms. Elkin held her tightly, his face pressed against her hair as her shoulders trembled.

"What happened?" he asked. When she only sobbed harder, he continued, "Are you hurt?"

"Olwynn." Innetha drew back, and he saw the tears on her cheeks. "He died."

Elkin's jaw clenched, his only betrayal. He'd heard that Innetha and Olwynn had become mates, and had specifically not thought further about the situation. "When? How?"

"We went to Nibika, to fight against Natreus," she began. "We were separated during the battle, and... And now I'll never see him again."

A fresh tear coursed down her cheek. Elkin wiped it away with his thumb.

"I heard Nibika was a victory," he said.

"It was, but at great cost." She dashed her hand across her eyes. "A great, great cost."

Elkin squeezed her fingers. "Go to my room and rest. I'll come get you for supper."

Innetha nodded, and without another word she unfastened her pack from the saddle and walked toward the Northern Contingent's keep. Elkin hoisted the bale of straw onto his shoulder again and grabbed her horse's reins, and brought both into the stable. He paused before the stable's entrance and watched Innetha enter the keep. Her walk was confident, the walk of someone who belonged here. Of someone who was at home in the north.

The north will never again be home to Innetha. If only it were.

Elkin entered the stable and dropped the bale onto the pile with the rest, then he started removing the tack from her horse. Wynnstead, Elkin's second, entered the stable.

"I see our Innetha's back," he said.

"Our?" Elkin removed the saddle and balanced it on the edge of a stall.

"I'm joking," Wynnstead said, clapping Elkin's shoulder. "Everyone knows she only has eyes for you. Unnatural behavior for a nymph, but there you have it."

Elkin grunted, then he grabbed a cloth and set about rubbing down the horse. "It's not like that between us," he said. "She took another as her mate."

"What? Who?"

"Olwynn. One of the *con'dehr*. He fought at Nibika, didn't make it."

"I'll be sure to offer my condolences," Wynnstead said. "But you must wonder why, when he died, she came to you."

Wynnstead left the stable. Elkin continued rubbing down the horse, but he admitted Wynnstead was right. He did wonder why Innetha was here. He'd been so happy to see her he hadn't questioned her motivations, but now he wondered: why had Innetha returned to the keep?

***

After the horse had been watered and fed, and the rest of the straw bales packed away in the loft, Elkin entered his room. He'd debated leaving Innetha alone with her thoughts, but that would be a cruelty. Innetha was a nymph on her mother's side, which accounted for her amazing tracking abilities. On more than once occasion Innetha's affinity with the land had made all the difference during a hunt, and more hunters than he could count owed her their gratitude.

Another aspect of her nymph blood meant that Innetha needed contact with others. It could be as fleeting as a caress, or something much more intimate, but without regular physical contact, she withered away like a flower denied sunlight. He recalled how fragile she'd felt in his arms, and wondered if she'd travelled the entire way from Nibika alone and was close to becoming touch starved.

He eased the door shut, and his gaze fell on the heap of her discarded clothing. He frowned and stepped around the pile, and found Innetha lying in his bed with her back to him. She'd put on one of his shirts, and he didn't know if that pleased him or if he wished she was bare.

He shook his head. She was a mated woman, and for all that her mate had died, he still shouldn't be imagining her naked in his bed or anywhere.

Elkin sat on the edge of the bed. Innetha rolled over and faced him, her dark hair fanned around her head and wide brown eyes rimmed in red. "I'm sorry."

"Thank you." Innetha took his hand, held it against her cheek. Before his eyes, a flush of pink returned to them. He'd been correct, then; she was touch starved.

"Innetha, why are you here?"

She laced her fingers with his. "I can't go back to Teg'urnan. Not right now, not with him so newly gone."

"Does Asherah know you're here?"

"Aeolmar does," she replied. "Asherah's too busy with her wounded mate to worry about where I am."

Elkin's brow pinched. "Asherah took a mate?"

"Yes. Finlay, the merchant from Cadogan."

Elkin remembered the fight in the desert village, and the brave shopkeeper. "He's a hunter now?"

"You really need to poke your head out of the keep more often," Innetha replied. "Finlay is Aeolmar's second. He nearly died as well." Innetha turned toward the wall. "While I was trying to save Finlay, Olwynn lay dying. Or maybe he was already dead by then. I'll never know."

"You haven't answered me." Elkin smoothed back her hair. "Why are you here?"

"Because you're here."

Elkin almost spoke, then thought the better of it. She was hurting, and he didn't want to add to that with his petty feelings of betrayal.

"I'll send one of the lads by with food," he said as he stood. "Get some rest."

He made sure he was in the corridor before she had the chance to speak.

***

The next day Elkin woke before first dawn. As always, there was much to do around the keep, and Elkin began by walking the boundary ditch. They'd never flooded the ditch—at least, it hadn't been flooded since Elkin arrived—and truth be told, he didn't think a moat was much of a deterrent against a demon. Although, watching them skidding across the ice next winter might be amusing.

Again, he felt her before he saw her. "I trust you slept well?"

"Why didn't you come to bed?" she countered.

"I'm not in the habit of lying with bound women," he said over his shoulder. When her only response was silence, he turned around. Innetha had left her hair loose, and she had more color in her cheeks than when she'd arrived. She was wearing her hunter's gear along with the shirt of his she'd claimed yesterday, and he couldn't explain how he felt about that.

"Olwynn and I weren't bound," she said at length. "It... it wasn't like that."

"You didn't love him?"

"I did. I do. But a binding is forever, and we were still new to one another." She took a step closer to him. "I don't regret taking him as a mate. It was what we both needed."

"If you needed a mate—"

Elkin turned around and resumed walking the boundary.

"Why are you so angry with me?" she called.

"You lied to me, and you promised you'd never do that!"

Innetha caught up to him and grabbed his forearm. "I have never lied to you!"

"You did, just now," he replied. "You say you don't regret things but I can feel it on you!"

Innetha stilled, her hand motionless on his arm. "What do you mean, you can feel it?"

"So you admit."

"Elkin. How do you know what I'm feeling?"

He shrugged, thus breaking contact with her. "I've always been able to feel you, ever since we said our goodbyes that day at Teg'urnan. I know when you're near, when you're happy or sad..."

Innetha moved in front of him, so close he could see the green and gold flecks in her brown eyes. "You know when I'm near?"

"And far. It feels different." Elkin raised his hand, his palm hovering over the base of his skull. "I don't see pictures or hear words, but the feeling of you is here."

"Elkin, you shouldn't be able to do that," she said, shaking her head. "That's something mates experience, not people like us."

Mates? Elkin looked at her, the only woman he'd never been able to get out of his mind. "How is that possible?" he asked. "Did you ever feel Olwynn?"

"No." She stepped closer, slipped her arms around his neck. "Show me?"

"How?"

Even as he asked the question, his eyes closed, and he searched for the feeling of her at the back of his mind. He set his hands on Innetha's waist and pulled her toward him until his forehead rested against hers. He gathered each and every sensation he had about Innetha and pushed them toward her.

"Oh," Innetha gasped. She felt it too, then. "You're angry with me?"

"I... no."

"You are." She placed her palm against his cheek. He opened his eyes. "Tell me why. Please."

He gritted his teeth and squeezed his eyes shut. Just as she'd promised she'd never lie to him, he was unable to keep the truth from her. "I'm angry you took a mate. I'm angry it couldn't be me."

"Why can't it be you?"

"It wasn't, was it?" He broke away from her. "Should we really be having this conversation? Your last mate's hardly cold and you're already looking for your next bed warmer?"

Innetha slapped him so hard his ears rang. "You're right. We shouldn't speak."

She turned on her heel and walked away from him. He wanted to call after her, but if his men heard him calling her name... No, best to let her go. He was good at letting her go.

***

Elkin took his time walking the rest of the boundary ditch before he returned to the keep. Even then, he didn't head straight for the structure, instead stopping by the stable. Inside he found Leofstan; if Wynnstead was Elkin's right hand, Leofstan was his left.

"Any word on your cousin?" Elkin asked. Leofstan's cousin had gone missing nearly two moons past, and none of the hunters or Elkin's contacts had been able to locate him.

"Nary a whisper," Leofstan replied. "Fear not. I will make my family whole again. About Innetha."

"What about her?" Elkin snapped.

"Wynn told me she was back," Leofstan replied, ignoring Elkin's tone. "She couldn't stay away too long, eh?"

Elkin's shoulders tensed. Of course Leofstan remembered when Innetha had first stayed here; he'd been the Northern Contingent's commander less than a season, and suddenly the new man in charge had a new woman in his room. Leofstan must also remember how inseparable they were, how Innetha ad Elkin spent every day together and never quarreled.

"It's not like it was before." Elkin rubbed his cheek. It still stung. "Things have changed."

"So what's it like now?" Leofstan asked.

Elkin looked toward where he'd last seen her. "I don't know yet."

Fettered, Part Two

Innetha Speaks

I stormed away from Elkin, mad and hurt and most of all, humiliated. Of all people, Elkin should understand me! I wasn't looking for a mate just now, or even someone to share my bed for a night. I only sought to understand why he could feel me, and I'd always learned best by touch. Elkin knew that.

And what had touching Elkin revealed? His anger, his fear I'd left him in the past, his deep affection for me. None of that had been a surprise, not really, but it didn't explain why Elkin could feel me in the first place. And why couldn't I feel him in return?

I recalled when I first met Elkin. I'd been newly escaped from Griselle, my former employer, who became my captor. After I'd gotten free of Griselle's estate, I made my way to the nearby village of Stonekeep and took shelter at the inn. I was warming myself near the common room's fire when a hunter strode into the room.

I wasn't surprised to see the fae demon hunter; after all, the village took its name from the nearby keep the hunters occupied. I was surprised by the set of this hunter's shoulders. From the way they slumped, something had gone poorly. That had likely been a demon hunt, and hunting was something I could help him with. I hoped that by assisting this hunter, I could earn some coin and leave this dismal northern waste behind.

I approached the hunter and claimed the stool next to his. "Bad day?" I asked.

"Yes." He glanced at me, and up close I noticed his sharp gray eyes that likely took in every detail. His brown hair was haphazardly tied back, and while he wasn't much taller than me, his broad shoulders and the sword at his hip made him look the part of a warrior. I hoped he could act the part, as well.

Satisfied with whatever he saw in me, he signaled the innkeeper. A moment later, two mugs of ale were set on the bar in front of us. "You like ale?"

"I do, but I have no way to pay for it," I replied.

"Where I'm from, a man buys a woman her ale. The first mug, at least," he added with a wink.

"Where are you from? Perhaps I should travel to this land of free ale."

"Western Parthalan. And only the first is without cost," he added.

"Hmm. What's a man from the warm and gentle west doing in the cold, dreary north?"

"Buying ale, for starters." He jerked his chin toward the mug in front of me. "The only payment I'll accept is your name."

"Innetha." I drew the mug closer. "Thank you, hunter."

"I'm Elkin, and you're welcome." He raised his mug; a moment later I followed suit, and we drank together. "How did you know I'm a hunter?"

"You have the look of one," I replied. "Tell me what went wrong with your recent hunt."

"How did you—" He shook his head, and continued, "I was tracking a demon. It was a big one, maybe a *mordeth*, and I lost it."

"So you came here to drown your sorrows?"

"I came here to find a better tracker than me," he replied. "I've only been with my contingent a short while, and I can't let word get back to Teg'urnan that I let a demon escape. I need to find this beast before it causes any more havoc. The sooner the better."

"You're in luck, Elkin of the west, because I can track anything." I finished the ale and set my mug on the bar. "Should we leave now?"

"You're a tracker?" he asked, looking over my attire. I was still wearing what I'd escaped in: a blue silk blouse, both too thin for the climate and too tight for comfort, and a full blue skirt made of many gauzy layers. I'd grabbed a green and gold vest on my way out of Griselle's manor as my only defense against the cold, and a pair of soft black boots. It wasn't a bad or inappropriate ensemble, but I looked more like a courtesan than someone who knew her way around a trail. If only he'd seen what I'd been wearing before I filched these clothes.

"I am the best tracker you'll ever meet, and I will find this demon for you," I said. "You have my word."

Elkin grunted and frowned at my boots. They were rather flimsy. "What sort of payment are you after?"

"Leave it for after you've dealt with this demon," I said. "Shall we?"

Elkin drained his mug, then he set it and a few coins on the bar. "Let's be off."

***

Soon enough, Elkin and I were astride his horse, and he brought me to where he'd last seen the demon. It was a clearing in the wood, bordered by a stream.

"There." Elkin pointed toward the water. "It went into the stream, and that's where I lost it."

"Then here is where I begin," I said.

Elkin swung himself down from the saddle, then he reached up to help me dismount. I quashed my short comeback; I'd been riding since I could walk, but he didn't know that. More, this hunter was helping me with more than just dismounting. This hunt was putting distance between me and Griselle's estate. The farther away I got from her, the better.

Once he'd seen me safely to the forest floor, I approached the stream. Elkin watched me walk, I assumed either to admire my form or wonder if he was a fool for bringing me along on his hunt. I raised my skirts to step over a mass of roots. When I glanced over my shoulder, I saw his gaze focused on the odd lumps near my ankles.

"What's wrong with your boots?" he asked.

"What? Nothing." I dropped my skirts and faced him. "The boots are fine."

"But they're not yours." He set his horse free to graze, then indicated I should sit on a nearby fallen tree. "I noticed your limp at the inn, but it's not a limp, is it? There's something in your boots."

I lifted my chin. "And what if there is?"

Elkin sat at my feet. "Whatever it is, it's hurting you." He sat at my feet and reached for my boot. "May I?"

I hesitated, unsure if he meant to help or merely send me back to the hell I'd so recently escaped. But his eyes were kind and his face was honest. I nodded, and he drew my foot onto his lap.

Elkin felt around my ankle, then he pulled off my boot and revealed a golden fetter. He stared at it for a moment, then he did the same to my other foot. That fetter still had a few links attached to it, further proof of my recent horror.

"You were shackled with golden chains?" he said. "Why would anyone go to such an expense for a prisoner, or a—"

He shut his mouth, not wanting to utter the word that came to mind.

"You can say it," I said. "Slave. You want to know if I was a slave."

"I was going to say hostage," he said, then he swept his gaze over my attire. "It would explain your clothing."

"This is not what I wore while fettered," I said, remembering the gauzy silks I'd thrown into the kitchen fire. "I stole these after I broke free."

"How did you get free?"

"Gold is a soft metal," I replied. "I found a bit of iron and worked at the chains whenever I had a moment alone. Eventually they broke."

"That must have taken some time."

"It did."

Elkin nodded, then he leaned closer to the fetter on my right ankle and ran his fingers along the edge.

"What are you doing?" I asked.

"Looking for the release." The fetters were well-made—Griselle would abide nothing less than perfection, especially with her torture devices—but he eventually found the hinge. He withdrew his dagger and used the tip of the blade to release the clasp, then he did the same to the other fetter.

"You were bound for a time," he said, noting the ugly red skin that encircled both of my ankles. He went to his pack and retrieved a small pot. A moment later my feet were again in his lap, and he rubbed balm onto my ankles.

"You carry balms for such wounds?" I asked.

"Actually, this is for my horse," Elkin replied. "He's prone to saddle sores." We laughed together. I rotated my foot, enjoying how the balm seeped into my flesh and warmed my stiff bones. I didn't know where a hunter had learned the delicate art of massage, but Elkin was a master. As he loosened my muscles, he also loosened my tongue.

"I was there for a time," I said softly. "You're right about that. And I was a prisoner; you're right about that, too. Thank you for removing the fetters, and for the balm. You can keep the gold."

"Don't you need it?" he asked. When I only looked at him, he continued, "I'm not trying to be cruel, but you obviously have nothing more than what you're wearing. Take the gold, use it to start over somewhere new."

I leaned forward, placed my palm against his cheek. "How are you so good?"

He shrugged. "Am I, or am I just better than wherever you came from?"

I smiled. "I suppose time will tell." I took both fetters and set them in my lap, watching the dappled sunlight play across the shiny surface. Based on their weight, I could use them to book passage all the way south to the sea. I might have enough to cross the sea, and start over in the lands beyond.

I offered one to Elkin. "Here," I said. Was it foolish to give this man I'd just met half of my gold? Most likely. But he was the best man I'd met in a good, long while. "We will each take one. That is fair, no?"

Elkin closed his hand around the fetter, testing its weight. "Yes. That is fair."

***

"This is where you last saw it?" I asked. We had moved on from our resting spot, and were standing on the stream bank. My ankles were still sore, but felt better than they had in a long time.

"Yes. It went into the water, and I lost the trail."

"Hmm."

I crouched down and dipped my fingers in the stream, and touched the mud beneath. I closed my eyes and felt the cool water ripple over my skin. Beyond that was edge of the streambed, the earth on the far side, and the many trees with their roots sunk deep into the ground. One by one, I asked them where our quarry was.

"He went east, then he doubled back and went south." I stood and wiped my hand on my skirt. "He moves southward still, but not so quickly we cannot catch up."

"How can you know that?" he asked.

"My mother was a nymph," I replied. "The trees, the ground, even the grass speaks to us. To me. I was not overstating when I said I could track him anywhere."

Elkin frowned. "This... this is much to consider," he said. "Stolen clothes, golden shackles, and now the trees speak to you."

"You're wondering if I'm a liar or a lunatic."

"I am," he replied, "but what if you're neither? I've always been a good judge of people. You don't seem like a liar."

I lifted my chin. "By default, that makes me a lunatic."

"Not necessarily." Elkin raked a hand through his hair, loosening the leather tie that bound it. It softened his appearance, making him less of a warrior and more of a man struggling to do the right thing, and I wanted to help him. Not because helping him might lead to me leaving the north, but for him alone. Thoughts like that were dangerous, especially to me.

Elkin took his time considering what I'd revealed. He was a careful man, this hunter, and I'd given him much to think on. "I am taking much on faith, but without faith, what do we have?"

That was not the sort of response I'd expected. For him to send me away, or demand I stay quiet until we found the demon, yes, but not a statement on faith. "You're not one of those wandering monks that squawk about the old gods, are you?"

He laughed through his nose. "Thank the gods, no. How far is this beast? Should we walk or ride?"

"Ride," I replied, and moved toward the horse. "Elkin, I mean it. I appreciate your help more than I can say."

"Don't forget, you're helping me, too." He helped me onto the saddle, and he swung himself up behind me. He put the reins in my hands, and said, "All right, then. Show me your appreciation by guiding me to my quarry."

***

"Tell me about nymphs."

I glanced over my shoulder. We'd been riding for the better part of an hour, Elkin's horse gingerly picking his way through the forest. "What do you already know about us?"

"I know there are brothels in the northern elflands filled with nymphs." He looked down, frowning. He worried he'd offended me. How sweet.

"That's true," I said. "We have a need for contact, you see. Any kind of physical touch will do, but the more intimate, the better. Without touch, we wilt like a plucked flower." I gathered the reins in one hand, then I drew off his glove and laced my bare fingers with his. "You don't mind, do you, Elkin?"

"N-No." His fingers tightened against mine. "What is this... this warmth?"

"When we receive pleasure, we give some in return. Now you understand why there are brothels full of us." I rubbed my thumb against his palm and found a tiny scar. An image of a young boy hammering away at a worn boot filled my mind's eye. "You once repaired boots?"

"My father was a cobbler," he replied. "How did you know to ask me that?"

"This scar." I pressed the bit of slick skin. "You got it mending a boot." When he remained silent, I continued, "When I feel another's wound—even a healed wound, like this scar—I can read how it happened on the bearer's skin."

Elkin grunted. "Must make for some awkward conversations in the brothel."

"*I* never worked in a brothel," I snapped, then shut my mouth. Elkin only knew what I'd already revealed, and we'd just been speaking of brothels. It was natural for him to draw that conclusion. Before I could apologize, I felt him move my hair to one side, then he spoke close to my ear.

"I'm sorry," he said, his warm breath making my spine shiver. "I didn't mean anything by that."

"I'm sorry, too." I squeezed his hand. "I shouldn't have spoken that way."

"We could forgive each other."

"I can agree to that."

"Now that we're friends again, about those awkward conversations."

I leaned back and met his gaze. There was laughter in his gray eyes, and curiosity. I grew more fond of this hunter with every passing moment. "Awkward conversations happen between all lovers," I began. "Usually, the pleasure one experiences far outweighs the impact of a few memories. Remember, it's the contact we're after."

"Were you chained to keep you in... contact?" he asked, suddenly wondering what kind of prisoner I'd been.

"No. That was to keep me away from others." I released his hand and adjusted the reins. "By the time I escaped, I was so skin starved I could barely speak."

"I'm sorry," he said. "I didn't mean to upset you."

"But you did mean to test me."

"Beautiful women don't often approach me in pubs offering to help track demons," he said. "Trust is earned."

"Am I earning yours?"

"So far."

"I'll never lie to you," I said. "It's an easy promise for me to make. I never lie to anyone. I can't."

"Why can't you?"

"It's part of my curse."

"Let me get this straight," Elkin said. "You're a nymph, a tracker, an escaped prisoner, and now you're cursed? Your life sounds like the worst ballad ever sung. What's next? Olluhm's handmaiden?"

"Of course not," I replied. "Olluhm wouldn't have a handmaiden. A god of his stature would have a body servant."

When he remained silent, I knew my attempt at humor had fallen flat. Eventually, he asked, "Was your curse what made you a prisoner?"

"The two are linked," I began, "but to understand, I must first tell you about my father. He was a null."

"Really?" I was surprised Elkin had heard of nulls, rare beings who could absorb and negate magic. "Did he pass that on to you?"

"In a way. I don't absorb magic—at least, I don't think I do—but I am immune to it, mostly. I can even see through concealment spells."

"And that, coupled with you talking to trees and dirt, is what makes you such a good tracker," he deduced. "No one can hide from you."

I tilted my head back and smiled. "Very good, my lord hunter. My next riddles will be much more difficult."

Elkin tightened his grip on my waist, no doubt trying to understand if I was flirting or merely toying with him, when he heard a rustle in the trees. "Quiet," he whispered.

"Oh, your demon's there," I said, pointing toward the sound. "He's with two others."

"Gods, woman," he muttered as he dismounted and rushed toward the copse of trees. I remained on the horse; while I could hold my own in a fight and against a demon, I was unarmed.

Elkin yelled and then cried out. My heart lurched, and I started searching the saddlebags for a weapon. I located a spare sword lashed to the back of the saddle, and was about to draw it when a lesser demon fled past me. By the time I had the sword out, it was gone.

"Elkin," I called. "Elkin, do you need me?"

I dismounted and ran toward the noise of fighting, cursing the fetters that had abraded my ankles and made my movements slow and uneven. When I pushed through the undergrowth, I saw Elkin struggling against a demon, while another lay unmoving on the far side of the clearing.

"Innetha, leave," he shouted.

"I came to help," I said, holding the sword aloft.

Elkin maneuvered out from under the demon, spun around and sunk his blade into the back of its neck. It fell forward, convulsed once, and didn't move again.

"Are you all right?" Elkin asked. He pulled out a rag from his belt pouch and cleaned his sword, then he dropped the bloodied cloth onto the beast.

"Me? How are you?"

"I'm fine." He winked. "It was only two."

I glared at him, which only made his smile widen. "If you want to help find me some kindling," he said. "We'll burn these two, then find someplace upwind to set up for the night. Tomorrow we can set after the one that escaped."

"The night?" I put the sword on the ground and picked up a few nearby sticks.

"Aye, the night. When people sleep. Don't nymphs and nulls sleep then, too?"

I kept on collecting fallen branches, careful to keep my face turned away from Elkin. I craved contact, and he was a handsome man, but this very handsome, very large and strong man had been asking about brothels and knew I was recently a captive of some sort. What sort of night was he planning?

"Innetha."

"Hmm?"

"Innetha, look at me."

I stopped what I was doing and faced him.

"It's obvious that you're wondering about my intentions," he began. I suppose I hadn't been so stealthy with my emotions after all. "Let me explain myself. We are too far from the Northern Contingent to get there before sun rest, and I'd rather not bump into trees while travelling in the dark. All I meant was that we should either locate an inn for the night, or find a place to camp. Nothing more."

I crouched down and placed my hand on the forest floor. "The closest inn is the one in Stonekeep, where we met," I said. "Honestly, I don't know if they've ever cleaned those rooms."

He smiled. "So it's camping then? Just camping," he added.

I returned his smile. I knew I would be safe with this hunter. "Camping it is."

***

It didn't take long for the bodies to burn, and after a quick ride Elkin, myself, and his horse found a suitable place to set up for the night. Ironically, it was the same clearing where Elkin had removed my fetters; he quipped that we should have baited the demons toward us and saved ourselves the journey.

Elkin spent some time circling the clearing, verifying that we were indeed alone. While he did that I built a fire, and laid out our meager dinner of hard travel bread and dried meat, and poured out some feed for the horse. The beast whuffled his thanks, then ignored his feed and grazed on the wildflowers instead.

"Beautiful, ungrateful horse." I combed my fingers through his mane. "Elkin," I called, "what's your horse's name?"

"You'll laugh."

"I like laughing."

"Buttercup."

At that I did laugh, and hugged the warhorse's massive neck. "Buttercup, the most terrifying of mounts." Buttercup continued munching on his namesake flowers.

"I believe we will be safe for the night," Elkin declared as he stepped into the clearing, having finished his final circuit. The fire blazed in the clearing, hot and bright enough to keep most of the lesser demons at bay. He grabbed one of the strips of meat and scowled at it. "I do wish we'd gathered more supplies before we set out."

"If we had, we may not have caught the beast. Beasts," I amended. I tore a portion from the loaf as I moved closer to the fire. "The next time I steal clothes, I will be sure to take a cloak."

Elkin spread out his blankets next to the fire. "I've only the one bedroll. You take it."

"Don't be foolish. We can share it." He opened his mouth to protest, but I continued, "We'll be warmer that way. And why should you shiver alone?"

"Earlier you questioned my intentions."

"And you have since reassured me." I pulled off my boots and rubbed my ankles. "The next time I filch clothing, I'll grab a cloak *and* stockings."

"Are they still sore?" he asked.

"I imagine they will be for some time," I replied. "What... what will happen tomorrow?"

"After we find the remaining beast, I'll return to my contingent," he replied. "Have you anyplace to go?" When I rearranged the blankets instead of answering him, he asked, "Would you like to come with me?"

I bit my lip. "Is that a good idea? What will your commander say?"

"I, ah." He rubbed the back of his neck. "I am the commander."

"Why didn't you tell me that earlier?" All of Parthalan knew how the queen valued her hunters. If Elkin led a full contingent of hunters, he was one of the most powerful men in the region.

"Sometimes, when I tell someone about my title, they think I'm something I'm not," he replied. "No matter what sort of work I do, I'll only ever be Elkin."

"Then what of your hunters, only Elkin?" I pressed. "What will they think of you bringing an unknown woman into their midst?"

"They're good men and will do as ordered, but we can worry about that after the suns rise." Elkin pulled off his heavy jerkin and then his boots, and lay beside me. "Sleep well, tracker."

I moved closer to his side, only partly for warmth. I'd already decided that if he asked me again in the morning, I would go to his contingent with him. "You too, hunter."

***

I woke with Elkin's arm around my waist, his body pressed against my back and his face buried in my hair. For the first time in moons, I woke warm and comfortable, for all that I could remember what comfort was. After Griselle had chained me to her throne, there I remained, spending every waking and sleeping hour as a decoration on her dais bereft of privacy's solace or even a cushion. How I would love to put her in chains and leave her to rot as I had.

As I imagined Griselle getting what she so richly deserved, my fingers tightened on Elkin's arm, waking him. He moved to roll away, but I held him fast.

"It's all right," I said. "I need contact, remember?"

He stilled, but stayed where he was. "I don't want to take advantage of you."

I rolled over. "What makes you think I won't take advantage of you?"

Elkin gaped at me, but before he could react, I took his hand and retraced the scar I'd found yesterday. "Why didn't you want to be a cobbler?"

"Would you want to spend your life mending others' worn boots?" he countered. "When I was younger, I convinced myself I was destined for great things. Since there was nothing great about my father or his workshop, I struck out on my own."

"How could your father not be great?" I asked. "He sired you."

Elkin took my hand and slid it underneath his shirt, halfway between his waist and shoulder. "What do those scars tell you?"

"Let me feel them."

I glided my fingertips across his skin, enjoying myself far more than was proper and wondering just how long we could remain in the bedroll, when my vision went red.

Black.

Pain! Something struck me—a cudgel, a stick?—again. And again. I wept, and passed out.

"He beat you?" I asked once I removed my fingers from the scars.

"He did." Elkin wiped my cheeks with the edge of the blanket. "When you experience these old wounds, how much do you see?"

"Enough. Too much." I chanced a look at him. "I also saw the real reason you became a hunter. You wanted to protect people."

"You're right." He smoothed my hair back. "Do you, um, need protecting?"

Before I could say that yes, I was feeling rather vulnerable and would gladly take shelter in his arms, we heard a rustle in the trees. I placed my hand on the earth and nearly choked.

"It's the demon," I said, scrambling to my feet. "The one that ran off."

"Get behind me," Elkin said as he leapt up and charged toward the rustling sounds, sword out. I scrambled free of the bedroll and darted toward the horse, then I changed course and ran toward the gear, and Elkin's other weapons. Elkin paused to check on me, but he watched me a moment too long. He cried out, a crossbow bolt stuck in his gut.

"Innetha, go," he yelled as he fell. "Take Buttercup and go!"

I grabbed Elkin's second sword from behind the saddle and planted myself in front of him. I brandished the sword, my bare feet asking the earth where the demon was hiding. "Stay down," I said. "There's only one."

"Have you ever killed one before?"

"Yes."

A second bolt whizzed toward us. I knocked it down with the sword, surprising myself and Elkin with that lucky strike, then I picked up a rock and flung it where the bolt had come from. The lesser demon fell out of the tree and landed with a bone-cracking crunch.

I strode toward it and shoved the sword's tip against the dazed creature's throat. "Do you need this one for anything?"

"No."

I pushed the sword forward, and that was the end of that demon.

I dropped the sword and rushed to Elkin's side. "Let me see the wound." I plucked the bolt out of his belly and used the barbed tip to rip open his shirt. The wound was small but bled like a waterfall; the bolt must have pierced one of the larger veins. I rested my fingers against the puncture and closed my eyes. "No poison. That's good."

"Nymphs can detect poison?" Elkin asked.

"No. We can't." I placed my hands on either side of the wound. Immediately, the bleeding lessened. "I told you I was cursed. It was meant to make me crave pain instead of pleasure, but I'm only half nymph. My nuller's blood somehow reacted with the curse. The good part is that I still crave pleasure, and now I can heal wounds in others."

"And the bad part?" he asked.

I smiled weakly, feeling my strength ebb. "I heal by absorbing those wounds into my own body." I fell against him, spent. Elkin pushed up my blouse and saw a wound on my torso identical to the one he'd suffered, bleeding freely. He demanded to know how I'd been hurt, why I hadn't said anything. Instead of answering him, I passed out.

***

When I next opened my eyes, I was lying in a proper bed instead of a bedroll, and the bed was in a room rather than the forest. My stolen clothes were gone, and I was wearing a linen tunic that had been washed so many times it was soft as silk. I would have remembered stealing such a thing.

"How did I get here?" I asked the room.

"I brought you here." Elkin strode into my field of vision, looking well and hale and positively furious with me. "We're in the Northern Contingent's keep, and this is my chamber."

And this must be his bed. "Thank you," I said.

"I don't need thanks. I need an explanation." He crossed his arms over his chest and glowered at me. "Why did you do that? You could have bled out. You almost did."

"If I hadn't healed you, you'd be just another corpse being swallowed up by the forest." I pushed myself up to a sitting position. Between the wound's pain and the tight bandages wrapped around me, it was quite the endeavor. "That sort of wound would have been fatal to you, but nymphs heal quickly. For me, it was nothing more than an inconvenience."

"Yes, you seemed quite inconvenienced while you lay in my arms, unconscious and soaked in blood." I turned my face to the wall. He was right. The wound had been worse than I'd realized, but I had a much better chance of recovering than he did. While I was ignoring him, he sat beside me.

"Innetha, please don't think I'm not grateful," he began. "I am, so much so. I owe you my life at least twice over, but my life isn't worth more than yours. Don't ever heal me again."

"Is that an order, hunter?" I asked. "I don't recall you having any authority over me."

When he remained silent, I dared to look at him. He was still frowning, but it was more of a contemplative frown than the furious glower of a few moments ago. After a moment, he placed his hand on mine. "Why did you do that? Take my wound as yours?"

I shrugged. "You were hurt," I replied. "You needed help, and I helped."

Elkin worked his fingers between mine. "You do realize that I am far more indebted to you, than you are to me."

"You're not," I replied. "We helped each other when we were needed. No debts are owed."

"Well, then." He moved closer to me. "How can I return the favor, and help you heal?"

"You are helping me," I said, indicating our joined hands. "I need contact to heal. The more the better."

Elkin nodded, then he repositioned himself so he was sitting upright against the wall and drew me against him. He rested his chin on the top of my head, and my arm found its way around his waist. "Better?" he asked.

"Yes. Much better."

Fettered, Part Three

Innetha Speaks

I stayed with the Northern Contingent for more than a year. During that first summer, my wounded belly was healing, and Elkin claimed it wasn't safe for me to travel. Then summer faded to autumn, and since I still didn't have a destination in mind, it only made sense for me to stay the winter. That season proved bitterly cold and our food stores ran dangerously low, but those moons were some of the happiest of my life. By the time the spring thaw came, I was through making excuses for my presence in the keep. I was there because Elkin was there. No other reasons were needed.

One morning, I waited for him in the ash grove. It had become our special place for when we needed more privacy than his chamber afforded us. Elkin joined me shortly before noon, bringing with him a wineskin and a scroll.

"A messenger's just been." He sat beside me on the fur I'd laid out and unrolled the parchment. "The queen has sent word from Teg'urnan."

"Has she?" Elkin handed me the scroll and I read how two *mordeths* and a host of lesser demons had attacked Teg'urnan, killing half of the soldiers and all but one hunter. One of the *mordeths* had escaped, and the queen meant to track him. The missive ended with Asherah requesting Elkin and four of his hunters accompany her.

"Did Asherah herself write this?" I glided my fingers across the precise script. The writing was as beautiful as any scribe's.

"She did," he replied. "I've seen her handwriting often enough to recognize it."

"And why does she request you accompany her?" I continued. "She can order you to stand on your head if she'd like."

"True, but orders aren't Asherah's way," Elkin replied. "She works with people, never assumes they'll work for her. She's very kind."

"You love her," I said.

"Everyone loves her," Elkin replied. "When you meet her, you'll love her too."

"I can't imagine how I would ever cross paths with the queen," I began, then I noticed Elkin's pensive stare. "What is it?"

"I thought you'd come with us to Teg'urnan," he said. "The queen needs a tracker, and no one's better than you."

I glanced down at the parchment. The missive really was a thing of beauty, and apparently Elkin had received several such messages from the queen. Enough to recognize her handwriting. I suddenly felt very out of place in his world. "Surely the queen already has trackers."

"She does, but she doesn't have an Innetha." He took my hands and kissed my knuckles. "Won't you come on an adventure with me? Even if you only come as far as the palace, it is a sight to behold. Not that it's anywhere near as beautiful as you."

My face warmed, and I ducked my head; only Elkin had ever made me blush. As for the queen's request, I had no interest in fae politics and their warring gods, and while I held no animosity toward the Faerie Queen I honestly didn't care if she captured the *mordeth* or not. But Elkin was a hunter, and this beast's capture was important to him. Therefore, it was important to me.

"I suppose, since tracking this *mordeth* is important to you, the least I can do is accompany you. Someone has to watch your back."

He grinned, and I fell a bit harder for him. "And no one watches my back better than you, love."

I kissed Elkin's cheek. "When do we leave?"

***

Some two moons later, we—the queen, her hunters, and I—were camped at the edge of the Southern Desert. I'd never been so far from where I'd been raised, and I loved the hot sands and dry winds. If only I could convince Elkin to build us a hut in the desert and leave the north behind, I'd never be cold or skin starved again.

That night I had the most peculiar encounter with Aeolmar, the First Hunter. He'd plunged into my tent to evade Brynne, the ghastly commander of the Eastern Contingent, and I soon learned he'd broken his hand. I healed him, but the healing went too deep, and I saw more of his memories than I intended. What's more, when Aeolmar questioned me, I told him Elkin was unaware of my abilities, and while that wasn't the complete truth, neither was it exactly a lie. Regardless, I needed to speak with Elkin before Aeolmar did.

I pulled my sleeping fur close about my body, then I went in search of Elkin. I found him alone in his tent; convenient, since I was only wearing the fur.

"Something happened," I began, and I told him everything that passed between myself and Aeolmar. By the end of my tale, we were sitting up on Elkin's bedroll.

"You took his broken bones?" Elkin took my hand, pressed it to his lips. He understood that the more skin to skin contact I had, the faster

I would heal. "Innetha, you can't go about absorbing every wound you come across."

"I know," I said. "He was so distraught, and I had to do something."

"Why did you tell Aeolmar I didn't know about your healing?" he asked. He moved to speak further, then paused. I knew what he was wondering. I'd told Elkin I couldn't lie, and now it seemed I had.

"There are two reasons," I began. "Firstly, I didn't know if you needed to advise him of my abilities before we set out. I didn't want you punished over me."

"Always defending my honor." He nuzzled my neck, his rough whiskers scraping my skin and delighting me. "What's the other reason?"

"You haven't experienced the full extent of what I can do."

"But you healed me from that crossbow wound," he said. "I remember it like it was just yesterday."

"All I did was heal your flesh," I said. "If you allow it, I can see every painful memory and cleanse them from your mind. I can heal your body and your soul. To know someone that deeply..." I shook my head. "I didn't intend to delve so deeply into Aeolmar's mind. It unnerved him, rightly so. It unnerved me."

Elkin smoothed back my hair. "Are you all right?"

"I am, now."

He smiled. "Good. This... This knowing." He frowned, his thumb stroking the thin skin of my wrist. "Is it a good knowing?"

"I suppose that depends on who you're with."

Elkin nudged me until I was flat on my back and lowered himself on top of me, holding me within the cage of his body. "I can't think of anyone I'd like to know better than you."

***

Another moon passed, and we were again within Teg'urnan's walls. The palace was everything Elkin had promised, and more. I had seen much of the realm before Elkin's path crossed with mine, though not much of the fae lands. After being inside their ancestral birthplace not once but twice, feeling the smooth gray stones that had been shaped by a god's hand, I understood a bit of the fae's arrogance. They were born of gods, and celebrated their heritage in every aspect of their lives.

I'd just left Asherah's receiving chamber where I'd been given news that left me elated and terrified all at the same time: the queen had been much impressed with my actions these past moons, and asked me to remain in Teg'urnan as a hunter. If I stayed, I would be further entrenched in fae business, something I'd successfully avoided most of my life... But if I stayed, I would be a hunter. Not just any hunter, but one of Asherah's own elite band of warriors. I would have the queen's ear, and while I would be tracking and killing demons by day, I would live in a palace again, this time not in chains but in a room of my own with servants to assist me and hot meals whenever I felt the slightest twinge of hunger. I could slow down and enjoy my life, rather than move from one small job to the next. I could breathe, and finally learn who Innetha really was.

As I stood in front of the hearth—my hearth, in my chamber!—and considered my options, Elkin strode into the room.

If I stayed in the palace, I would be here without Elkin.

"Found you," he said by way of greeting. "Why did the *saffira* move you into this room?"

"It was Asherah's idea." I stopped pacing and faced Elkin. "The queen wants me to have this chamber as my own. She wants me to stay in Teg'urnan, as a hunter."

Elkin's throat worked. "That's... that is a very great honor," he said. "You accepted?"

"I didn't. Not yet."

"But you want to."

"I do. For a hundred, maybe a thousand reasons, I do."

"Do you have any reasons not to?"

"One." I stepped closer. "Just one."

Elkin searched my face, then he hauled me into his arms and kissed me. No bed had yet been set up, so we tumbled onto the cushions by the window. We tore off our clothes, urgency having taken the place of our usual languid games, and made love as if we might never see each other again.

Afterward we lay relaxed on the cushions, warmed by the sunlight streaming in through the open windows. I had no idea what was on the other side of those windows, and was wondering if anyone had heard us. Then Elkin kissed the small of my back, and pleasure rippled up my spine. Let them listen. Let them immortalize us in a painting, for all I cared.

"I must return to the keep tomorrow," Elkin said.

"You must lead your hunters." I moved so I was facing him and traced patterns across his chest. "Asherah will name me tomorrow."

"Then I'll wait," he said. "I'll be here for your naming, and the celebration afterward, and whenever you need me."

I smiled, but it hurt. Gods, it hurt that he was leaving. "With all that staying, how will you ever get back to the keep?"

Elkin pushed back my hair and stared into my eyes. "Know this, Innetha, my heart, my love. No matter where my body may be, my heart will remain here with you." He pressed his lips between my breasts. "It always will."

I burrowed into his arms. "Will we ever see each other again?"

"Of course we will." He tucked my head under his chin and kissed my hair. "Of course we will."

Fettered, Part Four

After Innetha left Elkin alone in the grove, she found herself in the keep's kitchen. The Northern Contingent's cook, Tamil, was one of her favorite people, and when she'd previously stayed at the keep, she spent many hours helping her and listening to her stories. Since Innetha had been gone, Tamil had had a son, Mael, and like all children, he was forever getting into mischief. Innetha was healing a burn on Mael's arm when Elkin stalked into the room and dropped a leather pouch onto the table in front of her.

"What's this?" she asked.

"If you're going to stay here, you need to work." He upended the pouch, and a few maps and a compass tumbled out onto the table. "Since you're a tracker, I put together a kit for you."

Innetha glanced at the maps but made no move to pick them up. "I don't need a map. Or a compass," she added.

"Yes, I realize that, but don't you want to familiarize yourself with the area?"

Innetha arched a dark, delicate brow. "I spent several seasons here. Do you think I forgot everything?"

Elkin frowned, and Innetha's heart softened. She knew he hadn't meant to offend her; if he had, there were many other incidents he could bring up.

"I only want to help," he said.

She nodded and touched one of the maps. "Do you walk the border every morning?"

"Yes, I do."

"Good." She pointed to a location on the map. "I will meet you here at first dawn."

Elkin checked the location on the map. "The ash grove?" he asked. "Of all places you want to meet there?"

"Yes, I do."

Innetha swept out of the kitchens, leaving Tamil and Mael and the rest of the *saffira* staring after her. It was unnecessarily dramatic, but she wasn't about to wait for Elkin to come around to her. She hoped by meeting him in the ash grove—their special place from so long ago—she would learn if anything was salvageable between them.

She squeezed her eyes shut and offered up a small prayer. More than anything, she wanted to rebuild what they'd once had.

***

Innetha stayed near the keep for the rest of the day, and never once crossed Elkin's path. The keep was small, with the hunters usually packed one on top of the other, which meant Elkin was avoiding her. She knew she'd rattled him by asking to meet in the ash grove, but she hadn't expected outright avoidance. When she'd chosen the grove she'd hoped it would bring back a few fond memories, but he'd acted as if remembering their time there was the last thing he wanted to do. Innetha wondered if coming back to the keep had been a mistake.

But where else would I have gone? She couldn't bear to return to Teg'urnan, not yet. After Olwynn's funeral pyre had burned to the ground, the rest had gone out of their way offering kind words and sympathetic glances, all of them thinking a soft gesture or two could somehow offset her mate's death. Even Aeolmar had been kind; sitting up with her when she couldn't sleep, holding her when the tears came again. If she'd endured another moment of all that kindness, she would have gone mad.

Truth be told, she could have gone anywhere. She doubted Asherah would send anyone to apprehend her wayward hunter; if anyone understood the madness that followed a mate's death, it was the queen. A stronger truth was that Innetha didn't want to be anywhere else but with Elkin.

I've always wanted to be with him. So why did I remain in Teg'urnan when he returned here? She knew exactly why she remained in the palace: she loved being a hunter. For the first time in decades, others saw Innetha's worth as a tracker and fighter, and not as a pretty face and soft form. For too long, she'd been seen as nothing but a source of pleasure, and while she craved it, she was more than her nymph half. Even before she was cursed, Innetha had so much more to offer than a coy glance or soft caress. And Asherah valued all of her talents.

Elkin did, too. Elkin had never treated her as anything less than his equal. To him, she was strong, and brave, and cunning. At least, that's how he used to think of her. Now she worried he only saw her as a nuisance.

The supper bell rang, and Innetha made her way toward the hall. She deliberately took the corridor that led past Elkin's chamber. He opened the door and saw her. They stared at each other for a moment, then Innetha took her chance.

"Can we talk?" she asked as she brushed past him into his chamber. He frowned, then he closed the door and faced her, arms crossed over his chest.

"About what?" he asked.

"I know you don't want me staying here, in your room," she said. "Is there a guest room I can have?"

Confusion skated across his face. "There is, but you can stay here."

"But where will you sleep?"

"Why is it so important for you to know where I'm sleeping?"

"I came here to be with you, not to be ignored." Innetha grabbed her pack. "I know when I'm not wanted."

"Innetha, wait." Elkin reached for her. As she evaded him, she knocked over a small chest.

"I'm sorry," she said, bending to pick up the scattered items. "I'll clean this up."

Innetha fell silent. Underneath the scrolls and other items lay a golden shackle. Elkin's gaze alighted on the shackle, and he snatched it away before she could touch it.

"You kept the fetter." Innetha's gaze moved from the shackle to Elkin's face. "Why?"

"Why did I keep it?" Elkin turned the shackle over in his hands. "It reminds me of you."

She placed her hand on his. "You don't need a reminder. I'm right here."

"Why did you choose Olwynn?" he asked. "Why didn't you ever come back to me?"

"Why didn't you come back to me?" she countered. "You knew where I was. You knew *exactly* where I was. And before you drag Olwynn's name into this, tell me, have you been alone these past eight winters? Who are you to judge me for taking comfort with another? You all but refused me."

"I have never refused you anything," he said, then paused. "You really thought I abandoned you."

"How do you know this?" Innetha demanded. "You have no magic, and no way to know what I'm feeling. Yet, you knew this morning..." Innetha frowned. There was only one way Elkin could understand her emotions so thoroughly, but she wouldn't have thought it possible. "What am I feeling now?"

"Confusion, mostly," he replied. "And, hope?"

Innetha closed the distance between them. "Elkin, when we were together, did you choose me as your mate?"

"The woman does the choosing," he began, but she shook her head.

"The man chooses as well. It's not as if a woman can wish another into loving her, is it?" She raised her hand as if to touch his face, but he grabbed her wrist.

"What are you saying?" he asked. "Are you my mate?"

"I think... I suspect when you chose me, you became mine." She gazed up at him. "Why didn't you ever tell me?"

"I did," he replied. "That day in Teg'urnan before I left, I told you everything. I never thought of it as choosing you, not until just now, but... yes. I chose you."

Innetha watched him for another moment, then she slid her arms around his waist and rested her cheek against his chest. "Thank you," she said. "That is the most wonderful thing anyone could have ever told me."

Elkin hesitated, then he cupped the back of her head with his hand and kissed her hair. "I really am sorry about Olwynn," he said. "He was a fine man, and I'm certain he treated you as you deserve. I know how much you're hurting. I wish I could take the hurt from you."

"You do not want to start absorbing others' wounds," she said. "Believe me, it's not a fun process."

"I will take your word for it." He held her for a moment, relishing the feel of her in his arms. He'd missed her so much, at times wondering if he'd ever see his nymph again. "I'm glad you came to see me, but I do wish it had been for a different reason."

"So do I," she said. "So do I."

Fettered, Part Five

Elkin slept alone that night. He loved Innetha, and she him, but he didn't feel it was right to share her bed. Not yet, not while she was still mourning Olwynn. Besides, they had agreed to meet the next morning in the ash grove, and he could hardly wait. That was the place they'd first become close all those years ago, and he hoped they could still become like they were before.

No, not like before. This time will be better.

Elkin rose shortly before first dawn and spent an inordinate amount of time picking out his clothes and combing his hair. He was only going to walk the border with Innetha, but he wanted to show her his best self, and if he was honest with himself, he would admit hoping they never left the grove. He smiled as he left the guest chamber, and took the corridor that passed by his room. The door was open and the room empty; she had already left for the grove, then. Not wanting to keep her waiting any longer, he exited the keep and crossed the courtyard.

That was when he heard her scream.

"Innetha," Elkin yelled as he broke into a run. "Innetha!"

Elkin burst into the grove and found Innetha surrounded by four men. Her arm bled, her knife was out, and her face told him that whomever had dealt her that wound would soon be a corpse. Elkin drew his sword and advanced toward the men.

"Who sent you?" he demanded. "This is the queen's land, and you have no business here."

"They're from Griselle," Innetha said. "Seems she misses me."

Elkin remembered that name; Griselle was the woman behind Innetha's curse. He stared at the men. "Your mistress sent you to kidnap my huntress? She must like you four least of all."

"This is a servant what's run out before her debt's paid," the presumed leader said. "We were sent to retrieve our mistress's property."

"I am not her property," Innetha spat. "She hired me, then she cursed me!"

"That is not what we were told."

"Here is what I am telling you," Elkin said. "I, Elkin Savey, am the queen's hunter, and I command this contingent. Through Asherah the Ruthless I have lordship over all local landowners, including Griselle. Innetha is my huntress, and you will leave her be."

"She is a fugitive—"

"If she was indentured once, I hereby grant her freedom," Elkin said. "None of you will lay a hand on Innetha, not on this or any other day."

The leader lowered his sword. "We cannot return empty-handed," he said, and Elkin understood that they would be punished as Innetha once was.

"Tell your mistress I have overruled her in the name of the queen," Elkin replied. "If any of you wish to claim sanctuary, my keep is open to you." Elkin extended his hand to Innetha. She took it, and he caught sight of her bloodied arm. "Who cut you?"

Innetha pointed. "Him."

Elkin withdrew a throwing knife from his belt and flung it at the man, landing the blade in the exact spot where Innetha was wounded. The man cried out, but none of his companions moved to help him. *Mercenaries, then. What else has Griselle hired?*

"Our wounds are now equal," Elkin declared. "We have no reason to fight. Leave, before I change my mind."

Elkin turned his back on the men and led Innetha out of the grove. Once they were in the shadow of the keep, he stopped to examine her arm.

"It's fine," she said. "I've survived worse."

"I remember," Elkin said. "Has Griselle ever come after you before?"

"Not for a long time," she replied. "Teg'urnan is far out of her reach."

There's another reason why she wanted to stay at the palace, and why she refused to remain with me in the north. "Come. Let's get you bandaged."

They entered the infirmary, which was empty at the early hour. While Elkin searched for bandages and salves, Innetha stripped off her jerkin, and then her tunic. When Elkin turned around, she was seated with her back to him, bare from the waist up.

"Aren't you cold?" he asked.

"I am, so please hurry," she replied. Elkin examined the wound as he washed it; the cut was near her shoulder, long but shallow.

"Is Griselle known for using poison?" He spread a balm across the cut, and set about bandaging it.

"No, only badly worded curses," Innetha replied.

"You never told me why she cursed you."

Innetha laughed through her nose. "I was her best tracker. I found every one of her wayward servants, every debtor who'd refused to pay up, but the one thing I wouldn't do was go to bed with her. She took issue with that, so she cursed me to crave pain, dressed me as a whore, and put me in chains."

"Why did you refuse her?"

"Because she was a slaver," Innetha replied. "When she hired me, I thought I was retrieving those who owed her a debt. After a time, she referred to those debtors as indentured servants, and eventually she called them what they were. I thought Parthalan was the one place in this realm without slavery, thanks to Asherah, but I was wrong." Innetha's dark eyes met his. "Griselle is a terrible, terrible person. Time with her would not be pleasure, not in any way."

Elkin finished bandaging her arm, then he drew her against him. "If I'd known, I'd have had her stopped. I can stop her now."

"Isn't it strange that I can't hate her," Innetha murmured. "I should. By all rights, I should want her dead. But her curse became my gift, and if not for my time with her, I wouldn't be a hunter today, nor would I have been at the inn the day you needed a tracker."

"You think I wouldn't have found you?" Elkin was at heart a romantic, and he believed in fate.

"You never leave this keep, not if you can help it."

"Perhaps you're right, and it's time I ventured out into the world."

Innetha tightened her arms around him. "Perhaps we can stay here, together, just a little longer."

***

Innetha shoved the tracking kit across the table toward Elkin. "Why did you give me this?"

They'd retreated to the kitchens; blood loss had chilled Innetha, and the cooking fires meant it was the warmest room in the keep. That, and Elkin did his best thinking on a full stomach. Tamil had already served them two bowls of stew, a loaf of bread, and she'd just placed a joint of mutton between them. Elkin doubted he and his hunters would survive a moon without Tamil.

"I told you, to familiarize yourself with the area," he replied, but she shook her head.

"You forget, I've always been able to read you, too."

"That's right. You've always seen right through me." Elkin opened the leather pouch and took out the compass. "Two reasons, really. One, I wanted you to feel useful. I hoped that the more you had to do around here, the longer you'd stay."

"You want me to stay?"

"Of course I do." He turned the compass over in his hand. "But I wasn't reason enough last time, so I reckoned I wouldn't be enough now."

Innetha set down her tea. "I have only ever been here because of you. In fact, if it wasn't for you hauling me here when I was wounded, I never would have been here at all."

Elkin shuddered at the memory; after she'd absorbed the crossbow wound from his gut, and after he'd stopped the bleeding, he lashed Innetha to Buttercup's saddle and slowly and carefully walked back to the keep. The contingent didn't have a healer, but between himself and Tamil, they'd washed and sewn the wound and made Innetha as comfortable as possible. Elkin didn't sleep or leave Innetha's side until she opened her eyes.

"Surely my charms might have swayed you," he said, unwilling to speak aloud that she'd almost died to save him.

"If keeping me here was one of your reasons, the other must be that you need me to track something." She narrowed her gaze at him. "Or maybe, someone?"

Elkin leaned back in his chair and took a long draught of ale. "For the past few seasons, we've heard tell of people going missing. For a long time—too long, it seems—I ignored the tales. It's not so unusual for a body to leave everything behind to start a new life. It's what Aeolmar did."

"He had no other choice," Innetha said, then fell silent. While she knew that Aeolmar and Elkin had grown up together, she didn't know how much Elkin knew about what had happened to Aeolmar's family. It wasn't her place to reveal the First Hunter's secrets.

"What made you decide to pay attention to these stories?" she asked.

"The amount of them, for one," he replied. "It's unusual for so many to disappear from such a small area. And all of those who went missing shared similar traits."

Innetha sliced off a piece of meat from the joint they were sharing. "What sort of traits?"

"They were all young, many of them hardly more than children. All were described as especially handsome." Elkin frowned. "And we know one of the missing. Leo's cousin has been gone for near three moons now."

"His cousin? You mean Kenric?" Innetha asked, and Elkin nodded. "He's hardly more than a boy, but Griselle does prefer younger victims."

Elkin rose and refilled his bowl from the cauldron of stew hanging over the fire. "And now Griselle has sent her brutes after you."

"You think Griselle is capturing and then selling the villagers from Stonekeep?"

"You yourself said she's little more than a slaver. And what if she does have Kenric secreted away somewhere? We can't ignore the possibility he may be held by her." Elkin returned to his seat and set his bowl in front of him. Innetha tore off a piece of bread and dunked it in his stew.

"Pardon me," he said, staring at her gravy-soaked bread as if she'd committed the most grievous affront. "Ask first."

"Why bother? You love sharing with me." She picked up her spoon and fished a potato out of his bowl. "Even if Griselle is behind everything, what can we do? You're a hunter, not a magistrate."

"True, but I am the commander of this contingent." When Innetha merely raised her brows, he added, "There's precious little authority up here, love. I may as well be the local lord. Villagers from three days away come here to have me settle their disputes."

"So you think you can order Griselle to behave?" Innetha claimed another of his potatoes. "Not likely. Nor can you issue any sort of punishment."

Elkin grunted; Innetha was right. He could order Griselle to cease her operations, but she didn't have to listen to him. What's more, he had no way of enforcing such a judgement. His hunters weren't magistrates any more than he was.

A stray thought appeared in his head. "Do you think that would work?" he asked Innetha.

"Will you stop reading my mind," she snapped. "And yes, I think it might."

Elkin regarded her. Innetha thought he could return her to Griselle on the pretense of claiming a reward, then once he was inside her stronghold free all of her captives in one fell swoop. "This is a dangerous plan."

Innetha shrugged. "I was recently at war against Nibika. I'm sure this will be a much safer course of action."

"I don't like it," Elkin said.

"Have you a better idea?" When he remained silent, she continued, "We can't let those she's kidnapped rot away in her estate, and once we have freed them, her estate will grind to a halt."

"The entire estate?"

"Perhaps not all of it, but the lack of prisoners will set her back," Innetha said. "When I was there, precious few of her people were with her of their own free will. There were at least a hundred captives, and she bought and sold others every day."

Elkin spooned up some stew, and chewed thoughtfully for a moment. "How did she capture you?"

"I never told you?"

"No, and I've asked you several times." When Innetha only tore at her bread, he continued, "You're too cunning to allow yourself to be captured by such a snake, especially when you already knew she what she was. Tell me how she caught the sharpest woman I know, so I can hope to not be captured as well."

"Flattery will get you everywhere," Innetha said. "She caught me in a compromising situation, which was when she levied her curse. Because the curse was rushed, it didn't settle well. I fell into a stupor, and that was when she shackled me."

"Griselle herself cursed you?" he asked, and she nodded. "She's a sorceress, then?"

"She thinks she is. If she'd been any good with magic, the curse wouldn't have gone awry."

"We're both lucky it did. What was this compromising position?"

Innetha gave him her coyest smile. "She found me in bed with her lover. I got off easy with just a curse. I heard she had him unmanned."

Elkin grabbed Innetha's hand and kissed her knuckles. "Just as well. After being with you, all other women would have paled in comparison." To his utter delight, Innetha blushed.

"All right, my love," he said. Tell me everything you remember about this Griselle's compound, and sketch out a map of the place. I'll talk with the boys and see if any want in on this adventure."

"You'll really help me against her?"

"Of course. Officially, as a hunter in service to Asherah, it is my duty to punish villains in her name."

"And unofficially?"

"I can't let her actions against you go unpunished. A man must defend his mate, both with his body and his soul."

Innetha pushed their bowls aside and reached for his hands. "You really are my mate."

"I am," he said, the words settling on his heart as if they belonged. "Maybe, once all this is over, you'll be mine, too."

Fettered, Part Six

Elkin spoke with Wynnstead and Leofstan later that day. Both were eager to help them infiltrate Griselle's compound, the former because he loved a good fight, and the latter to hopefully find his missing cousin. They were also angered by Griselle sending mercenaries after Innetha, and so close to the keep.

The four of them departed for Griselle's compound the next morning. The men were dressed in their usual gear, but Innetha had donned one of Tamil's dresses. It was pale orange edged in blue, and it kept slipping off her shoulders and showed off her lovely neck. Elkin had a hard time looking away from her.

As Elkin admired Innetha, he thought about their time together, especially those last few days in Teg'urnan. He hadn't just stayed on for Innetha's naming but for a fortnight afterward, until he ran out of excuses and was forced to return to the keep. While he was proud of Innetha, he wondered if he should have ignored the queen's summons to help track Mersgoth and remained in the north.

"I never wanted to bring you to Teg'urnan," Elkin said.

Innetha glanced sidelong at him. "As I recall, it was your idea for me to accompany you."

"It was."

He remembered that day as if it was yesterday. A messenger had arrived bearing two shocking bits of news: demons had attacked the palace and killed nearly all the hunters and *nuvi*, and his boyhood friend, Aeolmar, was now First Hunter. Elkin couldn't say which facts had surprised him more.

"Then why did you bring me?" Innetha asked. "Why even mention it?"

"To answer your second question first, I had to tell you," he began. "You would have demanded to know where we were all going. As for the first, well, there's two parts to that answer."

"Are you going to start with the second part?"

"I just might." He paused. "I knew you'd prefer Teg'urnan to the keep. Hells, who wouldn't?"

"Anyone who's ever had Tamil's stew prefers the keep," Innetha said, and Elkin smiled. "And the first part?"

"I was afraid that if I didn't bring you along, you wouldn't be here when I returned. By taking you along on the mission, I got to be with you for a few more moons."

Innetha urged her horse closer to Elkin's. "If you'd talked to me then like you're talking to me now, I would have waited for you. Or gone on the hunt and returned here with you."

Elkin reached for her hand. "At least we're together now."

The road crested the hill, and Griselle's compound was laid out below them. The central enclosure was a long timber hall, and several outbuildings surrounded it. The whole of it was enclosed in a wooden stockade fence so tall that it was only by virtue of their place on the hill that Elkin could see inside at all.

"This isn't an estate, it's a fortress," Elkin said. "What goes on in there?"

"What doesn't?" Innetha countered. "Griselle deals in people. She needs places to keep them until they can be sold. Those she can't sell work for her until they escape or die."

"Perhaps we should burn it to the ground, put all of them out of their misery," Wynnstead said.

"Not while Kenric might be inside," Leofstan said. "Innetha, you said she deals in people. What does she do with them?"

"It depends on the individual." Innetha pointed to a roundhouse at the eastern end of the enclosure. "That's the pleasure house. Next to it is an ale room, where some dance and serve her customers. Sometimes, she sells them to the customers for an hour or two, if the price is right. If it's someone she's tired of she sells them off permanently."

"Then Kenric may no longer be here," Leofstan said.

"It's a possibility," Innetha said. "But if he was sold, there will be a record of the buyer. Griselle keeps detailed records on all transactions."

"He's a boy, not a transaction," Leofstan snapped. Elkin moved to reprimand him, but Innetha raised her hand.

"I'm sorry. I know he's not chattel, but that is how Griselle sees him and everyone else on her property. It's how she will see me, and it's how you will treat me." When Leofstan remained silent, Innetha urged her horse closer to his.

"Can you do that, Leo?" Innetha asked. "Can you drag me in and drop me on the floor like a useless piece of wood? Because if you do anything more, Griselle will suspect you."

"Wood isn't useless," Leofstan said. "Can burn it, carve it…"

"Leo," Innetha repeated.

He met her gaze and nodded, then he faced Elkin. "Maybe you shouldn't be here," Leofstan said.

"I'm not leaving Innetha," Elkin declared.

"If I'm to—"

"I am not leaving her," Elkin repeated. "If I can harden my guts for a few hours while we pull off this ruse, so can you."

"Now that we've established that Innetha is chattel for the rest of the day, shall we get on with it?" Wynnstead asked. "I've asked around, and those in the know claim the gates are barred after sundown."

Innetha turned back to the estate. "Yes, let's get this over with. I don't want to come back here tomorrow. Or ever again," she added.

"All right, beloved," Elkin said. "Wynn and I will go on ahead. Give us some time before you two follow."

The hunters nodded their assent, and Elkin and Wynnstead continued on toward the estate.

"Beloved, eh?" Wynnstead said. "I see things have returned to normal between you two."

"That's where you're wrong," Elkin said. "Nothing has or ever will be normal between myself and Innetha."

Elkin had worried Griselle's guards would refuse them entry, but the gold in his hand spoke their language. The guards didn't even confiscate their weapons, which made Elkin wonder if there was an arena somewhere on the property. Griselle wouldn't be the first landowner to set up a makeshift gladiatorial ring, and take wagers on the fights. In Elkin's experience in those situations, the only winners were the people holding the bets.

"Keep alert," Elkin murmured. "Based on what Innetha told me about this place, someone may knock us over the head and sell us to the highest bidder."

"That's where I've got the advantage." Wynnstead rapped his knuckles against his head. "Hard as a rock"

Elkin snorted, then he and Wynnstead stepped into Griselle's hall. It was a massive room, easily as large as the Northern Contingent's entire keep, with long tables on either side laden with food and drink while barely clad men and women moved among the guests. Wynnstead whistled at the abundant refreshment, but for Elkin, the most amazing part of the hall was in the center. A small woman draped in so much embroidered silk only her face was visible sat atop a dais on a golden throne.

"Excuse me." Elkin beckoned a passing server and jerked his chin toward the throne. "Is she our host?"

"Yes, that is our Lady Griselle," the server replied, then she held her tray toward Elkin and Wynnstead. "Wine? Or would you prefer something stronger?"

"Wine will do," Elkin said as he accepted a cup. Wynnstead waved the drink away. "Thank you." The girl dipped into a curtsey and moved on.

"Should we introduce ourselves?" Wynnstead asked.

"Let's wait for the other two. I want to look around a bit more." Elkin knew Innetha wouldn't have led them into a trap, but the hairs on the back of his neck were standing up. "Is Griselle nobility?"

"Not so far as I know," Wynnstead replied. "Wondering about the throne?"

"I am." Elkin wasn't well versed in the particularities of law, but he was certain that Griselle should not be presenting herself as royalty, being that Asherah didn't recognize her as such. In fact, there was very little fae nobility to speak of, since Asherah's predecessor had never mated or sired children. He wondered if Griselle sitting on a throne amounted to treason.

A commotion at the rear of the hall drew Elkin's attention; Innetha and Leofstan had arrived. He saw Innetha enter first, stumbling as

Leofstan drove her before him. They reached the carpet in front of the dais and Leofstan shoved Innetha into a kneeling position, then he pulled back the hood of her cloak. Innetha bared her teeth at Griselle and tried to rise, but Leofstan's hand on her shoulder kept her in place.

Elkin almost smiled. His first thought was that his brave mate was as strong as she was beautiful, and he couldn't wait to tell her so once all of this was behind them. Then he caught sight of her bound hands, and gritted his teeth. Griselle would pay for what she'd done, and dearly.

"Lady Griselle," Leofstan said. "I've got your wayward girl."

Griselle looked up from her throne. "Why, if it isn't the fair Innetha. We've missed you these past seasons."

Griselle gestured, and two of her men approached Innetha and hauled her to her feet. Elkin clenched his fists, but while he was angry, he wasn't worried. While they'd dressed, Innetha had concealed lock picks, a garrote, and several throwing knives within her clothes. He almost pitied her guards.

Innetha stumbled, and Leofstan steadied her with a hand under her elbow. As the guards dragged her out of the hall, Leofstan approached the throne. "I assume the reward still stands?"

"It does," Griselle said. A woman approached Leofstan and handed him a pouch of coins. "Please, stay. We'll be celebrating long into the night, and you may find someone you like."

"What are you celebrating?"

Griselle's face stretched into a smile. Elkin was close enough to note it didn't reach her eyes. "We're always celebrating here."

Leofstan glanced about the hall. "What about the one I brought in? This enough to buy her back?"

Griselle laughed. "That one is special to me, but we have many others. Perhaps you'll find another, or maybe two?" Griselle motioned to the girl, who guided Leofstan past the food and drink tables and toward a draped alcove. Griselle herself rose and made her way toward the servant pouring wine. Elkin followed.

"Wonderful evening, is it not?" he asked Griselle.

"It is," she replied. "Do I know you?"

"Elkin Savey, my lady," he replied with a shallow bow. "I've heard tell of your gatherings for some time, and I must admit they are more than idle talk suggests. You are a most gracious hostess."

"Elkin Savey." Griselle tapped her chin. "Aren't you the leader of that band of hunters? The very same hunters who were sheltering Innetha?"

"Correct, and correct," Elkin replied. "The man what brought her in is one of mine."

"Change of heart about the girl?"

"Change of priorities," Elkin replied. "I'm looking for a boy. Hardly a man, but thinks he is. Good with his hands, good with building things."

"Why tell me?"

"Word is that you take in waifs and strays," he continued. "Any way you can find out if he's here?"

Griselle pursed her lips. "And if he is?"

"I'll buy him from you, if he's for sale," Elkin replied. "I get a fair stipend from the queen. I'm sure we can come to an arrangement."

"I thought Teg'urnan frowned upon such matters," Griselle said. "Didn't the queen issue an edict against it?"

Elkin leaned close, and whispered, "I'm not the queen."

Griselle looked Elkin over as one would a horse. "Interesting. Do other hunters share your opinion?"

That you're a monster? Yes. "Of course. If this matter goes well, I'll make the introductions myself."

Griselle looped her arm through Elkin's. "I like you, Elkin of Savey. Come, walk with me, and tell me about this wayward boy. If he isn't here, perhaps we'll find something else to whet your appetite."

Elkin let Griselle lead him down a corridor and into a long, narrow chamber. Brackets of candles blazed against the whitewashed walls, and he saw Innetha on the far side of the room. Her hands remained bound, and they'd taken her cloak and boots, but the rest of her clothing was intact. That meant she still had her weapons.

"My Lord Savey, I have the most amazing treat for you tonight," Griselle said. Elkin noticed an open chest against the wall. It was filled with golden shackles. "You see, Innetha not only gives pleasure, she also absorbs pain."

"Pain?" Elkin repeated. "I've no pain to speak of. You mean to inflict some?"

"No, no," Griselle demurred. "Let us both inflict some pain on another."

A door opened, and two guards dragged Leofstan into the room. His head lolled to the side and blood crusted his ear and jaw. Elkin moved toward him, but Griselle stayed him with a hand on his forearm.

"This hunter of yours meant to dupe me," Griselle said. "He cares for this one. I saw how he helped her when she stumbled." Griselle's gaze narrowed toward Innetha. "This one does not deserve care."

"If that's true, why did he agree to bring her here?" Elkin asked.

"To steal from me," Griselle said, then she faced Elkin. "Are you here to steal from me, too?"

Elkin frowned; this plan, which hadn't been very good to begin with, was steadily getting worse. "Let me take my man and go," he began, but Griselle shook her head.

"Wait, dear Elkin," she purred. "Since you're already here, let's have Innetha show you a few of her tricks." Griselle gestured to the guards. "Bring her forward."

The guards grabbed Innetha's arms, but her attention was on Leofstan. Elkin knew she would feel responsible for his injuries and try to heal him, but Elkin had to keep that from happening. Leofstan was already down, and he needed Innetha to fight beside him.

"Found him!"

Elkin turned toward the voice, and saw Wynnstead hauling Kenric through the door by the back of his shirt. "Where was he?" Elkin asked.

"The ale house, enjoying himself far too much." Wynnstead released Kenric and surveyed the room. His gaze settled on Leofstan, and he frowned. Innetha, her hands still bound, craned her neck toward Leofstan.

"Uncle?" Kenric asked. When Leofstan didn't respond, Kenric turned to Elkin. "Will he be all right?"

"What is happening here?" Wynnstead demanded.

"What is happening is that we are putting Griselle out of business." Elkin drew his sword, then he strode up to Griselle's guards.

"The first thing you did wrong was only bringing four guards." Elkin said.

"You forget, I have scores outside these walls," Griselle said, but Wynnstead shook his head.

"Actually, all you had were hired mercenaries," Wynnstead said. "With a bit of gold and a promise of a full pardon from the queen, I convinced them to look elsewhere for employment. Luckily, they hate you as much as the slaves do."

Griselle spun around and faced Elkin. "You said you were here to buy the boy," she screeched. "You lied to me!"

"And you cursed me." The ropes fell from Innetha's arms and a knife dropped into her hand. "How many others have you cursed? How many lives have you ruined, all for your games?"

Griselle looked down her nose at Innetha. "I need not answer to the likes of you."

"But you do need to answer to me," Elkin said. "I've no interest in your lands or possessions. Maintaining my keep is quite enough work, and I'm not interested in adding more. Your people, however, now that's another matter."

Elkin crouched beside Kenric. "How old are you now?"

"Nineteen winters come midsummer."

"And how did you come to be here?"

"I was working the crops, like I always do, when these big hands grabbed me and tossed me in the back of a hay cart." Elkin patted Kenric's arm, but he wasn't done yet.

"There were others in the cart," Kenric continued. "Boys, girls, most of 'em younger than me. Some could barely walk they was so small. They all got tossed into the cart, and we all got brought here."

Elkin straightened and leveled his sword at Griselle. "Slaver. Kidnapper. What other crimes can we add?"

Griselle went white, then red. "You cannot judge me based on the account of a child," she shrieked. "They lie, tell stories!"

"What about my account?" Innetha said. "I was not a child when I came here. Am I to be dismissed as well?"

"You are nothing," Griselle began, but Elkin stepped between her and Innetha.

"Have a care how you speak to one of Asherah's hunters," he said. "I could take your head for less."

Griselle snatched a dagger from her robes and plunged it into Elkin's neck.

"No!" Wynnstead caught Elkin and lowered him to the ground. Innetha was at Elkin's side in an instant, pressing her hands on the wound.

"You can't die," she wailed. "I can't lose you. Not you!"

"Don't... heal me," Elkin rasped. "You promised... you wouldn't."

Innetha ripped off a length of her skirt and wrapped it around Elkin's neck. His bleeding slowed as a trail of red appeared on Innetha's shoulder."

"Don't." Elkin's eyes fluttered shut.

"Wynn," Innetha said. The front of her dress was soaked with blood. "Bring Griselle here." Wynnstead grabbed Griselle's arms and pushed her down beside Innetha. "Expose her neck."

Wynnstead held Griselle's arms immobile as he pulled away the gaudy silks. Innetha kept one hand on Elkin's neck and placed the other on Griselle's.

"What are you doing?" Griselle demanded. She struggled against Wynnstead, but he didn't budge. "What are you doing to me?"

Innetha's gaze remained on Elkin as she replied. "What you deserve."

Red droplets landed on Griselle's skirts as her neck opened up. Innetha had moved the wound from Elkin to Griselle. "You cannot do this," Griselle said. "You cannot... It's not..."

Griselle slumped against Wynnstead's legs. He lowered her to the floor, then he crouched beside Innetha. "How much blood did you lose?"

"Not much," she replied. "Not as much as Elkin." She looked toward Leofstan, then noticed Griselle's guards flanking the door.

"Are they yours?" she asked.

"They are," Wynnstead replied. "Elkin and me knew we couldn't fight our way out, so we brought plenty of gold to buy an escape route." He stood and approached the guards.

"You will have your pardons," he told them. "They will be signed by the queen herself. Is there any place we can hole up until those two can travel?"

***

The guards helped get Elkin and Leofstan to a safe room, but that was all. The next morning Innetha learned that word of Griselle's demise had spread quickly, and almost everyone had left the compound.

"I'm surprised there wasn't more looting," Wynnstead said as he and Innetha put together a meal in the kitchens. "I would have taken everything I could carry."

"Perhaps they did," Innetha said. "You forget, almost no one here was a soldier. Most were stolen children." Innetha's hand trembled as she set a loaf of bread on a tray.

"Don't let her haunt you." Wynnstead put his hand on her elbow to steady her. "She was evil, and now she's gone. You did the right thing."

"I know," she said. "It was an easy choice to save Elkin. I couldn't let him go."

"Of course you couldn't. We'd all be lost without him. Why do you think the whole contingent loves you? You look out for him."

Innetha raised an eyebrow. "All of you love me?"

"We do. Not as much as we love Tamil," he added, "but she's a special one."

Innetha laughed. "I understand. Let's bring the food to the rest, and see about leaving this wretched place."

***

Both Elkin and Leofstan were eager to leave the compound, and within a few hours, they were in the stables. Their four horses were the only ones that remained, and soon enough they were on their way back to the keep.

"I had no idea you could move a wound from one person to the other," Leofstan said as they rode. His cousin Kenric sat in front of him, and had complained about the arrangement until Elkin ordered his silence.

"Neither did I," Innetha said. "I didn't even realize what I was doing. I just knew that it was wrong for Elkin to die while that horrible woman lived."

"I am very glad you felt that way," Elkin said. His neck was still bandaged, but the bleeding hadn't resumed. "And, beloved, I won't even mention how you broke your promise. Perhaps I should have taken that chest of gold shackles so I can keep an eye on you."

"Try fettering me and you'll regret it," Innetha said. "And I'll break that promise again if it means saving you. We only need to ensure an enemy is at hand whenever you're injured."

Elkin laughed. "As you will it, beloved."

"Why do you keep calling her beloved?" Kenric asked. "Are you mates?"

"Yes, Kenric," Innetha replied. "We are."

Fettered, Part Seven

"A messenger's just arrived," Wynnstead said, as he entered the kitchens. Almost a moon had passed since Griselle's death, and both Elkin and Leofstan had long since healed. "He brought a scroll addressed to you," he said to Innetha, as he held out the item.

"Who would have sent me a message here?" she wondered as she unrolled the parchment. "Oh, Aeolmar."

"How goes things at the palace?" Elkin asked. Innetha leaned against him and they read the scroll together.

Innetha and Elkin, for I'm certain he is peeking over your shoulder,

I write to you today about the health of my second, and our most gracious queen. Finlay has recovered quite well from his wounds, and soon enough he'll be riding again. As for Asherah, her temperament has much improved, caused no doubt by Finlay's good health.

Please, Innetha, I understand that you have been privy to Asherah's most private thoughts, but she does wish to keep her union with Finlay quiet, at least for the time being. As you know, she worries he may be a target for her enemies, and the battle at Nibika only lent credence to her fears. I realize you have likely told Elkin everything, and I implore him to keep quiet about the queen's affairs. As we know, his tongue wags like an old washer woman's, but please do your best to convince him.

"My tongue does not wag," Elkin huffed.

"Sometimes it does," Innetha said, then she resumed reading.

As for you, Innetha, I know you don't want to hear it but you have my deepest condolences. My heart—no, Elkin, it is not made of stone—goes out to you. Please know that I will do anything in my power to help you. Your position as a huntress is held for your return, should you decide to come back to Teg'urnan. Wherever the coming days take you, I wish you w ell.

Aeolmar, First Hunter of Parthalan

"Odd, that Aeolmar has no surname," Innetha mused. "Shouldn't he use Savey, as you do?"

"Aeolmar has always done things his own way," Elkin said. "What of it, love? Will you return to Teg'urnan?"

"I... I don't know," she said. "I do enjoy being a huntress. After the life I've led, it's wonderful to be valued for one's mind and skill above all else. Not that you've ever not valued me," she added.

"But while you're here, you're my woman. It's hard for the rest to see you as anything more," Elkin surmised. "Perhaps the solution is for me to follow you to Teg'urnan."

"You'd do that?" Innetha asked. "But what about the Northern Contingent?"

"Before I could relocate, we'd have to find a new leader, and there would have to be room for me in the palace contingent," Elkin said. "But that will happen, in time." He brushed Innetha's hair back. "What do you say? Should I begin the search for my replacement? It may take many winters."

"If we were in Teg'urnan together, would I still be only your woman?" she countered.

He cupped the back of her head and drew her close. "If anything, I'll be your man. You could say my heart is fettered."

She halfheartedly swatted his arm. "That was awful. But yes, my heart is bound to yours, too."

Elkin grinned. "Best words I've ever heard, beloved."

***

Another moon passed before Innetha was ready to return to Teg'urnan. Elkin sent a messenger on ahead to advise the palace of her return, and walked his mate to where the keep's path met the main road.

"I know you won't be alone while we're apart," Elkin said. "I understand you will need companionship."

"I'm sure you will, too," she said. "For all that you're fae, you need comfort as much as I do."

"You're right. I do."

They stopped walking, and Elkin pulled her into his arms.

"I've sent word to Aeolmar letting him know I'd like to return to the palace, and he's already replied. He has agreed to watch the *nuvi* for a suitable replacement for me. It may not happen quickly, beloved, but it will happen."

"And you will visit me?" she asked. "First you will come to Teg'urnan, then I will come here. I don't want to be apart from you for so long ever again."

"Agreed, beloved." He kissed her, long and hard. "No matter how many times you fall in love while we're apart, please leave room in your heart for me."

"As you will for me?"
Always, beloved.
Always.

***

Did you like this story? If so you can get five more in Pieces of Parthalan, available here: https://books2read.com/PiecesOfP arthalan

About the Author

Jennifer Allis Provost is a native New Englander who lives in a sprawling colonial along with her beautiful and precocious twins, a dog that thinks she's a kangaroo, a parrot, a junkyard cat, and a wonderful husband who never forgets to buy ice cream. As a child, she read anything and everything she could get her hands on, including a set of encyclopedias, but fantasy was always her favorite. She spends her days drinking vast amounts of coffee, arguing with her computer, and avoiding any and all domestic behavior.

Find Jenn on the web here: http://authorjenniferallisprovost.com/

For up to the minute sale notifications, follow her on Bookbub here: https://www.bookbub.com/profile/jennifer-allis-provost

For exclusive content, follow her on Patreon: https://www.patreon.com/jenniferallisprovost/

Friend her on Facebook: http://www.facebook.com/jennallis

Follow her on Instagram: @jenniferaprovost

Happy reading!

Also By Jennifer Allis Provost

The Chronicles of Parthalan, a six volume epic fantasy (and one short story collection)

Heir to the Sun

The Virgin Queen

Rise of the Deva'shi

Pieces of Parthalan: Six All-New Stories From The Land Of Parthalan

Golem

Elfsong

Sunfall

The Copper Legacy, a four book urban fantasy:

Copper Girl

Copper Ravens

Copper Veins

Copper Princess

A duology based in the Copper world:

Redemption

Salvation

Poison Garden, an urban fantasy filled with seers, witches, and one seriously hot detective:

Belladonna

Oleander

Bleeding Hearts

Thornapple

Wolfsbane

Mistletoe

Mandrake

Gallowglass, an urban fantasy set in Scotland and New York:

Gallowglass

Walker

Homecoming

Winter's Queen, an urban fantasy set in Scotland and Elphame:

Touch of Frost

Giant's Daughter

Elphame's Queen

Merrowkin, an urban fantasy set in Ireland above and below

Merrowkin

Death's Door

Manannán's Pearl

Changes, a contemporary romance:

Changing Teams

Changing Scenes

Changing Fate

Changing Dates